BEETLE
BATTLES THE
BIOTOXIC
BULLDOGS

ANDREW ROLSTON

Don't become a mere recorder of facts, but try to penetrate the mystery of their origin.
—Ivan Pavlov

PROLOGUE

IT WAS THE SUMMER OF 1987. A young man by the name of John Michael decided to spend the summer single-handedly making the greatest and most epic movie of all time in the great state of Kansas, armed with an Arriflex 16SR2 with Kodak 16mm film, a Nagra IV-STC reel-to-reel tape recorder, and a few close friends filling in as non-union actors. It was going to earn him global notability and lifelong credibility.

John Michael had just finished his freshman year in college. His sophomore year wasn't going to happen, as he had spent his full student loan on making his masterpiece. It wasn't just the student loan he blew. He maxed out every credit card he could open. He also accumulated some massive debts with rental houses. All the equipment was on loan. Loans he couldn't pay back. The project cost $300,000. The equivalent of $650,000 adjusted for inflation. It ended up costing him far more because of accumulated interest that piled up on those credit cards. The project did gain him notability. Notability with collection agencies. As far as credibility, his credit score was in the deep negatives.

John Michael's goal was to shoot the most epic movie of all time that summer. One had to give it to him—he managed to shoot it. There was only one problem—he never put it together.

ONE

IT WAS A COLD DAY IN JANUARY OF 1998. Beetle sat in the
pew between his mother and father with his hands folded. Beetle
and his parents attended church every Sunday. His father drove him
and his mother in the early hours of the morning. When it was still
dark outside, the sun of Sunday had yet to peek in Kansas. Beetle's
mother always had been faithful to the Church. She made sure to
be in attendance at the first Mass every Sunday. She also made it
a primary concern to arrive at the church a full hour early to take
part in the prayer of the Rosary. Beetle's mother had a devotion to
the Church that made him feel guilty about his complete and utter
boredom during the service. He could not stay focused or control his
body or mind.

Those two hours every Sunday in church were complete torture for him. Sitting for a long time was difficult for Beetle. He was
tired from waking up so early to get dressed up nice and brush his
hair to be presentable. Despite being fifteen years old, his mother
still helped him pick out the clothes he was going to wear. She also
brushed his hair for him. The way his mother brushed his hair was
torturous. For years she used the same old brush with its thin, dark,
wooden handle and a bunch of sharp, black, spiky bristles. The
brush felt like someone was rubbing the quills of a porcupine on his

head. After his mother had brushed his hair, he could feel where the bristles had scraped his scalp for hours and hours into the day.

Beetle sat in church trying to behave and trying not to squirm, but it was hard because he felt like he was choking. It felt as though a choke collar was around his neck because the button-down shirt was so tight it was strangling him. It was so hard to button, his mother had to help him do it, but even she had struggled, as the shirt was too tight. Beetle's mother was not the type of woman to have long fingernails, but her fingernails were long enough because she felt it was feminine. His mother was still a purist, however, and never painted her nails, though occasionally she put a little gloss on them. Beetle's mother fastened the button on his collar with her ladylike, unpainted fingernails. He didn't know what was more painful, the collar strangling him or her thumbnail digging into the skin of his neck. After she had put the button through the hole for him, he looked in the mirror and saw that the skin around his neck was red and bulging from the tight collar. He saw on the right side of his neck a ladylike, crescent thumbnail indentation on his skin.

Beetle sat in church, hands folded, on his best behavior. He tried not to act weird. When Beetle grew bored, he became fidgety. He was fighting his compulsions. He sat there wishing it were over, thinking about how bad his scalp hurt. He felt the little scratches on his head from where his mother had brushed his hair this morning. He reached up and rubbed his hand along the grain of his parted hair that was still there from the brushing. He removed his hand from his head and examined his palm to see if there was blood. He thought about the girls in his class who said they loved getting their hair brushed, and Beetle concluded the girls were masochists.

All he could think about was how painful his scalp was, and how tight his collar felt. Beetle sat there in the pew trying to breathe

3

through his nose. He wondered if the number of breaths he was able to take were becoming more limited. Was his tight collar cutting off his circulation? Beetle held his breath as he sat sandwiched between his mother and father.

His father generally did not come into the church. Most Sundays he would drive his son and his wife to Mass. He would let them out at the entrance, park, and then just wait in the car until the service was over. When most people pull up to church, they look for the spot closest to the entrance. Beetle's father knew the best place to park was over near the basement of the church, where they held the reception afterward. Everyone attending the Mass would head down for donuts and coffee when Mass was over. Beetle's father never complained about the complimentary donuts and coffee. Except for this day—on this day he did complain about the donuts and coffee.

Although it was rare for Beetle's father to attend Mass, on this day he made an exception. After his father parked the car, he sat there listening to the radio like normal. And then he realized it was too cold and he was not going to sit in the car running the heater for two hours straight. He decided it was better to go inside and sit with his wife and boy. It was better than sitting in a running car, cranking up the heat as far as it would go, hoping he wouldn't freeze to death.

The church did not have central heat, so people wore their coats and jackets during Mass. Some of the older and stricter churchgoers found it disrespectful. The church ran window heaters in the back rooms on full blast to warm the place up. They couldn't put window heaters in the main area of the church because of the stained-glass windows. Although the window heaters worked reasonably well in the back rooms, everyone in the church pews remained moderately miserable. And though the heat could not reach far from the back room, the noise certainly could. The heaters were so loud, no one could hear the sermon.

Even on those rare occasions when Beetle's father would attend the service, he never participated in the Mass. He never said the prayers, and he never quoted along with the other Mass attendees. He never stood when everybody stood; he never kneeled when everybody kneeled. He didn't sing along to the songs, nor did he offer anyone a handshake during the Sign of Peace. He just crossed his arms and sat in the pew with a giant frown on his face.

Beetle inspected his palm again for any sign of a bleeding scalp. He remembered hearing about how you can tell a lot about somebody by the lines in their palm. He ran the tips of his fingers along his palm lines. Beetle's fingertips were automobiles on a freeway. They were making exits and merging into traffic. He could feel his father's stern gaze bearing down on him. Beetle did not even have to look up to know his father was staring disapprovingly at him. Beetle turned his neck, made a quick confirming glance, and made eye contact for a split second with his angry father, noting the tightened forehead and raised, dark eyebrows. Beetle sat up straight and folded his hands in his lap again. He looked straight ahead.

His father was intimidating, especially to Beetle. Beetle's father was a tall man. He stood six feet and two inches. If he stood upright, straightened his back, and stiffened his legs, he would measure about six feet and three inches. The man had worked laying bricks and mixing and spreading mortar since he was Beetle's age—fifteen. Beetle's father had worked the brutal and strenuous job for the past forty years. Those forty years of work had not worn him down the least. Quite the opposite—it made him muscular and strong and hard. Beetle's father was built like a giant refrigerator. Regrettably, his son did not inherit his father's size. Beetle inherited his height from his mother's side. Beetle's mother was only four feet and ten and a half inches. She told everyone she was five feet tall. Being the honest person she was, she told herself she was five feet tall. And she was—five feet tall when wearing the proper sized heels. Beetle bore a striking resemblance to his father because they both had the same dark hair and the same big noses. They also had similar ears. The large ears looked fitting on Beetle's father as he was a big man. Beetle's small head made the ears look quite comical. Pretty much everything about Beetle was comical.

Beetle looked over at his mother. She was thirty-five years old and beautiful. The lenses of Beetle's thick, black glasses were smudged. Looking through the smudged lenses gave his mother a soft-focus look. She sat there in her formal Sunday dress underneath the ambient lighting of the church. Beetle thought his mother resembled one of those actresses on soap operas. Beetle and his mother watched soap operas during the summer.

After he had pulled his gaze away from his mother, Beetle focused straight ahead again. Everything looked blurry because of his dirty glasses. Every Sunday as far as he could remember, he had come to this church.

He was told that his mother had taken him to another church when he was a baby. The other church provided a cry room where parents could hold their babies. They could sit and watch and listen to the Mass behind a two-way mirror. There was a speaker up in the corner amplifying what the priest said. The volume was not turned up on the speaker, and the crying babies usually overpowered the priest's voice. The cry room had rows of metal chairs, far more chairs than was ever needed. The room resembled a police interrogation room. The only difference was that the two-way mirror faced the opposite way.

Beetle had sat in this church every Sunday for as long as he could remember. He also sat there every Wednesday because Wednesday was the day his school had the all-school Mass.

It was ten past seven, and the Mass had still not started yet. Even Beetle's mother had never seen a service delayed this long, and she had attended church every single Sunday of her entire life. Beetle was tired from waking up so early, and his stomach growled. He hadn't eaten. He never ate before church. It was a rule his mother had. She always told Beetle you weren't supposed to eat before receiving communion. Beetle's stomach growled like a wild animal. He pressed his arms against his belly to silence the growl. Beetle's father gazed at him again with the angry look on his face. The growling stomach wasn't something Beetle could control. Beetle's father gave him a warning look then shifted his focus to the front of the church and began shaking his head in condemnation. Beetle was not sure if the disapproval was because of his behavior or to his irritation that the Mass was taking so long to begin.

Five minutes later, at fifteen past seven, the priest stepped out. A new priest no one in church had ever seen before. When a new priest began at a parish, he would make a tremendous effort to introduce himself to everyone in the community. Making his presence known was something this priest had failed to do. When everybody saw him, they assumed he was a fill-in for the regular priest.

This priest was a lot younger than the regular priest. He was in his late twenties, yet he looked even younger. He had an edginess everyone assumed was owing to his guilt for being late. But the priest was nervous. He was so nervous he had dry-heaved in the back of the church beforehand. He had almost called in to get a temporary priest to fill in for him, but he knew he could not hide from it forever. He couldn't call in a temporary priest every single time he had to do a Mass. The young priest had to go out there and face his fears. Talking to a broad audience and public speaking terrified him, but he knew that if he didn't go out there and talk to the public now then he would still have to do it the next day, and the day after that, and so on. He pulled out a slip of paper. He had written many notes on it to give the best sermon he could. He spent hours and hours planning and rehearsing. The day before, the young priest had felt he was prepared, but now he felt only fear.

Despite the cold in the church, the priest perspired profusely. He walked up to the podium, adjusted the microphone, and asked, "Can you hear me?" He saw about two or three people nod their heads. He bent down and moved his mouth closer to the microphone. "Testing, one-two, testing." He had intended this to be funny, but not one person smiled. "Is this thing on?" An old man in the audience nodded his head as if it was a serious question.

"Well, good morning, ladies and germs," the priest felt this would spark a laugh from the audience, but the nave was radio silence. "Not that I'm referring to all you gentlemen as germs . . . the only germs here with us today are on the hands of people sitting near you. The ones whose hands you're going to shake during the Sign of Peace."

The priest hoped this would get a chuckle, and his stomach sank when nobody reacted. "The germs on people's hands aren't what you should fear. It's the germs on their mouths that should scare you. I was talking with somebody, a man, the other day, and he told me he didn't like how the church started doing the Sign of Peace after Vatican II. I'm not going to say the man was old, but I will say he was older than I am, so his memory of this goes back further than mine and I wasn't even born when the Second Vatican Council occurred. He told me he didn't like how the Catholic Church started doing the Sign of Peace because he felt it was something the Church had stolen from the Lutherans. It's true, the Lutherans do something where they exchange handshakes, and it is called the Exchange of Peace. You know where they got that? They got it from an old Christian tradition called the Kiss of Peace. As I'm sure you can tell by the name of it, the Kiss of Peace is where you offer a sign of peace with a kiss. So you should all be grateful that all you have to do is shake each other's hand and not have to lay a big wet one on each other." The priest was hoping for a laugh, but the crowd was tough. "Look at all the people around you and think about what it would be like to kiss them." Nobody looked around nor did they show any signs of amusement. "That's where you get the germs! Not from holding hands . . . you get germs from kissing!"

He tried to be as funny as he could possibly be, but not one person in the whole place found him the least bit amusing. "Premarital kissing!" He regretted saying it as it came out of his mouth. "Luckily we don't have you touch your lips to those around you." He then checked his wristwatch and immediately felt it was a rude thing to do. "I'm completely opposed to kissing here because I have to hear all of your confessions and I'm fearful that if we had everybody here kissing one another then it would lead to a horrible herpes outbreak!" This not only did not receive a laugh from anyone, it fostered a lot of irate stares. "This place would turn into Cold Sore City!" When the priest said this, he even received a more negative response. "I don't want to be responsible for everyone here becoming sick!" There began much coughing and shifting in the pews. "We're safe here from any mouth germs unless you count all the germs that accumulate on the chalice during communion from everyone putting their mouths on it." The young priest immediately regretted this, too. "Don't worry about it because I blessed it and the blood of Christ will kill any of the germs. The blood of Christ is like antibacterial hand sanitizer. Except it tastes better. It's like wine-flavored mouth sanitizer."

Despite everyone taking offense to everything the young priest said, Beetle was transfixed. Beetle managed to hold back his amusement to not upset his father. "This is my first time doing this," the young priest confessed. "They say it hurts your first time." This was intended as a joke, but failed utterly. "The pain's not too bad. It just feels like a little pinch. I might bleed a little." Everyone looked up at the priest with concerned looks on their faces.

After Mass, all the church attendees headed down to the basement for coffee and donuts. Beetle's mother filled a white, foam cup with the brown, diluted coffee. She filled the cup to about seven and a half of the eight ounces it held. She opened two packets of sugar and poured them into her cup, then pulled back the label of a creamer container and poured that into the cup, as well.

"Why are you putting cream and sugar in your coffee?" her husband asked. "You don't need sugar if you have cream in it already."

She didn't answer him; she just sipped her coffee and then complained about it being cold.

Her husband gnawed on a donut as if he was eating a piece of raw leather. "I don't mind cold coffee," he said. "At work, I fill up a large water bottle full of coffee and keep it in the refrigerator, and then when I need a quick fix I pull it out and squirt it down my throat. I don't have time at work to sit around and enjoy a hot cup of coffee. When I need a caffeine buzz, I need it fast, and I need it large. When I need to just drink a whole pot of coffee, I chug it down cold, as quickly as possible, so that I can get on with work."

"Well," his wife said, looking down into her cup. "I don't like cold coffee."

Beetle removed his coat and placed it on a chair.

"It's not the cold coffee that bothers me." Beetle's father said to his wife. "It's these donuts! Geez! What happened to the donuts they normally have? These came from a supermarket bakery. They taste like they're a few days old. I wonder if the supermarket donated them to the church after they'd been sitting out for a few days."

Beetle pulled his coat off the chair and put it back on as church-goers glared at him.

"What are you doing?" asked his father in a harsh whisper with his teeth clenched.

"I just wanna put it on," Beetle said timidly as he struggled to prod his arm through the armhole.

"You just took it off! Why are you puttin it back on?"

"I took it off cause I was hot. Then when I took it off, I got cold, so I wanna put it back on."

Beetle's father gave his son another glare.

As they drove home from church, Beetle's father complained about the donuts and how he did not like the new priest. "He shouldn't have gone up there and made a jackass of himself," he said to his wife as he tried to stay focused on the road as he drove. "A man like that shouldn't have become a priest. If he wanted to act like that and try to be funny and make a fool of himself and be a jackass, then he should've gone and been some kinda standup comic."

Beetle's father had the radio tuned in to pregame coverage of the football game. Beetle's mother sat in the passenger seat. She worked on knitting pink and white thread in hopes that it would become a beautiful scarf. Beetle sat in the backseat looking out the window. He imagined he had a giant laser gun. He pretended he was shooting a laser beam out the window. Cutting down all the trees, signs, light-posts, bushes, and even houses. "I thought of something!" Beetle said to his parents, but they did not respond even though they heard him. "My birthday is in a few months, and I'm gonna be sixteen. I could be driving when I'm in eighth grade."

His parents still did not speak, but they did ponder what Beetle had said. Beetle did not enter kindergarten the year he was supposed to. He failed the entrance examination. His mother felt it was reasonable to wait a year because he was small for his age. Beetle struggled in school, and after he had finished with the fifth grade, he was held back to repeat it. His parents put a tremendous amount of thought into keeping him back. They never thought about how their son would be driving in the eighth grade.

When they arrived home, Beetle's father dropped him and his mother off. He then proceeded to drive to work. Beetle's dad usually had to work Sundays, so off he went to mix and spread wet mortar and lay bricks.

TWO

UNBUTTONING HIS SHIRT ALONG THE WAY, Beetle rushed inside the house to tune into his favorite television program. It was a local broadcast. The program showcased short movies made by local individuals, most of whom were students—primarily college students, though the show did feature some work created by high school students as well. Inspiring filmmakers not much older than Beetle himself. Beetle looked forward to seeing this show the whole time he was at Mass. He sat on the couch and fully unbuttoned his shirt, which was about to bust at the seams because of all the donuts and orange drink he had consumed after church. He would usually go and change his clothes, but he didn't want to miss his show. He decided to put on something more comfortable at the commercial break.

The television program started up with tacky, 90's computer graphics. Shoddy, synthesized keyboard music accompanied the graphics and Beetle's excitement.

—

The first short they showed opened with a girl wearing a yellow robe over red, lacy lingerie. She mixed soup in the kitchen of a tiny dorm room. The kitchen was so small, it was claustrophobic. The color balance was off in the shot, giving it an ugly, yellow tint. It was so bad the girl's yellow robe was in reality white. The camera angle moved upward, creating a down shot. The camera operator had tried for a side shot, but the kitchen was too small. There was no way they could cram the camera in for a wider angle. The majority of the shorts were shot with camcorders. The idea of using interchangeable lenses was unfathomable to most of the filmmakers in the program, and they wouldn't know how to use film to save their lives.

The girl mixed the soup. The camera shot down on her as she added spices, herbs, and whatnots into her pot of boiling broth. A boy walked in from behind and grabbed her by the waist. The boy looked younger than the girl. The girl looked pretty young as it was, but this boy looked not much older than Beetle himself. The boy had a patchy beard of dark, pubescent hair, growing thicker on his neck than on his face. As the boy kissed the girl's neck, the camera had to move outside of the kitchen to get the shot in the frame. This gave an even better notion of how small the kitchen they were in was. "I made you some soup," the girl said.

The sound in this short was better than the usual shorts on the program. Beetle didn't notice things like sound quality. The sound in the short was better because they were using a boom microphone. They mistakenly dropped the boom mic into the frame in a couple of the shots, but Beetle wasn't aware of things like that, either.

The girl pulled out a ladle, scooped the soup from the pot, and plopped it into a purple, plastic bowl. The boy grabbed the bowl and sat at a small table resembling the kind of table people would use for a game of poker. The boy began eating the soup as the camera cut over to him from the backside. This completely broke the 180-degree rule of filmmaking. Then they broke the 180-degree rule again by cutting back to another angle showing a close-up of the girl's face. The shot was so close it broke another film rule—biting the chin. Biting the chin is when you shoot so narrow and tight onto someone's face that it cuts the subject's chin out of the frame. The girl asked the boy as he shoveled spoonful after spoonful into his mouth, "How do you like the soup?"

The boy continued to eat, mumbling something because he couldn't speak—his mouth was too full. It cut back to the girl. Another close up of her face. She was supposed to be talking to the boy, but she was eyeballing elsewhere. She was not looking in the proper direction of where he was supposed to be. Once again, Beetle did not notice little things like that. Then the girl said to the boy as he ate, "Well, you better enjoy this soup because it is the last meal you will ever eat," and she reached into the pocket of her robe and pulled out a vial with some white powder inside. "It will be the last thing you ever eat because I filled it with cyanide!" The girl laughed an uncontrollable, wicked, evil laugh like that of a witch.

After the short was over, it cut to a commercial. A fat woman in a wheelchair with a neck brace looked into the camera and said, "I got hurt up real bad in a car accident, and I needed myself an attorney right… a…way!"

Beetle rushed to his room. He quickly changed into a baggy, orange T-shirt and long-legged, blue gym shorts. He rushed back to the television and hoped the show had not begun without him.

When he walked back into the room, he saw the tail end of a patent ad, showing a cartoon image of a caveman chiseling away at a stone wheel. It was the last commercial. The show's cheesy computer graphics faded in for two of three seconds and then faded out to black.

—

The second short film opened with titles that said THE GOVERNMENT IS WATCHING, THE CIA KNOWS YOUR SECRETS, and so on. The quotations all had a bright glow. Some were so bright, they were unreadable. What gave the words their effect was that the filmmaker used a camcorder to record images off his computer screen. He opened a word processor and typed large white fonts onto a black background. After the quotes had ended, the writer/ director's name popped up. Then the title of the movie appeared— THE WRECKK. The second K was an unnoticed mistype.

It opened with a handheld shot of a girl blindfolded. She was chained to a chair as the mysterious man behind the camera interrogated her. Not one word of what he said to her during the interrogation was discernible because the audio was so bad. The man poured some liquid on the girl in chains. The mysterious substance caused the girl to scream. She screamed so loud it rattled the single mono speaker on the television.

The remote control had been missing for years, so Beetle jumped up to turn it down. After Beetle sat back down, the movie cut to black-and-white stock footage of two old trains crashing into each other over and over as heavy metal music played. The music was so loud Beetle walked over to the television again and turned it down even more. He wanted to avoid his mother hearing it.

The looping, one-second clip of the trains crashing played 489 times total. Then it ended with another camcorder computer screen-shot of text that read: THE END? The question mark implied it was not the end because the government was still after us. The person who made *The Wreckk* also added the question mark because he had intended to make a sequel.

—

The next short featured a girl who looked gothic. She had jet-black hair, black lipstick, black fingernails, and black eyeshadow. Pretty much black everything. Her face was baby-powdered white. Her whole body was pretty much baby powdered, but her tattoos still stood out. There was little color in her tattoos. The color they did have wasn't visible since it was in black and white. She walked through an abandoned building. The video was double exposed, so there were many shadows of her going in all directions. One of the exposures showed her fully naked.

It was surprising to Beetle that they would allow it on television. It wasn't even cable—it was the regular network television he picked up with rabbit ear antennas. Beetle never had cable television growing up. His television was the same one he had watched since he was a little boy. His father bought it for his mother for their fifth-year anniversary. The picture quality always came in fuzzy and off-color. When Beetle watched the amateur movies on his favorite program, it made no difference because they were already off-color and fuzzy.

—

The short to follow was also colorless. The black-and-white ones were usually experimental. In the short, there was a bunch of darkly lit, old-fashioned, glass dolls. The dolls lay in strange places such as abandoned buildings, dirty basements, and in the dark woods.

This one was the shortest of the shorts. It was only about a minute and a half, but there was not much to it. The dolls never moved. They just lay there. In the background, there was a voice with massive amounts of echo and reverb to give it a scary sound. The voice was intended to sound like a little girl's voice, but it was the filmmaker's. He was the only person involved with the project. That is, apart from his roommate. His roommate lent a helping hand with recording the music by using an organ effect on his keyboard.

Beetle was no critic, but one thing he had noticed was a lot of the shorts on this program involved creepy dolls.

—

The fifth short film they showed would have been pretty scary if it had been nighttime while Beetle was watching it. A sunny Sunday morning did not create the intended effect. Sometimes Beetle would stay up late on Saturday nights because occasionally they would show a short film program at two o'clock in the morning. When Beetle watched it then, it seemed a little scarier.

Beetle wished they had saved the scary one for the two in the morning broadcast. The problem with the program they showed at two o'clock in the morning was that occasionally they didn't even show it. Sometimes they would show it, and sometimes they played an infomercial instead.

Despite it being daytime outside, the short film was still quite creepy. It was about a girl who was alone in a house, and the house was pretty scary. It was an old house. It looked like a house nobody would want to be alone in and that was what it was about—a girl being alone in the house. She heard a creaking noise, and thought there was an intruder in the house. At the end of the film, it was revealed that it was not a person in the house but a ghost. It being a ghost made Beetle feel less scared. He felt an actual person breaking into the house was far scarier than a ghost being in the house.

—

The last film in the showcase was Beetle's favorite of the six. A director named Christopher HC made it. This director stood out to Beetle because his short films were always far more interesting than any of the others on the showcase.

One time during the two o'clock in the morning broadcast, instead of showing two hours of short films, they showed just one of his movies. It was a full-length flick about a little boy who fell into a well. When pulled back out, he realized he was forty years old, but he was still in the body of a little boy. It was an interesting take on the body-switch genre. The boy not only knew everything he would know when he would be forty, but he also had the ability to see the future. He told everybody in the town what would happen in the future. The movie took place thirty-five years before being shot. They shot it in 1996, but the events of the film occurred in 1961. The early sixties was believable in the film because they shot it on a farm. Shooting on a farm could pass for being any historical place in time.

The thing that made the movie enjoyable was that it not only focused on the five-year-old boy who was as smart as a forty-year-old, but it also focused on him knowing the future. Either of these subjects alone would have made for an entertaining movie. Combining the two made it even more enjoyable. The movie was beautifully made, Beetle thought, and wonderfully acted. The five-year-old actor gave an incredible performance for being so young.

The Christopher HC film that played that day on the shorts program was a film about a man trying to force his wife to move to a small town. It wasn't the most original concept ever, but it seemed very creative and unique to Beetle. He felt the two actors gave good performances. It was, as were all Christopher-HC productions, beautifully made. Beetle could always spot a Christopher-HC production. They looked far superior to all the other films presented on the program. The acting was always a lot better, as well. Probably the most distinguishable aspect of his work was his actors. He seemed to use the same actors over and over again. They all did well and were always diverse in their performances, so there were no complaints on Beetle's end for seeing the same actors in different films.

This short was the last one they showed; it was as if they saved the best for last. After the short was over and the credits rolled, Christopher HC appeared on screen holding a long microphone with a red, furry wind cover on it. The microphone was a boom microphone, which he used to record the sound in all his movies. Beetle was surprised to see what this man looked like. He was younger than Beetle imagined. He also resembled the college student who tutored Beetle in math over the summer.

Christopher HC looked into the camera and thanked the audience for watching the program. He thanked the television channel. He also thanked the people who put together the short film showcase program. Christopher HC thanked them for allowing him to present his films on their show. Then he told everyone to come to some event going on next weekend. Beetle failed to pay attention to what Christopher HC said. He was thinking about how much Christopher HC resembled the math tutor. He could not focus on what Christopher HC said. Beetle had an insufferable impediment when it came to staying focused.

THREE

THE NEXT DAY WAS MONDAY. Beetle sat in the back of his classroom. He was hands-down the oldest in the eighth-grade class as he was fifteen years old. He was also the shortest, even shorter than all the girls, and he looked underdeveloped for his age. Beetle wore his thick, black glasses because ever since he got them he could see so much better. He used to sit in the front row voluntarily because he couldn't see the chalkboard. With his new glasses, he was able to sit in the back row where he could see all the other students. When he sat in the front row, kids would throw stuff at him, including balled-up pieces of paper. They would shoot rubber bands and project spitballs they made out of the milk straws they brought back from the cafeteria after lunch. No one used straws to drink milk because they drank it straight from the little paper carton. The straws were wrapped in white paper. They were made for aerodynamic spitball projectiles. Because of this, Beetle was relieved when he received his new glasses. He could sit in the back row and still see the blackboard. He did not have to worry about his classmates teasing him from behind his back.

Another reason he wanted to sit in the back of the class was so he could look at a beautiful girl. The most beautiful girl in the class—the most beautiful girl he had ever seen in all his life—was Latricia, and she sat at her desk wearing a soft, pink sweatshirt with pockets on the front. She had her hands buried in the pockets as she sat sideways in her wooden desk with her legs crossed. Latricia had long, beautiful legs. Her legs were on display all the way up to her short, plaid, Catholic-schoolgirl skirt. She was the second tallest person in the class. A boy named Cage was not only the tallest person in the class, but he was a borderline giant.

—

The first time Beetle saw Latricia was when he was in first grade, and she was in kindergarten—four years before being held back and ending up in the same grade with her. Latricia played the Virgin Mary in the school's yearly nativity scene. The school performed this with their kindergarteners, who depicted all the biblical characters present on the night of Jesus' birth in the manger. The teacher chose Latricia to play the role of the Virgin Mary. This caused some controversy among the faculty. They did not find it fitting to have the mother of Jesus portrayed by a black girl. Some did not consider it a proper casting choice. A petition was put up requesting that instead of playing the role of Mary, Latricia should take the part of one of the three wise men. Some felt it would be more suitable as she was the only black person in the class; she would be a proper fit for the part of the black wise man.

The kindergarten teacher argued that Latricia would fit the role of Mary. She said the real Mary was probably closer in resemblance to Latricia than she was to any of the Caucasian girls in the class. They couldn't argue her case. Except for one teacher who pointed out that the doll they used every single year to represent the baby Jesus was white. The white baby would confuse everyone. The dissenting teacher said the audience wouldn't know why this black girl had a white baby. The kindergarten teacher disputed that the baby was the Son of God and he could be any color he wanted. This argument did not go over well. The white baby doll was then replaced with a black baby doll. This resulted in even more confusion. The following year, no one could find the white baby doll. They ended up having to use the black baby doll despite having an all-white production.

Latricia was cast as the part of the Virgin Mary. The part of her Joseph went to a boy named Bullet. Bullet was a nickname he gave himself because he did not like his birth name, which was Joseph. Being named Joseph was the reason he was given the role in the first place because the teacher thought it would be fitting for a Joseph to play Joseph. He unwillingly did so. Bullet was on display in front of all the parents, faculty, and students—first-through-eighth grade. He stood there with an exasperated expression on his face. One of the mothers pointed out how he appeared troubled. Much to the offense of many people in the audience, one of the fathers joked that he looked upset because he must have found out the baby wasn't his. A few let out soft but controlled laughter. The role of the black wise man went to Cage, the borderline giant even at the age of five. He played the part with black makeup on his face. Once the teacher saw everyone lined up in front of the audience, she decided her choice to pick him to play the black wise man was not a great one because the whole audience's attention was on him. He was the gigantic boy in blackface.

—

Fifteen minutes passed. The teacher was not there. Beetle was thankful none of the other students were picking on him like they normally did when the teacher was not in the room. He guessed it was because he was now sitting in the back of the room and no one looked back there to notice him.

The teacher, Heather Cole, finally showed up.

Heather Cole hated when the students referred to her as "Miss Cole." Because she was a self-proclaimed feminist, she required all her eighth graders refer to her as Ms. Cole.

Ms. Cole was twenty-three years old, two weeks away from twenty-four. She was a traveling train wreck on track to derail. She was only one day away from destination disaster. Ms. Cole had an addictive personality. Ever since she was the age of her students, she had been co-dependent on attention. She had always demanded to be the center of attention. If she failed to get attention one way, she was determined to get it another, however she deemed necessary. Since her early teen years, she believed being loud, obnoxious, and crazy would make everybody notice her. She felt she always had to be on the edge of things. She thought of herself as a risk-taker, a go-getter, a show-off, and most of all a partier. She started smoking when she was twelve to impress her friends. By the age of thirteen, she convinced them she had become a full-blown chain-smoker.

It was also at age thirteen when she started drinking. At fourteen she had not only her friends, but also her family convinced she was an alcoholic. Nobody seemed to take her seriously. They had known her and grew wise enough to realize her shenanigans were nothing more than desperate cries for attention.

Around the age of fourteen, she developed a devoted passion for boys. At fifteen, she was known to be the kind of girl who liked to kiss and tell. At sixteen, she became the kind of girl who wanted to brag about her escapades with the opposite gender, which involved a lot more than just kissing. When she went off to college, she tried her hardest to fit in with the rich and popular girls. She even joined a sorority. Though it was not her top choice house, she made the most of it and knew she was fortunate to get into the one she did. Teenage Ms. Cole had spent her whole life trying to fit in with the upper echelons. The old-money girls with lifelong inheritances passed down from a long line of the affluent and the wealthy. Her father made a good living. He worked hard his whole life. He made enough money to provide his daughter with a proper upbringing. The other girls still looked down on her for being the poor girl. She wanted to fit in, and the whole *BE YOURSELF* platitude was not going to cut it in her situation.

She had to be more than herself. She had to stand out. She not only had to stand out from the crowd but stand out in the crowd. She had to be crazy. She knew she couldn't be one of the rich girls, but she could be the rich girls' crazy friend. That is what she became. The crazy one! The one who would go out with the rich girls and drink too much. She was the one who would drunkenly flirt with boys. The rich girls would pull her away as they apologized to the boys for the way she had been acting. The boys would tell the rich girls it was fine. Deep down inside they were mad at the rich girls for pulling away their chance at getting some action.

Girls like her gave the rich girls a sense of responsibility. As they carried her out to the car when she had too much to drink or when they held her hair back as she vomited, the rich girls believed they were being good friends. That they were part of the solution. They would haul her drunk from parties and bars. They would pull her by her arms with her legs dragging on the concrete. The concrete would scratch the flesh off her one bare foot. It would be bare because she was missing a shoe. A shoe she had unwittingly left behind. The rich girls would shout to the crowd of gawkers, "We're sorry about our friend!" Even if she was intoxicated beyond recognition, just hearing the rich and attractive girls identify her as "our friend" made it all worthwhile.

It was a miracle that Ms. Cole earned her teaching degree. Becoming an eighth-grade teacher did not sober her up the least. It did the opposite. Now she had a little spending money not coming from her daddy. She went out every weekend and blew her paycheck three days faster than it took her to make it. It wasn't just the weekends. Ms. Cole never missed an opportunity to party. It gracelessly grew to where it was no longer about her impressing her friends. It became something she came to enjoy. She developed a real love for partying. She had an addiction to partying, drinking, smoking, and sleeping with men.

Ms. Cole was late for work because she had overslept. Where she had overslept was in the bed of a stranger she had met the previous night at a club. She woke up and realized she had to be at school and was late. The only good thing about sleeping over at this guy's place was that she was now actually closer to the school than her own apartment. Ms. Cole threw on the dress she wore out clubbing the previous night. She then threw a black leather jacket over it and headed to work. The dress was something she thought she could pull off at school. That was until she arrived at the school, walked into the restroom, and looked in the mirror. She was a disaster, and there was nothing she could do about it. Ms. Cole took off the jacket and stood there in the red dress she had worn out the night before. It was sleeveless and low-cut. She realized she was going to be leaving the jacket on for the rest of the day. The dress was not appropriate for teaching a group of eighth graders. Ms. Cole observed her pale and freckly skin in the restroom mirror, and only hoped that under the black lights and the dark ambiance of the club the night before she had appeared more alluring. She looked a lot different than she had in her bathroom mirror the night before she left for the evening out. It was as if she had aged ten years in the course of one night. She put her jacket back on and headed toward the classroom. As she walked into the room, a mousy little girl with curly blond hair named Nova shouted, "You're late!"

"Duh!" said Ms. Cole. "You think I don't know that?"

All the boys in the class had a crush on Ms. Cole. They would never admit it to any of their classmates. Deep down inside they had a hard time admitting it to themselves. Even Beetle had a secret crush on her. Beetle would have thoughts about his teacher that made him feel guilty. Whenever one of those suggestive ideas would come to his mind, he would switch his thoughts toward something different. Beetle's mind was always filled with thoughts. So whenever an ill thought crossed his mind, he had no problem switching to a new one.

—

Beetle once had a dream about Ms. Cole. He dreamt he was on a deserted island with her, and she was wearing a strapless, tie-around, red bikini top with a hula skirt. She wore nothing underneath the hula skirt. On the island, the trees all caught on fire. The flames spread until the whole island was ablaze. Beetle and Ms. Cole stood ankle deep in the ocean water. They watched the whole island become engulfed in flames. Ms. Cole told Beetle they had to swim or they would burn to death. Beetle told Ms. Cole he couldn't swim. Ms. Cole told Beetle he didn't have to worry about swimming. Ms. Cole said she could float on her back and he could ride on top of her like a raft. The idea of floating out in the ocean scared Beetle. The thought of staying behind and burning alive scared him more. So Beetle decided to use Ms. Cole as a flotation device if it granted him safety from the island inferno.

Beetle and Ms. Cole dove into the sea. The tide removed both Beetle's swim shorts and Ms. Cole's hula skirt. Knowing he couldn't swim, Beetle tried his best to paddle to keep himself afloat, but he couldn't hold out for long. Ms. Cole floated calmly on her back as she lay on top of the ocean water. She turned her head, squinting over at Beetle. He kicked and flailed his arms in panic. His naked body submerged up to his chin in blue ocean water. Ms. Cole lay there on the surface of the water, wearing only her strapless, tie-around, red bikini top. Her hula skirt lost at sea. Squinting from the scorching sun, Ms. Cole looked down at Beetle and told him to swim over to her. She instructed him to get on top of her so he wouldn't drown. Despite being embarrassed because of his nakedness, he swam over and hopped on top of her. He rode her like a raft. As he rode on top of her, she kept asking him if it felt good to be on top of her. All of a sudden something happened. Beetle woke up from his dream. He found he was wet. Beetle had been a lifelong bedwetter, but this was different.

He only had a dream like that one other time. He dreamt he was in a graveyard. In the graveyard, there was a playground with swings and slides. Beetle climbed the ladder of one of the slides. When he was at the top, he looked down. A girl in his class was at the bottom of the slide. Her name was Jennifer. She went by the name Jenny. Then she changed her name to Jenni. She dotted the *i* in her name with a star. She would draw the star in one single swipe. One day a boy asked if she was Jewish. She told him she was not. He asked, "If you're not Jewish, then how come you write your name with a Jewish star?" The star dotting her *i* resembled the Star of David. Jenni started taking more time to dot the *i* with a star. She spent lots of time spacing out every single point of the polygon shape, making sure to not leave a single mark in the center of the star.

Beetle was at the top of the slide, and Jenni was at the bottom. She was naked. Beetle looked down at himself. He was naked, too. Jenni told Beetle to come down the slide. She said she would catch him. Beetle did not want to go down the slide because he was nervous. He did not like going down slides. He was also embarrassed about being naked. Jenni said it would be fine because she would catch him. Beetle went ahead and slid down the slide. When he reached the end, Jenni caught him. Beetle knocked her down. They fell onto the woodchips. Beetle plopped his body on top of her, their naked bodies in the dirt and chunks of wood shavings. Jenni asked

Beetle if it felt good to be on top of her. She asked him the same way Ms. Cole asked him in the ocean dream. Then, he woke up, and his underwear was sticky wet. Those were the only two dreams of that sort that he had dreamt.

—

"Did y'all finish the reading assignment?" Ms Cole asked the classroom. When no one responded, she looked at them with her eyes wide open with confusion. She looked at Nova. The blond girl was playing with a strand of her curly hair. She twirled it around her finger as she gazed up into the fluorescent light. "Nova? Earth to Nova! Did you read the reading assignment?"

"What reading assignment?" Nova asked.

"Did anybody here read the reading assignment?"

All the students were silent except for one small voice that asked "What assignment?" so quietly it was impossible to make out which one of the students said it.

"What assignment?" Ms. Cole pointed to the chalkboard. "The assignment I wrote down on the board! Like I do every single day! Now get out your books and start reading!"

All the students pulled out their reading books. They opened to the pages Ms. Cole wrote down on the board. As they did so, Ms. Cole reached up and squeezed the stem of her nose. She squeezed her eyes shut. She didn't realize how bad her hangover was until she started screaming. It was not a good idea to drink so many Mountain Blackberry Clearly Canadians with Grey Goose on the rocks.

Ms. Cole began to take off her jacket without thinking. When it was down to her shoulders, she realized she was wearing the dress underneath. The dress that was not appropriate for school. She threw the jacket back over her freckled shoulders and zipped it up. She slid the office chair on wheels out from behind her desk. Ms. Cole sat on it discreetly. She crossed her legs as tightly as they would cross. That morning she couldn't find her panties when she woke up, despite having help from her new male companion. He helped her look all over his place. The lacy pair of pink underwear was nowhere. She intended to stop and pick some up along the way, then realized there was no place from the loft to the school where she could stop and buy underwear. Because she was so late for work, she decided to go commando.

Ms. Cole had a wide-open desk on the bottom. Her legs were visible to every student in the classroom. The open desk was why she usually wore pants when teaching. The young teenagers were stunned to see how beautiful her legs were. She had stems worthy to model nylons. Her legs grew numb from keeping them crossed so tightly for so long. It was necessary to keep her legs crossed. Ms. Cole was not in the mood to add an anatomy lesson to the students' daily curriculum.

FOUR

AFTER SCHOOL, Beetle headed down to the custodial closet along with a boy named Brownie. Brownie was the third shortest in their class. Beetle and Bullet were the only ones shorter. Brownie was the smartest in the class. He also had the poorest parents. Brownie was rebellious. He embraced his smartness to the point of being a show-off. Brownie had a superiority complex because of his intelligence. In reality, he used his aptitude, his quick wits, and his ability to thrive in academics to hide the fact he came from a poverty-stricken family. Brownie was not only book-smart, but he was incredibly street-smart as well. He had never caused physical harm to anyone, but Brownie was verbally abusive to those around him. Brownie never yelled or raised his voice or showed any signs of anger, but his sharp, mean tongue was worse than any angry outburst.

Assisting with custodial work after school was something Beetle and Brownie had to do to help compensate their tuition costs. Brownie came from a low-income family who could not pay the tuition costs. So he had to work after school, unlike Beetle's father. Beetle's dad made enough money working bricks and mortar to pay the school for his son's education comfortably. However, Beetle's father felt this was a good program for his son. So they signed him up to be a Junior Janitor.

Beetle and Brownie sat in the custodial office in the basement of the school. They waited a few minutes until Gary, the school's one and only custodian, showed up. Gary was an older man, but there was no telling exactly how old he was. He was bald but had gray hair on the sides of his head and a thick, gray mustache. There was a stack of mail in his hand as he walked over to his desk. The desk had fake, wooden laminate on top; it was bubbling up and chipping, exposing the plywood underneath. He sat at the desk in his old chair, covered in gray cloth and stains. The chair had holes in it from where mice had chewed through the material. The little rodents dined on the sweat-soaked orangish foam padding underneath.

"You know that public high school down the street? Well, it's been crazy over there. They've got a bunch of janitors over there, and one of them got in trouble for taking a leak in the girls' locker room showers. The people runnin the place over there wanted to embarrass the guy, and they fired him in front of all the other janitors, and this guy being fired goes, 'How do you know I did it?' and they go, 'Cause we saw you on the security camera!' Then the guy being fired goes, 'Why do you have a security camera in the girls' showers?' Then the people firin him from the school didn't know what to say to this. Then all the other janitors got upset and asked why the school would have cameras in showers where fourteen- and fifteen-year-old girls are showerin, and you know the bosses didn't know what to say to this. Then the janitors all tried to blackmail the bosses by tellin em they were goin to call the news and let em know that the school had cameras in the girls' showers and locker room. They said they would do it if the school didn't pay em not to say it. Ain't that crazy?

"Now they're all on some kinda strike. The place there looks like some kinda trash jungle. There's nobody cleanin the place up, and it's just covered in trash. They just brought me over there to help out durin the day, and there's trash overflowin from the cans and the halls are just filled with trash. It's like you're walkin through trash. It's like each one of the halls is like just a big river of trash and you're just walkin through it like you're walkin through the water in like a pond or somethin."

"So they were paying you to help them clean up because all the janitors were on strike?" asked Brownie.

"Yep, they were."

"You actually did work?"

"Yep, I did work for em cause the other janitors weren't there."

"Why didn't you just tell them that you would go to the news and police and whatever the janitors are all saying they would go to, and then have them pay you for not doing it like they're paying their own janitors?"

"I'm not into blackmail. I prefer good old-fashion mail." Gary held up a pink envelope with glitter all over. "I like pink mail."

On Gary's desk was a stack of papers with handwritten complaints. The papers were criticisms of things not properly handled over the previous few nights. There were also two books on his desk. Books he read for pleasure: *The Basics of Winning Lotto/Lottery* and *Winning Lotto/Lottery for Everyday Players*. The books had well-worn spines. On the wall was a Vietnam War calendar exhibiting a gruesome painting of soldiers in the jungle fighting. Many lay on the ground dead or barely alive, suffering from bad battle wounds. Some gushed blood from blown-off limbs. Gary was injured in the war in Vietnam. He had the Purple Heart gold-framed under glass in the custodial office to confirm it. Gary tossed the mail on the desk. He scooted his chair over to face the two boys. "I have my mail delivered here cause I don't trust it comin to my house cause I don't know who goin to steal it cause it's always gettin stolen."

Glitter from the envelope stuck to Gary's dirty fingernails. It caught in his mustache from where he had been scratching it. Beetle thought he saw glitter on his bald head, but that was tiny, glistening specks of sweat.

Gary reached into the open envelope and extracted a greeting card. The card had a cartoonish illustration of an overstuffed teddy bear holding over inflated balloons in its paws. He opened the card up, and two photographs fell into his lap. He picked the pictures up and handed one to Beetle.

"Here's a picture of my new grandchild," Gary said as he handed the photograph over to Beetle.

Beetle looked at the picture in confusion. The girl in the picture was not a baby like he was expecting. "This is your new grandchild?" asked Beetle.

"Well, she ain't new to God's green earth, but she's new to me."

"She's your son's daughter?"

"That's right. My son does tattoos, and some girl came in and wanted a tattoo and this little angel was the result of their exchange."

"She exchanged her baby for a tattoo?" Beetle was completely confused.

"Well, what happened was this baby's mother had a bad drug addiction and she didn't have any money and she had to give up her baby. But I'm not talkin about a real baby, I'm talkin about a baby pit bull. She had a pit bull puppy. She had a baby pit bull that she loved, but it was sad cause she loved drugs more. So in order to get drugs and cause she didn't have any money, she had to sell the pit bull, but she felt so guilty bout sellin the pit bull that she wanted to have a way of rememberin it. So she went and got herself a tattoo of the pit bull. She went to my son cause he did tattoos, and she asked him if he could do a tattoo for her but since she didn't have no money they worked out the payment through another exchange that ended up resultin in the birth of this little angel right here," Gary yanked the photograph out of Beetle's fingers. "They only did it once."

"They only did what once?" asked Beetle.

"They only did *it* once. You get what'um sayin? Then she came to him last week and said she's sick of the baby and she told him if he wanted it he can take it back and handed him this precious little six-year-old. He went and had a paternity test done to prove that it was his and sure enough it was, so now he's taken legal actions and it's now in full custody of his care."

Beetle still didn't understand how Gary's son ended up with the little girl.

"My son just got married! Not to the pit bull baby woman who had his baby. He just got married to the most wonderful woman you've ever seen. She's beautiful too. They have a baby, and it's only one. Here's a picture of em." Gary handed Beetle another photograph. In the picture, Gary's son held the new six-year-old. His blond wife held the one-year-old. "Well, that's enough of my stories. You boys ready to work?"

Beetle and Brownie headed out to do their daily routine. Beetle cleaned the restrooms, and Brownie cleaned the classrooms. There was no argument between Beetle and Brownie about who would take on which job. Beetle willingly took the restrooms because he was allergic to chalk. Cleaning the chalkboard would result in a horrible allergic reaction. Brownie was happy to take the classrooms over the bathrooms. The idea of cleaning a toilet repulsed him. What he found more disgusting was emptying the boxes filled with used tampons. Emptying the feminine hygiene boxes did not seem to bother Beetle. He didn't understand what it was he was emptying.

Brownie always finished before Beetle. On that day he finished so quickly, he offered to help Beetle. He thought helping him clean would be better than standing around doing nothing. "I'll help you do the floors and I'll spray the urinals, but I'm not scrubbing them and I'm definitely not touching the toilets," explained Brownie. "I'm hella not touching the blood boxes."

Brownie mopped the floors and sprayed the urinals as Beetle scrubbed the toilets. As Beetle scrubbed, Brownie told him his great ancestor came over on the Mayflower. Brownie said his pilgrim ancestor brought opium over on the ship. "He made heroin. It was different back then," said Brownie. "You wouldn't light it up with a pocket lighter; you'd use a candle or maybe a fireplace. Also, you wouldn't use a silver spoon to boil it. You'd have to use a wooden spoon." Brownie also told Beetle his great uncle was the one who dropped the atomic bomb on Hiroshima. "My great uncle received a certificate from President Reagan back in 1981 congratulating him on murdering more people than anyone else in human history. That's pretty cool, ain't it?"

After running out of stories, Brownie walked over to a dirty window. He killed time by killing hundreds of ants crawling up and down the windowsill. Brownie squashed each ant with his thumb one by one. "I bet this was what it was like when my great uncle was flyin that bomber plane and blew up all those Orientals."

Cleaning the restrooms resulted in many large trash bags filled with paper towels along with many buried treasures hidden inside. The giant trash bags were rather lightweight. Even though they hardly weighed anything, Beetle still preferred to drag the bags across the floor. He had to bring the bags to the back of the school. The trash had to be thrown away in the dumpster by the loading dock. As Beetle stepped outside, he propped the door open with one of the five trash bags he brought. Beetle threw the other four trash bags in the dumpster. He realized he could not throw away the fifth bag without having the door shut behind him. That was when he had the idea to brace it open with his shoe.

Beetle removed his once black sneaker. The sneaker was so worn out, the black paint had almost come all the way off. The shoes looked white because the cotton was fully exposed. Beetle placed the shoe down and shut the door so it would be propped open. He was proud of himself for coming up with the idea. Beetle grabbed the last trash bag. He hopped over to the dumpster on one foot to throw it away. As he was hopping, Brownie pranked him. When Beetle was jumping up and down on one foot with his back to the door, Brownie snatched the shoe out from where it held the door open. Beetle was unaware it happened. He only saw the door was shut when he returned. Brownie always said things that were rude, but Beetle never assumed he would do something like this. The thought of somebody pulling his shoe out from the door never crossed Beetle's mind. He believed the door's own pressure pushed it out of the way and then it shut and locked on its own. Beetle was in a panic.

Beetle was in the back of the school. He had to walk all the way to the front to the school's main entrance. As he walked the side of the school building, he hopped on one foot until it wore him out. He thought about hopping again when he stepped down and realized how wet and cold the ground was on his sock. After his sock had gotten soaked and muddy, he pulled it off and toddled along with one exposed foot. The side of the school building was lined with pine trees. All the pine needles had turned brown and fallen to the ground. They poked the bottom of his naked foot. He decided it was best to put his muddy, wet sock back on.

When Beetle finally made it to the front of the school, he realized the doors were locked. Brownie and Gary had left. It was cold, and his jacket was inside. Beetle banged on the school's glass doors, but no one was inside. He knew pounding on the doors was not going to get anyone's attention because all the lights in the school were off. Beetle was certain nobody was inside.

Beetle's mother finally pulled up in front of the school. "Why aren't you wearing a coat?" she asked.

"I left my coat inside."

"Why do you only have on one shoe?"

"My shoe was left inside too."

"How did you leave only one shoe inside? Why did you even take your shoe off in the first place?"

Beetle explained the whole story about trying to hold the door open with the shoe.

FIVE

THE FOLLOWING DAY AT SCHOOL, Beetle found his jacket in the Lost and Found, but there was no sign of his sneaker. When Brownie snatched Beetle's shoe, he tossed the shoe into one of the restroom's trash cans. He thought this would be a funny joke because Beetle would find the shoe while pulling out the trash the next day. After putting the shoe in the trash can, Brownie thought Beetle might overlook the shoe because when he threw it in, it had a trash can liner inside of the can. He thought about how people would fill the trash can with trash and Beetle would pull the bag out and never see the shoe down at the bottom of the can. Brownie pulled the shoe out of the empty trash bag and tugged the trash liner upward and dropped the sneaker directly into the inside of the trash can. This way, when Beetle would remove the trash bag, he would see the shoe at the bottom of the bagless trash can.

Beetle asked the girl working the office if anyone had turned in his shoe.

"I haven't seen it."

"Has somebody turned in a little Troll with green hair with glitter on it?"

"No."

Beetle used to have a pencil with a little Troll at the end over the eraser. The Troll was not even an inch tall—unless measured by the tip of its hair. At a school assembly, the Troll fell off the pencil and dropped underneath the bleachers. Gary mopped it up off the gymnasium floor right after the assembly and threw it out. It had been over a year since Beetle lost it. He still went into the office a couple times a week to ask if somebody had found it.

Ms. Cole was late for class again. In fact, today she would not show up at all. The previous night she had gone out alone. She was sick of clubs and meeting guys. Ms. Cole was in the market to meet some real men. She decided to put on a baseball jersey and designer blue jeans, and head down to the sports bar across the street from her apartment.

Sitting alone at the bar, she watched the game on the little box TV mounted to the wall above. A charismatic man sat beside her. They talked, and Ms. Cole hit it off very well with the charming stranger. He seemed interested in her, even after she had knocked back numerous shots of Rumple Minze peppermint schnapps and chased them with many bottles of Zima. The guy she was sitting with said he was waiting for his friend to show up.

His friend finally arrived and invited Ms. Cole to join them at their table. They all sat and drank beers. Ms. Cole was hitting it off with this guy she had just met. Then the guy's friend told her about how the man she had taken a fancy for was in fact married. This news deeply affected Ms. Cole, even if she had only known the man for a little less than two hours. She still hung out with the duo until they got up and left, and then she followed them out and tried to drive home.

Ms. Cole was in a bad situation, but things ended up just getting worse. As she drove home drunk, she saw the flashing lights behind her. She pulled over, and the police officer asked her to step out of the car and gave her a Breathalyzer test. She failed. The police brought her into jail and slapped her with a Driving Under the Influence charge. This was her second DUI. The first one she had received was when she was in college. Her family was so disappointed. They called an intervention and eventually dragged her to Alcoholics Anonymous. She stopped going to AA. The speakers stood up and told stories about narcotics, prostitution, multiple suicide attempts, etc. She believed she was nowhere near as bad as these people just because she had a few drinks and got pulled over.

She was now in the same situation. She was getting her second DUI charge. She used her one phone call to call her parents. Her father picked up the call. She told him that she got pulled over for drinking again. Her father remembered how horrible it was the last time. He remembered how she swore to them that she would not do this again. Her father hung the phone up on her, leaving her to solve the problem herself. The last time she was in this situation, her father came and bailed her out. She had no idea she could bail herself out by calling a bondsman. She ended up spending two days in the holding cell because the court was not in session until Thursday. That is why Ms. Cole failed to show for school.

In class, the students all sat in their desks. There was a reading assignment written on the chalkboard. Ms. Cole had written it out the day before, right after school let out. The students talked amongst themselves on whether they should pull out their readers and read the assignment. Latricia suggested one person read it and then tell everybody else in the classroom what it was about. Everyone seemed to like this idea. Latricia volunteered to read the story and give the class a summary. As she began reading to herself, Brownie pulled out his book and started reading as well. Brownie was showing off how he could speed-read. Once he finished the reading assignment, Brownie turned around and started telling everyone what it was about. "It was about this guy named Pavlov," Brownie announced to the class. "He had this dog. Every time he would show his dog a bowl or plate of food, the dog would salivate."

A boy named Billy sang out, "Sa-li-vate good times, come on!"

"A salivation," sang Brownie, "to last throughout the years."

"So what happened with the dog and its food?" Nova asked Brownie.

"So the dog would salivate when it was shown its plate of food," Brownie explained. "Then this Pavlov guy, the guy who owned the dog, he showed the dog the plate and the plate didn't have any food on it and the dog still started droolin. It drooled just cause it saw the plate, not cause there was food on it or anything. Then Pavlov started ringin a bell every time he'd give the dog food. Then he just started ringin the bell without givin the dog food just to tease it, and the dog salivated just by the sound of the bell."

"What was the point of the story?" Nova asked. "Why would they even have us read something like that?"

"That dog was a retard!" said Bullet. "I bet if we rang a bell every time Beetle went to the restroom, we could ring a bell and then he would pee and poop his pants."

Most of the class laughed

Latricia was still three pages away from completion.

The students sat in the classroom for hours alone, without a teacher. They all kept their eyes on the clock and when lunchtime rolled around, they headed down to eat. None of the other teachers questioned why they were going down there teacher-less. The eighth graders were a little more rowdy than usual, but none of the teachers questioned it. This class of students was notorious for being boisterous.

Even at lunch, they all kept their eyes on the clock. When it was time to head back up, they all progressed back to the classroom. Around two o'clock in the afternoon, the music teacher came up to the classroom after waiting a half an hour for the eighth graders who never showed up to the music classroom. Had they just planned the music class out, they could have skimmed through without anyone noticing they went all day without being supervised. The music teacher was outraged. She couldn't believe they had not had a teacher all day long and she reported it to the central office. The principal deemed it was necessary to address the eighth-grade class on why they did not contact the main office within the first few minutes of not having a teacher present when school started. However, the principal was not in the mood to give a disciplinary lecture. He decided to plan out an impassioned speech to give the students the next day. He sent his secretary up to watch them for the remaining hour or two left in the school day.

After school was over, Beetle and Brownie went down to the custodial office as usual. A new man was working there who looked nervous when he saw them. He advised the two boys they should head up and talk to whoever was in the office before coming back down there. The principal told the two boys that Gary was not in today because he was sent to the public high school. A temp service sent the school a temporary janitor to fill in. The principal told the two boys they would be paid for the day but didn't have to work because Gary was not there. They would normally have the two kids work with the temporary janitor, but the school had been informed that the janitor they had been sent was a convicted sex offender. So they found it best if he was not left alone in the school at night with the two boys.

Beetle asked the principal if he could use the office phone. He needed to call his mother. She did not know to pick him up early. The principal reminded Beetle that students were not allowed to use the office phone. They had to use the pay phone out in the hall. Beetle was not a confident boy. He did not explain to the principal that he did not have a quarter for the pay phone.

Brownie lived not far from the school. He walked every day. The principal told the boys they could go. Brownie darted out the front door and headed home as quickly as possible. He was so relieved not to have to clean up the classrooms after school.

Beetle was frightened about having to wait five hours for his mother to come pick him up. He walked to the door slowly because he was not in any rush. As he passed the pay phone, he stuck his finger into the coin return slot. He checked to see if by luck there might be a quarter inside. It was empty, but it didn't really matter. Even if there was a quarter, Beetle did not know his own phone number.

Waiting in the cold, Beetle stood in the grass in front of the school. He looked down at the tight dress shoes he was wearing. Beetle was relieved when he was called out of having to clean the restrooms tonight. His feet were killing him from wearing his nice shoes all day. Beetle did not want to have to do janitorial work in the pair of shoes he wore to church. They were the only pair of shoes Beetle now had because his sneaker had been found earlier in the day by the temporary custodian who threw it way. The sneaker was so old and worn out that when the temporary custodian saw it, he did not for a second question whether or not the shoe was trash.

As Beetle looked up, he filled with dread when he saw Bullet and his sidekick Cage walking toward him. Bullet was the biggest bully in the class despite being the second shortest. Cage was Bullet's sidekick. Cage was the borderline giant. Cage was not a mean person, but he was definitely a follower. Cage would do anything Bullet told him to do. He was like Bullet's personal bodyguard. Had Bullet told Cage to beat somebody up, Cage would beat him or her up. Bullet and Cage walked over to Beetle. "Hey, Beetle," said Bullet, "are you and that Brownie guy lovers? Everyone says you're lovers. And it would make sense that you're lovers cause you both hang out every night alone in the school."

"No, we're not lovers! We only hang out in the school to work cleaning the school up."

"Why do you guys hang out after school n clean it up?"

"Cause we're poor."

Both Bullet and Cage laughed out loud at what Beetle said.

"Yeah, I heard your parents were really poor," said Bullet. "Guess when your mom's as ugly as your mom is she can only make it as a cheap hooker."

"Stop picking on him!" a girl's voice said out of nowhere.

Beetle turned around and saw Latricia walking up behind him.

"Oh, Beetle! You've sent your girlfriend after me?"

"You say one more mean thing to Beetle," Latricia gave Bullet a mean glare. "and I will slit your throat from ear to ear."

"You're kinda hot for being black," Bullet said to Latricia. "You're not one of those scary blacks."

"Pick on me or pick on Beetle and I can get scary."

"Are you and Beetle doin it?" Bullet asked Latricia. "If you and Beetle are doin it, then I have to say that Beetle's a lucky guy."

"No!" huffed Latricia. "We're not doin it!"

Bullet told Latricia all the perverse things he would like to do to her.

"You're a pig!" Latricia told Bullet.

"I may be a pig," said Bullet, "but you're a monkey. A porch monkey."

"You're an animal!"

"I know! I'm a pig. You've said that already."

"You're the sort of guy that's never going to get any because you're so mean to girls."

"Girls like it when you treat em like that! Girls like a man who's in charge."

"No, they like a man who will treat them with respect."

"I can get some whenever I want."

"The only way you could ever get some is if you pay for it. I'm sure you're going to be the sort of guy that pays for it. It's going to be the only way you could ever get some and even then you'll most likely be so rude when you're paying for it that whoever you're paying is going to tell you to hit the road the second they meet you because of how gross and mean and rude you are."

—

Latricia was on to something. The following year Bullet would receive a check from his grandmother for Christmas. He would go and cash the check. With the money, he bought a newspaper and a day bus pass. He used the back of the newspaper to contact a woman named Lady Lacey. According to the description in the ad, Lady Lacey was quite attractive. He called Lady Lacey and set up an appointment with her for the same evening. Over the phone, she sounded attractive. Bullet used his bus pass to ride out to where she was located. Lady Lacey had told him which bus stop to get off on. The bus stopped against the road. There was a long forest area. Bullet had to walk down a gravel road for about a half an hour. He was cold and wished he had brought a coat.

When he finally arrived, the structure was a metal shed. Now the sky was merging from a blood red to the dark of night. Bullet knocked on the door. No one answered. He knocked again. Finally, Lady Lacey came to the door. She poked her head out. She was naked. "I'm busy right now," Lady Lacey said. "I need for you to wait for me 'nother half hour, k?"

Bullet waited in the back of the shed for over a half an hour. The door opened up, and a big, tall man with a long beard walked out of the shed. The man had tattoos all over his neck. Bullet's heart started pounding when the man looked over at him. The man gave Bullet an irate stare. The mean look was because of the man's embarrassment for seeing Bullet. The man got into a pickup truck parked in front of the shed and quickly drove off. As he did, Bullet kept an eye on him. Bullet had not realized Lady Lacey was standing in the doorway of her shed. "Come on in!" said Lady Lacey. "It's freezing cold outside, and I'm buck naked."

Bullet walked inside. The shed was only one windowless room. Portable heaters lined the floor. There was a shower out in the open. There was a large, square, industrial sink. The lights came from a twin halogen light stand. Only one light was turned on. The light was shown on the wall, and it bounced off to give it a softer ambiance. The only piece of furniture in the shed was a full-size bed. On it was an old blanket with bright colors now deeply faded. The blanket had an image of an illustrated tiger. The tiger was cartoonish but looked mean and happy at the same time. It had long, sharp fangs. Resembling a cross between a vampire and a saber-toothed tiger with black and orange stripes. The tiger gave an ornery smile as if ripping a man apart was going to be the most fun it ever had in its life. The ornery grin on the tiger's face bore a resemblance to the look Bullet would give Beetle before beating him up.

Lady Lacey had a tattoo up the side of her left leg. It overlapped onto her bare buttocks. Bullet recognized the symbol. It was an emblem of an eagle standing on a globe with a roped anchor behind it. It was the insignia of the United States Marine Corps. He knew the seal very well as his father had been a US Marine Sergeant. Seeing the symbol reminded him of his father who had passed away three years ago the very same week.

Lady Lacey sat on the bed with her naked legs crossed. She asked Bullet for the donation. Bullet gave her the money. As he did, he saw two tattoos on her right chest. One was a tiny unicorn. The other was a red and blue hibiscus flower. This reminded Bullet of his grandmother—the one who had given him the check he cashed. The unicorn reminded him of his grandmother because she collected glass unicorns. The hibiscus reminded him of her because she always had them in a vase on a stand when he would enter her house.

"You look young," said Lady Lacey. "How old is you?"

"I'm twenty-two," Bullet lied. The then high school freshman was only fifteen but thought twenty-two would be an age he could pass off.

"Twenty-two?" Lady Lacey gave him a questioning stare. "You look like a ten-year-old! I've got a ten-year-old grandson. He looks older than you."

"No, I'm twenty-two," Bullet lied again. He felt justified lying about his age as Lady Lacey's ad said she was twenty-nine years old. Clearly, she was not if she had a ten-year-old grandson. Bullet noticed Lady Lacey's voice was significantly different than it had been on the telephone. Lady Lacey was not the one he spoke with when he called. It was Lady Lacey's daughter who had a much younger and prettier voice who had set up the appointment by phone.

"You ain't a cop are you?"

"No, I am NOT a cop."

"You look like a cop!"

Bullet found it strange how Lady Lacey had just told him he looked like a ten-year-old and now she said he looked like a cop.

"If you ain't a cop," Lady Lacey said as she fixed her eyes on him sideways, "prove it!"

"Prove it?" Bullet was confused on how she wanted him to prove it. How do you prove you're not a cop? Do you pull out your wallet and show the absence of a badge?

"Prove it! Pull it out!"

"Pull it out?"

"Yea! Pull it out! Unzip your pants and show it to me. If you're a cop, then you can't show it to me."

Despite being embarrassed, Bullet did as she requested.

She never actually looked at him or it during the unveiling.

After Bullet had put it away and zipped it back up, Lady Lacey said, "How old do you say you is?"

"Twenty-two."

"Let me see your ID."

"I don't have an ID."

"You don't have a driver's license?"

"No. That's why I asked about taking the bus. I don't drive."

"Why don't you drive?"

"I got my driver's license taken away for drinking and driving." Bullet was impressed with himself for coming up with such a quick lie.

"They won't take your license away for drinking and driving. They just suspend it. They let you keep it. You just can't drive with it."

Bullet could not come up with any more lies.

"You got the protection?"

"Do I have what?"

"Protection. I told you to bring it over the phone." Lady Lacey's daughter did not tell Bullet to bring what her mother had instructed her to tell all of her clients.

"No."

"Well, then, I'm just going to have to tell you to go."

"Really?"

"If you come in here the way you come in here and tell me stuff that freaks me out, then I ain't havin none of it. Go!"

"Can I have my money back?"

"No! Go!"

"But if we didn't do anything, then I should have my money back."

"I ain't givin it back! You bought my time and you come here and you waste my time. Now if you don't get out of here, then I'm gonna call somebody to come here and grab your head and twist it around in a circle like an owl until it pops right off of your neck."

This frightened Bullet. He walked out of the shack and back through the snow until he arrived at the bus stop. When he stood at the bus stop, he began to cry. It was so cold outside; it felt like his warm, salty tears were freezing to his face.

—

Latricia advised Beetle to come inside the school with her. Beetle did as she told him. Once inside, Latricia said, "You can come in here, and the boys won't pick on you. Are you waiting for somebody to pick you up?"

"Yeah, my mom is comin to pick me up, but she's gonna be a little bit late."

"A little bit late? School let out over an hour ago."

"Yeah, she's not gonna be here until five o'clock."

"Five o'clock? You should come with me. On Tuesdays now, the new priest here, he shows foreign films in the gym. You can come sit by me."

Beetle followed Latricia into the gym. They each grabbed a plastic folding chair, leaning against the wall. They brought the chairs toward the stage. The new priest who gave the Mass on Sunday came out and stood in front of the crowd. Apart from Latricia and Beetle, there were only six other people in the audience. Latricia and Beetle were by far the two youngest people there. The rest of everyone else was middle-aged to elderly. After he had greeted the audience, the priest told everyone they were in for a real treat. He had two great movies to show. He also bragged about how good the two films were going to look. They were remastered, and they would be presented on LaserDisc. He told the audience, "Watching these on LaserDisc is second only to seeing the films projected on thirty-five millimeter."

The priest walked over to the projector. He hit PLAY on the LaserDisc player. He manually pressed the button reading FF >> to fast-forward through the white texts against the red background, declaring the FBI Warning. When the first few frames of the movie appeared on screen, he let go of the button. The movie resumed back to normal speed.

The movie was a black-and-white French film made in the '50s. It was about a man who meets a girl. That was about as much of the plot as Beetle could make out. Beetle had a hard time reading the subtitles. He had trouble reading, but it was even harder for him to read these because they were going fast. He was also not wearing his glasses. Beetle chose not to wear his glasses because he felt he looked better without them. He wanted to look good with Latricia around. So he kept them in the pocket of his black, wool coat.

The second movie that was screened was an Italian film. It was also black and white. The movie was about a man who meets a little girl. That was all the plot Beetle understood. He was not able to sit through the entirety of the film because his mother was there to pick him up. Beetle spent more time watching the hands on the clock in the gym than watching the movies.

Beetle's father insisted they sit down together for a family meal, homemade and prepared by his wife every night. After they said grace, Beetle's mother looked at her son and asked, "Did you find your shoe?"

"No."

"Where's your shoe?" Beetle's father asked.

"Don't know," confessed Beetle. "I lost it."

"How do you lose a shoe?" Beetle's father said as he slapped a large helping of mashed potatoes onto his plate.

Beetle did not answer.

"We're going to have to get him new shoes," his mother said as she looked at her husband.

Beetle's father poked a hole in his mountain of potatoes with his spoon. He spun the spoon until he could see the white glass of his plate through the hole.

"I'll need money to get him shoes," Beetle's mother said.

"Why can't he just find the shoe he lost?"

"It's gone," proclaimed Beetle. "I've looked everywhere."

Beetle's father kept his eye on Beetle as he stood from the table. He stuck his hand into the pocket of his black jeans. The jeans were stained with mortar powder and covered in holes. Beetle's father would wear the jeans with the most holes when it grew cold. He wore his black, long underwear underneath.

"I'm sure I can find a pair on sale," his wife said. "Especially this time of the year."

Beetle's father threw the wad of cash he had extracted from his pocket at his wife as she sat at the dinner table. It almost landed in her food. He then sat back down and reached for the blue and white gravy boat with the floral design.

Beetle's mother un-balled the wad of cash. She examined the wrinkled bills. "There's not enough here to get him a new pair of shoes."

"Then don't get him a new pair." He tilted the gravy boat. Thin, brown gravy sludge fell into the potato nook. The gravy filled to the top and then overflowed. Beetle's father's potatoes looked like a volcano entirely covered in lava. "Go to the thrift store. Get 'im a pair there. You might get lucky and find a pair like the pair he had and only have to get one and only have to pay half for it."

His wife laid the bills out on the dinner table. She ran her hands over them to make them less wrinkled.

"What did you do today in school, son?" he drove a hefty spoonful of gravy-soaked potatoes into his mouth.

"Nothin."

"What did you learn?"

"Nothin." This was Beetle's stock response. Every night at dinner his father would ask him what he learned in school. Beetle would always respond by telling him he learned nothing. With the teacher being absent that day, Beetle's answer was justified. "I watched a movie today at school."

"We send you to a nice private school and they show you movies?"

"Was it an educational movie?" Beetle's mother asked.

"It was a French movie."

"What was it about?" asked Beetle's father.

"Nothin," said Beetle as he poked his broccoli with his fork. "It was French. French movies are all about nothin."

SIX

IT WAS WEDNESDAY. Much to the eighth-grade class's dismay, not only did the new teacher show up on time, she was thirty minutes early. This was the first time all year the kids arrived to class and saw a teacher in the room. The new teacher was named Sergeant Powers. She demanded the students refer to her as Sergeant Powers because she was a ranked US Army E-5 Sergeant. Sergeant Powers explained to the class how she was brought up with not only a strict military upbringing but also a strict militant Catholic upbringing. She said she had been informed of their horrific behavior. It was evident by her demeanor she was not going to stand for it. She even explained how she was told of a student who exposed himself to the last teacher. When she mentioned this, the classroom let out an uproar of laughter. The way she described it made it seem far worse than what really happened. What Sergeant Powers referred to was a time when Ms. Cole was writing on the chalkboard and Bullet said, "Ms. Cole, I have a question!" When Ms. Cole turned around, she saw Bullet with his pants down. He was mooning her. Bullet asked, "What does my butt look like?"

Sergeant Powers had a stable build. She had big, thick shoulders and muscular arms. Her cheeks were so large she resembled a chipmunk storing nuts. She had large acne craters on her cheeks. It looked as if some wild animal had been chewing on them. There was a mannish quality about Sergeant Powers. Her flattop crew cut did not help this impression. If it weren't for her large mammaries resembling overinflated water balloons being held back by an industrial-strength sports bra, Sergeant Powers would have unquestionably passed for a male.

With a long stick, Sergeant Powers smacked the chalkboard so loud every student jumped in their desks. "There's the reading assignment!" Sergeant Powers said. "I want every single one of you to have it finished by Mass."

The assignment consisted of reading three stories from the reader, which was three times more than Ms. Cole ever assigned. Ms. Cole never assigned more than one reading assignment a day from the reader.

Sergeant Powers reached into her desk. She pulled out a yellow rubber ring. It looked like a swim ring. No one could actually use it to keep afloat because it was too small for a doll. An action figure might fit in the hole and be able to float in a pool. Sergeant Powers unplugged the clear air spout and began to blow heavy breaths into the yellow rubber ring. She blew as if she was trying to blow up a Navy Seal raft in order to save her life. It didn't take too many huffs and puffs for her to get the thing fully inflated. She pushed in the nipply air spout and flipped it around. What she inflated resembled a donut with pink frosting and colorful sprinkles. It looked liked the donut had a bite taken from it. She placed the inflated donut on her chair and sat on it. She had to sit on the donut to avoid the pain of her hemorrhoids.

None of the students managed to finish the reading assignment except for Brownie. He was a speed-reader. Sergeant Powers reprimanded the class for being lazy and slow. She was outraged they had not taken her orders. Reaching into her desk, she removed a sheet full of stickers. The sheet had three rows of different color stars. The stars were silver, gold, and red. As she removed the sheet from the desk drawer, she examined it and questioned whether to award Brownie with a gold star or a silver star. She was leaning toward the silver star. Sergeant Powers believed the silver star would be appropriate because reading the reading assignments was hardly deserving of any sort of honor. She thought her students should follow her instructions without being rewarded for doing so, but this was her first day, and because this was the first star she would give out, she felt a gold star would do well for now. As she observed the group of students, she knew there would not be many gold stars given out.

Sergeant Powers walked over to Brownie's desk. She said, "Stand erect."

The students laughed at the word *erect*.

"Stand up!" Sergeant Powers' tone sounded more like she was punishing rather than honoring him.

"Why?" Brownie asked.

"Don't talk back to me!" demanded Sergeant Powers. "Stand erect!"

The students laughed again at the word *erect*. It was even funnier the second time.

"I'm already erect," said Brownie. "That's why I can't stand."

This triggered every student in the room to let out an uproar. Even Beetle laughed, and he didn't understand the joke. He laughed because he found Brownie's delivery to be timed quite well.

Sergeant Powers grabbed Brownie by the front of his shirt collar where the buttons were sewn and yanked him out of the desk. She held him so high, his feet dangled above the ground. She dropped him, and Brownie landed with catlike reflexes. "I am presenting you with a star," the teacher said to the boy as he looked up at her with a frightened face. "A gold star."

She stuck the star to his chest and then slapped his face. The slap was very hard. It knocked Brownie to the ground. She clutched him by his collar and put him back up with both hands. Holding him close to her face, the teacher looked him in the eyes and said, "Next time you talk back to me I'm going to punch you. You feel how strong I am? You don't want me to punch you!" Sergeant Powers dropped Brownie back down to earth. "Congratulations on your star. It's quite an honor."

Brownie sat back down in his desk. He looked down at his shirt to make sure the star had not fallen off.

The teacher looked up at the clock. She then instructed the students to line up for Mass.

At the all-school Mass, the new priest came out. This was his first all-school Mass. He stood at the pedestal and read a passage from Mark nervously, stumbling on the words. The whole school, even the younger students, laughed at his folly. Usually, when the old priest was finished reading the Bible passage, he would then explain the meaning behind it. The former priest was very dry and dull in his explanation. He did not make it entertaining or understandable for the students. Even the older ones struggled with following him owing to their boredom. The new priest walked over and pulled out a reddish pink balloon. It had not yet been inflated. He held it up to the full student body, kindergarten through eighth grade. "What the Gospel of Mark says to us is, it says, and I quote," the priest looked back down at the Bible to make sure he quoted it correctly. "'You must love your neighbor as yourself.' Mark 12:31. What does that mean? This is your heart," he said to his audience as he held up the limp sliver of reddish pink rubber. He inserted the balloon onto a miniature hydrogen tank. "It starts off weak and flaccid. You have to let your love grow. You have to let your heart grow," the balloon sluggishly inflated. "It's not about what it is; it's about what it can become. You've got to feed your heart with love and compassion."

As the balloon grew, it started to take form. When it was about halfway filled, the balloon began to take shape. When the balloon reached its maximum capacity, the priest unplugged the nozzle and tied the knot. He wrapped a kite string around it then let it go. The heart-shaped balloon floated slowly above the students. The balloon moved slower than it would have if filled with helium. The kite string was long, allowing the balloon to float all around the church. The priest lectured the students on what it means to love and how having a full heart doesn't matter unless you let it out. "If you have a big heart, it is wasted unless you let the world see it."

The priest dragged the balloon back to the altar by its kite string. He pulled it down and held it in his hand and walked over to one of the large, lit altar candles. He raised the balloon up to the flame. It took a few seconds. When the fire burned through the rubber, the balloon exploded in a ball of fire. All the kids squealed with excitement.

When the eighth graders returned to class, their new teacher was not in a good mood. She was very upset because she had left her inflatable, pink-frosted-with-colorful-sprinkles, hemorrhoid donut cushion in church. She did not want to walk over there because she did not want to leave the students unsupervised. She called, and the priest checked the pews and found it. He told her he would bring it to her. He explained how he had planned to come up there anyway. He wanted to introduce himself to the students. Also, he wanted to talk to them about something.

The priest entered the classroom with a paper bag in his hand. The teacher's inflatable donut was inside. He put it in the bag because he knew what it was and didn't want to touch it. The priest turned to the class and told them how he was surprised at the lack of altar boys and girls in the church. The priest before him had only two altar boys, and they were high school students. The new priest thought this was strange. He felt it was appropriate to enlist seventh and eighth graders to help out with the services. The priest before him also insisted they have only altar boys—not girls. The new priest thought this was strange because he had come from a church with both girls and boys serving. He saw no reason why a girl should not be able to do it as well. "So girls can do it too?" Latricia asked.

"Yes, of course they can."

"Even if they aren't Catholic?"

"I . . . don't . . . see why not," the priest said slowly because he knew he would have to think it through. "You might have to check with your parents first."

"I'm sure they'd be cool with it."

"Well, whoever is interested, training is Monday, right after school."

"I would love to be an altar boy," said Beetle. "I can't, though."

"Why can't you?" asked the priest.

"Cause I gotta clean up the school after school."

All the students laughed at Beetle.

"Well," said the priest. "I'll see to it that you can get off from doing your after-school chores."

"I don't know," said Beetle. "I've gotta clean the toilets. Who's going to clean the toilets if I'm not there?"

The students laughed at Beetle again.

"I'm sure they'll work it out."

"You're going to leave me with having to clean the toilets," said Brownie.

"Do you want to come down for training?" the priest asked Brownie.

"No way!" Brownie said. "I would rather clean toilets than become an altar boy. At least when you're scrubbing toilets, you're dealing with actual crap instead of made-up crap."

"That's one way of looking at it," said the priest. "So, if anyone else is interested, just come down to church Monday after school.

Also, on Tuesdays, I do a film screening in the gym at four o'clock. We show some great foreign films. I want to thank these two for being there yesterday," the priest pointed to Latricia and Beetle. "Did you two enjoy the movies?"

Latricia nodded her head. Beetle looked over at her. When he saw she admitted to enjoying the movies, he too nodded his head.

"You have to come next Tuesday," the priest told Latricia and Beetle. "We've got a French sci-fi movie called *Alphaville*. You have to check that one out."

"Do I get out of cleaning the school after school if I go see the movie?" asked Beetle.

"I don't know about that," the priest said with embarrassment as he scratched the back of his head. "You'll probably have to check with the principal on that one."

"He better not get out of his duties for watching a movie," said Brownie. "I don't mind scrubbing the toilets for him if he's training to dance around the church in a white dress lighting candles and whatever. I am NOT going to scrub his toilets for him just because he's gone off to watch some movie about French aliens."

Both the priest and the teacher pretended to ignore Brownie's comment. There was a moment of silence as the priest thought of something to say to ease the tension. "Also, this weekend," began the priest, "there's a film festival going on, and if anybody is interested I would recommend you go. If you're a student here, they gave me passes and everything, and you get complimentary admission. If anyone's interested, just let me know, and I'll give you a pass."

"I'd like to go," said Latricia.

"I wanna go too," Beetle said, jumping at the opportunity to attend an event with his classroom crush. "Can I get out of my cleaning duty for the festival?"

"When do you have your cleaning duties?" asked the priest.

"After school."

"Well, then it'll work out fine because the festival is on Saturday."

After school, Beetle went to the school's central office. He asked again if anyone had turned in his missing sneaker. Beetle's mother had to send him to school in his dress shoes once again. The thrift store did not open until eleven. As she dropped him off, Beetle warned her he had gym class in the afternoon. She told him that she would try to get the sneakers to him in time for gym class. It did not happen. She had to go to three different thrift stores to find a sneaker in Beetle's size.

—

The rule was that when students did not wear the proper shoes to gym, the teacher would have them play in bare feet. They stopped doing this after the school experienced an overwhelming outbreak of athlete's foot and other fungal infections. The eighth graders played dodgeball in gym class. Beetle was more than happy to sit it out. He did not care for the game. It was embarrassing getting hit by the ball. What was even more embarrassing was always being the last one picked. Two years prior they had a boy in their class with a broken spine. He was in a wheelchair and couldn't even move his neck. He was picked before Beetle.

Before they began picking teams for the dodgeball game, the gym teacher had the students climb the giant ropes. Beetle could not climb the ropes. As he would try, all the kids laughed at him. What Beetle despised most about climbing the ropes was not that he couldn't do it nor was it that all the other kids could do it and he couldn't. The thing he detested most about the ropes was that he was afraid they were going to get hurt. He was afraid someone was going to get to the top and fall off and crack their head open like Humpty

Dumpty. The other thing he feared was that someone was going to get rope burn. This was a justified fear because back when Beetle was in third grade, there was a girl in his class who climbed the rope to the top. She slid down it fireman style. When she hit the mat at the bottom, she stepped off and started screaming. Everyone turned around. They saw she had blood all over the insides of her legs. Rope burn ripped the flesh off her legs as she slid down. It was the principal's fault. He had bought rope from a hardware store. Rope that was not intended for climbing. The problem had since been resolved. The ropes in the gym were replaced with ropes ordered from a school-supply catalog. The new ropes had been approved for their safety. Beetle still feared it could happen again.

—

The woman working the office said, "Nobody has turned in a shoe, but your mom did drop something off for you."

Beetle was excited and confused when she pulled out a K·B Toy Store bag. The bag was donated to the Disabled American Veterans thrift store where Beetle's mother bought the shoes. Inside the bag were two slightly worn sneakers. They had new laces his mother had put in them. The shoes cost more than the cash her husband gave her to purchase them. Luckily she had some extra money saved up. Beetle tried putting the shoes on, but they were too tight. He still had his one sneaker. Beetle decided to wear it on one foot and the dress shoe on his other foot to do his custodial chores. Beetle and Brownie cleaned the school as usual because Gary was back. Brownie made fun of Beetle for wearing two different shoes until he realized it was his fault Beetle's shoe was missing.

Brownie, as usual, finished cleaning the classrooms before Beetle was finished with the restrooms. Brownie stood over Beetle as Beetle scrubbed a toilet, and Brownie told Beetle about how he was a huge prankster. "I have these cousins that come to town, and they're a lot older than me," Brownie began to tell Beetle. "When they come to town we pull these pranks that are of epic proportions. One time we found this Hamburglar costume. It was like a Halloween costume, and I put it on, and we went to the McDonald's drive-thru, and whenever anyone was going through the drive-thru I would pop up and grab the food when the person working there was putting it through the drive-thru window and the person in the car was reaching for it. I popped up from underneath their car wearing the costume, and I would take it from them and then run off, and I ran to my cousin's car and we drove off. It was hilarious.

"Then one time I got this spaceman costume, and I looked like I was like from the future or something, and we climbed this ladder. It was like one of those ladders on the backs of a building so people can get on the roof. I'm on the roof of the building and whenever people walk by I would jump off the roof of the building and then I'd fall to the ground and nobody knew where I came from and they would all run over cause nobody saw me jump off so they ran over to see what was wrong and it was real funny because the costume was all silvery and I had these big shoes on and they were like these platform shoes like Spice Girls shoes and they would run over to me and I had on this purple cape and I looked like I was from the future and I would start telling them I just fell from the sky and I just came from the future and I had to come back because I couldn't live in future earth anymore cause there wasn't any air and I couldn't breathe and then I started taking really big, deep breaths and I would act like it was the best thing in the world that I was able to breathe fresh air and then I pretended like I was getting really dizzy like the modern-day air was really so good that it made me dizzy."

Gary came into the restroom and said, "Beetle, they'll be sendin you over to work at that public high school where they have em cameras in the girls' showers."

"What about me?" asked Brownie.

"You're gonna stay here with me."

Beetle was excited. He was even more excited when Gary told him he was going to ride over in a limousine. Beetle had always wanted to ride in a limousine his whole life.

Beetle's mother picked him up on time. "Did you get the shoes?" she asked her son.

"Yeah, they didn't fit."

"They were your size."

"I think my feet have grown."

"Are you wearing two different shoes?"

"I was thinkin they'd work better this way."

"Did it work better with two different shoes?"

"No."

"On Saturday I'll take you to get new shoes. I don't want to do this but I'm going to have to go to your grandma's house, and I'm going to have to ask her to give me some money so I can get you some shoes because your dad's not going to provide us with the money. I really hate doing this because I know she has never liked your dad and she's angry I married him and is always looking for fault in him, but I don't think I really have another choice because I don't think your dad's going to give me the money for your shoes."

They went home, and she made dinner. It was ready in time for her husband when he arrived home from work. Beetle and his parents sat for their nightly family dinner. Barbecue tofu. Beetle's father despised tofu. He wished his wife would not make it. Not only did he not like the way it tasted, he thought it was turning him into a woman. He believed tofu was packed full of estrogen and other female hormones. "What did you learn in school today?" Beetle's father asked him.

"Nothin," responded Beetle

SEVEN

THE NEXT DAY AT SCHOOL, the students disappointingly saw that
Sergeant Powers remained their teacher. They assumed she was a substitute teacher. No one informed them, Sergeant Powers included,
that she was their permanent replacement teacher. The new priest,
Father Michael, came to the eighth-grade class. He brought the film
festival passes. They were nothing more than a stack of laminated
paper flyers.

Latricia slid out of her desk. She walked up to the teacher's desk
where the priest had placed the passes. She pulled the top flyer from
the large stack, then proceeded to walk back to her desk and slip
back in. Beetle waited a few seconds before he mustered up the nerve
to walk up to the desk himself to take a pass. When he stood from
his desk, he moved quickly. He worried his classmates were going
to make fun of him for taking a pass. He sat back down and hid his
head underneath his folded arms like a fox in its hole.

"I'm really excited about this," said Latricia. "That's really what I
want to do when I grow up. Become a movie director."

"They'd never let a black woman direct a movie!" Bullet said
rudely.

"Maybe she'll win an Oxcurr," Brownie chimed in. "At the Cad-
a-me Wards."

"What you two numbskulls are saying is very biased," Latricia
said to the two troublemakers. "It's also very bigoted."

"Well, you're bein a big hypocrite!" Bullet said.

"How am I being a hypocrite?"

"What you said was bigoted!"

"How was what I said bigoted?"

"You called us numbskulls!"

"I called you numbskulls," Latricia reminded Bullet. "I didn't call you honky crackers!"

"Young lady!" Sergeant Powers shouted. "I will not have that talk in this classroom."

"Sorry."

"What is your name?"

"Latricia."

"Is that really your name?"

"Yes, I wouldn't just make that name up."

"It sounds like you just made that name up."

"No, it's really my name."

"Why were you named that? Was your mother trying to decide between Lucinda and Patricia and just combined the two?"

"No. It's a real name. You can look it up."

"You've got quite a mouth on you, don't you, girl?"

"She's got a big mouth," Bullet said to the teacher as he looked at Latricia. "It isn't as big as most black girls' mouths."

"You don't need to talk like that," Father Michael said. "We shouldn't be judgmental of somebody because of their skin color. If we judge people because their skin color is different than ours, then we would judge every single person because no two people have the same skin color. Look at your parents. Your parents all have different skin colors. I'm serious. Look at your parents. You'll see how their skin tones are different and their coloring is different. And then what happens is they have a kid and their kid is you and you're a mix between the two of them and your skin color is a balance of the two of them. I mean, if you have sisters or brothers, of course, you would think they would have the same skin color because they come from the same parents and even though it's very close, it is still not the same skin color because some people get more from their mother's side and some people get more from their father's side. It just really all depends because no two people have the same skin color. So you cannot judge people with different skin color than yours because, like I said, you would be judging everyone.

"Everyone is like a snowflake. Have you ever stuck your tongue out and caught a snowflake on it? There is something invigorating about it. Something exciting. When that snowflake hits your tongue, it's like magic. It's like electricity. You feel a shock, but it's like a good shock, like you feel it, like there's something magical about it because every single snowflake is different and it just so happens that only one of a kind just fell on your tongue. I'm serious. If you've never done it, next time it snows go outside and stick your tongue out and catch a snowflake on your tongue, and you will understand right then and there the importance of being different and not only that but the importance of respecting people and respecting those around us for their differences. Our differences are what make us unique. If we were all the same, then it would be incredibly boring. And we don't want that. We want variety. We want mystery. We want something new and something different.

"So putting somebody down for not being like you is incredibly closed-minded. The most closed-minded people are the people who just remain in one place and see only what is around them and don't see outside of their bubbles. They don't look beyond the horizons on the hills. People who throw insults and take cheap shots at others only do it because they have inferiority complexes about themselves.

"I know you are all young and it's hard being young. You don't have any choices. You can't even drive a car. At least not drive a car legally. Getting into the line of work I got into has really opened my eyes and opened my mind to how beautiful and wonderful of a world we live in. But it's not all beautiful. I know this for a fact. I have been all around this world. Sent on missionary trips all over. I worked with Mother Teresa in India. I know everyone's talking about how great of a woman Mother Teresa was because she died a few months ago. I met her, and I knew her, and I can truthfully say that she was indeed an amazing woman. *Amazing* is too weak of a word to describe her.

"I want to advise all of you to travel. I'm serious! Create your own adventure. Get out there and see the world. Go out and get yourselves passports. Go out and get on a plane or even a boat and let it take you all over. Go backpack through Dharamsala or go ride a motorbike throughout the nooks and crannies of Thailand. See what the lifestyles of people in other places are like. See what their food is like. When you return back here, you will see everything differently. That is, if you even want to come back. Who knows? Maybe you'll end up liking wherever you go so much, you'll decide you don't want to come back. But if you do end up getting homesick and deciding that you do want to come back home, you're going to see your home in a new light. You'll see it completely differently. Right now you're seeing the world as just a microscopic speck of what it has to offer. The world is like a puzzle!"

"What's the capital of Thailand?" Bullet asked.

Ignoring Bullet's rude outburst, Father Michael pointed to a framed puzzle in the back of the room with an image of the Earth as viewed from outer space. There was a puzzle piece missing from it. "See that! That is what the world's like. It's like a puzzle. It doesn't make sense to you unless it is all together. Your whole view of the world is just like a single piece of that puzzle. Getting out there and seeing it for yourself is going to be an experience that will change you. You will learn more than you ever would from any schooling or all the books in the world.

"While I was in India, I spoon-fed hungry babies. They were babies without limbs who were sick with disease and were blind. There was a little tiny baby who was not even two years old. I held the little guy in my arms and spoon-fed him flavorless oatmeal. He was born blind. But in his case, it may have been more of a blessing than a curse. He didn't have to see what was around him.

"I remember holding him in my arms and looking down at him. He weighed practically nothing in my arms. I put that spoon in his mouth and the second his taste buds reacted to that bland oatmeal, you know what he did? He smiled at me. He had such a straight row of little tiny baby teeth, and he smiled, and he was happy. If any one of you were ever in that situation I was in where you had a kid who was dying in your arms and saw him or her smile at you, then none of you would ever name call again. If any of you took a trip with me to Bangkok or cruised with me down the streets of Amman, it would completely change you.

"I know being the age you all are and with your absence of wisdom, witnessing people different than you is something you think's awkward or even weird. I recognize that. I believe you're all this way because you feel ill at ease with it. If you and I took a trip to the places I've been and I showed you around, then when we would come back both God and I would grant you full permission to name call and make fun of whoever you want. You know why? Because you won't be able to. Your heart and your brain will have grown so large that they will prevent you from being so ignorant. I mean, I've been places where I've seen real people. I've seen women walking around with fabric wrapped around their heads, Middle Eastern women. We find that amusing because we're not familiar with that lifestyle. I've been there, and I've worked with those people. I've understood their culture. I lived in India. I lived in Iran. I lived in Iraq. I have been to war-stricken places where I feared for my life. But it wasn't my life I was there to protect.

"I've been to villages in Africa with starving children and starving adults who were lucky enough to even make it to adulthood. I've been to villages where the children were starving to the point that their rib cages poked out of their stomach because they're so malnourished and their legs were as thin as toothpicks, and they couldn't even walk. I've seen mothers and fathers drag their sons and daughters in the dirt because their children did not have the strength to walk on their own legs. I've been to villages where the children were covered with flies and had kwashiorkor to the point that it looked as if the babies were pregnant with babies."

The students laughed.

"We see these random strangers that seem foreign to us, who are alien to us. We see them, and we even mock them and make fun of them. We see Asians and their gestures and the way they talk, and we laugh, and we think it's funny because we don't know better and it's different to us. It's weird and alien to us, but that's because we are clueless."

A few of the students in the class laughed.

"If we're at the mall and we see Chinese or Koreans, and they're talking to each other, we find it funny because it's so strange. But it's not really as strange as we think. We only feel like it's strange because it's so foreign to us. We see the way they talk and behave." Father Michael did an impersonation of the kind of people he was talking about.

The class laughed at his impression.

"Right after the Second World War my mother signed up to go over on a missionary trip to China. She went over to China in the early '50s—I think it might have been 1950. Keep in mind that this was almost two decades before Americans were even allowed to go to China. China was a strange mystery. Americans were fascinated with China in the '50s and '60s. China was like a distant planet we would see on filmstrips and in pictures, and it was a fascinating place because we all knew that no American had ever been there. And my mother was one of the first Americans to go over to China, and she was scared to death. But being afraid of death is being afraid of losing your life. It wasn't her life she was going over there to save."

———

After school, a white limousine pulled up to take Beetle to the public high school. The limousine was something the high school purchased. They thought it would be a sound investment. Their students were always renting limousines for events such as football games and dances. Even actors in the school plays would take limousines to their performances. The school thought it was a good idea to buy its own limousine. They rented it out to the students. This way they and their families could save money and the school could make a little cash on the side. Because the school had the limousine parked in its garage, it wasn't doing much with it on the weekdays. That was why the principal of the public high school thought it was a good idea to send the lead custodian out to the Catholic grade school to pick up the eighth grader who was going to be cleaning their school. They thought Beetle would enjoy the limousine. The lead custodian they sent out to act as Beetle's chauffeur (unknowingly to the school he worked for) had a suspended license. His driver's license was suspended after he had been pulled over and did not have proof of insurance. He then failed to be present on the court date issued to him. Had anyone at the school known this, he most likely would not be allowed to drive the school's limousine.

Beetle felt he was the envy of all the other students of the school when he hopped into the limousine. It was even better than he imagined it would be. There was a little TV with a talk show on and a bucket of ice with bottles of Josta soda inside. Someone at the high school recommended they put this soda into the limousine. It contained caffeine and guarana. They hoped when the young custodian came over, he would be pumped up and ready to work. There was a minibar in the limo. Beetle pulled a champagne glass from the bar and poured the soda into it. The long car drove off. Beetle could not believe he was riding in a limousine. Drinking Josta and watching *The Ricki Lake Show.* He knew this was how rich people lived.

The public high school was tucked away in its neighborhood. Beetle had never seen the school before. It was only a few blocks from his school. He found it odd that when driving with his parents, he had never passed it. It was hard to miss because it was so big. When the car pulled up and parked, Beetle was sad about having to leave the limousine. At least he was excited about working in the high school. He had always wanted to see what high school life was all about.

As Beetle walked toward the entrance of the school, he noticed how drastically different high school was compared to grade school. He saw a group of kids standing outside the school smoking. Some of them were freshmen who were even younger than Beetle. They all talked funny, looked funny, and had funny haircuts. Some of them had long hair. They wore strange jackets and dressed like punks. Girls wore skirts that would not be allowed in his school. The skirts were cut way too high. Some of the girls were walking around with shirts so short you could see their belly buttons. It was cold outside, and Beetle had no idea why these girls would dress like that. Even though he found it strange, he was intrigued. This made him look forward to attending high school even more. The thing Beetle did not understand was that the high school he would attend was not a public school. It was a Catholic school. Just like the school he was attending at the time. There wasn't much difference between eighth grade and high school in the Catholic schools. Some of these public school kids came from elementary schools even more outrageous than their high school.

When Beetle entered the building, there was a stationary trash can outside the front door entrance. The trash can was dressed up as if it were a person. It had two sticks for arms—similar to a snowman—and a paper-stuffed, black trash bag placed on top of the trash can to give the appearance of a head. Two googly eyes had been put on it along with a long, black, rockstar-esque wig. It had nickel candy wax lips. A hole was poked out on the right side of the mouth. The hole was just big enough to squeeze a cigarette butt into it. That was just what they did. A half-smoked Misty Light was placed in the wax candy lips' hole as a finishing touch. This gave the trash figure an edge. Beetle could not believe the teachers would allow students to do something of the sort. Not only did the teachers let the students do it, they encouraged it. The trash mannequin was actually an assignment for an art class. It received an A+ grade.

As Beetle entered the building, he walked the hall called the Avenue of the Arts. Down the Avenue of the Arts hung paintings and photographs. Beetle found some to be extremely risqué. He once again could not believe the teachers would allow it in a high school. Seeing creativity and freedom made him anticipate going to high school even more. There was one photograph Beetle found very disturbing. It was taken by a student. The art class was asked to photograph something on their minds. One student had recently had eye surgery. Her eyeball was all stitched up. She photographed her stitched-up eyeball, then blew it up to eighteen feet and hung it on the school's wall for everyone to see. As Beetle walked down the hall, he reminded himself not to walk this way again. He did not want to see the picture of the stitched-up eyeball.

One of the administrators came up to Beetle and asked Beetle if he needed help. "They sent me here in a limo," said Beetle.

The administrator looked at Beetle as if he was a crazy person. Fortunately, an office assistant was standing behind the administrator and overheard their conversation. She turned around to explain to the administrator about how Beetle was the custodial fill-in. The office assistant also explained how the lead custodian drove the limousine to the Catholic school to pick Beetle up. The administrator politely assisted Beetle over to the primary custodial office, which was a storage closet with brooms, dust pans, and a couple of vacuum cleaners.

The administrator told Beetle to wait in the closet and somebody would come. He went to find the person who had to check Beetle in. It was some guy named George. Beetle wished they had not left him in the closet. It was freaking him out being in there alone. Luckily for Beetle, it didn't take George too long to return to the office/closet.

George extended his arm to shake Beetle's hand and introduced himself. "This is an excellent school," said George. "We've gotta lotta nice stuff coming in here, too. We just installed this tank that puts out electric water. Have you ever used electric water before? We call it Jesus Juice. It's some great stuff. It works better than regular water. Electric water cleans a lot better. The problem is they say it only works for a few hours. I heard it only works like three or four hours. It's like the electricity runs out. Like the electric water has electricity and then the electricity runs out so basically all you're left with is just water. But when it does work when you're working those three or four hours, it really cleans up good and does a good job. It smells kind of good, too. It smells like that clear Pepsi stuff. You remember that when they had the clear Pepsi?"

"No."

"Do they still make it? I know I had it a few years ago. I haven't seen it in some time. Remember those silly commercials? They had like naked women in bathtubs, and it is like filled with the clear Pepsi, and they had like a naked baby swimming under water, and they had like a man shave with the clear Pepsi. They had that song 'Right Now' in the commercials. Every time I hear that song on the radio, I think about the clear Pepsi stuff. Well, when I first had the stuff I thought it was pretty gross. But I was working at the hospital at the time, and they had it in the vending machines there. I had to drink it whenever anything else ran out because it was something that nobody in the place liked so they would always drink all the other pops. So I had to drink it. But then I started drinking it, and I kind of started liking it, like it kinda grew on me and was one of those things. It was like a taste that grows on you. So then I started actually drinking it like even when there was other pop in the machine, like when all the pops were all stocked up I still went for the clear Pepsi cause I thought it was pretty good, but then they took it out. I thought it was probably because they stopped making it or something."

"Maybe."

"But, yeah, this school is really up to date. We've got some pretty cool stuff here. Oh, do you clean bathrooms at your school?"

"Yeah. I clean bathrooms."

"Them some nice shoes you have, by the way."

"Thanks. They are my dress shoes. They're really uncomfortable. I really don't like to wear em, but I have to cause I lost my sneaker."

"I got you."

There was a short silence.

"What was I talking about again?" asked George.

"You're asking me if I clean restrooms."

"That's right. You clean restrooms where you're *at*?"

"Yeah, I clean them."

"You scrub toilets?"

"Yeah, I scrubbed toilets."

"You scrub floors?"

"Yeah, I scrubbed floors."

"We got this cool new thing comin in. We actually don't even get it in til Monday. They might send you back here on Monday to see it. It's basically a machine, and all you have to do is turn on the switch and it's like a gun, and you just shoot it at the toilet, and you shoot the floors, and it cleans them without you havin to do anythin. All you do is take a gun and shoot it. It's a brand-new product called a Kaivac."

Even though there was a lot of work to do, Beetle and George didn't do any work. They just walked around. George pointed out the different parts of the school. The school was rather big. They barely had enough time to walk through it. George gave Beetle a few small, transparent, trash can liners for the trash cans underneath the desks in the main office. He asked Beetle to replace them. Beetle ran in and checked beneath each desk and changed the trash cans. He even had to unlock office doors to get to a lot of the trash cans. Beetle liked the job. The thing he liked most about it was how some of the people had treats on their desks. Beetle didn't mind helping himself to the treats. After he was finished changing out all the trash cans, George handed him a roll of black, fifty-five gallon bags. George told him to change the large trash barrels in the girls' locker room. "I already got the boys'," he told Beetle.

There were four large trash barrels in the girls' locker room. One of the trash barrels had half of an uneaten bologna submarine sandwich. Beetle was so hungry. He ate it quickly so nobody would catch him.

When Beetle came out of the girls' locker room, George informed him his four hours were up.

The bell went off. Beetle was told he could leave.

"Do I get a ride in the limo again?"

"Yes, of course you do!"

Beetle hopped in the limousine and went back to his school. He waited on the school's steps for his mother to come pick him up.

The weekend was only minutes away.

EIGHT

THE NEXT DAY WAS SATURDAY. Beetle's mother drove him to her mother's house. Beetle's grandmother lived quite far away, but according to his mother it was a necessary trip. Beetle's mother had him wait in the car while she went in to speak to her mother. Beetle was all right with waiting in the car. He would rather sit there and listen to the radio. It was better than going inside. His grandmother's house was boring.

Sitting in the car and listening to the radio grew old after a while. Beetle wondered what was taking so long. Then horrible images popped into his head. He had visions of something bad happening to his mother and grandmother. He got out of the car and walked inside the house. Her house was a tiny little townhouse nestled in a community filled with elderly citizens. Beetle walked through the door. His grandmother saw him and looked surprised. "Oh, my! Look who's here!" his grandmother squealed. "It's my grandson."

Her surprise was faked. She knew he was waiting in the car because his mother had told her. Knowing her grandson, she was sure he could not sit out in the car for more than a few minutes. He was a hypochondriac, destined to come inside. "What have you been up to?"

"Nothing," Beetle replied.

"How is school going?"

"Fine."

"Well, we've got to get going," Beetle's mother said to her mother. She grabbed the credit card her mother had loaned her. "We've got to get this boy some new shoes."

Beetle's mother was quite relieved when he walked in. She and her mother had been in a heated argument over Beetle's father. When Beetle walked into the house, it eased the tension.

With her arm around her son's shoulders, Beetle's mother walked him out the door. She said her goodbyes to her mother.

Beetle's mother drove him to Payless Shoes. He picked out a pair of white imposter leather tennis shoes. They checked out and went to the Osco Drug next door. Beetle's mother allowed him to pick out candy as she went to find a thank you note from the bargain card section. She walked up to the counter and handed the cashier the thank you card tucked inside of a purple envelope. "Did you pick out some candy?" Beetle's mother asked him.

He handed his mother a pack of Butterfinger BB's. This was a big deal for Beetle. His mother never let him have sweets. Beetle's mother handed the candy over to the cashier at the checkout lane. The cashier removed the thank you card out of the purple envelope. She needed to scan the barcode. The cashier saw the illustration of the white, puffy cat on the front of the card. "Aw, that's so cute," the cashier said as she put the card back into its envelope. Beetle's mother paid for it with the remaining change from the money her husband had given her to buy Beetle's thrift store shoes.

When they got out to the car, Beetle's mother said she couldn't give her mother a blank card. She had to write a note inside. As they sat in the car Beetle's mother dug under the seats looking for a pen. After a few minutes, she gave up and walked back into the drug-store. She walked back to the checkout girl and asked if she could use her pen. The pen was on a small stand. It had a black plastic wire attached to it to prevent people walking out with it. Between the pen and the black wire was silver tape wrapped around the base, where someone yanked the pen from the wire. The pen was there for people to write checks. Beetle's mother stood there awkwardly. People checked out and attempted to squeeze past her as she used the check-writing pen to scribble a note on the card. It was difficult for her to write on the 10x6 check-writing stand. The check-writing stand had an illustration under the laminate that showed the proper way to write a check.

After finishing personalizing the card, Beetle's mother rushed out to the car. They drove back to her mother's house. Her mother was inside, but she didn't bother knocking on the door. She walked up and slid the purple envelope under the door. Inside the envelope was the thank you card. Inside the thank you card was the borrowed credit card.

She ran back to the car. Beetle said they were late for the film festival he wanted to attend. Beetle's mother rushed him home. He threw on some new clothes. "Aren't you going to wear your new shoes?" his mother asked.

"No, I think I'm going to wear my dress shoes." Beetle knew Latricia was going to be there, and he wanted to look his most dapper in her presence.

Beetle's mother drove him to the public high school. Beetle had never even seen the place before the day before yesterday. Now here he was, going there two days in a row.

As Beetle exited the car, his mother reached over and gave him three shiny quarters to use the pay phone when it was over. The pay phone only cost a quarter. Knowing her son, it was likely he was going to lose at least one of the quarters.

Beetle walked up to the school building. There were six doors out front, and he tried five of them until he found one he was able to open. With his standard luck, it was the last door he tried.

When he walked into the building, there wasn't anybody in view, but voices were audible down the halls. He walked to where he heard the voices. Suddenly, he remembered he made a mental note to avoid this hall. It was the one with the giant picture of the stitched-up eye. Beetle forgot to take another route.

He came to the spot where all the people gathered. It sounded from afar like more people were there than were. It was because everyone was talking so loudly. "Did you fill out a name tag?" a man in his early twenties with a short-sleeved, button-down white shirt asked Beetle.

"No."

"Well, you gotta fill one out. So we know who you are. The table over there has all the name tags on it. Just fill one out. There might be somebody sitting there, but there might not be. If there's not someone sitting there, just fill one out."

Beetle walked over to the table. It was a long folding table with a dark navy, plastic tablecloth over it with a sign taped to the top declaring the film festival with a side note indicating name tags. The sign was taped to the middle of the table. It was printed on printing paper. Judging from the streaks in the front, it was printed using a printer with a cartridge low on ink.

A heavier than heavy-set, middle-aged woman sat at the table. She had black hair like straw and wore so much makeup you could not see one pore on her natural skin. She was friendly. She gave Beetle a name tag along with a black marker to write his name. Beetle scribbled his name down sloppily. He asked the woman if he could have another name tag and try it again. The woman had no problem giving him another name tag. They had expected far more people to attend this event than showed up. Therefore, they were left with quite an abundance of name tags. For all she cared, he could take a whole box of them and try it as many times as he wanted.

The guy with the short-sleeved, button-down white shirt came up to Beetle. He asked if Beetle was ready for the screening. Beetle responded by nodding his head. The guy then pointed to where the screening was, and Beetle walked into the room. There were a few people in the room, but there were plenty of chairs. Beetle looked around the crowd to see if he could spot Latricia. She wasn't there. People then took a seat toward the front, near the screen. Beetle sat toward the front because he was nearsighted and had left his glasses at home. Partially because he thought he looked better without them. Partially because he just totally forgot. It would have been nice to have them.

Looking around the room, Beetle only counted eleven people. There were at least forty chairs. A boy walked out wearing blue jeans and a red T-shirt. The boy looked like he was about high school age. He was a year or two older than Beetle. The boy thanked everybody for coming out and said, "This program is going to be extremely exciting." The boy asked if anybody had watched the television program on Sunday mornings where they show local short films. Beetle raised his hand and looked around only to find no one else was raising his or her hand. He thought maybe he did not understand the question. He slowly lowered his arm back down. "Well, that's good," the boy said. "We have someone who's a fan of the show. What we have for you is, like I said, is really exciting. These are some of the short films that were submitted to that show, but the TV station wouldn't let us show them. These ones are a little racier than what was shown on television."

As Beetle looked around, he wondered what the room was used for. Was it an immense storage room? The room was actually a black box theater for the high school to put on performances.

The lights dimmed. A movie was projected onto the screen.

—

The movie started off with a man and a woman eating dinner at a location the filmmakers believed they could pass off as being a fancy restaurant. One could tell right away this was a slapstick comedy. The man and the girl were talking back and forth. They seemed like they were hitting it off. Nothing they said was important to the plot. The conversation was just to show they were compatible.

The next scene was of them in a park playing with a Golden Retriever. The dog belonged to the man. Just like the previous scene, nothing said between the two was crucial to the plot. The dialogue merely reinforced that the two were developing a stable relationship. Beetle found the part where they were playing with the dog to be funny. It was a good thing the dialogue in the scene with the dog in the park was not important to the plot because it was so hard to hear over the sounds of the cicadas. Beetle found the lead actor to be rather annoying. He was a little too funny. The actor seemed to be impersonating Jim Carrey.

As the two characters in the short movie's relationship developed, the man invited the girl back to his apartment. They went into the man's bedroom and began kissing. You could tell the male actor was enjoying this, but the female seemed to be grossed out with having to make out. The girl took off her shirt, revealing a white bra. She was thin and rather flat chested. She had a nice set of abdominal muscles. "I have got something to tell you," the girl said to the man.

"Are you married?" asked the man.

"Oh, my heavens! No! Nothing like that!"

"Then what is it?"

"It is something about me."

"You don't have any diseases, do you?"

"No, gosh! The things you are saying are far worse than what I'm actually trying to say."

"What is it you're trying to say?"

"I am just too embarrassed to say."

"Too embarrassed?"

"I am afraid you'll judge me."

"I am not one to judge."

"I am afraid you won't like me anymore."

The man observed the woman's body. "Looking at you, there is no way I cannot . . . not like you."

"I am afraid it is going to make you not happy."

"You know what would make me happy? If you took these pants off." The man unbuttoned her jeans.

"Oh, boy. Here we go."

The man tugged her jeans down. She stood there in the white bra and matching panties.

"Oh, boy!" the girl said. She turned around to face the camera. There was a huge bulge in her underwear.

"Oh, boy?" the man said in comedic terror with a wide-open mouth. "Oh, man!"

The film then cut to black without any credits.

The boy in the red T-shirt came out after the movie was over. "We're lucky to have the filmmaker of that film here with us today." The boy pointed over to the guy who was the person who played the leading role. "He's the writer and director and starred in this movie. Give him a hand."

Everybody softly clapped as he stood. He now had a beard. He waved bashfully. It was funny how he was so outgoing in the movie but so shy and crowd conscious in real life.

"What inspired this film?" the boy in the red shirt asked the filmmaker.

The filmmaker just shrugged.

"Was this based on a real-life experience?"

"Yes, it was," the filmmaker said, stroking his beard. "I was the girl."

"We're really honored to have this next guy here," the boy in the red shirt pointed to the door. "He's standing outside. I don't know why. I think he thinks he's too good for us or something. I'll let him come in here and introduce himself."

A man with a bandana wrapped around his head, a long beard, and tattoos down his arm walked through the door. He wore a black, button-down shirt with the sleeves completely cut off, which showed off his tattoos. Bright, colorful tattoos. The man walked over to a microphone stand. He removed the microphone and held it up to chest level. It wasn't necessary for him to hold the microphone because there were only eleven people in the room. It was also unnecessary for him to hold the microphone because it was not turned on. He did it anyway. "I just want to clarify, I don't think I'm better than you guys. I just, unfortunately, I'm worse than you guys because you are all on time and I was late. I, unfortunately, had to attend my daughter's ballet recital and it ran a little over on time, so I am a little late now coming to this, but I'm really glad I'm here. I did see that last one. It was really good. I walked in when it was starting, and I didn't want to be rude, so I just stood out there and watched it from outside. It was very funny."

"So tell us about your film you're going to show."

"Yes, I'm showing a film called *Your Mother's Eyes,* and I made this a while back. I actually made my first film . . . I made it . . . it's been five years now. I can't believe it's been that long, but yeah. I made a film five years ago when I was twenty-nine, and the whole movie was backward, which I could really relate to at the time because I spent my whole twenties as a mover, moving tables, so I pretty much spent my whole twenties going backward. So I made that film—it was called *Backwards*, and it would kinda introduce me to the whole film circuit and film world, and then I got a job working for these two brothers on a film called *Bound*, and while I was working on that film I got access to all their cameras and stuff they were using. I was able to shoot my new film, *Your Mother's Eyes* with Panavision cameras and all the cool stuff that we got to use. All their cool lenses. It was shot on 35mm film, which was a real pleasure to use. I mean, it looks like a real, big-budget movie. Like a big-budget, Hollywood movie."

"Well, let's see it!" the boy in the red shirt said as he stood up and walked back to the projector. "Do you mind hitting the lights for me?"

"I'm screening my own film, and I have to work the lights too?" the man with the beard said. "Well, I guess I did work lights on my movies. I guess I am a lights expert."

The man with the beard flipped off the lights. The movie started.

The title popped up: *Your Mother's Eyes*. It opened with a short credit scene. A short but impressive credit scene. Bare-naked dancers were dancing on a stage in a club. Beetle had thought the shorts they showed on television were a little edgy, but nothing was ever like *Your Mother's Eyes*.

After the credits were over, the camera focused on a man sitting at a bar in a shady strip joint. A girl walked over to him and started talking. She asked him what he did. He told the dancer he was retired. "Well, what did you do before you retired?" the dancer asked.

"I was a doctor."

"What kind of doctor?"

"What is with all these questions?"

"I'm curious."

"You don't see me asking you what your profession is."

"You don't need to ask. You are looking at it."

"Fine. I delivered babies."

"That is a cool job."

"I delivered every single baby in this town in the last thirty years."

"I was born in this town."

"I bet I delivered you. What is your name?"

"Marcy Mahoney."

"What year were you born?"

"1976."

"A Bicentennial baby."

"Yes, I was."

"I remember you."

"Get out of here!"

"No, I do."

"You do not."

"Your parents were named Anne and Carl."

"Oh, wow! You are right."

"Your mother was very pretty. You look like her."

"Do you want a dance?"

"I would love a dance."

"You want to go to the VIP? I take it all off in the VIP."

The doctor and the dancer stood from their bar stools. They walked to a dark back room. The doctor sat on a black leather sofa. The dancer took it all off and straddled him. The song started playing. The dancer moved her hips to the rhythm and the beat. "You have your mother's eyes," the doctor said to the dancer.

"I know, people tell me that."

"You also have your mother's coochie," the actor playing the doctor delivered the line as if it was destined to be the most quoted line in movie history.

It cut to a close-up shot of the dancer's face. She had a shocked expression. The shot was only a second or two and then cut to black and heavy metal music began to play as title credits filled the screen. Then rolling credits started to roll. It was surprising how many people worked on this short, little film.

After the credits had finished, the guy in the red shirt flipped on the lights and turned off the projector. He walked up in front of everybody and said, "We have another special guest here with us who looks like they just got here as well, or at least they think they're too good for us to sit through the whole program, but we have another special guest. Come on out," the guy in the red shirt waved to the door, and Latricia walked in. Beetle's heart started racing. Latricia was not the special guest. The special guest walked in behind her. The special guest was Christopher HC. He wore faded blue jeans and a teal T-shirt. The shirt said Junior Citizen. It had a cartoon drawing of a grinning, nose-less boy. The boy had vortex eyes and a yellow helmet with a star on front and antennas protruding from the sides. Latricia looked slightly embarrassed. She waved at Beetle. She looked surprised to see him. She walked over and sat next to Beetle. Beetle's heart beat harder. His palms began to perspire. He rubbed his sweaty hands on his corduroy pants.

Christopher HC went up and introduced his film. It was called *Deliver Me to Evil.* The film projector started it up. The opening shot was a man in a dirty robe, a dirty white undershirt, and boxers with a cherry print. He sat on a dirty couch with his hand in his pants as the glow from the television lit him. There was a knock at the door. The man opened the door to reveal a pizza deliveryman. The pizza deliveryman had a pizza box in his hand. The man in the robe stuck his hands down his boxer shorts and pulled out a bill. He gave the bill to the pizza deliveryman. The pizza deliveryman pulled out salad tongs to take it. There was a close-up of the bill. Devil horns were drawn on Alexander Hamilton's head with a red marker. A thin and long devilish mustache was drawn to his face along with a pitchfork at his side. "Keep the change," the robed man said.

The pizza delivery guy looked at the bill. He rolled his eyes and walked away.

The robed man slammed the door behind him. He brought the pizza into his kitchen. The pizza was thrown onto the kitchen counter. A close-up shot revealed the artwork on the pizza box. It said *Evil Pizza*. There was an illustration of a slice of pizza with long, sharp fangs, dripping droplets of blood.

The man walked out of his kitchen. A wide-angle shot of the kitchen was shown. It was filthy. The man sat back down on the couch and turned on the television. There was a roar from the kitchen. The man jumped in fright. He tiptoed to see what made the noise. There was a dim light shining out of the kitchen. The man peeked his eye through the kitchen door as he opened it ever so slowly. It was only the innocent-looking pizza box. The man walked into the kitchen more confidently. "I could really go for a slice of pizza right now," he said. He slowly opened the pizza box. It was a close-up shot of the pizza. A full pizza. It looked rather good. The man reached for a slice. The pizza box slammed down and bit his fingers off and began to roar. The pizza box opened back up, and a big, yellow tongue made of rubber emerged from the box. Though the tongue was made of rubber, it closely resembled pizza cheese. The tongue had round pepperoni slices all over it. The cheese and pepperoni tongue protruded from the box and licked the blood that had spurted onto the man's face from his now fingerless hand. The man began to cry. The pizza box lunged forward and bit the man at his neck. As the cardboard box clenched down, it completely decapitated the man. Blood squirted all over the kitchen. The blood dripped down the camera lens until the screen was completely red. A title card popped up that read: *The End*.

Beetle and Latricia both clapped furiously. They both enjoyed that short film. Christopher HC stood up. "Does anybody have any questions for me?" asked Christopher HC.

"What kind of camera do you use?" asked Beetle.

"That's the one question you're never supposed to ask a filmmaker."

Beetle was embarrassed.

"I use a 16mm camera."

"Do you use a 16mm camera for all your movies?"

"Pretty much. I like to shoot on film because it gives it a more movie look. I feel like shooting on videotape makes it look more like a home movie."

"Was the movie made about the kid who fell into the well, was that shot on film?"

"Wow! I'm surprised you've seen that!"

"It was on TV late one night."

"Yeah, I know. I didn't think anybody would watch it." Christopher HC looked at Beetle with fear in his eyes. As if Beetle was a vampire for staying up so late. "I can't believe you saw that."

"I watched the whole thing."

"I'm really impressed." Christopher HC eyeballed the strange boy. "That really means a lot to me."

"Did you shoot that one on film?"

"Oh yeah, sorry. I forgot about your question. No. I actually did not shoot that one on film. I shot it using a beta camera. Remember those old tapes called Betamax?"

"No."

"Well, they still use them now for doing television and stuff. I was working for a news station, and they had all these cameras they use, and I used one of the beta cameras. They're really high-tech. I know the beta tapes didn't really make it, but the cameras are still widely used and still shoot quality video. That's why I used one to shoot it, and then I sent it off to a person who did work on the color of it, and they color corrected and color graded it, and it was a real professional job. I think it turned out looking quite . . . quite good if I do say so myself."

"Yeah, it was really good."

The guy in the red shirt came back up. "Alright, I want to thank everybody for coming out. There is a workshop that is next. If you'd like to go to that, it'll show you the ins and outs of filmmaking and how to make movies and how to do all kinds of stuff including industrial stuff and commercial stuff. So if you're interested, then you can head over to room 316. Once again that was room 316. Thank you, and I hope everybody enjoyed the films. I'm sure you did. They were some great ones."

Latricia and Beetle sat there waiting for the crowd to leave. Once the eleven audience members had worked their way to the door, Beetle and Latricia stood and headed to the exit. They stood shoulder to shoulder. Beetle tried standing on his tiptoes to make himself look as if he wasn't so drastically short compared to Latricia.

"I really like that one about the pizza that ate the guy," Latricia said.

"Yeah!" said Beetle. "That Christopher HC guy is pretty good."

Christopher HC walked up to Beetle and Latricia. "I want to thank you two for coming out."

"Thank you for showing your film," Latricia said.

"Oh, sure thing."

"I really liked your movie," Beetle told him.

"Thank you, that means a lot. I'm really impressed that you

were so familiar with my work."

"Yeah, I've seen all your movies on TV."

"Well, not all of them show on TV. I have some on my website. You have a computer?"

"Yeah, my dad does. He sometimes lets me play on it, but he only lets me play educational games. I have Mario on it. But it's *Mario Teaches Typing*, and it's not that much fun because you have to type in order to play it."

"Does the computer have the Internet?"

"Yeah, I think it does."

Christopher HC reached into his wallet and extracted two calling cards. "Here's my business card. I've got two of them. I got this one that looks like a frame, maybe a couple of frames from a reel of film. I also have this one. This one looks like a slate board, like you know in the movies when they say action, and you clap down on that white . . . that black thing with the white stripes on top. It's called the slate board. Do you want to take one of these cards?"

"Yeah, sure!" Beetle picked the card where Christopher HC's information was presented in a film frame.

"It's got my www.com on it too," Christopher HC pointed out. "If you go to that address on there, then you can actually . . . it's actually my website, and I have movies on there that you can watch. Other short movies that you may not have seen on TV. You'll have to download a RealPlayer, though. The movies don't look the best because the frames get stuck on them but if you can, compress the RealPlayer so that it's small. Don't make it too big. If it's small, then it plays a little faster, and you can see the movie better."

Beetle put the card into his pocket and walked with Latricia and Christopher HC to the filmmakers' workshop. As the instructor of the seminar conducted his presentation, Beetle could not stay focused. He was nervous about sitting with both Latricia and Christopher HC.

After the presentation, Beetle walked over and called his mother on the pay phone. He only lost one of the three quarters. His home was not too far away from the school, so his mother was there in only a few minutes.

NINE

WHEN BEETLE RETURNED TO SCHOOL ON MONDAY, he, along with the rest of the class, was disappointed to see Sergeant Powers. She had returned as their teacher once again. They still believed she was just a substitute teacher.

The students were relieved when Father Michael entered the classroom. "I'm just here to inform you the altar boy or altar girl practice will be postponed to next Tuesday because I have to do a last-minute funeral service tonight. I don't know why they are doing it on a Monday night."

The priest had brought a mysterious case with him. The case looked like a black, plastic briefcase. Father Michael carried it from a handle. In his other hand was a caseless VHS tape with a white sticker label that said *A Production Of World Wildlife Fund ©1988.* Above the font was their logo of a panda bear.

"May I have a volunteer go and fetch me a television?"

A boy, named Brian, quickly shot his hand up before Father Michael had finished his question. Brian loved leaving the classroom for any random reason.

Father Michael told the boy he could transport the television. Before the priest was even halfway finished with his sentence, Brian was out the door.

"You shouldn't have sent him out there alone," the bossy girl named Nova said. "He's probably not going to come back."

Father Michael sent Nova out to make sure Brian returned.

Sergeant Powers told them the television was outside in the hall and should not take them more than a second. She went out after Brian and Nova. Once she was out in the hall you could hear her yelling at the two. Brian and Nova ran back into the room and quickly sat down at their desks. Sergeant Powers trailed behind them. She pushed the black, steel, A/V cart with the television strapped on tightly. The television was bound down with a thin, yellow, come-along strap.

"Who wants to plug it in?" the priest asked.

Everyone raised their hand, except for Beetle. Ms. Cole used to always ask the students if they wanted to plug in the cords. All the teachers before her did, as well. They asked as if it was fun to plug in the cords. The reason they had the students do it was they were too lazy to do it themselves. Beetle never liked plugging in cords. He always assumed he would get electrocuted. Father Michael asked Bullet to plug in the cord. Bullet jumped up and eagerly plugged it in. Beetle thought choosing Bullet was a good choice. If there was one kid in the class to be electrocuted, it was Bullet.

Father Michael hit the "on" button. Staticky snow filled the screen. "Is it on Channel 3?" the priest asked.

Without waiting for an answer, he stuck the VHS tape into the VCR. It began to play automatically.

—

A lighting bolt shot across the television screen. Transparent type emerged. Behind the see-through font, there was a panning shot of rainforest tree leaves. The title card read: RAINFOREST RAP. The font panned to the left and shot off the screen. It opened with a funky beat. It cut between stock footage clips of the rainforest. A young man came on screen with a bunch of young children.

He began to rap about the rainforest. It was made to look like the rapping young man and the children were in the rainforest. They looked to be in some urban, indoor greenhouse. Whoever shot it gave up on the rainforest look. They ended up taking the rapping young man out of the greenhouse. They put him on the street where he rapped in front of graffiti-covered walls. He rapped while standing on a fire hydrant. He rapped by hiding behind a phone booth.

The students all mocked the video at first. After six minutes of hearing this guy rap about the rainforest and how it would be completely destroyed by the year 2000, it became unbearable for them to watch.

The students universally agreed it was really bad.

"You think you could do better?" the priest asked.

The students all agreed they could do better.

"Well," Father Michael said, "here's your opportunity. I want everyone here to go home and shoot a video about the rainforest. I want you to do a video on how we can save the rainforest. Did you know by the year 2000 the rainforest will be completely destroyed because of all the paper we are using?"

"But we're getting to the point that we aren't even going to be using paper anymore," said Latricia. "We're about ready to hit the digital age. We'll be doing everything by computers."

"Yes, but what do all computers have?" asked the priest. "They all have printers. And what do printers print? Paper! We're not going to stop using paper."

"We won't need paper because everything is going digital," Latricia explained.

"I know that sounds fine and dandy," said Father Michael. "I just don't see that happening in my lifetime."

"Aren't there other issues worse than the rainforest that we should be worried about?" asked Brownie.

"You can make a video about them instead of making it about the rainforest. You don't have to make it about the rainforest."

"There are a lot worse issues," said Brownie. "Like how the world's going to end in the year 2000."

—

What Brownie was referring to when he said the world was going to end in the year 2000 was a video they watched a month prior. Ms. Cole had come to work a little hungover and was not feeling up for teaching. She allowed the class to watch a video. She sent Latricia and Brownie down to the library to pick out a video. She picked those two students because she promised whoever had the highest grade on the quiz could go. Those two both received one-hundred percents.

As they browsed the VHS collection in the school's library, the two were disappointed to see there were no actual movies. The library only had a bunch of educational programs and documentaries. Latricia gave up and told Brownie he could pick whatever he wanted. Brownie went through a phase where he was fascinated with doomsday, judgment day, and anything apocalyptic. Brownie found a video on Nostradamus. He read the blurb on the back. The summary told about Nostradamus predicting the end of the world. End-of-the-world material was right down Brownie's alley. Brownie selected the video and brought it back to the classroom. The eighth-grade class watched it.

The video talked about how Nostradamus predicted many things. He predicted the World Wars, the rise of Hitler, and the assassinations of both President Lincoln and Kennedy. This aroused the curiosity of the young teenagers. Then the video announced Nostradamus had predicted the end of the world. Much to the shock and dismay of the class, the video said Nostradamus predicted the world would end in the year 2000. This terrified them. After the video was over, their hands shot up with questions aimed at Ms. Cole. Questions such as, "If the world's gonna end in the year 2000, then why do we have to go to school?" Well, that was pretty much the main question they all had.

Nostradamus had predicted the end of the world was in the year 2000. Because he correctly predicted all the other stuff mentioned in the video, the eighth graders were convinced their days were numbered.

—

"What if you don't have a movie camera?" asked Billy.

"I'm glad you asked that," said Father Michael. The priest pulled up the black case and opened to reveal a Panasonic OmniMovie HQ VHS camcorder. "I found this at an estate sale. It's ten years old but still works great. That's about as old as that Rainforest Rap. They probably shot the Rainforest Rap with this camera. So what I'm trying to do here is I want you all to go out and shoot. I've explained this before. I want for you to shoot a video like the Rainforest Rap cause you all claim you can do better and I want to see it. If you need a camera to use, you can use this one. Just contact me and let me know, and I will let you check it out. If you have your own camera, if your family has a camcorder, then you can use that one. All that I ask is that they are put onto a VHS tape. I don't care what you have shot them on, just as long as you can give me a copy on VHS. If it's shot on one of those 8mm tapes, great. Just convert it to VHS. I think we can do this. I think we can make some great little movies here. I think we can do better than that Rainforest Rap crap."

All the students nodded in agreement.

"Can I record over the Rainforest Rap tape?" asked Bullet.

"It was so bad, I wish you could," said the priest. "Unfortunately, it's not a blank tape so you can't record over it."

"Yes, you can," Bullet assured the priest. "I know how to do it."

—

Bullet knew how to record over a VHS tape because soon after his father died he found a video in his father's closet. The video was a movie called *Easy Money*. The title looked pretty funny, and Bullet was feeling gloomy over the loss of his father. He thought a comedy might lighten the mood. When he popped in the movie, he realized it was actually a pornographic film his father had recorded. Bullet ejected it and looked at the video cassette. The cassette had tape over the hole in the back. He then realized he could record over a professionally recorded video. All he had to do was place a square of Scotch tape over the hole in the back.

Bullet had an aunt that he did not like. It was his mother's older sister. His aunt had a daughter who was a drug addict. The drug addict daughter ended up having a baby. Because the drug addict daughter was in no condition to take care of a baby, Bullet's aunt ended up having custody of the infant. His aunt drove him so crazy, he too believed he would be a drug addict had he grown up with his mean aunt as a mother.

After Bullet's father died, his aunt would come over at least once or twice a week. She would sit with her sister and complain about everything. The aunt would rent children's videos and plop the baby down in front of them. Bullet would take the dirty tape his father had recorded and hook up two VCRs. At the end of every children's video, Bullet would record the money shot from the *Easy Money* tape to the children's videos. He would always record it at the end of the video. Only about two or three minutes of the actual dirty video would end up on the children's video. He always made sure to remove the Scotch tape from the hole in the back of the VHS tape. Bullet thought this was a fun prank. He also hoped he could frame his aunt. She would be falsely accused of some kind of crime. Bullet hoped his aunt would get incarcerated.

———

All the students were excited about the project of making a movie.

"And remember," said Sergeant Powers, "this counts as a grade. These will be graded."

After school, Beetle went outside when the limousine pulled up. As he walked to the long automobile, the principal grabbed him by the shoulder and turned him around. "You're going to have to go back inside and talk to the office," the principal said.

Beetle went into the office. The girl working the front counter explained that they were sending Brownie to the public high school. "How come?" asked Beetle.

The girl working the office was blunt and to the point. She explained to him how the public high school contacted them. The high school requested they didn't send Beetle back again. "They complained that you didn't pick up all the trash in the trash cans," said the girl in the office. "They said you left trash bags in the teachers' trash cans and the rooms. They said you also didn't clean the desks. They said that like, kids were writing on the desks and stuff and you didn't scrub any of it off. They also said you forgot to lock doors. There were like four doors that you forgot to lock. And they also said that you ate somebody's cookies. Someone in the office . . . I think they said she was like a counselor or in the registrar's office. They said that the lady in one of the offices was mad because you ate like five of her cookies. And she said they were expensive cookies, too. Oh, and they also said that they caught you on video eating a sandwich out of the trash."

ANDREW ROLSTON

Beetle was overcome with the need to defend himself. He thought those cookies were complimentary. The way people leave candy and dishes at their desk for people passing by to enjoy. And as far as eating the sandwich out of the trash can, he only took one bite of the sandwich. And it was in the trash can where somebody was throwing it out. What was the problem with eating something that somebody was throwing out? Beetle felt the urge to defend himself. Then he felt it wasn't worth it. The sandwich Beetle pulled from the trash can was in the girls' locker room. This proved to Beetle they did, in fact, have cameras in the girls' locker room.

TEN

A WEEK PASSED. It was Monday again. Beetle's mother dropped him off early at school. As he entered the school building, he saw Father Michael walking the halls. He approached Father Michael and explained that he had a problem with his project. Father Michael asked what kind of problem he was having. Beetle told him he had difficulties converting his movie to VHS.

"We don't screen them until the end of the day," Father Michael said. "If you want, I can convert it for you. Do you have what you shot? What did you shoot it with?"

"I shot it on film."

"What kind of camera did you use?" Father Michael asked the question you are never to ask a filmmaker.

"I don't know things like that."

"Do you have the footage?"

"Do I have the what?"

"Do you have what you shot?"

"Yeah, it's in my backpack."

"Well, let me have a look."

Beetle unzipped his backpack and extracted a metal film canister. He opened it up to reveal a 16mm film. "I tried to take it somewhere so somebody could turn it into or put it onto videotape. I tried to get it on one of those videotapes like you said. But they wanted more money than I had to do it."

Father Michael's jaw dropped when he saw the film stock. "I think you may be in luck," he told the boy. "I actually have a projector in the back of the church."

At lunch, Beetle noticed Latricia was not present. He never sat by Latricia nor ever had the nerve to do so. Beetle would always sit at the boys' table. Latricia would always sit at the girls' table. Beetle made sure he always had a spot at the boys' table where he could have a good view of his crush. During lunch, Bullet asked Beetle if he masturbated. Beetle said he didn't know what the word meant. Bullet explained it meant you played with yourself. "Yeah," admitted Beetle. "I do that all the time." All the boys laughed. Even a few of the girls at the opposite table who overheard it laughed as well.

After lunch, the whole school met in the gymnasium. Beetle looked around and saw Latricia was not present. This made him nervous because they were about to screen the short movies. Latricia was not even there. Beetle spent the last week doing everything shy of dying to make his film. The reason he put so much hard work into it was because he wanted to impress Latricia. He even spent all the money he had saved to buy film and pay Christopher HC to help shoot and edit his school project.

Father Michael came out and introduced himself to the school. The introduction was pointless as all the students had already seen him before at Mass. How could a group of kids forget a priest who created a fiery explosion in church?

The priest's introduction did not last long. He got right to the student shorts. They were all immature and amateur. For the most part, they were all just downright bad. Most of them were parodies of television shows. Most of them tried to be funny, and most of them ultimately failed.

The worst film was the only one not trying to be funny. It was an upward shot of a circulating ceiling fan. In the background, a voice was speaking through a toy that distorted the voice, so it sounded burly. The voice was also so distorted that no one could make out what was being said.

Beetle's was saved for last. Mostly because they had to turn off the VCR and flip on the Bell & Howell 16mm projector the priest had brought over on a dolly.

—

Beetle's film opened with him standing in a fancy dining room wearing an oversized tuxedo. The suit belonged to his next-door neighbor. It was the next-door neighbor's house where Beetle shot the film. His next-door neighbors were a friendly, middle-aged couple who never had any children of their own. They were always kind to Beetle. They even gave him presents for his birthday and Christmas. The neighbor lady had a condition where she could not conceive children. Beetle's parents had moved into the neighboring house when Beetle was three years old. The neighbors had played a significant role in Beetle's upbringing over the past twelve years. He was the closest thing the couple had to a child of their own.

The suit hung on Beetle. The next-door neighbor was not a big man. He knew Beetle was small but thought the suit would fit him better. Beetle wore the suit because he was trying to look like an actor from a soap opera. The neighbors had a beautiful dining room with a mahogany dining table. From the ceiling hung a sparkling crystal chandelier. Beetle always thought the room looked like something from a soap opera. That idea was what inspired the soap opera theme of his film.

Beetle stood there in the oversized tuxedo looking into the camera. He explained how he usually drank scotch straight but occasionally would have it on the rocks. If he were drinking it from a disposable cup, he would see to it the cup was biodegradable. He introduced the second part of the film he made as if the soap opera star doubled as a television host presenting a movie that was about to be shown. The movie he made was called *Mother Nature/Mother Evil*. It was about a boy who had Mother Nature as his mother. Beetle had thought about asking his own mother to play Mother Nature but felt she would not approve of what he was doing. That was when he asked the neighbor lady if she would do it. The neighbor lady truly loved the idea. She had majored in theater in college. After graduation, she even traveled with a group of thespians. They were part of a cross-country tour of an off-Broadway comedic play about the deadly dangers of not shaving your legs.

Beetle did the costume design himself. His outfit for Mother Nature was a green dress he found at a thrift store. The neighbor lady had to wear jeans with the bright green dress. The dress was made for a freckled-face child who went to the Renaissance Festival dressed as a fairy. The dress was so short, it actually looked more like a shirt on the neighbor lady than a dress. Behind a dumpster of a florist, Beetle found some floral fillers such as statice lavender and Queen Anne's lace. He decorated the neighbor lady's hair with the flowers he found in the garbage. They really gave her a Mother Nature look.

In the movie, Mother Nature told her son that a boy at school had invited him over to play. Beetle (or the character he played who seemed to be pretty much Beetle winging it) went over to the boy's house only to find out the boy was dead. His mother had eaten him. His mother was named Mother Pollution. Beetle's character addressed her as Mother Pollution. The neighbor lady also played Mother Pollution. Beetle was limited on the number of actresses he had at his disposal. The neighbor lady's husband said he didn't want to be in the movie. Beetle was relieved because he did not have a part for him.

The neighbor lady's wardrobe for the role of Mother Pollution consisted of a black dress, black lipstick, twigs, sticks, and dirt in her hair. Beetle found the black dress at the thrift store. A teenage girl first wore the black dress for her grandmother's funeral. Beetle had turned it into the universal uniform of Mother Pollution. The black lipstick she wore was not lipstick. It was black Halloween makeup. Beetle was given a Frankenstein makeup kit for Halloween the year before. The color makeup pens were wrapped in gold foil. He mostly used the green and yellow makeup that Halloween. There was a lot of black makeup left over. Fortunately, it came in handy for a fill-in for black lipstick. The sticks, twigs, and dirt all came from the park across the street from where they all lived. In the movie, Beetle walked into Mother Pollution's kitchen.

"Would you like a non-environmentally friendly snack?" Mother Pollution cackled like a witch. She opened the refrigerator. Significant amounts of black and yellow smoke poured from the open door. This effect was created by lighting three smoke bombs (two black and one yellow) left over from the Fourth of July. The result did not look as impressive as Beetle had planned.

In the movie, Beetle's character rushed home to his mother, Mother Nature, to warn her about Mother Pollution. When he arrived home, he found Mother Nature lying on the couch dead. The way Beetle and Christopher HC shot this was all in chronological order. This was frustrating for the neighbor lady. She had to change in and out of wardrobe and makeup to transition between characters.

When the main character in the movie looked up from his dead mother on the couch, he saw Mother Pollution standing nearby, looking at him. They couldn't show Mother Nature and Mother Pollution in the same shot because the same actress played both roles.

Mother Pollution looked at the Beetle character and said, "I killed your mother. I am your new mother now."

Without even cutting to black, it cut to a shot of Beetle swinging on a rope swing over a frozen lake. "If you don't protect the

Earth," Beetle began with an improvised narrative voiceover, "then pollution will kill you."

The movie cut to black.

—

"Who made that one?" Beetle overheard one of his classmates ask.

Was it not obvious by who the star of it was? Beetle thought to himself.

Sergeant Powers grabbed the eighth graders and lined them up in a single file. They were the first ones to be taken out of the gym. They were always first to leave the gym as they were the oldest class and sat in the back. This time Sergeant Powers moved them out quickly. It was as if she was concerned their safety was in danger from younger students reacting negatively toward their projects. A lot of the teachers considered the content in the eighth-graders' shorts not suitable for an all-school assembly.

Like a train conductor, Sergeant Powers walked her students back to class like a conductor fronting a train. Beetle was in the back of the line. He trailed like a caboose. When he saw Latricia step out of the nurse's room, he derailed. "You weren't at the thing," Beetle said to Latricia as if he was informing her of her absence.

"I know," said Latricia. "I was having girl-problems."

"Huh?"

"Did you see the one I made?"

"What one did you make?"

"Guess?"

"Du-know."

"I made the one with the fan and the creepy voice."

"Oh…"

"Did you see that one?"

"Yeah."

"Did you like it?"

"Uh-huuuuh," Beetle lied.

Latricia walked with Beetle back to the classroom.

When the students arrived back to class, Sergeant Powers discovered the priest had beat her back to her room. He had since left, but he placed a note on her desk. The letter asked if she could excuse Beetle and have him report to his office in the church. Sergeant Powers dismissed Beetle right away. The way she saw it, it was just one less annoying student she didn't have to deal with.

Beetle trotted to the church. He was afraid the priest would discipline him for making an inappropriate film. When making it, Beetle did not think the film was inappropriate. When he watched it in front of all the children in the school, he then felt maybe he went a little overboard. Then again, maybe the priest just wanted to talk about being an altar boy.

Father Michael stood inside the large church doors as Beetle entered. "I thought I'd stand here and greet you," said the priest. "I didn't think you'd know where my office was. I didn't want you wandering around the church aimlessly looking for it. It's right back here."

Beetle followed Father Michael. They passed the Tabernacle. Father Michael genuflected. Beetle was so nervous he almost forgot to genuflect as well. Father Michael brought Beetle back to his office. The office did not look like the kind of office a priest would have. It was modern and looked more like it should be in a bachelor pad loft. It definitely did not look like a room that would be or even should be in a church. "Have a seat," Father Michael said as he pointed to the chair in front of his desk.

Beetle sat. The boy was so nervous he could feel his legs shaking. He wiped his moist palms on his knees. Was Father Michael going to talk to him about the film he made? Hopefully, he was going to talk to him about being an altar boy. The priest sat on the chair at his desk. The futuristic chair looked like it should have been in a space-ship. He looked over at Beetle. "I want to talk to you about your film," he said.

Beetle could feel his stomach clench when he realized the priest did not want to talk about being an altar boy.

"I really liked your film."

There was a long moment of silence. Beetle was waiting for him to say, "but . . . it was inappropriate," or "but . . . it was in bad taste," or "but . . . you're getting kicked out of school for making it!"

"Thanks." This was the only thing Beetle could muster up the nerve to say.

"Did you do that all yourself?"

"Yes," Beetle did edit it himself. Even though he did have the help of Christopher HC. Beetle felt like getting help on it was like cheating on the project.

"Oh, look what I got!" the priest stood from his chair and walked over to the closet. "I was doing some charity work in Chicago. They have this old building that was one hundred years old. Well, maybe it wasn't a hundred years old, but it was really old. They had all this old stuff that they were storing there, and I found this. I guess you could call it artwork." Father Michael removed a large, rectangular board that was once white. It had faded to a yel-lowish brown.

"I found this thing, and it was made by a child and has their name written on the back here." The priest pointed to where the child scrib-bled its name and age. Age 8. "It's like a mosaic. I guess it's not really a mosaic. It's more like a collage. But look what this child did. This child did this in the '20s. They took all these candy bars and candies and these wrappers, and they glued them to this piece of paper.

"I know somebody looking at it back then would think that it was crazy. But when I see it now, it looks beautiful. I have never seen any of these candy bar wrappers before. I recognize a lot of the names. But I've never seen these designs and these logos. The way they wrote things out. The way they wrote the names of the products. It is beautiful to me. I love this more than anyone could have loved it back then. Who would have known that one day this little time capsule would be a cherished piece of art that this eight-year-old child made? It's like some kind of artifact. It's like I've gone to an archeological dig and I just unearthed this amazing artifact. It's like I am a paleontologist and I just discovered this amazing crop of dinosaur fossils."

The priest observed all the candy bar wrappers glued down. "This is absolutely amazing!" He ran his hand softly and smoothly over the candy wrappers. His hand grazed the top of the wrappers. "Some of the glue looks like it's coming off. I feel guilty gluing these cause it's kind of like defacing a piece of art. I don't need to look at it as defacing the art, I guess. If I glue these, it will be more like restoring the art like they do in museums when they get a piece of art in need of some love and attention."

The priest hung the collage of candy bar wrappers on the wall of his office.

"So you shot that movie yourself?"

"Well, I had somebody shoot it for me," Beetle confessed. "I couldn't shoot it myself because I was in it."

"That's a good point," Father Michael said as he rubbed his chin. "And you edited it yourself?"

This made Beetle nervous. He didn't want to tell the priest Christopher HC pretty much did most of the editing. He was afraid this would get him in trouble. There were two boys last year in the eighth-grade class. Beetle knew them from when he was in the same class with them in fourth grade before he was held back. The two boys were caught paying a student from their class who was on honor roll to do their homework for them. Beetle did not want to get expelled from school.

"I did a lot of the editing," Beetle explained to the priest. "It was really hard."

"I know," the priest agreed. "I've tried my hand at editing film and I just couldn't do it. I admire you for being able to."

Beetle felt the priest was trying to set him up. As if he was trying to make him confess to not editing it. This was not Father Michael's intention at all. The priest was truly impressed with the work Beetle had put together. "It was so hard to do," Beetle said. "It was so hard that I actually had to get the help of somebody to kinda help me through it. But I did edit most of it. I just needed help." Beetle hoped this would convince the priest not to expel him for paying someone to do his homework for him.

"I tried to have somebody help me and show me how to edit," Father Michael explained. "I just couldn't do it. I just couldn't learn how to do it. It was just a big jumble. I had all this footage and all the stuff and I just couldn't piece it together. It's like piecing together a puzzle, and I don't have that kind of intricate brain that could put it together. I also didn't have the patience and the attitude. I got distracted too easily. I just couldn't do it. Not even with help could I learn how to do it. I mean, I've kind of learned how to do it, but I just didn't have the attention span to devote myself to actually doing it. That's why I deeply admire you."

"Thanks."

"I shot a movie a long time ago. I could never put it together. I shot it long before you were even born."

"When did you do it?"

"It was in the '80s."

"I was born in the '80s."

"It was in 1987. What year were you born?"

"March 3rd, 1982." Beetle revealed more information than requested.

"I guess I made it after you were born. You would've been five, I guess."

It offended Beetle that the priest took him for being under ten years old.

"I have a proposition for you," Father Michael said as he leaned forward. "How would you like to help me?"

"Help you with what?"

Father Michael sat forward in his chair. "I need you to edit my passion project."

"I don't know."

"You need to say you will."

"I don't know if I can."

"I know you. I've seen the film you made. I know you can."

"I don't have time?"

"Don't have time? You're a kid. You've got all the time in the world."

"I gotta do things like school work, and I have to go to school, and I have to clean up the school after school. I also got homework and stuff."

"What about the weekends?"

"I have to go to piano lessons on Saturday and church on Sunday. I have to do homework, too, on the weekends."

"Church isn't an all-day thing," said the priest. "I know because I control how long it is."

"I guess I can do it after church."

"After church doesn't work for me. After church, I have to do church again."

"I don't know if there will be time."

"I have an idea. How about instead of having you clean the school, you help me edit?"

"I don't know if I can do that."

"Why not?"

"Cause I have to clean the school after school."

"You don't have to do anything you don't want to."

"No, I have to clean the school cause it pays for me to go to school."

"I know, I'm familiar with the program. How about this—I'll pay for you to not have to clean the school and that money will go to your education. Then I will double it and pay you the same amount so you can have some spending money. What do you think about that?"

"I don't know."

"What don't you know?"

"I don't know if I can do it by myself."

"Why can't you?"

"I need help."

"Who do you need help from?"

"There's this guy who helped me. His name is Christopher HC. I'm gonna need him to help me edit it."

"Fine. We'll get him involved."

"He's gonna want money."

"That's fine. I'll pay him."

"I don't know how much he's gonna want."

"You have his number?"

Beetle poked his hand into the pocket of his school pants. He pulled out his Tasmanian Devil wallet and pulled back the Velcro. He opened it and pulled out Christopher HC's calling card. Beetle looked at the contact information in the film frame.

"Let me see that!" Father Michael extended his hand to take the card from Beetle. "Mind if I call him?"

Beetle leaned forward to give him the card. "Yes, you can call him."

"Do you mind talking to him? I'm not good at talking to people I don't know."

"Yeah, I'll talk to him."

The priest picked up the receiver of his desk phone and hit the speaker button. The dial tone hummed out. Father Michael held the calling card up to his face. He was nearsighted, but never wore glasses. Father Michael dialed the number.

The phone rang. Christopher HC picked up. "Hello?"

"You talk," Father Michael whispered to Beetle.

"Hello," Beetle said nervously into the phone's speaker. "This is Beetle."

"Oh, hey. How's it goin?"

"Good. How are you?"

"I'm doing well."

"That's good."

"Ask him about editing," Father Michael whispered to Beetle.

"Oooh, yeah."

"Oh, yeah, what?" Christopher HC asked.

"I wanted to know if you'd be able to edit something."

"What are you talking about?"

"There is this guy and he's wanting us to edit something for him."

"What does he want us to edit?"

"I don't know."

"Tell him it's a movie," Father Michael whispered.

"It's a movie."

"What kind of movie?" Christopher HC asked as he chewed on ice.

"I don't know."

"Tell him it is the most awesome movie ever made!" Father Michael said loud enough for Christopher HC to hear him.

"It's the most awesome movie ever," Beetle said to Christopher HC in a dull tone.

Christopher HC sucked a few more cubes of ice. "How much does it pay?"

Beetle looked at Father Michael.

"Tell him," he told Beetle.

Beetle told Christopher HC how much he was getting paid, assuming the payment would be the same for Christopher HC.

"I want twice that," Christopher HC said.

"Deal," Father Michael whispered.

Beetle sat back in his chair.

"Tell him!" Father Michael said to Beetle.

"Tell him what?"

"Tell him it's a deal."

"It's a deal," Beetle said into the phone's speaker.

"So," Christopher HC's voice crackled through the speaker. "What's the name of this movie?"

Father Michael rose from his chair. He walked over to the closet. He unlocked the door with a long, golden key. The priest walked in and flipped on the light. He walked over to a black, waist-high refrigerator. Pulling out a little silver key, he unlocked the refrigerator. When it opened, a gust of cold steam escaped. It formed in the air like one's breath on a bitter winter day. Inside the refrigerator was a stack of silver, metal film canisters. He pulled one out and brought it over to Beetle who examined the canister. He flipped it over. On the side of the film canister was a long strip of masking tape. It read: Attack of the Biotoxic Bulldogs.

ELEVEN

THE NEXT DAY AT SCHOOL, Sergeant Powers assigned an essay
about Napoleon in the reader. She was nice and only assigned one
story. Well, nicer than usual. The piece was longer than most in the
reader. Beetle learned about Napoleon when he was in kindergarten. Beetle always admired Napoleon for his ability to take charge
of a situation. He was able to be a leader despite being small. Beetle
could relate to Napoleon because he was small and a good man.
Napoleon along with Paul Bunyan and Johnny Appleseed were
Beetle's three biggest idols. Paul Bunyan was the complete opposite
of Napoleon. Beetle was eager to read the story about Napoleon.
He was disappointed to learn Napoleon was not really short. It was
just a rumor. Beetle was even more disappointed when he read that
Napoleon wasn't that nice of a guy.

In math class, Beetle turned in his assignment. He got every
single problem wrong because he didn't work them out correctly.
He was afraid he was going to have to go back to summer tutoring.
He was probably going to have to do it anyway. He wondered if he
would get the instructor who looked like Christopher HC again.
Now, after actually meeting Christopher HC and working with him,
Beetle didn't think the two even slightly resembled each other.

At lunch, Beetle bought a bag of nacho-cheese-flavored corn
chips with the money he had saved up from being paid a dollar
per day to clean the school. Receiving the ten-dollar check on the

school's payday once every two weeks was more of an insult than a reward. The worst part was it wasn't even ten dollars because they removed taxes from it as well. Beetle was happy, though, to have a little bit of spending money. It meant a great deal to him to be able to purchase even something as minor as a bag of chips from the vending machine. Beetle dropped the coins into the slot. Beetle had to scrub five-and-a-half toilets to raise the money to buy the bag of nacho cheese corn chips. He eagerly watched the spring turn. It eventually loosened the air-filled bag until it dropped down to the bottom of the vending machine. Beetle pulled his corn chips out from the swinging, vending machine door.

Within two seconds of having them out, Bullet ran over and grabbed them out of his hands. Bullet used his fingers and thumbs to smash up every single chip inside the bag until it was nothing more than yellow cheese powder and crumbs. He impressively did it without even popping the bag. Beetle was so sad, he almost started crying. He knew his mother didn't like him eating junk food. He was convinced it was God's way of punishing him for not honoring his parents. Bullet gave Beetle the bag of chips back out of fear he would tattle on him. They were of no use to Bullet. What would he want with a bunch of corn chip powder? Beetle sat at the table and ate his turkey sandwich on rye his mother had made. He opened the bag of chips. The chips were not even crumbs. They had been crushed to dust. To eat them, Beetle had to pour them from the bag into his mouth. The nacho-cheese-flavored dust was nowhere near as satisfying as eating a full-sized chip. His eyes grew wet with tears as he chewed on the powder. He would never again buy junk food from the vending machine and disobey his mother.

In gym class, Bullet continued his pranks. He threw Beetle's gym shorts up behind a water pipe in the locker room. The gym teacher made Beetle sit through gym class. He was not allowed to participate. Beetle did not have a problem with this because they were playing dodgeball again. Beetle would much rather sit and watch the game instead of actually playing. The gym teacher gave Beetle a note to bring to his mother. It was in a blue envelope. The envelope was licked shut so Beetle could not read the note. Even if Beetle had access to the note, he would still not be able to read it. The gym teacher's handwriting was illegible to Beetle. Beetle had difficulty reading people's writing.

After school, Beetle and the rest of the interested students headed over to church for the altar boy/altar girl practice. Father Michael was notorious for being late. That day was no exception. When the group of twelve seventh and eighth-grade students entered the church, Harry greeted them. Harry was a thirty-one-year-old man. The Church took custody over Harry after his smack-addicted mother disowned him as a child. Harry's brain never worked properly owing to his mother's drug abuse while she was expecting him. Harry's nickname in the town was Harry the Halfwit. This name was insulting, but it was actually giving Harry more credit than he deserved. His wits were not even half there. Harry's name was appropriately fitting because he was in fact very hairy. He always wore a white polo shirt, similar to the ones the schoolboys wore. The difference was Harry's shirt always had a bushel of hair protruding from the collar. He wore short-sleeved polo shirts even when it was cold outside. Harry did not even need sleeves because his arms were hairier than a grizzly bear.

All the students sat in the pews. Harry walked out in the white altar boy robe the older boys would wear. They had to special order one for Harry because he was so tall. His face was dabbled with torn shreds of toilet paper. Each little piece of two-ply was dotted in the middle with little round droplets of blood.

"Harry," Nova said with concern. "What happened?"

"I cut m'self shavin," explained Harry.

Father Michael eventually showed up, forty minutes late. He told all the students the practice would only take one hour. Therefore, he had to cram everything into a quick twenty-minute session. He went over how to wear the robes and tie the rope belts. He went over lighting the candles and holding the Bible. The former parish where Father Michael had served as the priest didn't have a podium where the priest stood and read from the Bible. They instead had altar boys and altar girls stand beside the priest, holding the Bible up for him to read. Father Michael liked the approach where they held the Bible. So he did away with the podium. He was going to have them go over the Sacraments of the Holy Eucharist. Unfortunately, they ran out of time. Father Michael spent five minutes telling them about his pilgrimage to Japan. He told the group of bored teenagers how he and a Japanese translator journeyed to Aokigahara to talk people out of committing suicide.

It was a cloudy and rainy day. When Beetle left the church, it was almost night. He walked back to the school. Beetle thought he could lend a helping hand to finish his janitorial duties. He banged on the door. Nobody answered. He stood out in the cold. In the distance, he saw two figures walking toward him. When they arrived closer, Beetle could see they were Bullet and Cage. His stomach sank. He thought about running but knew it was not a good idea. Bullet and Cage could easily outrun him. They walked straight toward Beetle. He froze like deer in headlights. When the two approached Beetle, Bullet asked Beetle, "What are you doin here?"

Beetle did not answer.

"Look at what we got," Bullet said as he reached in his pocket. He pulled out a cigar and a box of thirty-two diamond matches. "I stole this stuff. Cage stole a Butterfinger."

Cage pulled the candy bar from his pocket. The chocolate had melted and had molded to the shape of Cage's leg.

Bullet struck a match on the side of the box. He lit his stolen cigar. "You like to smoke?" he asked Beetle as a puff of smoke clouded around his mouth.

"No."

"You're not cool if you don't smoke," Bullet said and then coughed because his young lungs couldn't withstand the carcinogens. "Hold him down!" Bullet said to Cage between coughs.

Cage grabbed Beetle by the shoulders and spun him around. He knocked Beetle's feet out from underneath him. Beetle hit the ground hard. It knocked the wind out of him.

Beetle assumed they were going to de-pants him.

—

The previous year, the seventh-grade class had a bowling party. The party was unsupervised. Beetle went up to roll the ball down the lane, and Bullet told Cage to shove Beetle and hold him down. Cage did as Bullet had instructed. As Cage held Beetle down, Bullet ran over to the lane and pulled Beetle's pants and underwear off. Bullet had difficulty tugging Beetle's brown corduroys over his rented bowling shoes. Bullet yanked the pants so hard, they turned inside out as they dangled from Beetle's feet. Beetle kicked his naked legs furiously as Cage sat on his back. It was something the students would never forget. They all perceived it as being the most horrifying and hilarious thing they had ever seen.

—

Bullet and Cage did not de-pants Beetle in front of the school. Cage pushed Beetle's left cheek into the dirt. He pushed so hard there would be gravel imprints on Beetle's jaw and forehead for days.

Kneeling down next to Beetle, Bullet removed the cigar from his mouth. He held it to Beetle's face. "I'm gonna burn your eyeball out."

"Hey! You two!" Gary shouted as he walked out of one of the school's front doors. "Get off him!"

Bullet and Cage ran off. The students were all afraid of Gary. Rumor had it he had killed so many people in Vietnam, he had developed an addiction to killing.

TWELVE

THE WHOLE NEXT DAY AT SCHOOL, Beetle was nervous because he was going to Christopher HC's house after school. He was skittish when thinking about going over there with Father Michael to edit *The Attack of the Biotoxic Bulldogs*.

The note Beetle's gym teacher had given him the day before was to inform his mother she had to buy him new gym shorts. Beetle checked with the Lost and Found to see if they had his gym shorts. The girl in the office checked the box and brought out a pair of gym shorts. "That's them!" Beetle said. They were not Beetle's gym shorts, but he thought they were them. The shorts the girl working the office had given Beetle were a pair that had been in the Lost and Found for the past two years. Beetle never even noticed they had another boy's name written inside on the elastic with a permanent marker. Something only his mother would see when Beetle would bring them home for her to wash. Beetle asked the girl working the office if they had his black shoe. She informed him they did not. "Do you have my—"

"Troll with green hair and sparkles?"

"Yeah."

"No."

After school, Father Michael drove Beetle to Christopher HC's house. He did not live too far from the school. When Father Michael pulled up to the house, Christopher HC was standing in the driveway. Father Michael manually hand-cranked the window of his old pickup truck. "You have a projector?" Father Michael asked without even introducing himself to Christopher HC.

"No."

"Well, I assumed you didn't, so I brought one," Father Michael told Christopher HC as he turned the key in his pickup to shut off the ignition. "I also brought a projector screen as well."

"Looks good."

"You want to carry the screen, and I'll bring in the projector?"

Christopher HC walked over to the bed of the truck and lifted the Bell & Howell projector out of the truck's bed. "This is heavier than it looks."

"You want to carry the projector, and I'll carry the screen?" Father Michael said this as a joke because the projector was far heavier than the screen.

"No, thanks."

"That's what I thought."

Christopher HC struggled to lift the screen. Father Michael fought, even more, to carry the projector. The projector weighed three times more than the screen. Christopher HC had already brought the screen inside when Father Michael wasn't even half-way across the yard with the projector. Beetle and Christopher HC walked over to ask Father Michael if he needed help. "No. I got it!" Father Michael grunted modestly.

Father Michael pushed his way past Christopher HC and Beetle. He banged the projector against the door frame. "Don't worry," he said to Christopher HC. "It did more damage to the projector than it did to your house."

Once Father Michael was inside the house and out of earshot, Christopher HC asked Beetle, "Why's that guy wearing a priest's uniform?"

"Cause he's a priest."

Christopher HC walked inside his house as Beetle followed.
Father Michael paced in circles as he stretched his arms and rubbed
his shoulders that were sore from lifting the bulky projector. He
then ran back out to his truck. He returned with a hulking, red,
Budweiser foam cooler. The cooler was once used for catering until it
was donated to the church.

Father Michael checked each one of the film canisters. He
examined the masking tape labels on each one of them. "Here it is!"
he said, holding up a canister. "Reel #1." He grabbed the cord of the
projector and plugged it into a power strip behind Christopher HC's
television. The light of the projector lit up. "It works! I was afraid I'd
have to change the bulb."

The walls in the house were white. Father Michael didn't bother
with setting up the projector screen. Instead, the priest aimed the
projector against the white wall. A Ziploc bag with two cloth gloves
inside appeared in Father Michael's hands. He opened the bag and
put on the gloves. Beetle thought the gloves resembled the kind
Mickey Mouse would have worn. The gloves' purpose was to prevent
any fingerprints on the film stock. Father Michael opened the film
canisters and gently extracted the reel. He had spun the film through
all the projector's obstacles. The film was ready to project. Father
Michael switched it on, and the reel began to spin.

—

Two teenage boys were sitting on a street curb talking. One
boy said his girlfriend had just broken up with him. The other boy
attempted a pep talk to comfort him. The dialogue was blocky. It
was obvious the actors had memorized their lines word for word.

Father Michael pointed to the image of the two boys sitting on
the curb. "That boy on the right, that's my brother. He's my little

brother. He's two years younger than me. His name is Rory. And the other guy, his name is Mark. Mark was in the class between Rory and I. Mark was a friend of both of ours. Alright! Enough standing around and watching this! Let's get to the editing."

They walked down to Christopher's basement. Beetle was familiar with his basement. He had been down there to edit his school film project on nature.

"This basement is really cool," Father Michael said. "This reminds me of when I was in the Middle East. I stayed in this guy's basement. It was a basement just like this. It had no windows or anything. I lived there for weeks. Months even. The guy whose basement it was, was this guy who was some kind of scientist. He thought I would go crazy if I slept without any windows because he claimed that you had to see the sunrise while you were sleeping in order not to go crazy. I don't know if I believe that or not, but he put a TV down in the basement right next to the bed where I slept. He left it on all night. It was set to dim so it wasn't too bright because I'm kind of a light sleeper and having a giant glowing nightlight would definitely distract me.

"So he left his TV on, and the TV was hooked to a surveillance camera outside. He was some kind of scientist, and he was always paranoid that somebody would come in and steal his patents. He was working on this one patent that he thought was going to make him super rich. So I would sleep with the TV with the outdoor surveillance camera showing me the sunrise. The surveillance camera was in black and white. I don't know if that really affected anything or if it would have been better if it was in color. Even though his whole idea of sleeping without seeing the sunrise is a really crazy thing, I think, but he was a scientist, so I took his word for it.

"The basement downstairs, I'm serious the basement was just like this, but it was filled with all these balloons. It was filled with all kinds of balloons. Different kinds, different shapes, made from different materials. This guy invented a machine that could inflate a balloon and have it float without actually using helium. He had some way of filtering out, I don't know how he did it, but he would filter out regular air with an air pump. It was just a regular air pump, and he had a way to filter the air. There wasn't any kind of gas in it or anything. There was just a filter that would just suck in regular air and then blow it out. Somehow this filter removed something in the air that you put in it that would make it fill up a balloon and make it float. It was the strangest thing. I don't know how it worked. I'm not the scientist.

"He would test it out with all these balloons, and every time he would set up a new filtering machine that would inflate the balloons, he would inflate a bunch of them and keep them down in his basement and test them, and they all had little notes on them with dates and times so he could monitor each one and see how long it would float, and he'd also filled some up with helium to see the comparison between the helium and his filtered air. His were nowhere near as effective as helium. He still had a great invention nonetheless."

Beetle, Christopher HC, and Father Michael all sat at Christopher HC's desk to edit the film. Christopher HC spliced together the scene of the two teenage boys sitting on the curb.

"I don't know what is going on with these labels," Father Michael said while examining the masking tape on the film canister. "I think these are not labeled correctly. This is number one, but it's not the first reel. I know there's a reel before this. I'll have to go through and check."

Father Michael insisted Christopher HC wear the Mickey Mouse gloves while splicing the film to avoid fingerprints and smudges.

After they had finished editing the scene with the boys on the curb, the three headed back upstairs. Father Michael had Christopher HC remove the white gloves so he could use them to handle the next reel of film. Father Michael pulled out the film canister. It had #2 scribbled on the masking tape with a black marker. Father Michael proceeded in loading the second reel of film into the projector and flipped it on.

—

In the second scene, the two teenage boys from the previous scene were walking through a parking lot. It was a parking lot of a giant hardware store. It was late at night, and the store was closed. The hardware store's lights were turned off. The name of the hardware store was not even visible because the lens blurred it out of focus. As the two boys walked up the sidewalk, they bumped into two teenage girls. With the two girls was a teenage boy standing by crates of bagged soil in front of the hardware store. The five teenagers introduced themselves. They briefly reminisced back and forth in a typical deadpan, poorly scripted dialogue.

The teenage boy who was with the two girls whistled bird sounds. He was acting like he was trying to hold them back.

Father Michael pointed out that the one girl, the blond girl, the one who seemed the more talkative of the two girls, was named Sarah and was his then girlfriend. Her name was Sarah, and her character in the movie was named Sara. She named the character herself. The other girl, the brunette girl who appeared somewhat shy, was his girlfriend Sarah's best friend. Her name was Amy, and her character in the movie was named Amy. The boy who chirped like a bird was his girlfriend's little brother. His name was Arnie. Arnie's character did not have a name. "He has a tic where he says words and they just come out," Father Michael said about the boy in his movie who impersonated a bird.

Christopher HC asked, "Tourette's syndrome?"

"Oh, you're familiar with it?"

"I saw it on the Maury Povich Show. They always have weird stuff on the show like primordial dwarfs and stuff."

"I saw a primordial dwarf once," Beetle added. "He or she, I'm not sure, but the primordial dwarf worked at Builders Square, and I saw it when my dad took me there."

The two boys and the priest cut together the second reel. As Christopher HC did all the splicing, Father Michael asked if he could let Beetle try his hand at it. Beetle was nervous at first because he was not familiar with the editing process, but he warmed up to it.

Christopher HC turned out to be a good teacher. It impressed Father Michael and Christopher HC how fast Beetle had learned the craft. It impressed Beetle more than anyone how quickly he had picked up the skill. Beetle managed to edit the whole second half of the scene without any help.

Once they had the two scenes cut, they used the projector against the white wall again. They screened what they had pieced together. Father Michael was pleased with the finished product. He pulled out his wallet and paid the two boys the cash he had promised. Without asking Christopher HC or Beetle for help, Father Michael carried the screen for the projector out to his truck. They had not even used it. "I don't think we'll be needing this tomorrow," Father Michael said.

Once Father Michael was outside and out of earshot, Christopher HC said, "I don't know if I like this guy."

"What do you mean you don't like him?" asked Beetle.

"I just don't like him."

"He's a priest. How could you not like a priest?"

"I don't care if he's a priest or not. I'm not even Catholic."

"You're sayin you don't like him cause you're not Catholic?"

"Being Catholic has nothing to do with it. I don't dislike somebody because they're Catholic. But I also don't give somebody undeserved praise just cause they're a priest. If I met someone who was a priest and they were a real cool guy, then I'd be all cool with that, but this guy is weird, and I have no problem or regret saying it."

"He's not that weird."

"Really? Did you see the movie he made?"

"It wasn't that weird."

"Really?"

"Well, we really can't judge it cause we only saw two scenes from it."

"He made a weird movie."

"Well, you make weird movies too."

"But mine are a good kinda weird."

Father Michael came back into the house. The boys remained silent. Without saying a word, Father Michael picked up the massively heavy projector. He tried to act casual as he carried it out the door, nonchalantly trying to hide how weak he was.

"You need help with that?" Christopher HC asked, accurately guessing the priest's self-esteem would prevent him from saying he did.

"I've got it!" Father Michael grunted the refusal. "If Jesus could carry the cross across the desert, then I can carry this projector out to my car."

"I think that projector weighs more than the cross did?" said Beetle.

"I think you may be right," Father Michael groaned as he exited the door.

He dropped the projector into the bed of his truck slowly.

Christopher HC stayed inside, without giving either of the two verbal farewells.

Father Michael drove Beetle to his house. Beetle's mother was grateful he was dropped off before his father arrived home.

THIRTEEN

AFTER LUNCH THE NEXT DAY AT SCHOOL, Beetle was standing
at one of the urinals. As he relieved himself, he observed how gross
they had become owing to his two days of being absent from cleaning them. As he did so, a violent shove to his back caused him to
lunge forward into what he always thought looked like a miniature
bathtub on the wall.

It was no surprise to Beetle when he turned around; Bullet stood
there. A Cage-less Bullet. Cage had been out sick with strep throat.
Beetle turned around and grabbed Bullet by his white, parochial
school uniform shirt. He swung Bullet around until the bully's
pelvis banged against the protruding porcelain sink. Bullet fell to
the ground, his body flushed because of pelvic pain. He could not
believe Beetle's strength. Beetle even impressed himself with being
tough enough to stand up to the bully. Beetle was filled with so
much hot adrenaline, it blew steam out of his ears. He had tasted
a nibblet of revenge, and now he was hungry for the main course.
As Bullet fell to the urine-stained restroom floor, he cried in pain.
Beetle bent down and grabbed the collar of the black shirt Bullet
wore underneath his polo. Beetle grasped the collar with his fists.
He pulled it so tightly that it sent Bullet into a gagging convulsion.
Convinced he was going to die, Bullet could not believe his cause
of death—Beetle murdering him. Bullet's face grew tomato red. He
became light-headed.

"You're not so tough without that big ol' oaf," Beetle said as he continued to strangle Bullet. "I can hold this all day long."

The bully was now being bullied by the bullied. Bullet tried to squeeze his fingers underneath the front of his collar. He hoped it allowed enough slack for him to breathe. It was hopeless. Beetle mustered up more strength to pull the collar even tighter. Bullet resorted to full-blown panic. The bully flung his arms in all directions. He did so by gyrating his hips back and forth. His pelvic bone still throbbed in pain. Beetle caved in and let his collar loose. Beetle did not stick around to observe the bully's reaction when he released him. Beetle walked out of the restroom without turning around. He rushed down the hall to get to his classroom. Beetle grew worried when Bullet never returned to class for the rest of the day. Part of him wondered if he had killed Bullet. Another part of him wondered if Bullet would be waiting for him outside after school.

When the final school bell of the day rang, Beetle rushed down to the main office to get a ride from Father Michael. He avoided going outside or even going into the restrooms where he felt Bullet might be hiding. This was all getting to his head. He then took a deep breath. Beetle thought about how he shouldn't be so concerned about Bullet. He was clearly stronger and a better fighter than the bully.

When Bullet got home, he took off his polo shirt and looked in the mirror. He saw that the left armpit of his *Appetite for Destruction* T-shirt had been ripped. Tears filled Bullet's eyes. Bullet's father gave the shirt to him last year for Christmas just two weeks before his father took his own life. This was the last gift his father would ever give him. Bullet grabbed his mother's mossy green ceramic soap dish off the bathroom sink. He slammed it down on the tile floor. The soap dish shattered into a countless number of pieces. Bullet broke into an uncontrollable crying fit. He missed his father. The thought of never having him back ever again caused a sharp pain in his stomach, which made him cry more. He tried to hold it back. His sobbing grew so thick he had difficulty breathing. He suffered from depression. Something he had inherited from his father.

FOURTEEN

DESPITE IT BEING ONLY THE SECOND DAY of working on *The Attack of the Biotoxic Bulldogs*, Christopher HC was already getting bummed out with the project.

Father Michael set up his projector. He projected a scene with his friend Mark who played the role of Mark and his old girlfriend Sarah who played the role of Sara. In this particular scene that he showed to Beetle and Christopher HC, however, Mark played a character named Jeremy and Sarah played a character named Bianca. The two actors attempted to differentiate these two characters from the other two characters they played in the film. They did so by wearing black wigs. Sarah wore a long wig with thick bangs. Mark had a wig cut short on the back but was thick and messy on top. They also attempted to mask their identities with thick sunglasses. The two walked through a cemetery looking for the headstone of the girl's great-aunt. They found the marked grave, and both stopped to observe it.

"Tell me about your great-aunt," Mark's character Jeremy asked.

"She was a real bulldog," Sarah's character Bianca replied. In less than a second after the words came out of her mouth, a bulldog flew out from behind the tombstone. The bulldog bit her right in the neck. The bulldog latched its teeth into her as she screamed for help. The Jeremy character ran. She stood screaming in panic. She attempted to tug away the gore-soaked canine with its fangs deep into her trachea. The blood squirted so high that it squirted off screen. Even when the camera cut to a wide-angle shot, the blood still spurted so high, it sprayed off screen.

Christopher HC looked away once the attacking bulldog emerged. Halfway through the attack, Christopher HC walked into his kitchen. He pulled a plastic pitcher of ice tea from the refrigerator and poured himself a glass. After he had heard the film reel end, he walked back into the living room.

"Pretty exciting," Beetle said to Christopher HC. "Isn't it?"

"Beetle," said Christopher HC. "I think you should edit this one yourself."

The priest and the two boys went down into the basement. Beetle was nervous about trying his hand at editing all by himself. Once he did his first couple of cuts, he became confident.

After Beetle had finished editing the scene, he walked upstairs. He had the finished product tucked under his arm. Father Michael trailed behind him. Christopher HC waited down in the basement. He did not want to see the scene again. Once he heard it was over, Christopher HC walked upstairs. As he walked into the living room, Father Michael had queued up another reel. The projector started. Beetle walked up close to it in excitement to see what was going to happen next. Christopher HC did the opposite and stood in the back of the room with his arms crossed. He wanted to be as far away from it as possible.

—

The scene opened up in a darkly lit laboratory. A mad scientist stood in front of a large table. The scientist was another character played by Mark. He wore a green lab coat, screw ring goggles, a white wig with the hair sticking straight up, and a head mirror. Across the table were Bunsen burners with lit flames, beakers containing unknown substances, Erlenmeyer flasks overflowing with colorful, bubbly foam, and preserved brains, eyeballs, fetal pigs, and bull testicles floating in formaldehyde.

Standing behind the mad scientist were his two voluptuous assistants in cleavage-revealing outfits. The two busty girls were squeezed like sausages into white, rubber nurse costumes. The outfits were obtained from an adult novelty shop.

"Where is my stethoscope?" the mad scientist asked.

"What is a stethoscope?" the assistant behind him to the left asked.

"It is the thing I use to listen to people's hearts."

"A heart-hearing thingy?"

"Yes. A heart-hearing thingy."

"Your heart-hearing thingy is around my neck," the busty assistant behind him to the right answered.

The mad scientist reached his hand behind him without looking back. The assistant with the stethoscope around her neck leaned forward. "Can you feel it?" she asked.

The mad scientist's attention focused on pouring a red liquid from an Erlenmeyer flask into a beaker with blue liquid. When the two mixed, an overflow of froth formed. The mad scientist reached blindly behind him for his stethoscope. He accidentally grabbed the science assistant's right breast. As he squeezed the boob, it made a honking noise. Using a children's bicycle horn created the sound effect.

The scientist's eyes grew big with the "honk." The mad scientist turned around and removed the stethoscope from the assistant behind him to the right's neck. "I apologize for being so hands-y."

"It was fine with me," the assistant behind the mad scientist to the right said. "I needed a quick massage."

Father Michael laughed loudly at the one-liner. Beetle and Christopher HC both looked up at the priest at his unexpected reaction.

Father Michael headed down to the basement. Beetle followed him until Christopher HC pulled him aside. Christopher HC brought Beetle into his kitchen to talk to him. He didn't want Father Michael hearing them. "I'm out," Christopher HC whispered to avoid Father Michael hearing him.

"You're out of what?"

"I'm out of *The Attack of the Biotoxic Bulldogs*. I'm out! I'm not doing any more."

"What are you saying?"

"I don't want to have any part of this thing you guys are working on. I don't want to be credited for having worked on this. This will totally tarnish my reputation. This is my mom's house. I don't want her coming here and seeing this. I've also been dating this girl and she's religious and doesn't drink, and she's like really sweet and nice and stuff. I just met her, and we started going out. I met her in a chat room, and I don't want her coming over here like she does occasionally and seeing what is going on with whatever you guys are doing. I want out. I'm not working on it anymore."

"But how are we going to finish it?"

"You can finish it yourself. I showed you how to edit. You're good at splicing and doing everything. You finish it."

"Yes, you can. But you have to stay in the basement. If you guys come over here, you go right down into the basement, and you don't come up. The projector goes down in the basement too. When you guys get here, you have one minute to get down to the basement, and you stay down there until it's time for you to leave."

"What if I have a question?"

"Call me. The number on my business card is to the phone in my bedroom. This house has two phone lines."

FIFTEEN

THE NEXT DAY, Cage returned to school despite doctor's orders not to because of still being highly contagious.

The class was assigned a three-part reading on the Donner Party. Beetle was feeling depressed all day. Reading the story about cannibalism did not help.

After school, Beetle walked into the boys' room. Bullet and Cage followed him. "Give him a wedgy!" Bullet shouted to Cage.

Cage ran over and pulled Beetle's underwear up with so much strength it lifted Beetle off the floor. His new white sneakers kicked frantically.

"Take em into the stall," Bullet said, pointing to the toilet. "Dunk him!"

Cage forced Beetle into the toilet stall. Beetle tried to grab both sides of the stall's door frame. His weak little grip was no match for Cage's strength.

"I said dunk him!"

Then Cage flipped Beetle upside down and dunked his head into the toilet like a cookie in milk. Beetle tried to push himself back up by pressing his hands on the toilet seat. It was of no use. Cage's strength outpowered Beetle's. Beetle's head was soaked. "Maybe you'll think twice next time before goin and rippin someone's favorite shirt."

With his hands around Beetle's ankles, Cage yanked his head out of the bowl. Beetle gasped for a breath of air. Beetle exhaled and then screamed. The very second Beetle's voice cried out, Cage dropped Beetle's head back into the toilet. His head went down so hard his forehead was bruised, and his neck was whipped back so hard on the impact that it was sore for a full week. Bullet reached past Cage and through Beetle's upside down legs and flushed the toilet. When the water bowl filled back up, Bullet was disappointed to see there was now very little water in the bowl. Beetle still screamed, but inside the bowl, his voice was muffled and quiet. "Hold him still. I'm gonna drown him." Bullet unzipped his pants. As Beetle screamed, Bullet managed to shoot a urine stream directly into Beetle's open mouth like some sort of carnival game. The second the rank urine hit Beetle's tongue, he immediately closed his mouth and squeezed his eyes shut. Bullet didn't micturate enough to fill the bowl very high. Bullet was sick of play torture and told Cage to drop him.

Cage dropped Beetle's legs, and they landed with a thump.

As Bullet and Cage walked out of the restroom, Beetle remained kneeling there with his head in the bowl like an ostrich's head in the sand.

When Beetle stumbled down to the school's office, Father Michael was waiting for him. It was unusual for somebody to keep Father Michael waiting. He was always the one who was late.

"What happened?" Father Michael asked Beetle when he walked into the office.

"I'm sorry I'm late."

"I'm not talking about being late. I'm asking what happened to your hair?"

Beetle bashfully put his hand on his wet head. "I wet it down."

"Boy, you soaked it down!" Father Michael said, trying to be funny. He was concerned. The boy smelled of urine. The yellow urine droplets ran down the back of Beetle's white, uniform shirt's collar. A few dropped all the way down the back of his shirt. The priest did not say anything about it. He just followed Beetle outside and walked him to his pickup truck.

When they went over to Christopher HC's house, they did as they were told and went down to the basement with the projector and screen. Father Michael pulled out some random reels, and they edited the film together. Father Michael had learned from watching Christopher HC edit. He had picked up more of an understanding of the process than Beetle had acquired. Whenever Beetle found himself in a rut, Father Michael was able to help him out.

The priest and the boy stayed down in the basement and cut together scene after scene of biotoxic bulldogs. There was not a method to their madness. The priest just pulled out random reels and pieced them together. Most of what they cut was scenes of the biotoxic bulldogs terrorizing the city. They managed to cut a record-breaking four scenes in one night. Beetle began to think about what Christopher HC had told him about not wanting to be affiliated with the project. Beetle himself questioned his affiliation with the project as well. He was afraid of the reputation it would cause him. He wondered what his parents and the people at his school would think of him, knowing he helped edit *The Attack of the Biotoxic Bulldogs*.

After they had finished editing, the priest left without even saying a word to Christopher HC and took Beetle home.

As they ate dinner, Beetle's mother noticed her son seemed gloomy. Beetle had a bad day, and it showed. Right after dinner, Beetle headed straight for bed. His mother listened outside the door of his bedroom. She heard him sobbing. She knocked on the door and slowly entered the room. When Beetle heard his mother walk into his room, he turned on his stomach and buried his tear-covered face in his pillow.

"Is everything alright?" she asked her son.

"No."

"What's wrong?"

"Everything."

"Everything's wrong?"

"Yes. Everything's bad."

"Not everything is bad."

"Yes, it is."

"Don't say that."

"It is."

"Stop."

"I hate everything!"

"Stop talking like that!"

"I do!"

"Stop that!"

"I hate everyone."

"That is a terrible way to talk."

"I want everyone to die."

"No son of mine is going to talk like that."

"I want to die."

"Why would you even say such a thing?"

"Every day when I wake up I just want to die!" Beetle broke out crying. Out of embarrassment, he hid his head into his pillow. He sobbed hard into it. Then he tilted his head to the side to gasp for a breath. "I just want to kill myself."

"Why would you say that?"

"Cause, like I told you! I wanna die."

"Why do you want to die?"

"Because I hate everything about my life."

"What's going on with you and that priest?"

"I don't know."

"What do you mean you don't know? You've spent the last three nights with him."

"I don't want to talk about it."

"Why not?"

"I don't—" Beetle almost said he didn't like Father Michael but felt guilty saying such a thing about a priest.

"What is he having you do?"

"Weird stuff."

"What sort of weird stuff?"

"He's making me go down in this guy's basement and do weird stuff."

"What weird stuff is he making you do?"

"He has this weird movie . . . "

"What sort of movie is it?"

"It's a really horrible movie."

"Do you want to stop working with him?"

"I don't think I can!"

Beetle was overwhelmed with all the mayhem going on in his life. Struggling with his schoolwork, dealing with bullying, and now having to edit a project he was embarrassed to have people see. Afraid of how their reaction would be, he cried himself to sleep.

His mother was deeply concerned about his relationship with the priest. She felt she needed to contact an authority.

SIXTEEN

BEETLE'S MOTHER DROPPED HIM OFF AT SCHOOL the next day at the side of the school by the entrance to the cafeteria. The doors were not always opened, but it was a risk Beetle and his mother would take. It saved time from waiting in line with all the other cars at the main entrance. Beetle pulled himself out of the car and walked up to the door. He tugged the handle, and it swung open. He waved to his mother and walked inside the warm building as his mother drove off. The cafeteria was dark. All the lights were off because it was still early morning on that cold and cloudy day. There was not a lot of light coming through the windows.

Beetle walked in a line as he pretended to tightrope-walk on a light-colored row of floor tiles. He was looking down at his feet when he passed a pillar with somebody unexpected behind it. As Beetle passed the pillar, Bullet popped out and grabbed him by the shoulders. Cage stepped out from behind the pillar in front of the one Bullet was behind. In his hands was a Super Soaker 60. Bullet let go of Beetle's shoulders as Cage tossed Bullet the Super Soaker. Before Bullet even shot the water gun, Cage had Beetle in a choke-hold. Cage dragged Beetle by his neck backward as Beetle's new white shoes became scuffed from dragging on the dirty cafeteria's tile floor. Bullet walked into the locker room the boys used for gym class. Cage followed him, pulling Beetle along. Bullet opened one of the lockers, and Cage threw Beetle inside. Beetle was so small, he fit inside the locker so tightly it was as if it was custom made to fit him. Cage held Beetle against the metal wall of the locker. "What's the capital of Thailand?" Bullet asked with is fist up, as if to punch Beetle.

"I don't know," cried Beetle.

"Tell me or I'll punch you in your mule!"

"I don't know," sobbed Beetle, as tears ran down his cheeks.

"Bangkok!" Bullet punched Beetle in the penile region, and then hosed Beetle's crotch with the Super Soaker 60. The water gun's tank was filled with Bullet and Cage's urine. They slammed the locker door. Beetle was locked inside. He screamed and panicked. Bullet and Cage didn't need to squirt him with their own micturition because within a minute of being inside the locker, Beetle wet his pants. He went into shock and passed out. He was out cold for hours.

Two hours before the final bell rang, Beetle came to. When he woke up, he began screaming. The art teacher heard the screams from down the hall. She walked through the cafeteria to see where it was coming from. When she noticed it was coming from the boys' locker room, she felt going in there was not a good idea. She went to the principal's office. The principal was on his computer when she entered.

"There is screaming coming from the boys' locker room," she told him.

"I will be there in a second," the principal waved her out to the hall. "I just need to finish this up."

The principal finished his game of Ski Jump and walked out into the hall.

The art teacher reminded him of the noise came from the boys' locker room. The principal casually walked down to where the art teacher claimed she had heard the screams.

As the principal and the art teacher walked to the cafeteria, they could hear the screams coming from the locker room. They slowly walked into the locker room. They walked up to the locker with Beetle stuck inside. The principal tried to ask questions to the boy stuck in the locker, but Beetle was too panic-stricken to explain who he was or how he ended up in the locker. The principal told the art teacher to go back to what she was doing—he had it from there. The art teacher returned to her class, and the principal searched the school for Gary. When he found him, he asked Gary if he could get one of the lockers in the locker room open.

"You got somethin stuck in there?" asked Gary.

"I got someone stuck in there!"

The principal explained there was a combination lock on the locker. Gary grabbed his bolt cutter. They went back to locker room, and Gary cut the lock off the locker, freeing Beetle from his metal casket. Even after the principal freed him from the locker, Beetle was still in an emotional frenzy. The principal did not know what to do. He brought Beetle up to his office and gave him the bottle of Diet Dr. Pepper he had only halfway finished before being called down to rescue the boy. He also gave him two oatmeal raisin cookies that had been sitting out for days and had grown quite stale. Neither the principal nor any of the other staff in the school's office would have eaten the cookies. Beetle did not seem to mind the cookies' staleness. He thought the cookies were good. The principal allowed Beetle to play Ski Jump on his computer as the boy enjoyed his snack.

"Are you goin to tell my mom about this?" asked Beetle. "About me gettin stuck in a locker?"

"You don't want me to tell her?" the principal asked.

"No. I think it would be embarrassing."

"I won't tell her," the principal assured Beetle. This was a relief to the principal. He didn't want Beetle's mother to find out her son had been thrown into a locker and left there all day without anyone noticing he was missing. "She doesn't need to know about it."

The school's young receptionist walked into the principal's office. "His mother's coming to pick him up early today," she said to the principal as she pointed to Beetle. Both the principal and Beetle were shocked.

"Why is she picking him up early?" the principal asked out of fear that Beetle's mother had been contacted regarding the locker incident.

"He has a doctor's appointment."

"Did you know you had a doctor's appointment today?" the principal asked Beetle.

"Nope!" Beetle said watching the computer screen as the Abominable Snow Monster shredded his skier apart. "She didn't tell me anything about that."

SEVENTEEN

BEETLE'S MOTHER ARRIVED AT THE SCHOOL to pick up her son about a half hour before school dismissal. She walked into the office to find her boy already waiting for her. "Are you ready to go?"

"Should I let Father Michael know?" asked Beetle.

"Do you mind letting Father Michael know that Beetle has a doctor's appointment?" Beetle's mother asked the girl working the office's front desk.

The girl assured Beetle's mother she would let the priest know.

Beetle and his mother walked out to her car. "Are they gonna give me a shot?" Beetle asked his mother as he sat in the car's passenger seat.

"No," she said.

"Good."

"I don't think they'll give you a shot," Beetle's mother said. She thought about how she didn't know what specific procedures the doctors would be performing on her son.

Back at the school, Father Michael showed up to the office to pick up Beetle. He was disappointed to hear Beetle had left with his mother to go to the doctor. Father Michael decided to rummage through the box of items teachers confiscated from students. Things the teachers found to be inappropriate. A vintage *Penthouse* stolen from a student's father's private collection. The magazine was six years older than the boy who took it. There were also two or three *Playboys*. Technically, only one of the *Playboys* was in its full page-for-page entirety. The other two *Playboys* were well worn. Most of the pages were missing, including both of the centerfolds and a good chunk of the pictorials. The most popular thing among the confiscated items were *Victoria's Secret* catalogs. They filled the large, brown, cardboard box. Father Michael sifted through all the R-rated VHS tapes. He didn't find anything too interesting. He ended up settling with a CD-ROM game called *Leisure Suit Larry: Love for Sail!*

———

The doctor checked Beetle in and introduced herself to him. She walked Beetle back to her office. She tried to explain all the tests she was going to give him. "Am I gettin a shot?"

"No, we are not giving you a shot."

The doctor pulled out a clipboard from her desk. Clipped to the clipboard were four pieces of paper. The pages consisted of a questionnaire. The doctor knew she wasn't going to go through all the questions. Next to each question was a yes and no box, and under the yes and no box was a line for the doctor to make her own notes. She asked Beetle the first question on the list. "Do you have a lot of friends?"

"I wouldn't say I have a lot of friends," Beetle said, looking down at the carpet.

"Do you have any friends?"

"Yes."

The doctor marked the yes box. "Who are your friends?"

"I just have a few friends."

"What are your friends' names?"

"You wouldn't know em."

"I know I wouldn't know them. I'm just curious to know their names."

"Why do you wanna know their names?"

"I'm just curious."

"I have a friend named Brian. And I also have this guy, and he's kinda one of my friends. His name's Brownie."

"What makes them your friends?"

"What do you mean?"

"Why would you consider these two people to be your friends?"

"I don't know what you're saying."

"What do you do with these people?"

"Do you mean what do I do with Brian and Brownie?"

"Yes. What do you do with them?"

"Well, we talk and stuff like that. They tell me stories. Sometimes I tell them stories. But they mostly tell me stories. Especially Brownie. He's always tellin me stories about stuff."

"What kind of stories does he tell you?"

"All kindsa stories."

"Can you give me an example of a story he has told you?"

"There's this puzzle of the world. You know what I'm talkin bout? Like the whole round world?"

"A puzzle of Earth?"

"Yeah, a puzzle of Planet Earth."

"What about the puzzle?"

"Well, Brownie told me that where they were puttin the puzzle together last year he was cleaning the room. He was vacuuming it and he sucked up one of the puzzle pieces that'd fell on the floor up in the vacuum cleaner. Now the puzzle is missing a piece."

"Have you ever been to either one of these boys' houses?"

"What boys?"

"Brian and Brownie?"

"What about em?"

"Have you ever been to either of their houses?"

"No."

"Have you ever been to any of the boys or girls in your class's house?"

"No."

"You haven't been to anyone in your class's house to play or anything?"

"No. I think I'm too old to go over to peoples' houses to play."

"How long have you been going to your school?"

"I've been going to the school since I was five."

"So you've been going to the same school for ten years?"

"Yes."

"And you haven't been to anyone in your class's homes?"

"No. I got held back. Before I got held back, I went over to play with boys at their houses and even a couple of them came to mine. But my house is kinda boring. They even said it was kinda boring. But they still came over anyway. I got held back, and I've never gone over to anybody else's house ever again. I guess I've gone and gotten too old for that."

"Do you do anything with any of the people in your class?"

"What do you mean?"

"Do you do anything with them after school or on the weekends or anything?"

"I clean the schools after school. I don't have a lot of time on the weekend because I'm always busy with homework and church and stuff like that."

"Do you ever get into fights at school?"

"No."

"No one ever picks on you or calls you names?"

"Not really."

"What do you mean by not really?"

"I don't know what you're sayin."

"So you've never been in a fight before?"

"Yeah. I guess I've been in a fight before."

"What kind of fights?"

"What do you mean?"

"Can you tell me about one of your fights?"

"I can't remember."

"You can't tell me anything about a fight you've been in?"

"I don't know."

"I think if I was in a fight, I would remember the fight."

"I don't know."

"Have you been in any fights recently?"

"What are you saying?"

"Have you been in a fight that wasn't that long ago?"

"Yeah. I got into a fight."

"What kind of fight?"

"I grabbed somebody by their shirt, and I threw them."

"That doesn't sound nice."

"Well, the guy with the shirt I grabbed wasn't being nice."

"Why wasn't he being nice?"

"I was in the bathroom, and he was being mean to me."

"How was he being mean to you?"

Beetle had to stop and try to remember what it was Bullet did to provoke him. "This guy in my class came up, and he shoved me when I had my back to him, and I got mad and turned around and grabbed him by the shirt and I threw him."

"So it was in self-defense?"

"Yeah. I guess."

"Why did you do what you did? Why didn't you just tell somebody?"

"Because I had to defend myself."

"I see."

"I also grabbed him by his shirt and choked him with his own shirt. I was like," Beetle did an impersonation of how he strangled Bullet with the T-shirt. "I choked him real good."

"Why did you do that?"

"Like I said. He deserved it."

"Did you think that using that kind of force would prevent him from picking on you later on?"

"I don't know what you're sayin."

"Did you think that if you choked him, then he would no longer push you and be mean to you?"

"Yes."

"You really did?"

"Yes."

"Did this stop him from pushing you and being mean to you?"

"Yes."

"Your mother tells me you have become friends with a priest."

Beetle was silent.

"Is this true that you have become friends with a priest?"

"No."

"You have not become friends with a priest?"

"No."

"Well, your mother tells me that you have been spending a lot of time after school with a priest."

"Yes."

"Yes, what?" The doctor had begun taking mental notes because the questions she now asked were off the paper.

"I have been spendin a lot of time with a priest after school."

"Why are you spending time with the priest?"

"Because I'm doin work for him."

"What kind of work are you doing for him?"

"It's hard to explain."

"Can you explain it to me?"

"I can't. It's hard to explain, and kinda top-secret."

"I see."

"It's kinda hard work."

"Interesting."

"Yeah."

"Has the priest ever made you feel uncomfortable?"

"What are you sayin?"

"Has this priest ever made you feel weird?"

"I don't know what you're sayin."

"Has the priest ever said anything to you that was weird?"

"He's a priest. They always say weird stuff."

"Has he ever touched you?"

"No."

"Has he ever touched you?"

"You just said that."

"I know. You answered it so quickly. I want you to stop and think about it. I want you to be truthful with me. Has the priest ever touched you?"

Beetle stopped and thought about it. He could not recall the priest ever touching him. "No. He never touched me."

"He never touched you in any way?"

"No. You just said that. I just said that he hasn't touched me. He hasn't touched me in any way."

"Has he ever said anything to you?"

"About what?"

"Has he ever said anything to you that made you feel uncomfortable?"

"Like what?"

"Has he ever said anything in reference to your body?"

"My body?"

"Yes. Has he ever said anything about your body or your body parts?"

"No. Why?"

"Has he talked about any other boys' bodies?"

"No. He talked about the body of Christ."

The doctor laughed a forced laugh.

"We're going to go into another room and take another test."

The doctor stood and gestured for Beetle to stand up as well. She asked him to follow her out the door. She walked him down the hall so they could proceed taking another test another doctor had lined up for him.

The next exam for Beetle was in another room. The new doctor had Beetle follow him a couple of rooms down. Inside he walked into a room that was similar to the last room he was in, except it had gray walls. The doctor sat at a desk, and then immediately realized that he had left the test that he was supposed to conduct on Beetle on his file cabinet. The doctor jumped up from his desk. He walked over to the black file cabinet. He removed the black plastic easel with laminated flashcards attached by two metal hook clips. The doctor sat and positioned the plastic easel in front of Beetle. The doctor slid the easel over his desk. The first of the test cards was an introduction.

The doctor explained to Beetle the rules of the test. "What I want you to do with this test is I want for you to tell me . . . I'm gonna show you some pictures and I want you to tell me if the pictures make you feel one of three things. Do they make you feel happy, do they make you feel sad, or do you think they're funny." The doctor flipped the first laminated card over to reveal a drawing of a sad-looking billy goat. The goat was standing on top of a very narrow, snowcapped mountain. "How does this picture make you feel? Does it make you feel happy, sad, or do you think it's funny?"

"It makes me feel happy," Beetle confirmed.

"It makes you feel happy?"

"Yes."

"You feel happy when you see this goat, and he is frowning and crying?" The doctor pointed out a cartoon tear protruding from the goat's eye.

"I didn't even see that."

"So why did you say it makes you feel happy?"

"Because when I saw it," Beetle said looking at the picture again, "it made me think of being on top of a mountain and looking out and seeing a goat on top of a mountain and that made me feel happy."

"I see," the doctor said as he flipped another laminated card over the easel. "What about this next one? Does it make you feel happy, sad, or do you think it's funny? Same rules as the first one."

The next card was similar to the previous card. The only difference was now the illustrated billy goat had slipped and was falling down the mountain. Beetle smiled when he saw the drawing.

"Does this make you feel happy, sad, or do you think it's funny?" asked the doctor. "I assume from your laughter you find it funny."

"Yeah, I guess."

"Why do you say you guess?"

"Because it's kinda funny."

"Why do you think it's funny?"

"Cause it's fallin down."

"You think it's funny when people and animals fall down?"

"Yeah, I guess."

"Why?"

"I mean," Beetle said nervously. "I don't think it's funny when people and animals fall and get hurt."

"Why?"

"Because gettin hurt's not funny."

"No, why do you think it's funny when people and animals fall down?"

"It just is."

"Why?"

"I don't know how to explain it."

"Try to explain it to me."

"You ever seen that show *America's Funniest Home Movies*?"

The doctor nodded his head. He restrained himself from correcting Beetle on his mispronunciation of the television program.

"Well, on that show," Beetle explained, "people and also animals are always fallin down, and it's funny. They have, like, a dog running and a dog like runs into the glass. It's like, one of those glass doors in people's homes, and then falls down, and they have like a bride who has like her wedding dress on, and she throws those flowers in the air that brides throw, and like, she falls off the stage, and it's funny, and then they have like, a little kid walkin, and the little kid is walking through the kitchen and slips on a puddle, and it's funny. You have a man walking outside carrying somethin and he slips on the ice and he falls and it's funny."

"Why do you say that's funny?"

"Because it is."

"Why?"

"Because the audience laughed when they are showin the home movies."

"So you think this picture is funny?" The doctor pointed to the illustration of the billy goat falling.

"Yes, I think it's funny. I think if somebody did a home movie of it, then it would be funny."

"What about this next picture?" The doctor flipped a third laminated card over. The card revealed an illustration of the same billy goat who had fallen. In the third illustration, the billy goat had fallen on top of one of the mountaintops. The tip of the mountain pierced his body. It penetrated all the way through to where the tip was sticking outward. The first two illustrations did not have any color to them. The third illustration, however, had red ink added to it to symbolize blood. There was a lot of red ink representing a lot of blood. The doctor asked Beetle, "How does this picture make you feel?"

"Yuck."

"Does it make you feel happy, sad, or do you think it's funny?"

"It's sad."

"Why do you say it's sad?"

"Because it's hurt."

"But look at the expression on his face," the doctor pointed out that the billy goat had a large, happy, toothy smile and big, bright, happy eyes. "Doesn't the expression on his face look as if he is happy?"

"No."

"Look at his face. Doesn't he look happy?"

"It doesn't matter if it looks happy or not. He's dead."

"Why do you say he's dead?"

"Look at him. He can't have that sharp thing goin all the way through his body and not die."

"And why do you refer to it as him? As he? Does something about this animal indicate to you that it is a male?"

Beetle looks at the drawing and shakes his head.

"Do you think this animal could possibly be a female?"

"I guess it could be."

All three pictures of the billy goat had an illustrated penis. The doctor was trying to get Beetle to identify the billy goat's reproductive organ.

The first doctor that saw Beetle, the female doctor, entered the room. She told Beetle he needed to follow her.

Doing as he was told, Beetle left the room and followed the first doctor down the hall. He followed her into a room with brick walls covered in gray paint. There was a small, wooden table with some kind of a strange device sitting on it. The doctor pulled out the chair for Beetle to have a seat. She walked to the opposite side of the table. She sat opposite Beetle with the strange device separating the two of them. "Do you know what this thing is?" she asked Beetle.

"No."

"It's called a polygraph."

"Oh."

"Do you know what a polygraph is?"

"No."

"Do you know what a lie detector is?"

"Yes," Beetle looked down at the machine and instantly recognized it. "Oh, this is a lie detector test."

"Yes," the doctor said as she extracted wires from the side of the polygraph. "I just need to put these on your fingers."

Beetle looked a little nervous.

"Are you all right?" she asked Beetle.

"Yes."

"You're not nervous about this, are you?" the doctor knew when she said it that it was not the proper thing to say to him.

"No."

"Well, there's no need to be nervous. You should be excited. Are you excited about this?"

"Yeah, I guess."

"Have you ever taken a lie detector test before?" the doctor said just to ease Beetle's nerves. If Beetle actually said he had taken a polygraph before, then she would assume that he was in fact lying.

"No. I haven't taken a lie detector test before, but I think I have seen one in the movie where they were, like, in war, and they were trying to get the enemy to confess somethin, and that's where I saw it. So is this one kinda like that?"

"Yes, they're pretty much the same thing." The doctor said as she slipped little metal brackets attached to wires over Beetle's fingertips. "This one is probably very similar to that one because this one is actually pretty old. But they never really go out of date because they were very reliable. They make new ones now, but they pretty much just do the same thing the old ones do. In some ways, the old ones are better than the new ones. Does that feel good on your fingers?"

"Yeah. They're fine."

"What I'm gonna do here is ask you a few questions. Now I just want for you to give me a quick yes or no answer. If I ask you if you are a boy, you say yes. If I ask you if you go to school, you say yes. If I ask you if your name is Strawberry Shortcake, you tell me no. Do you understand?"

"Yes."

"Very good, just like that. Just yes or no answers."

The doctor flipped on the machine. A small piece of paper started running through it. Little needles remained stationary, drawing lines on the paper as it dragged itself across. "Are you fifteen years old?"

Despite being asked the question, Beetle did not respond.

"Are you fifteen years old?" the doctor asked again.

Beetle gazed up at the doctor with a look of confusion.

"I'm asking you the questions now," said the doctor. "I need for you to just answer each question with yes or no. Can you do that for me?"

"Yeah."

"Can you answer every question I ask you with yes or no?"

"Yeah."

"Can you answer this question that I'm asking you right now with a yes or no answer?"

"Yeah."

"Let me ask you this again," the doctor tried to refrain from exhibiting irritation. "Can you answer this question with a yes or no answer?"

"Yeah."

"That is not a yes or no answer. I'm going to ask you one more time. Can you answer this question with a yes or no answer?"

"Yes."

"Very good."

Beetle looked down at the moving paper and the lines being drawn on it.

"It might be better if you don't stare at it," the doctor advised Beetle. "You can if you want to, but it may just be a distraction. I'm going to start giving you some questions now. I'm going to ask you a bunch of them, so give me just a bunch of quick yes or no answers. Are you fifteen years old?"

"You already asked me that."

"Are you fifteen years old?"

"Yes."

"Are you six years old?"

Beetle laughed at the question.

"Are you six years old?"

"No."

"Do you live in the United States of America?"

"Yes."

"Do you ever have bad dreams?"

"Sometimes."

"Do you ever have bad dreams?"

"I do sometimes."

"I'm going to ask you questions, and you are going to give me only a yes or no answer. Remember?"

"Oh, yeah."

"Do you remember?"

"Yeah."

"You're only gonna give me yes or no answers. Do you remember?"

"Yes."

"Very good. Do you have bad dreams?"

"Sometimes."

"Do you live in France?"

"No."

"Do you like broccoli?"

"Sometimes."

"Do you have a lot of friends?"

"Not really."

"Do you have a lot of friends?"

"No."

"Do you like your teacher?"

"Yes," Beetle looked down and saw the needle jump. This made him nervous because he realized he had just lied.

"Is your teacher named Cole?"

"No," Beetle's said. His mother had filled out the form wrong when the doctor asked for the name of his teacher. Beetle's mother had not realized the school had switched eighth-grade teachers. "She was my old teacher. They got a new teacher now instead. I don't know if she's gonna be my teacher for the rest of the year or not or if she's just there for a short time while Ms. Cole is away."

"Do you like Miss Cole?"

"Yeah," Beetle looked away out of embarrassment. "But she, like, always smells like smoke, though."

"Do you have a crush on Miss Cole?"

"She doesn't like it when people call her Miss Cole. She likes to be called Ms. Cole."

"Do you have a crush on Ms. Cole?"

"No!" Beetle became more nervous because the polygraph needle moved even more.

"Have you ever thought about Ms. Cole naked?"

"No," Beetle answered quickly. He held back a laugh. His heart started beating at a fast pace owing to his nervousness.

"Have you ever seen any of your teachers naked?"

"No."

"Have you ever seen anyone in your class naked?"

"No," Beetle said quickly without thinking. He then remembered the time Bullet mooned Ms. Cole and he saw Bullet's bare buttock.

"Have you ever seen your own mother naked?"

"Oh, you know what? When you asked me if I'd seen anyone in my class naked. I think I actually have. Because in gym class we have to get dressed before that and so like, I see boys in my class like change their underwear. So I have actually seen em naked before," Beetle laughed uncomfortably. "I wasn't like lookin at them or anything. I just saw it out of the corner of my eye, I guess."

"Have you ever seen your mother naked?"

"No."

"Have you ever seen your father naked?"

"No."

"Has your mother ever spanked you?"

"No." This was a flat out lie. Beetle's mother spanked him all the time.

"Has your father ever hit you?"

"What do you mean by hit me?" Beetle did not know why he

was asked this question. It was a pretty clear question. Beetle knew the answer to it was a definite yes. Beetle's father hit him all the time. He was trying to dodge the question.

"Has your father ever hit you?"

"Yes. I mean no."

"Has your father ever hit you?"

"No." Beetle was afraid he was going to be taken away from his parents at this point.

"Have you ever seen a grown adult naked?"

"Does it count if I've seen them naked in a movie?"

"Have you ever seen an adult naked?"

"Does it count if I see an adult who is naked and they are like in a movie or a magazine or something?"

"Have you ever seen a grown adult naked?"

"No."

"Has anyone ever asked you to touch them, in a way you felt was uncomfortable?"

"What do you mean?"

"Has anyone ever asked you to touch them in a way that you felt uncomfortable touching them?"

"No."

"Have you ever bled before?"

"What?"

"Have you ever bled before? Have you ever had blood come out of your body?"

"Blood come out of my body? What part of my body?"

"Have you ever had a cut before that bled?"

"Yeah, I guess."

"Has anyone ever caused you to bleed?"

"What?"

"Has anyone ever made you bleed?"

"I don't know."

"Has anyone ever hurt your feelings?"

"What do you mean?"

"Has anyone ever said or done anything to you that has embarrassed you?"

"I don't know. I can't think of anything right now."

"Has anyone ever said anything to you that hurt your feelings?"

"I guess so."

"Has Father Michael ever made you do anything you felt uncomfortable doing?"

"Yeah, he made me work on his movie."

"Has Father Michael ever asked you to touch him in a weird way?"

"No."

"Have you ever had sexual relations?"

"What?"

"Are you fully aware of what sexuality is?"

"Yeah, I don't know. I guess I do."

"Has Father Michael ever asked you to do anything sexual?"

"No. He's a priest. Why would he do that?"

"Have you ever hurt an animal?"

"I don't like these questions."

"Have you ever hurt an animal?"

"No! I would never do that."

"Have you ever touched an animal's genitalia?"

"I've never even had an animal. My parents won't let me have pets."

"Have you ever caused pain to a small baby or small child?"

"I really don't like this. These questions are making me feel weird."

"Have you ever caused pain to a baby or small child?"

"No."

"Have you ever tried to touch the genitals of a baby or a small child?"

"I don't even know why you would ask me these questions."

"Have you ever tried to touch the genitals of a baby or small child?"

"No."

"If you saw a small child or baby in public and there was nobody around, would you touch them?"

"No."

"Have you ever been touched by a stranger?"

"No. You mean like if someone like brushes up against you when you're like walking down the street or like walking through the mall or something?"

"I'm not talking about accidentally touching you. Has anyone ever, has a stranger ever purposely touched you?"

"No. That's weird."

"Have you ever laid down with Father Michael?"

"No. These questions are weird."

"Have you ever seen Father Michael take off his clothes and reveal his genitals?"

"What?"

"Has Father Michael ever exposed his private parts to you?"

"No. He's a priest. He wouldn't do that."

"Does Father Michael ever do anything strange to you that doesn't seem like something a priest would do?"

"Yeah, he's made a movie about these biotoxic bulldogs who are killing people."

"I think I'm going to stop the test here."

"Good. I don't like these questions."

The doctor and Beetle walked back into her office for a couple of minutes. Beetle explained to her about *The Attack of the Biotoxic Bulldogs.*

She brought Beetle back to the lobby where his mother was waiting. The doctor told Beetle to wait in the waiting room while she brought his mother back to her office to discuss their session. Beetle did as he was told. Beetle's mother followed the doctor back to her office. Once inside the office, the doctor gestured for Beetle's mother to have a seat in front of her desk. Once Beetle's mother was seated, the doctor walked over and sat in her own chair right behind the desk. The doctor looked at Beetle's mother and gave her a concerned smile. "We think your son may have an attention deficit disorder."

"I already know that," Beetle's mother said. "That is not why I brought him in here."

"We ran some tests on him."

"What did you find out?"

"We did a survey with a bunch of men. Just normal men between the ages of early and mid-twenties to middle-aged. The survey we did, it was more like a test. Keep in mind that these were normal men. None of them had any sexual abnormalities to our awareness. They were all straight, and a good portion of them were even married. I think most of them are married if I recall correctly. They ran a test and we gave them photos of young girls. Like photos from yearbook pictures and random pictures of young girls. They were very young girls. I'm talking like thirteen and fourteen years old. And we asked the men which one of the girls they would prefer to be in a physical relationship with and we discovered that the men all gravitated toward the girls whose teeth had braces."

"What does this have to do with my son?"

"We don't think that the priest was involved with your son. Are you familiar with what your son is doing for the priest?"

"My son doesn't talk to me about that kind of thing."

"We feel that you should discuss this with him. How well do you know this priest?"

"He just began at our parish. I don't know him at all."

"You have met him before?"

"He has conducted the Mass on Sundays the past few weeks."

"You've never actually introduced yourself to him?"

"After Mass, I went up to him and introduced myself. Everybody was introducing themselves to him. He wouldn't know me if he saw me. I'm pretty sure he wouldn't."

"I am surprised that you came here before even meeting him. Are you going to meet him?"

"It was one of those things I didn't want to take a risk on."

"I can understand. I just want to clarify that I am not saying that I am positive he's not doing anything with your son. It is just that I feel after talking to your son that there is not much going on for you to be concerned about. I highly recommend that you meet with this priest and get to know him."

"I'll try to do that."

"If you're really concerned, this is something that you're going to have to do as soon as possible. I recommend doing it tomorrow."

"I will try to do it tomorrow."

"This is your son we're talking about. This should be the most important thing on your agenda. I want you to do this tomorrow. I want you to sit down and talk to the priest tomorrow."

"I will do it tomorrow."

"There's also something else that concerns me."

"What's that?"

"Have you explained to your son about sex?"

"I don't think that's my job," Beetle's mother said with a soft, uncomfortable laugh.

"You're his mother," the doctor reminded her. "This is your job."

"I sent him to Catholic school."

"I'm not sure what that has to do with anything."

"I went to Catholic school, too. They explain it to the students there."

"I don't believe they do."

"They did when I was there."

"I want for you to talk to him about it."

"I will do."

"I want you to talk about it tonight with him."

On the drive back home, Beetle saw a stork flying through the sky. He pointed it out to his mother as she drove. "The stork was probably goin to pick up a baby," Beetle said. "I think it was going to go pick one up cause I saw its beak and it didn't have a baby wrapped up in it."

His mother found this a good time to explain to him what the doctor had advised her to discuss with her son. However, his mother approached the subject with a sterile and medical approach. This caused Beetle's mind to drift. He did not pay much attention nor did he absorb any of the concepts his mother was trying to describe.

EIGHTEEN

THE NEXT DAY BEETLE'S MOTHER HAD ARRIVED EARLY to drop him off at school. Beetle's mother was proud of herself for being able to get her son there so early; she could drop him off in front of the building without having to wait in a long line. Once Beetle had walked inside, his mother drove over to the church to make a surprise visit to Father Michael.

It was so early that she felt guilty about showing up uninvited. She decided to walk back over to the school to use the pay phone outside of the school's gym to call him. One of the doors to the gym was unlocked. This was on accident because of Gary not checking the doors to make sure they were locked before leaving the school. Beetle's mother walked in the school with the directory in her hand. She considered memorizing the priest's direct phone number before going in, then realized it was easier just to bring the small stapled book in with her. She pushed past the unlocked door and over to the pay phone. She picked up the receiver and dropped her quarter down the hole. With a glance at the number in the directory, she replicated it on the pay phone's number pad with such lightning speed she probably could have broken a world record or caused her finger to catch on fire. It only took three rings until the priest picked up.

"I didn't wake you up," she asked, "did I?"

"No," replied Father Michael. "I've been up for a long time."

It was true. The priest had been up for a long time. He actually hadn't slept all night. He had spent the whole night playing computer games.

Beetle's mother introduced herself to the priest. She explained she was Beetle's mother and asked if there was a good time to set up a meeting with him so they could discuss her son.

The priest said anytime was good for him. "Are you willing to meet me today?" he asked.

"That would be great."

"What time?" Father Michael was concerned about how the meeting would affect his chances of getting a sleep break.

"How about now?"

"Now's good with me."

"May I come over now?"

"Fine with me."

"I'll be over in a minute." She added as somewhat of a warning, "I'm just over at the school. It's literally going to be just a minute."

She walked over to the rectory. Once there, she knocked with a hard fist upon the thick, wooden door. It only took Father Michael a few seconds before he answered. As he swung it open, the priest looked honestly happy to meet Beetle's mother. "Come on in," he gestured with a swipe of his arm.

Walking in, Beetle's mother looked around the office. The reaction she had was the same as her son's when he first entered the room. They both felt this was not your typical office for a Catholic priest.

"May I take your coat?" asked Father Michael.

"Yes, please," she said, removing her wool jacket and handing it to Father Michael. "Thank you."

Father Michael hung her coat on a stand a few inches shorter than himself. He suggested she have a seat in front of his desk. Beetle's mother sat down. Father Michael quickly walked over and sat in his chair, facing her. Father Michael started an introductory chitchat with Beetle's mother. Basic talk, such as: "Where are you from? Where did you go to school? What part of town do you reside in?"

"My son has told me a lot about you. "This slipped out of her mouth before she processed it. She immediately regretted it because it was a lie. Beetle had not said anything about the man.

"Good things?" the priest asked. "I hope."

"One thing he hasn't told me," she leaned forward trying to gauge his attention with her eye contact. "He hasn't told me what he's doing to you."

"Doing to me?"

"I mean," she embarrassingly stumbled as she tried to correct herself. "He hasn't told me what he has been doing with you."

"He's helping me edit a movie I made a long time ago."

"That's interesting."

"Yes," Father Michael agreed. "He's a great editor."

"That's news to me."

"He really is."

"How did you find out about this hidden talent?"

"He made a short film."

"Really?"

"Yes, it was really good. Actually, it was more than really good. It was incredible."

"Incredible?"

"It was a class assignment that I had the eighth graders do. I asked the eighth graders to do a short video using a video camera. Your son did not opt for using the video camera. He instead went out and found a professional cinematographer." The priest knew referring to Christopher HC as a professional was a stretch. "Then your son went and edited this beautiful film together."

"Really?"

"Your son is an amazing film editor."

"I'm not sure how he learned it. I couldn't even get him to play 'Twinkle, Twinkle, Little Star' on the piano. Despite putting him through years and years of piano lessons."

"Well, he edited this film, and he did such a good job. Do you know how hard it is to find someone nowadays who can edit film? He brought this big film canister and showed it to me. I was just completely floored. Then when I saw the film, I was even more, I don't even know the word to use, I was just absolutely stunned."

"This is a real surprise to me."

"It was a surprise to me, and I didn't even know your son. I shot this movie a decade ago and have never been able to edit it together. Then I saw what your son did. I saw the film your son made, I saw the film that your son edited together, and I felt like it was some kind of sign. I talked to him and told him I would pay him to put together my movie."

"I wonder why he hasn't told me any of this."

"He might be a little embarrassed."

"Why should he be embarrassed?"

"This movie I made was my passion project. I made it ten years ago. I mean, I was a teenager when I made it. And I mean, it's silly, and it's even a little dated now. I kind of feel he feels a little bit embarrassed about being part of my movie."

"Why do you think he feels embarrassed?"

"I think he thinks my movie is silly. I also believe he's nervous about you and his father seeing the movie. I think he thinks you are not going to like it. And maybe even be mad at him for editing it. May I show you something?" without even waiting for a response, Father Michael stood and walked into the other room. Beetle's mother followed behind the priest.

In the other room, the film projector was set up. There were not any reels of film on it. Father Michael rushed over to the film cooler where he stored his film and pulled out the environmental film Beetle had made. He put on his white cloth gloves and loaded the film into the projector. He started up the projector and showed the mother the film her son had made. It brought a tear to her eye. She could not believe that her son was capable of putting together something as remarkable as the goofy short film he had made.

Afterward, Beetle's mother walked back to the school and walked into the office to talk to the principal. She asked him if she could take her son out to lunch. Remembering the incident that had happened the day before, the principal was more than willing to excuse her son for lunch.

Beetle was excited when he found out his mother was taking him to a restaurant. He had only been to a restaurant one time in his life. It was with his grandmother. She had taken them to a steak restaurant inside of a shopping mall. The restaurant had big barrels of peanuts when you walked in, and the floor was covered in peanut shells. As Beetle had never been to a restaurant again, he always assumed that every restaurant had peanut shells all over the floor. Even when he watched soap operas, he assumed when the soap opera characters were in a fancy, candlelit restaurant where all the tables were clad in linen cloths, he always believed the floor was blanketed with peanut shells.

They went to Hot 'n Now for lunch. The restaurant was drive-thru only. This was not a problem as they had to eat quick in order to get Beetle back to school. They sat in the car and ate their hamburgers, fries, and sodas. As they did so, Beetle's mother confessed to him that she had seen the environmental film he had made. Beetle was so embarrassed his face turned bright red. His face quickly resorted back to its original color after his mother declared the film very good and complimented her son by saying how proud she was of him for making such an intriguing piece of art. That was how she described it. A piece of art.

Beetle opened up to his mother and told her all about *The Attack of the Biotoxic Bulldogs*. His mother was intrigued at first, but after his ranting had progressed, she found the subject matter and his enthusiasm to be rather grating on her nerves.

"Am I going to help Father Michael edit tonight?" Beetle asked his mother.

"Do you want to help him edit tonight?"

"Yes."

"Well, then, you should do so." It was at this point when Beetle's mother realized that she had jumped to conclusions and overreacted.

With his belly full of fast food, Beetle's mother dropped her son back off at the school before lunch had ended.

After lunch, Beetle went up to Latricia to brag about how he had eaten Hot 'n Now for lunch. She told him he was lucky. Latricia told Beetle about how some high school boys were going to shoot off a rocket behind the school right after school. Beetle told her he would be there.

Back in class, Sergeant Powers had left for the day after developing an unpleasant stomach bug. Filling in for her was Sister Bea, a hunchback nun who followed the old rules of the Church and still wore a habit with the black tunic. She was sixty-five years old. Her face was so wrinkly and leathery, everyone assumed she was two decades older. Sister Bea hunched down to read the class roster with all the students' names. "Joseph Domitius?" the old nun said. "Is Joseph Domitius in this class?"

Behind Bullet's back, Latricia pointed him out to the nun.

"Young man," the holy sister said as she looked at Bullet with a closed-mouthed grin. "I haven't seen you since you were a small little boy."

Bullet ignored her.

"I don't know if you all know this or not," Sister Bea announced to the class. "His family runs a large warehouse that supplies all the inventory to all the Catholic churches in the area."

All the students laughed loudly because Bullet was not the person who they would assume came from a strictly religious background. They all started chanting at him. Calling him "Bible Boy" over and over again. Even Beetle joined in on the chant. Beetle was actually the loudest of all the students chanting. Beetle was the one who was most amused to discover Bullet came from a staunch Catholic background.

After school, Beetle decided to go out and see the high schoolers who were going to shoot off the rocket. He knew Father Michael was usually late. Beetle felt that because Father Michael had him wait so long after school every day, even if the priest was on time that one day it would be fair for him to wait a few minutes while Beetle watched a rocket launch.

As Beetle turned the corner of the school, Bullet and Cage unexpectedly and unpleasantly greeted him. Bullet was holding a rusty pipe. "So you thought it was funny to call me Bible Boy, huh?"

Beetle did not respond to Bullet's question.

"Well, maybe you'll think it's funny when I strangle you to death," Bullet said and then laughed loudly. "It's better to be called Bible Boy than Dead Boy." Beetle still did not say anything. He just stood there big eyed. His whole body vibrated with fear.

"Don't try any funny business," Bullet advised. "If you try more of your tricks, I'm going to have Cage strangle you. You don't want Cage strangling you."

Bullet dropped the rusty pipe and started strangling Beetle with both hands. Beetle grabbed Bullet's wrists with his thumbs. Beetle was luckily strong enough to pry them off of his neck. Bullet then told Cage to grab Beetle's arm and twist his wrist back. Cage did as Bullet ordered and grabbed Beetle's right arm and twisted his wrist back. The bent wrist hurt far worse than the strangulation.

"Do you think it's funny now? You think it's funny to call me Bible Boy? You think it's funny to poke fun at me? You think it's funny to call me names? You think it's funny to rip my favorite shirt? You think it's funny to make fun of my dead dad? You think it's funny to make fun of my family for bein white trash? You think it's funny? You think it's funny to pick on me for being small when you're smaller than I am? Do you think it's funny to make fun of me and call me names and make fun of me for bein stupid when you're the stupidest person anybody's ever seen? Do you think it's funny? I don't think it's funny! I don't think it's funny at all! I think it's sick! And I think you're sick! I think you're sick in the head and you need to die! I don't think a person like you should go on living. I don't wanna see a person like you going on living. I want to see you dead. I want to see you dead more than anything. That's why I'm gonna see to it that I kill you," Bullet said to Beetle as he began to squeeze his neck as hard as he possibly could. "My life's goal is to choke you to death!"

As Bullet continued to wring Beetle's neck as tight as he could squeeze, Beetle grew dizzy.

"I need some help here," Bullet said to Cage.

"What do you want me to do?" asked Cage.

"I want for you to help me choke him!"

Cage wrapped his big hands around Beetle's neck and squeezed along with Bullet. Cage's hands were far larger than Bullet's, and he could definitely squeeze a lot tighter. Cage squeezed down on Bullet's hands and Bullet made him stop so he could pull his hands out. "You're going to break my fingers," Bullet said to Cage.

Then Bullet placed his hands around Beetle's neck so the tips of his fingers were overlapping Cage's fingers and not under them like before. The two bullies gripped their hands as tightly as they could around the poor boy's neck. Beetle had gotten far past the point of dizziness and lightheadedness. He was about to pass out.

Right before everything went black for Beetle, Bullet's body slammed against his. Bullet removed his hands from Beetle's throat and placed them behind his back and let out a high-pitched squeal.

This frightened Cage—he let go of Beetle, as well.

"My back!" Bullet cried as he slowly stumbled around. Standing behind him was Gary. With a twist-punch to the nose, Gary cracked every single bone in Bullet's schnoz. Bullet's head swung back-and-forth as if his neck was rubber with a large spring down his throat. The pain was so much it caused Bullet to fall backward into the grass. He covered his nose with both hands. The same two hands that only seconds before were locked around Beetle's throat. He pressed his hands against his nose to plug the outpouring of blood. It didn't help much because blood was squirting out the crevices between his fingers. Blood sprayed like a fountain.

Cage took off running, but didn't get far. Not only did Gary outrun him, Gary ran in front of him and stuck his leg out, causing Cage's huge body to fall to the ground. In a desperate attempt to escape, Cage stumbled back up to his feet. His problem was Gary was right in front of him with both fists up as if Gary was ready for a boxing match. Gary swung a punch at Cage's face. The punch was so hard it split open his cheek. Bloody fat tissue oozed out. Cage decided to lay on the ground. Gary kicked Cage so hard in the ribs he broke three of them. Cage then stumbled up with hopes of running away. It was hard for Cage to stand with broken ribs. Cage miraculously managed to erect himself on both legs. He stood there for a few seconds. His weak legs swayed in a circular motion as if caught in a tornado. He remained upright for only a half minute because Gary swung a side-punch, knocking Cage's right supraorbital ridge so hard it split open his eyebrow and the bone underneath protruded outward. Blood flooded out from slits, one on his cheek and one on his eyebrow.

After wasting the two bullies and draining their body of vital fluids, Gary went over to check to see if Beetle was safe. "Don't worry about those guys," Gary said. "I dealt with guys like that when I was in the war. I just can't stand it. Don't worry about them. They'll never pick on you again. If they do, come to me. I will be there."

Although Gary's statement was comforting, it wasn't entirely accurate. Bullet and Cage would continue to pick on Beetle, but Gary was never there to defend the boy because he would be fired the next day for his violent attacks on the two teenagers.

—

Beetle ran back inside the school. Father Michael was waiting inside the office. When the priest saw the boy he questioned the bright red marks around his neck. He thought it could have been some bad infection. "Is that why you went to the hospital yesterday?" Father Michael asked in reference to the rings around the boy's neck.

"Look what somebody found!" the girl in the office pulled out a green-haired Troll the size of a quarter.

"Wow!" Beetle said, taking it from her. "Where'd they find it?"

"I don't know."

It was not Beetle's Troll as Gary unknowingly threw Beetle's Troll out with the trash. The girl working the desk had been checking out at the grocery store and saw a display of Troll pencils. She bought a green-haired one for Beetle to make him think it was the one he had lost. She did it partially to be nice, but mostly because she was tired of Beetle coming in for a year and half asking if anyone had found it.

Beetle looked at the small Troll and said, "I don't think this is mine."

"Why not?" the girl said with concern.

"The one I had had glitter on it."

"It's been gone so long," the girl said. "All the glitter has come off."

Beetle thanked her for finding the Troll then went out with Father Michael to his pickup truck. They headed to Christopher HC's house to partake in the final editing session. "After tonight," Father Michael said as he drove, "the movie will be finished. *The Attack of the Biotoxic Bulldogs* will be in the can."

Christopher HC was sitting on the couch watching a daytime talk show.

"Today's the last day!" Father Michael said to Christopher HC. "Tonight's the last night!"

"Good," Christopher HC said, not pulling his focus away from the television.

"You want to help us finish it?"

"No, I don't want to work on that movie."

"Why not?"

"Because I don't want my mom or my girlfriend coming in here and seeing what you guys are doing because it's crass!"

On the talk show was a naked woman with gigantic implants pixelated out for television. The host of the talk show was taking questions from the studio audience. A young man in the audience stood up and asked the naked woman with the monstrous breasts if they were real. "They're real all right," the large-breasted woman said with a backwoods accent. "They're real. Real expensive."

"So you're saying my film is crass and this isn't?"

"Everybody watches this," Christopher HC pointed out. "No one's ever seen your movie."

"What if my movie becomes the next this?" Father Michael pointed at the television.

"Well, then I would say that I knew it back when it was nothing."

"You knew it back when it was nothing." Father Michael shook his head. "And you refused to help with it."

"That's right."

"Are you sure you don't want to help finish this thing up?"

"Fine," Christopher HC caved in. "I'll help you, but if anybody comes home, I am coming up here, and I'm having no part of what is going on down there."

Christopher HC went down in the basement as Father Michael followed. The three of them sat down without any interruptions through the night. Christopher HC's mother did not show up nor did his girlfriend. They edited the movie until they finished it. They all three admitted after viewing it in its entirety—it was splendid.

NINETEEN

FATHER MICHAEL USED THE SCHOOL'S GYMNASIUM to screen
The Attack of the Biotoxic Bulldogs for its world premier. After the
film was finished being edited, he submitted it to a lab to do color
correction and sound mixing. The priest had wanted to rent an
actual movie theater, but after doing some research he discovered it
was not in his budget. The gymnasium worked perfectly well and
with the money he saved from renting the movie theater, he was able
to buy a giant screen to project his movie. The screen he bought was
actually bigger than the screen at the movie theater.

There was quite a large crowd who showed up for the premiere.
The gymnasium was packed. Father Michael came out and gave the
audience a quick introduction. A very quick introduction because he
did not want to waste any time or hold back his passion project that
he had so vigorously been working on. "I have spent over ten years
preparing this movie," Father Michael said. "I don't want to wait any
longer."

The audience clapped.

The lights dimmed.

The projector fired up.

———

The opening scene featured Mark and Sarah playing their
characters Jeremy and Bianca. They walked through the cemetery

in search of her aunt's gravestone. The audience gasped in joy as the biotoxic bulldog lunged from the back of the tombstone and dug its teeth into the woman's neck. They loudly squealed when the blood erupted from her jugular. On the new big screen, it looked tremendous.

Both Beetle and Christopher HC were present in the audience, and they watched from a new perspective because they had never seen it with the remastered color and contrast or heard it with the fine sound quality. A professional composer had even added an amazing score to go along with the film.

After the first bloody bulldog kill, it cut to black. A title card popped up: THREE DAYS EARLIER. The title card was Christopher HC's suggestion. He told Father Michael that the audience would be confused about why there was a biotoxic bulldog in the opening scene when the biotoxic bulldogs are not even released until the third scene. The suggestion was in itself worth every penny Father Michael had paid Christopher HC to work on the film.

The next scene featured his brother Rory and his friend Mark sitting on the curb. This was the first scene Beetle and Christopher HC were shown before editing. In the scene, Rory and Mark sat and chatted.

"My girlfriend, Vanessa, broke up with me today," Mark said.

"I am sorry to hear that. I thought you two were in love."

"I thought we were in love, too."

The movie cut to the third scene with the mad scientist and his lab. There was the gag about the stethoscope and the massaging of the mammary.

A new scene cut to a shot of Sarah who played a third character in the movie named Vanessa. Sarah wore a bob-cut wig when playing the Vanessa character. The wig was similar to the wig she wore when playing the Bianca character, except the Bianca character's wig was black and the Vanessa character's wig was red. The Vanessa character also wore red, heart-shaped sunglasses. Liquid Paper was used to draw zigzag lines through the heart-shaped lenses of the sunglasses. The glasses represented broken hearts.

She walked into a coffee shop. The coffee shop was intended to resemble a flea market. The coffee shop owner allowed them to shoot in his coffee shop because they could not find a location resembling a flea market. The film crew brought in a truckload of random household items to fill the coffee shop to give it the appearance of a flea market. The Vanessa character walked up to the counter. Mark was behind the counter, but he once again was playing a different character as well. He had a bald wig on and makeup to give the impression of an old man.

"What can I help you with today, young lady?" said the old man.

"I just dumped my boyfriend," Vanessa said. "I am looking for something to destroy him."

"I have dynamite."

"No. I am looking for something more witchcraft-y."

"I had a voodoo doll, but I sold it this morning to a nun."

Sister Bea was in the audience. She, along with all the other spectators, laughed loudly at the joke.

"Here is my phone number," Vanessa said, handing over a slip of paper to the flea market peddler. "Give me a call if something good shows up."

The next scene was back in the mad scientist's lab. "I have created some rather odd and wild inventions," the mad scientist laughed. "This, I have to say, is my most strange and most wicked invention ever."

"What is it?" asked the buxom assistant to his right.

The mad scientist reached under his lab table and pulled out a dog cage that was painted with green Day-Glo. The color shined brightly under the black light. There was a sound effect of a dog growling inside the dog cage. "I reveal to you," the mad scientist announced with a wave of his hand, "a biotoxic bulldog."

The mad scientist opened the cage. A white stuffed animal covered with green Day-Glo paint was yanked from the cage by a fishing wire.

"Oh, no!" one of the seductive assistants said.

"It is running off!" the other seductive assistant said.

"Oh, no!" the mad scientist said. "We have to stop it before it gets to the toxic waste dump."

"What happens if the biotoxic bulldog gets to the toxic waste dump?" one of the assistants asked and then ran off before she could hear the answer.

"If the biotoxic bulldog gets to the toxic waste dump, then it will multiply, and there will be millions if not billions of biotoxic bull-dogs roaming the world."

"Oh, no!" said the remaining assistant. "We do not want that to happen."

"I think it is too late!" the assistant who ran off said as she ran back into the room. "I looked out the window and saw that the bio-toxic bulldog has got into the toxic waste dump, and now there are millions of biotoxic bulldogs all over the place."

The next scene was back at the coffee house/flea market. The old man was still behind the counter. The Vanessa character walked in and said, "Thank you for calling me."

"Thank you for coming down. I came across something today I thought you would be interested in purchasing."

"Can you tell me what this item is?"

The old man pulled out the Day-Glo-covered dog cage. There is no explanation on how he came across the dog cage from the mad scientist.

"I was walking through the woods today, and I found this," said the old man.

"I do not know about this," said Vanessa. "I do not want some piece of junk you found out in the woods."

"This, young lady, is not a piece of junk."

"Then what was it doing out in the woods?"

Growling sounds grew louder.

"I am no dog expert," the old man said, looking into the cage, "but this, to me, looks like it may be a biotoxic bulldog."

"A biotoxic bulldog?"

"That is what I said."

"That would be absolutely wicked if I mailed it to my ex-boyfriend."

"That does sound absolutely wicked. And you are in luck today because I am willing to give you a good discount."

The next scene was the part where Mark and Rory walked through the hardware store's parking lot and came across the two girls and the boy with Tourette's.

"What are you two beautiful girls doing out here so late at night?" asked Rory.

"We were just hanging out here because there is nothing to do in this town," Sarah's character Sara said and pointed to the boy making bird sounds. "This is my brother."

"Do you want to come back to our place and have a party?" asked Mark.

"I do not know about that," said Amy, who played the role of Amy.

"That sounds like it may not be a good idea," Sarah's character Sara said. "What kind of party are you boys having?"

"We were not really planning on having a party. It would just be the five of us. We can hang out at our house and listen to records and tapes and stuff and drink bottles and cans of soda pop. It may not be the most fun party ever, but I think it would be more fun than hanging out here in a parking lot at night."

The next scene was in a large living room, evident by the room's décor. It was not a place where teenage boys were living alone. The film crew had knocked door to door on houses in a wealthy neighborhood asking people if they could shoot a movie in their homes.

Mark and Rory went into the kitchen and pulled out multiple bottles of cola and orange soda. Mark went over and pulled out a record. It was a classical orchestra record from the house owners who were letting them use their house's personal record collection. Mark lowered the vinyl onto the turntable and dropped the needle as the record spun. Classical orchestra music did not play on the film. What played was electronic dance music. The five teenagers all danced to the music. Everyone laughed at the scene. They especially laughed at Arnie because he had a very spastic dance method.

The composer and post-production service had added the electronic music. Beetle and Christopher HC had never seen the scene with the music added, and they both found it less strange and even a little less funny with the music put in. The way they had watched it, there was just people dancing without any music playing.

As the teenagers danced, they were interrupted by a loud thump at the door. They walked over and looked through the glass door to see a biotoxic bulldog sitting in the backyard. The stuffed animal was dragged through the grass by a fishing line.

"Oh, no!" Amy said. "What was that?"

"I do not know," Rory said. "I think we should go check it out."

The five teenagers set out and walked through their neighborhood and ended up in the woods. Mark shined his flashlight between two trees, and a bunch of biotoxic bulldogs popped out and tried to eat him and the other four teenagers.

Stricken with panic, the five teenagers ran back to the house.

"We have to warn everybody," Sarah's character Sara said.

"What are we going to do?" asked Amy.

"The sun is starting to come up," observed Rory.

"It will be easier to see those things in the daytime," explained Mark.

"We need to go outside and warn everybody," Rory suggested.

The next thirty minutes of the film was nothing but bloody and violent footage of biotoxic bulldogs ripping apart innocent bystanders.

The five teenagers returned to the house with their clothes in shreds, covered in red and green blood.

"It is crazy out there," said Amy.

"We are lucky we did not die," said Rory.

"It is too bad that all those other people were not so lucky," said Sarah's character Sara.

"Oh, no," said Mark. "The sun is going down. We cannot see them through the windows if it is dark."

"Does this place have an attic?" Sarah's character Sara asked.

"Yes, it does," said Rory.

"That is a good idea," said Mark.

The five teenagers went to the attic.

"What are we going to do in this attic?" asked Amy.

"We can have a dance party," suggested Rory.

It cut to fifteen minutes of the five teenagers having a dance party in the attic.

"What do you think is going on outside?" asked Amy. "Do you think they stopped all those biotoxic bulldogs?"

The movie cut to thirty minutes of night shots of people being bludgeoned and torn to shreds by biotoxic bulldogs' claws and teeth.

After the brutal and gruesome thirty minutes, the film cut back to the five teenagers up in the attic. They were still enjoying themselves and having a dance party.

The party was interrupted by the ring of the doorbell.

"What was that?" asked Sarah as Sara.

"What if it is one of them?" asked Amy.

"One of the biotoxic bulldogs?" Rory asked Amy.

"Yes. What if it is one of them?"

"I do not believe that they can ring doorbells," Mark joked.

The audience laughed at the line.

"Everybody, come with me," said Rory. "You will be safe. I have a gun. Guns make everything better."

The five teenagers slowly walked down the stairs. They were walking very quietly, except for Arnie. His Tourette's caused him to bark loudly like a dog.

"I want everybody to stand back," said Rory as he held out his rifle. "Mark, I want you to open the door slowly. If it is one of those biotoxic bulldogs, I will shoot it dead as a doornail."

Mark slowly opened the door as Rory aimed his rifle. As the door opened, it creaked loudly.

"Do not shoot me!" the mad scientist said when the door opened and it was revealed he was the one behind it. "I am here to help."

"How can you help?" asked Sarah as Sara.

"I created those biotoxic babies," the mad scientist explained. "I assure you I can uncreate them."

The audience applauded with excitement.

"How do you plan on doing that?" Sarah/Sara asked the mad scientist.

"With a bell," the mad scientist explained.

"A bell?"

"If you ring a bell," the scientist told the five teenagers as a dramatic musical score played in the background, "it will put them to sleep."

The five teenagers and the mad scientist all ran around the city ringing bells and putting bloody biotoxic bulldogs to sleep.

There was a close up of Mark and Amy. They stood close together smiling because they had just defeated the biotoxic bulldogs. "I cannot believe it!" Mark said to Amy. "We saved the world."

"Yes, we did," Amy said.

Mark grabbed her by the blood-drenched shirt and pulled her toward him. They locked lips in a long, passionate kiss.

A title card popped up: THE END.

EPILOGUE

IT HAS BEEN THIRTY YEARS SINCE *The Attack of the Biotoxic Bulldogs* was shot. It has been twenty years since its world premiere. None of the people involved in the making of the movie went on to work on any other movies. Christopher HC ended his moviemaking career after falling deeply in love with the girlfriend he had met in the chat room who was very religious and did not drink. It may be a surprise to find out that the girl he fell in love with was actually Ms. Cole. She had cleaned up her act after her run-in with the law and got her life back together again. She resumed teaching, and Christopher HC finished college and has spent the years since working IT.

After being terminated from the school, Gary never found employment elsewhere. In 2005 he died from a blood clot in his brain.

Father Michael is still a priest at the church. He has straightened his act up, too, and in the last sixteen years has not been late for a church service once. It took him a few years to develop his time management skills. Father Michael has conducted Mass every Sunday since the release of *The Attack of the Biotoxic Bulldogs*, except when he went on tour with the movie and screened it at film festivals all over the world.

Bullet and Cage were kicked out their freshman year of high school after a run-in with the law. They threw a brick over an overpass. The brick went through a windshield and almost killed an elderly woman. They were sent off to juvie. Today, Bullet runs the family business he inherited. Cage works in the warehouse, checking in shipments coming in from Thailand. Cage spends most of his workday removing Made In Bangkok stickers from the feet of miniature statues of patron saints.

Billy dropped out of high school his freshman year to become a musician. He played with many bands until he quit his musical dreams at the age of thirty. He now lives in a camper out in the woods where he doesn't have to deal with humanity.

Brian went on to work at a local auto shop for seven years, before inheriting it. He still owns it to this day. He still gets lost when off by himself.

Brownie sailed through high school with help from his high intelligence and photographic memory. By the age of eighteen, he learned to speak Japanese, and do so fluently. After high school, he moved to Japan and opened a bar. He still lives there to this day. His bar is only a few miles away from Hiroshima were his great uncle dropped the atomic bomb. Where he lives was located on the puzzle piece of the Earth he sucked up into the vacuum.

Beetle went off to the Catholic high school, but only spent one year there. He dropped out and went to the public high school instead. He did not enroll as a student there; he applied as a custodian. They hired him, and he still works there to this day. He still uses a Kaivac and drives their limousine. It is the same limousine he rode in twenty years ago. The school still has cameras in the girls' locker room, and Beetle still eats out of the trash can when nobody is looking. He married Latricia, and they now have a ten-year-old son named Michael. One year for his birthday, Latricia gave Beetle a DVD copy of *The Attack of the Biotoxic Bulldogs*. She found it online.

The Attack of the Biotoxic Bulldogs is now their ten year old son's favorite movie of all-time.

Tristram and Coote's
Probate Practice

Tristram and Coote's Probate Practice

Twenty-Ninth Edition

2005 Supplement

R D'Costa

District Probate Registrar, Oxford

J I Winegarten

The Chief Master of the Supreme Court, Chancery Division

T Synak

IR Capital Taxes

Members of the LexisNexis Group worldwide

United Kingdom	LexisNexis UK, a Division of Reed Elsevier (UK) Ltd, Halsbury House, 35 Chancery Lane, LONDON, WC2A 1EL, and 4 Hill Street, EDINBURGH EH2 3JZ
Argentina	LexisNexis Argentina, BUENOS AIRES
Australia	LexisNexis Butterworths, CHATSWOOD, New South Wales
Austria	LexisNexis Verlag ARD Orac GmbH & Co KG, VIENNA
Canada	LexisNexis Butterworths, MARKHAM, Ontario
Chile	LexisNexis Chile Ltda, SANTIAGO DE CHILE
Czech Republic	Nakladatelství Orac sro, PRAGUE
France	Editions du Juris-Classeur SA, PARIS
Germany	LexisNexis Deutschland GmbH, FRANKFURT, MUNSTER
Hong Kong	LexisNexis Butterworths, HONG KONG
Hungary	HVG-Orac, BUDAPEST
India	LexisNexis Butterworths, NEW DELHI
Ireland	LexisNexis, DUBLIN
Italy	Giuffrè Editore, MILAN
Malaysia	Malayan Law Journal Sdn Bhd, KUALA LUMPUR
New Zealand	LexisNexis Butterworths, WELLINGTON
Poland	Wydawnictwo Prawnicze LexisNexis, WARSAW
Singapore	LexisNexis Butterworths, SINGAPORE
South Africa	LexisNexis Butterworths, DURBAN
Switzerland	Stämpfli Verlag AG, BERNE
USA	LexisNexis, DAYTON, Ohio

© Reed Elsevier (UK) Ltd 2004
Published by LexisNexis UK

A CIP Catalogue record for this book is available from the British Library.

ISBN   1405700084

Typeset by Etica Press Ltd
Printed and bound in Great Britain by Hobbs the Printers Ltd, Totton, Hampshire

Visit LexisNexis UK at www.lexisnexis.co.uk

Preface

This supplement covers the recent spate of activity in probate practice.

Part I explains by reference to rule 32 of the Non-Contentious Probate Rules 1987 the acquisition of parental responsibility by a father not married to a child's mother following the amendment to s 4 of the Children Act 1989 by s 111 of the Adoption Act 2002. The amended s 4 is set out in Appendix 1. The changes effected by the Inheritance Tax (Delivery of Accounts)(Excepted Estates) Regulations 2002 and 2004 include the extension of the concept of 'excepted estates' in specified events to persons who died on or after 6 April 2002 and who were never domiciled or treated as domiciled in the United Kingdom and increase the threshold of such estates to £1,000,000 of persons who died on or after 6 April 2004 domiciled in the United Kingdom. These regulations are included in Appendix 2.

The Non-Contentious Probate Rules were amended in 2003 and 2004. Firstly rule 60 was amended to provide that Parts 43 to 48 of the Civil Procedure Rules replace with modifications RSC o.62 in respect of the assessment of costs in non-contentious probate matters. Secondly on 7 December 2004 the definition of 'probate practitioner' was extended and for the time being the combination ss 53 and 55 of the Courts and Legal Services Act 1990 (by (Commencement No 11) Order 2004) and the Probate Services (Approved Body) Complaints Regulation 2004 allow a licenced conveyancer to prepare probate papers if he /she has been granted exemption from the provisions of s 23(1) of the Solicitors Act 1974. The Non-Contentious Probate Rules 1987 as amended are included in Appendix 2.

The Non-Contentious Probate Fees Rules 2005 come into force on 4 January 2005 and can be found in Appendix 3 of this supplement.

Various forms have also been inserted at the suggestion of practitioners for which I am grateful.

The law is at 4 January 2005.

RRD'C

PART I

The Common Form Probate Practice

CHAPTER I

The probate jurisdiction of the Family Division

COMMON FORM BUSINESS

1.30

See para **2.58** *post* for an update of District Probate Registries.

1.31

The Non-Contentious Probate Rules 1987 which incorporate the Non-Contentious Probate (Amendment) Rules 2003 are reproduced in Appendix II to this supplement.

Rules

1.39

The Non-Contentious Probate (Amendment) Rules 2003[1] with effect from 24 February 2003 disapply the Rules of the Supreme Court to costs in non-contentious probate matters and apply Parts 43, 44 (except rules 44.9 – 44.12), 47 and 48 of the Civil Procedure Rules 1998 with certain modifications to those matters. eg by rr 3 and 67). Rule 3 applies the Rules of the Supreme Court 1965, with the necessary modifications, in respect of matters not specifically dealt with in the Non-Contentious Probate Rules.[2]

1   SI 2003 No 185 (L.3).
2   NCPR 60 see para **A2.1**.

1.40

The Civil Procedure Rules 1998 which came into force on 26 April 1999 generally replaced the Supreme Court Rules 1965 but save as mentioned in the noter-up to para 1.39 above they do not apply to non-contentious or common form probate proceedings.

1.41

The current rules are the Non-Contentious Probate Rules 1987, as amended by the Non-Contentious Probate (Amendment) Rules 1991, 1998,1999 and 2003.

1.42

The Non-Contentious Probate Rules 1987, as amended, are printed in Appendix II.

Table of fees

1.44

The current table of fees incorporating the changes made by the Non-Contentious Probate Fees Order 2004 is printed in Appendix III.

Vesting of property prior to issue of grant

1.57

Substitute 'p 903' in place of 'p 898' at the beginning of line 2.

CHAPTER 2

General procedure in registry

AT THE PRINCIPAL REGISTRY

By whom application made

2.02

With effect from 7 December 2004, a licensed conveyancer will qualify as a probate practitioner if he is granted an exemption from the provisions of s 23(1) of the Solicitors Act 1974. On that date, ss 53 (and Sch 8 Pt 1) and 55 (and Sch 9) of the Courts and Legal Services Act 1990 come into force. The effect of this confirms the Council of Licensed Conveyancers as an approved body for granting exemption to a licensed conveyancer in accordance with criteria mentioned in the Act.[1]

1   Courts and Legal Services Act 1990 (Commencement No 11) Order 2004 and the Probate Services (Approved Body) Complaints Regulation 2004.

Lodging papers for grant

2.08

The Inheritance (Delivery of Accounts)(Excepted Estates) Regulations 2002 (as amended) replaced and revoked the Captial Transfer Tax (Delivery of Accounts) Regulations 1981 and subsequent amendments with effect from 2 August 2002. The later regulations extended the concept of 'excepted estates' to specified estates where the deceased died domiciled outside the United Kingdom on or after 6 April 2002. The Inheritance (Delivery of Accounts)(Excepted Estates) Regulations 2004 further extend the scope of 'excepted estates' in respect of persons dying on or 6 April 2004 (see noter-up to Ch 8). Form IHT205 (IHT207 in foreign domicile cases) must now be filed with all excepted estate applications.[1] In the Principal Registry payment of court fees may now be made by credit or debit card.

The Table of Fees which came into force on 4 April 2005 is reproduced in Appendix III to this supplement.

1   Practice Direction, 27 October 2004.

Postal, or document exchange, applications

2.11

The Principal Registry is a member of the British Document Exchange and its box number is DX 941 London/Chancery Lane.

2.13

Insert 'summary (form D18) after 'account' in the penultimate line.

2.14

Insert at the end of this paragraph:

Helpline telephone number 0845 3020 900 may assist with general enquiries.

2.30

The Non-Contentious Probate Fees Order 2004 is reproduced in Appendix III to this supplement.

2.31

Substitute for this paragraph:

In those cases in which an Inland Revenue is not required to be delivered (see noter-up to Ch 8) the oath to lead the grant should state either the gross and net amounts or the value of the brackets into which the estate falls. Every oath must contain a statement as follows either:

(i)   'To the best of my knowledge, information and belief the gross estate passing under the grant does not exceed [the limit applicable to the date of death] and the net estate does not exceed [the net value rounded to the next whole thousand]' 1 and this is not a case in which an Inland Revenue Account is required to be delivered or

(ii)   'To the best of my knowledge, information and belief the gross estate amounts to [exact value] and the net estate amounts to [exact value]' and this is not a case in which an Inland Revenue Account is required to be delivered [used where the date of death was on or after 6 April 2004 and the gross value of the estate plus chargeable value of transfers made within seven years of death does not exceed £1,000,000 and the net chargeable after deduction of spouse and/or charity exemptions is less than the IHT threshold]

Official errors in grants

2.47

Substitute '30' for '14' in the second line.

2.53

Insert '(see Chap.13 ff – grants de bonis non)' at the end of this paragraph.

AT DISTRICT PROBATE REGISTRIES AND SUB-REGISTRIES

Situation of registries

2.58

District probate registries and sub-registries are now situate at the following places[1]:

Registries	Sub-registries	Addresses, telephone numbers, fax number and document exchange number
Birmingham		The Priory Courts, 33 Bull Street, Birmingham B4 6DU
		Tel: 0121 681 3400
		Fax: 0121 236 2465
		DX 701990 Birmingham 7
	Stoke on Trent	Combined Court Centre, Bethesda Street, Hanley, Stoke on Trent ST1 3BP
		Tel: 01782 854065
		Fax: 01782 274916
		DX 20736 Hanley
Brighton		William Street, Brighton BN2 2LG
		Tel: 01273 684071
		Fax: 01273 625845
		DX 98073 Brighton 3
	Maidstone	The Law Courts, Barker Road, Maidstone ME18 8EW
		Tel: 01622 202048/7
		Fax: 01622 754384
		DX 130066 Maidstone 7
Bristol		Ground Floor, The Crescent Centre, Temple Back, Bristol BS1 6EP
		Tel 1: 0117 927 3915
		Tel 2: 0117 926 4619
		Fax: 0117 925 3549
		DX 94400 Bristol 5
	Bodmin	Market Street, Bodmin, Cornwall PL31 2JW
		Tel: 01208 72279
		Fax: 01208 269004
		DX 81858 Bodmin
	Exeter	Second Floor, Exeter Crown and County Courts, Sothernhay Gardens, Exeter EX1 1UH
		Tel: 01392 415 370
		DX 98442Exeter 2

Registries	Sub-registries	Addresses, telephone numbers, fax number and document exchange number
Cardiff–		PO Box 474, 2 Park Street, Cardiff CF10 1TB
Probate Registry		Tel: 029 2037 6479
of Wales		Fax: 029 2022 9855
		DX 122782 Cardiff 13
	Bangor	Council Offices, Ffordd, Gwynedd, Bangor LL57 1DT
		Tel: 01248 362410
		Fax: 01248 364423
		DX 23186 Bangor 2
	Carmarthen	14 King Street, Carmarthen SA31 1BL
		Tel: 01267 236238
		Fax: 01267 229067
		DX 51420 Carmarthen
Ipswich		Ground Floor, 8 Arcade Street, Ipswich IP1 1EJ
		Tel: 01473 284260
		Fax: 01473 231951
		DX 3279 Ipswich
	Norwich	Combined Court Building, The Law Courts, Bishopsgate, Norwich NR3 1UR
		Tel: 01603 728267
		Fax: 01603 627469
		DX 5202 Norwich
	Peterborough	1st Floor, Crown Buildings, Rivergate, Peterborough PE1 1EJ
		Tel: 01733 562802
		Fax: 01733 313016
		DX 12327 Peterborough 1
Leeds		3rd Floor, Coronet House, Queen Street, Leeds LS1 2BA
		Tel: 0113 386 3540
		Fax: 0113 247 1893
		DX 26451 Leeds (Park Square)
	Lincoln	360 High Street, Lincoln LN5 7PS
		Tel: 01522 523648
		Fax: 01522 539903
		DX 703233 Lincoln 6

Registries	Sub-registries	Addresses, telephone numbers, fax number and document exchange number
	Sheffield	PO Box 832
		The Law Courts, 50 West Bar, Sheffield S3 8YR
		Tel: 0114 281 2596
		Fax: 0114 281 2598
		DX 26054 Sheffield 2
Liverpool		Queen Elizabeth II Law Courts, Derby Square, Liverpool L2 1XA
		Tel: 0151 236 8264
		Fax: 0151 227 4634
		DX 14246 Liverpool 1
	Chester	5th Floor, Hamilton House, Hamilton Place, Chester CH1 2DA
		Tel: 01244 345082
		Fax: 01244 346243
		DX 22162 Northgate
	Lancaster	Mitre House, Church Street, Lancaster LA1 1HE
		Tel: 01524 36625
		Fax: 01254 35561
		DX 63509 Lancaster
Manchester		9th Floor, Astley House, 23 Quay Street, Manchester M3 4AT
		Tel: 0161 837 6070
		Fax: 0161 832 2690
		DX 14387 Manchester 1
	Nottingham	Butt Dyke House, Park Row, Nottingham NG1 6GR
		Tel: 0115 941 4288
		Fax: 0115 950 3383
		DX 10055 Nottingham
Newcastle upon Tyne		2nd Floor, Plummer House, Croft Street, Newcastle upon Tyne NE1 6NP
		Tel: 0191 261 8383
		Fax: 0191 230 4868
		DX 61081 Newcastle upon Tyne 14
	Carlisle	Courts of Justice, Earl Street, Carlisle CA1 1DJ
		Tel: 01228 521751
		DX 63034 Carlisle

Registries	Sub-registries	Addresses, telephone numbers, fax number and document exchange number
Middlesbrough		Teeside Combined Court Centre, Russell Street, Middlesbrough TS1 2AE
		Tel: 01642 340001
		DX 60536 Middlesbrough
	York	Duncombe Place, York YO1 2EA
		Tel: 01904 671564
		Fax: 01904 624210
		DX 61543 York
Oxford		Combined Court Building, St Aldates, Oxford OX1 1LY
		Tel 1: 01865 793050
		Tel 2: 01865 793055
		Fax: 01865 793090
		DX 96454 Oxford
	Gloucester	2nd Floor, Combined Court Building, Kimbrose Way, Gloucester GL1 2DG
		Tel: 01452 834966
		Fax: 01452 834970
		DX 98663 Gloucester
	Leicester	90 Wellington Street, Leicester LE1 6HG
		Tel: 0116 285 3380
		Fax: 0116 285 338
		DX 17403 Leicester 3
Winchester		4th Floor, Cromwell House, Andover Road, Winchester SO23 7EW
		Tel 1: 01962 897024
		Tel 2: 01962 897029
		Fax: 01962 840796
		DX 96900 Winchester 2

District probate registries and sub-registries are open daily, except weekends and bank holidays, from 9.30 am until 4 pm.

1   The District Probate Registries Order 1982: SI 1982/379 as amended (see para **A2.28** ff).

Administration pending determination of a probate claim

2.64

A grant of administration pending determination of a probate claim (formerly administration pending suit) can be made only at the Principal Registry[1].

1   NCPR 7(1).

Add to this paragraph:

It is anticipated that payment by credit and debit card will be introduced in the near future following the successful implementation of this method of payment in the Principal Registry.

PERSONAL APPLICATIONS

2.91

Add to this paragraph:

A telephone helpline (0845 30 20 900) operated jointly by the Probate Service and the Inland Revenue will provide information about probate and inheritance tax.

CHAPTER 3

Wills and codicils

REVOCATION OF WILLS

Revocation by subsequent marriage

Will made on or after 1 January 1983

3.40

Add at the end of s 18(3) of the Administration of Justice Act 1982 as quoted

'the will shall not be revoked by his marriage to that person'.

3.88a

Practitioners who are instructed to draft a will but do not supervise its execution are under a duty to check that it is properly executed when it is returned to them for safekeeping[1].

1 *Humblestone v Martin Tolhurst Partnership (a Firm)* (2004)Times, 27 February (it was found on examination after the death of the deceased that the will was not signed by him).

Knowledge and approval

3.125

Insert after the first sentence 'More recently this proposition was qualified when it was held that a will was validly executed even though the testatrix did not have testamentary capacity when she signed it. In *Clancy v Clancy* [2003] EWHC 1885 the court found for the validity of the will which had properly been drawn up in accordance with the instructions of the testatrix who had at least the capacity to understand that she was executing a will prepared in accordance with her instructions[1].

1 Applying *Parker v Felgate and Tilley* (1883) 8 PD 171. See also *Minns v Foster* [2002] All ER (D) 225 where a testator suffered short-term memory loss but 'understood the business in which he was engaged' at the time he executed the will.

CHAPTER 4

Probates

EXECUTORS

Executor's title

Limitation as to subject-matter

4.09

Substitute '11.277' for '11.279' in the last line of this paragraph.

4.46

Add to this paragraph:

A similar difficulty arises where the partnership firm has been replaced by a limited liability partnership. In the absence of a contrary expression in the appointment clause the probate registries do not treat the members of the limited liability partnership as partners for the purpose of the appointment.

At the time of going to print this matter is under review.

REQUIREMENTS ON PROVING A WILL

The executor's oath

Recitation of judgment in a probate action

4.140

After 'postal address' in the second line insert 'including the post code if known'. This information will appear in the grant (*President's Direction 22 March 2002*).

Amount of estate in oath

4.200

Insert 'and the Inheritance Tax (Delivery of Accounts) (Excepted Estates) Regulations 2002, as amended'[1] after 'Capital Transfer Tax (Delivery of Accounts) Regulations 1981, as amended'.

Insert at the end of the paragraph:

In applications made on or after 1 November 2004 where the deceased died after 5 April 2004 Form D18 must be stamped and authorised by the Inland Revenue Capital Taxes Office before it is submitted with the application'[2].

1   The Inheritance Tax (Delivery of Accounts)(Excepted Estates) Regulations 2002 (as amended) is reproduced in Appendix II to this supplement.
2   Inheritance Tax (Delivery of Accounts)(Excepted Estates) Regulations 2004 (See Appendix II to this supplement.

4.201

Substitute for this paragraph:

DEATH BEFORE 5 APRIL 2004

In all cases in which an Inland Revenue account is not required to be delivered, the oath will recite the gross value of the estate as not exceeding the limit applicable to the date of death (see para 4.202) and the net value rounded to the next whole thousand[1].

DEATH ON AND AFTER 6 APRIL APRIL 2004

In those cases in which an Inland Revenue is not required to be delivered (see noter-up to Ch 8) the oath to lead the grant should state either the gross and net amounts or the value of the brackets into which the estate falls. Every oath must contain a statement as follows either:

(i)   'To the best of my knowledge, information and belief the gross estate passing under the grant does not exceed [the limit applicable to the date of death] and the net estate does not exceed [the net value rounded to the next whole thousand]'[1] and this is not a case in which an Inland Revenue Account is required to be delivered'; or

(ii)   'To the best of my knowledge, information and belief the gross estate amounts to [exact value] and the net estate amounts to [exact value]'[2] and this is not a case in which an Inland Revenue Account is required to be delivered [used where the date of death was on or after 6 April 2004 and the gross value of the estate plus chargeable value of transfers made within seven years of death does not exceed £1,000,000 and the net chargeable after deduction of spouse and/or charity exemptions is less than the IHT threshold]

Where an estate qualifies as an 'excepted estate' Form IHT205 must be filed with the application.

1   *Practice Direction* 22 March 2002.
2   *Practice Direction* 27 October 2004.

4.201A

The concept of 'excepted estate' in respect of deaths after 1 April 2002 where the deceased died domiciled had never been domiciled in or treated as domiciled in the United Kingdom and the estate is attributable to cash or quoted shares or securities which do not exceed £100,000[1].

1   Inheritance Tax (Delivery of Accounts) (Excepted Estates) Regulations 2002 – see Appendix II to this supplement.

4.201B

Every oath must contain a statement by the applicant as follows:

'To the best of my knowledge, information and belief the gross estate passing under the grant does not exceed/amounts to* £ and that the net estate does not exceed/amounts to* £ [and that this is not a case in which an Inland Revenue Account is required to be delivered]*'.

The alternatives marked with an asterisk should be deleted as appropriate[1].

1   *Practice Directions* [1981] 2 All ER 832, [1981] 1 WLR 1185. In relation to a death prior to 13 March 1975, a sworn Inland Revenue affidavit is still required (see NCPR 42).

4.202

The relevant dates and gross limits are:

Death on or after	Gross limit
6 April 2004	£1,000,000/263,000[1]
6 April 2003	£240,000
6 April 2002	£220,000
6 April 2000	£210,000
6 April 1998	£200,000
6 April 1996	£180,000
6 April 1995	£145,000
6 April 1991	£125,000
1 April 1990	£115,000
1 April 1989	£100,000
1 April 1987	£70,000
1 April 1983	£40,000
1 April 1981	£25,000

and the relevant net limits and court fees payable are:

Exceeding	Not exceeding	Court fee
£————	£5,000	(no fee)
£(nearest whole thousand)[2]	(relevant gross limit stated above)	£50

1   Or prevailing inheritance tax threshold: see para 4.201.
2   Practice Directions 22 March 2002 and 27 March 2004.

Notice to Treasury Solicitor

4.222

In any case in which it appears that the Crown is or may be beneficially interested in the estate of a deceased person, notice of the intended application for a grant must be given by the applicant to the Treasury Solicitor. The district judge or registrar may direct that no grant shall issue within 28 days after such notice has been given[1].The notice should be sent to: The Treasury Solicitor (BV), Queen Anne's Chambers, London SW1 9JX *or* DX 123240 St James Park (tel: 020 7210 3000).

1   NCPR 38.

4.225

In certain special cases, however, an engrossment or a 'fiat copy' of the will must be lodged by the solicitor.

Inland Revenue account

4.249

Substitute for this paragraph:

'Unless dispensed with pursuant to the Capital Transfer Tax (Delivery of Accounts) Regulations 1981, as amended or the Inheritance Tax (Delivery of Accounts)(Excepted Estates) Regulations 2002 as amended, or the Inheritance Tax (Delivery of Accounts) (Excepted Estates) Regulations 2004 an Inland Revenue account in Forms IHT200 and D18 (a sworn Inland Revenue affidavit is required in cases of death prior to 13 March 1975) must be submitted pre-grant together with any tax payable to the IR Capital Taxes. Form D18 will be receipted and authorised and returned to the probate practitioner for inclusion with the probate papers and it will be retained by the probate registry. Where the estate qualifies as an 'excepted estate' Form IHT205 (or IHT207 if the deceased died domiciled abroad) must be lodged with the probate papers. The subject of Inland Revenue accounts is dealt with in detail in the noter-up to Ch 8.

Payment of inheritance tax

4.249A

With effect from 31 March 2003 it has been possible to draw on funds in a deceased's bank and building society accounts to pay inheritance tax before the grant can be issued. Where the deceased had sufficient funds the in the accounts the bank or building society will transfer the amount of inheritance tax due directly to the Inland Revenue. Details of this scheme may be obtained from the IR Capital Taxes. (See also noter-up to para 8.133.)

FEES

Fees on the grant

4.250

The NC Probate Fees Order 2004 as amended is included in Appendix III to this supplement.

4.251

Exemption of an asset from inheritance tax or capital transfer tax does not give exemption from court fees unless it is expressly directed by statute or otherwise[1].

1 Direction (1940) 10 April. As to property excluded in assessing the fee for a grant, see paras **4.218–4.221**.

4.252

The Principal Registry accepts payment of fees by debit/credit card and in all likelihood it will be introduced throughout the Probate Service in the foreseeable future

Remission of probate fees

4.255

Under the NC Probate Fees Order 2004, the Lord Chancellor has power to reduce or remit a prescribed fee where it appears that its payment would, owing to the exceptional circumstances of the particular case, involve undue hardship. The Fees Order allows for an application for reduction or remission to be made retrospectively. The application should be made within six months of paying the fee. However the Lord Chancellor may extend the period if he considers that there is good reason for the application being made after the end of that period[2]. All requests for reduction or remission of fees payable in the Principal Registry will be referred to the probate manager of the probate department; those made in the district probate registries should be referred to the registrar[3]. The power is, however, discretionary and cannot be exercised unless the Lord Chancellor is satisfied that the circumstances of the particular case are exceptional *and* that undue hardship would be involved unless a reduction or remission is made.

1 NC Probate Fees Order 2004, para 4.
2 NC Probate Fees Order 2004, para 5(1).
3 Registrar's Direction (1976) 22 June, as amended 8 June 1981 and 27 March 1995.

Members of HM forces and other persons 'killed in war'

4.264

The Non-Contentious Probate Fees Order 2004 corrects an anomaly in the Non-Contentious Probate Fees Order 1999 in respect of members of armed forces of the Crown killed on active service. Paragraph 3 in the Schedule 1 of the substantive Fees Order (Special Applications)is reclassed as 3(1) and Fee 3(2) provides that on an application for a grant in an estate exempt from s 154 of the Inheritance tax Act 1984 (exemption for members of the armed forces etc) the fee shall be £8. The Fees Order is reproduced in Appendix III of this supplement.

COSTS OF NON-CONTENTIOUS PROBATE PROCEEDINGS

Solicitors' charges

4.266

The Rules of the Supreme Court (Non-Contentious Probate Costs) 1956, which applied to all non-contentious or common form probate business for which instructions were accepted on or after 1 May 1956 were revoked as from 1 September 1994[1]. A solicitor's charges in such matters are now governed by the Solicitors' (Non-Contentious Business) Remuneration Order 1994[2], which came into force on 1 November 1994 and applies to all non-contentious business for which bills are delivered on or after that date.

1   Rules of the Supreme Court (Amendment) 1994, r 24 (SI 1994/1975).
2   See para **A5.01**.

4.267

Add to footnote 2:

In *Jemma Trust Co Ltd v Liptrott* [2003] ECWA Civ 1476 the Court of Appeal held that it was open to solicitors to charge a scale fee based on the value of the estate as well as for time spent on administration. Taking into account all the factors in the Remuneration Order the question to be determined was whether the overall remuneration was fair and reasonable. The Court suggested the following guidelines be applied by solicitors: it would be best practice for the solicitor to obtain the prior agreement as to basis of charges from the executors and entitled third party; in complicated administrations provide in the terms of retainer for interim bills to be rendered for payment on account but subject to reviewing the overall charge at the end of business to ensure that it is fair and reasonable; charges may be based on value of the estate or the hourly rate or mixture of these two elements but it is important to ensure clarity to show how value is taken into account and it is not to be charged twice; if charges are made by reference to value they should be on a regressive scale; when a separate element of the charge is based on the value of the estate it would be helpful to specify the number of hours that it would notionally take to achieve that amount and where there is no relevant and ascertainable value factor it may be helpful to consider the Law Society's guidance in 'An Approach to Non-Contentious Costs' (February 1995) at para 13.4' *The guidance is in the process of being updated.*

4.268

Notes for the guidance of solicitors in assessing their charges for obtaining grants of representation and administering estates have been issued by the Law Society[1].

1   *An Approach to Non-Contentious Costs* (February 1995) now in the process of being updated.

Assessment/Taxation of costs

4.271

Proceedings for the assessment (previously taxation) of a solicitor's bill of costs under the Solicitors Act 1974 must be commenced in the Supreme Court Taxing Office[1]: for the practice, see the notes under the Solicitors Act in Volume 2 of the Civil Procedure Rules.

1   NCPR 60 excludes taxations in probate matters under the Solicitors Act from the jurisdiction of district judges or registrars or taxing officers of the Family Division.

4.272

On any assessment of costs it is the duty of the solicitor to satisfy the taxing master as to the fairness and reasonableness of his charge.

Legal aid and inter parties costs—non-contentious probate applications

4.273

Legal aid under the Legal Aid Act 1988 may in certain circumstances be given in respect of non-contentious probate matters.

4.274

The solicitor must by regulation file the legal aid certificate and, to obtain payment, lodge his bill of costs for assessment.

4.275

An application for a grant to make title in probate claim will be regarded as a step in the claim, and the solicitor should file his certificate and tax his bill in the Division in which the action is proceeding.

4.276

If proceedings are confined to the Family Division the certificate should be filed in the probate department at the Principal Registry or at the district probate registry where the order for assessment of costs was made.

4.277

With effect from 24 February 2003 the following rule was substituted for NCPR 60:

60 Costs

(1) Order 62 of the Rules of the Supreme Court 1965 shall not apply to costs in non-contentious probate matters, and Parts 43, 44 (except rules 44.9 to 44.12), 47 and 48 of the Civil Procedure Rules 1998 ("the 1998 Rules") shall apply to costs in those matters, with the modifications contained in paragraphs (3) to (7) of this rule.

(2) Where detailed assessment of a bill of costs is ordered, it shall be referred—
   (a) where the order was made by a district judge, to a district judge, a costs judge or an authorised court officer within rule 43.2(1)(d)(iii) or (iv) of the 1998 Rules;
   (b) where the order was made by a registrar, to that registrar or, where this is not possible, in accordance with sub-paragraph (a) above.

(3) Every reference in Parts 43, 44, 47 and 48 of the 1998 Rules to a district judge shall be construed as referring only to a district judge of the Principal Registry.

(4) The definition of "costs officer" in rule 43.2(1)(c) of the 1998 Rules shall have effect as if it included a paragraph reading—

   "(iv)   a district probate registrar."

(5) The definition of "authorised court officer" in rule 43.2(1)(d) of the 1998 Rules shall have effect as if paragraphs (i) and (ii) were omitted.

(6) Rule 44.3(2) of the 1998 Rules (costs follow the event) shall not apply.

(7) Rule 47.4(2) of the 1998 Rules shall apply as if after the words "Supreme Court Costs Office" there were inserted ", the Principal Registry of the Family Division or such district probate registry as the court may specify".

(8) Except in the case of an appeal against a decision of an authorised court officer (to which rules 47.20 to 47.23 of the 1998 Rules apply), an appeal against a decision in assessment proceedings relating to costs in non-contentious probate matters shall be dealt with in accordance with the following paragraphs of this rule.

(9) An appeal within paragraph (8) above against a decision made by a district judge, a costs judge (as defined by rule 43.2(1)(b) of the 1998 Rules) or a registrar, shall lie to a judge of the High Court.

(10) Part 52 of the 1998 Rules applies to every appeal within paragraph (8) above, and any reference in Part 52 to a judge or a district judge shall be taken to include a district judge of the Principal Registry of the Family Division.

(11) The 1998 Rules shall apply to an appeal to which Part 52 or rules 47.20 to 47.23 of those Rules apply in accordance with paragraph (8) above in the same way as they apply to any other appeal within Part 52 or rules 47.20 to 47.23 of those Rules as the case may be; accordingly the Rules of the Supreme Court 1965 and the County Court Rules 1981 shall not apply to any such appeal.

4.278

The Civil Procedure Rules Parts 42, 44 (except rules 44.9–44.12) 47and 48 apply to the assessment of costs in non-contentious probate matters. Apart from events where summary assessment of costs apply every bill of costs and supporting papers should be lodged in the Registry where the order for assessment was made. If it is not possible for the registrar to assess the bill it will be referred to a district judge in the Principal Registry. An appeal against a decision of the registrar in assessment proceedings lies to a judge of the High Court. Permission for such appeal is required and may be applied for at the assessment or by way of notice of appeal to the High Court judge.

4.278B

The provisions of RSC Ord 62 continue to apply to costs arising out proceedings which began before 24 February 2003.

CHAPTER 5

Letters of administration with the will annexed

PERSONS INTERESTED IN THE RESIDUARY ESTATE

Adopted persons

5.36

Insert at the end of this paragraph:

The Adoption and Children Act 2002 was enacted on 7 November 2002. In addition to introducing amendments to the Children Act 1989 it will in due course on a day to be appointed repeal and replace the Adoption Act 1976 except for Part 4 and paragraph 6 of Schedule 2.

5.56

Insert at the end of this paragraph:

Sections 1, 3, 8 and 12 of the Adoption (Intercountry Aspects) Act 1999 which came into force on 23 January 2003 substituted the definitions for 'the Convention' and related expressions. Except in relation to a 1965 Convention adoption order or a 1965 Convention adoption (as defined by s 17(2) of the 1999 Act the Convention is the Hague Convention on Protection of Children and Co-operation in respect of Intercountry Adoption which was concluded at the Hague on 29 May 1993.

5.57

See noter-up to para 5.56. The scope of the Convention has now extended to several countries a complete list of which may be found at the Department for Education and Skills website at www.dfes.gov.uk/adoption/intercountry or linked sites. (See also noter-up to para 6.242ff.)

5.58

See noter-up to para 5.56 as to modifications to the Convention and related expressions by reference to the Adoption (Intercountry Aspects) Act 1999 with effect from 23 January 2003.

Insert after para 5.89:

Contingency age

5.89A

Words in a will initially may appear to create a vested gift by reference to the beneficiary attaining a specified age and a direction to advance interest and capital. However a direction to limit the amount of interest and capital and the creation of a discretionary power rather than a gift of income cuts the benefit to a contingent gift with postponed payment. The effect of this is that if the beneficiary dies before attaining the specified age his interest fails and subject to a gift over a partial intestacy is created[1].

1   *Harrison v Tucker* [2003] EWHC 1168, Ch.

Conditional gift

Insert after para 5.130:

5.130A

A condition subsequent which divested a benefit if the beneficiary challenged the will was not an adequate ground for holding the condition void as contrary to public policy because it deterred an applicant from making an application under the Inheritance (Provision for Family and Dependants) Act 1975. That is a statutory right and the court would have regard to the effect of the condition when it decided the application[1].

1   *Nathan v Leonard* [2003] 4 All ER 196.

Residuary legatee or any beneficiary a witness. Forfeiture

5.149

Add to this paragraph:

However in respect of any death after 31 January 2001 section 28(4) of the Trustee Act 2001 provides that a trustee's attestation does not invalidate the charging clause in his favour.

5.151

See noter-up to para 5.149.

Death by murder or manslaughter

5.160A

The court refused to modify the rule where the residuary beneficiary was convicted of manslaughter on the grounds of diminished responsibility. The court took into account the conduct of the offender in having spent large amounts of the deceased money for his own benefit and not providing formal medical care for the deceased who suffered from dementia. Further the manslaughter verdict had not extinguished the offender's responsibility but merely reduced it[1].

1   *Dalton v Latham* [2003] EWHC 796, Ch.

5.183

Notice of the application should be sent to: The Treasury Solicitor (BV), Queen Anne's Chambers, 28 Broadway, London SW1H 9JS *or* DX 123240 St James Park. Tel: 020 7210 3000.

Rule 20, Class (e)

Undisposed-of estate vested in spouse who has since died

5.196

Insert 'intestate' in the second line of this paragraph after 'died'.

Grant to assignee

5.217

Add to the end of this paragraph:

The Finance Act 2003 introduced Stamp Duty Land Tax which came into effect on 1 December 2003. The effect of this tax does away with the requirement of the Stamp Duty Act 1891 to original deeds unless they relate to the transfer of shares and securities. The Stamp Taxes enquiry line tel. 0845 603 0135 will provide assistance about particular deeds or transactions.

5.219

See noter-up to para 5.217. It appears that the endorsement of certificates on deed of assignment is no longer required.

REQUIREMENTS ON OBTAINING ADMINISTRATION (WITH WILL)

Inland Revenue account

5.246

See noter-up to para 4.249.

Fees

5.247

The Non-Contentious Probate Fees Order 2004 is reproduced in Appendix III to this supplement.

Solicitor's charges

5.248

See noter-up to para 4.267, and as to assessment of bills of costs see noter-up to para 4.278.

CHAPTER 6

Letters of administration

TO WHOM GRANTED

Assignment of life interest or reversion

6.25

Add to footnote:

A voluntary disclaimer of benefit in a person's estate before his death is ineffective (*Re Smith, Smith v Smith* [2001] All ER 2).

RIGHT TO THE GRANT

6.98

Add to the footnote the further reference of: *Jemma Trust Co Ltd v Liptrott* [2003] EWCA Civ 1476.

Adopted persons

After para 6.229 add:

Children and Adoption Act 2002

6.229A

The Adoption and Children Act 2002 which received the Royal Assent on 7 November 2002 will when implemented repeal and replace the Adoption 1976 except for Part 4 and paragraph 6 of Schedule 2. On the day that Chapter 4 of the later Act comes into force adoptions effected on and after that day shall mean[1]:
(a) adoption by an adoption order or a Scottish or Northern Irish adoption order;
(b) adoption by an order made in the Isle of Man or any of the Channel Islands;

(c)   an adoption effected under the law of a Convention country outside the British Islands, and certified in pursuance of Article 23(1)of the Convention (referred to tin the Act as a Convention adoption);

(d)   an overseas adoption, or

(e)   an adoption recognised by the law of England and Wales and effected under the law of any other country.

But these references do not include an adoption effected before the day on which Chapter 4 comes into force[2]. Such adoption will continue to attract the meaning given by the Adoption Act 1976 or earlier legislation.

1   Adoption and Children Act 2002, s 66(1).
2   ACA 2002, s 66(2).

6.229B

Section 46(1) of the Children and Adoption Act 2002 defines adoption order as an order made by the court on an application under section 50 (application by couple) or 51 (adoption by one person) giving parental responsibility for a child to the adopters or adopter.

6.229C

The Convention means the Convention on Protection of Children and Co-operation in respect of Intercountry Adoption concluded at the Hague on 29 May 1993[1].

1   ACA 2002, s144 (1).

6.229C

Under section 67 of the Adoption and Children Act 2002:

(1)   An adopted person is to be treated in law as if born as a child of the adopters or adopter.

(2)   An adopted person is the legitimate child of the adopters or adopter and, if adopted by

    (a)   a couple, or

    (b)   one of a couple under section 51(2),

is to be treated as the child of the relationship in question.

(3)   An adopted person

    (a)   if adopted by one of a couple under section 51(2), is to be treated in law as not being the child of any person other than the adopter and the other one of the couple, and

    (b)   in any other case, is to be treated in law, subject to subsection (4), as not being the child of any person other than the adopter or adopters; but this subsection does not affect any reference in this Act to a person's natural parent or to any other natural relationship.

(4)   In the case of a person adopted by one of the person's natural parents as sole adoptive parent, subsection (3)(b) has no effect as respects entitlement to property depending on relationship to that parent, or as respects anything else depending on that relationship.

(5)   This section has effect from the date of adoption.

(6) Subject to the provisions of this Chapter [4 of the Act] and Schedule 4, this section

    (a) applies for the interpretation or instruments passed or made before as well as after the adoption, as so applies subject to any contrary indication, and

    (b) has effect as respects things done, or events occurring, on or after the adoption.

Convention adoption orders

6.241

Add to this paragraph:

With effect from 23 January 2003 and by virtue of the Adoption (Intercountry Aspects) Act 1999 Convention and Convention Orders are defined by reference to the provisions of the Convention on Protection of Children and Co-operation in respect of Intercountry Adoptions concluded at the Hague on 29 May 1993. Accordingly in the following paragraphs the provisions of the later Convention are applicable when referring to 'Convention', 'Convention country' and 'Convention order'

6.242

Substitute for the last sentence of this paragraph:

The Convention applies to the following countries:

States	S [1]	R/A [2]	Type [3]	EIF [4]	Ext [5]	Auth [6]	Res/D/N [7]
Argentina	28-I-1991	19-III-1991	R	1-VI-1991		1	D
Australia	29-X-1986	29-X-1986	R	1-I-1987		1	D
Austria	12-V-1987	14-VII-1988	R	1-X-1988		1	
Belarus		12-I-1998	A*	1-IV-1998		1	Res26
Belgium	11-I-1982	9-II-1999	R	1-V-1999		1	
Bosnia and Herzegovina	27-IX-1991	27-IX-1991	Su	1-XII-1991		1	
Brazil		19-X-1999	A*	1-I-2000		1	Res24
Bulgaria		20-V-2003	A*	1-VIII-2003		1	Res42

States	S [1]	R/A [2]	Type [3]	EIF [4]	Ext [5]	Auth [6]	Res/D/N [7]
Canada	25-X-1980	2-VI-1983	R	1-XII-1983	9	1	
Chile		23-II-1994	A*	1-V-1994		1	D
China (People's Republic of)			C			2	D,N
Croatia	27-IX-1991	27-IX-1991	Su	1-XII-1991		1	
Cyprus		4-XI-1994	A*	1-II-1995		1	
Czech Republic	28-XII-1992	15-XII-1997	R	1-III-1998		1	Res
Denmark	17-IV-1991	17-IV-1991	R	1-VII-1991		1	Res
Estonia		18-IV-2001	A*	1-VII-2001		1	Res
Finland	25-V-1994	25-V-1994	R	1-VIII-1994		1	Res
France	25-X-1980	16-IX-1982	R	1-XII-1983		1	Res,D
Georgia		24-VII-1997	A*	1-X-1997		1	
Germany	9-IX-1987	27-IX-1990	R	1-XII-1990		1	Res,D
Greece	25-X-1980	19-III-1993	R	1-VI-1993		1	Res
Hungary		7-IV-1986	A*	1-VII-1986		1	
Iceland		14-VIII-1996	A*	1-XI-1996		1	Res
Ireland	23-V-1990	16-VII-1991	R	1-X-1991		1	
Israel	4-IX-1991	4-IX-1991	R	1-XII-1991		1	Res
Italy	2-III-1987	22-II-1995	R	1-V-1995		1	

States	S [1]	R/A [2]	Type[3]	EIF [4]	Ext [5]	Auth[6]	Res/D/N[7]
Latvia		15-XI-2001	A*	1-II-2002		1	Res24
Lithuania		4-VI-2002	A*	1-IX-2002		1	Res24,26
Luxembourg	18-XII-1984	8-X-1986	R	1-I-1987		1	Res26
Malta		26-X-1999	A*	1-I-2000		1	
Mexico		20-VI-1991	A*	1-IX-1991		1	
Monaco		12-XI-1992	A*	1-II-1993		1	Res26
Netherlands	11-IX-1987	12-VI-1990	R	1-IX-1990		1	Res26
New Zealand		31-V-1991	A*	1-VIII-1991		1	Res24,26
Norway	9-I-1989	9-I-1989	R	1-IV-1989		1	Res24,26
Panama		2-II-1994	A*	1-V-1994		1	Res26
Peru		28-V-2001	A*	1-VIII-2001		1	
Poland		10-VIII-1992	A*	1-XI-1992		1	Res26
Portugal	22-VI-1982	29-IX-1983	R	1-XII-1983		1	
Romania		20-XI-1992	A*	1-II-1993		1	
Serbia and Montenegro	27-IX-1991	27-IX-1991	Su	1-XII-1991		1	
Slovak Republic	28-XII-1992	7-XI-2000	R	1-II-2001		1	Res26
Slovenia		22-III-1994	A*	1-VI-1994		1	
South Africa		8-VII-1997	A*	1-X-1997		1	Res24,26

States	S [1]	R/A [2]	Type[3]	EIF [4]	Ext [5]	Auth[6]	Res/D/N[7]
Spain	7-II-1986	16-VI-1987	R	1-IX-1987		1	
Sri Lanka		28-IX-2001	A*	1-XII-2001		1	Res24,26
Sweden	22-III-1989	22-III-1989	R	1-VI-1989		1	Res26
Switzerland	25-X-1980	11-X-1983	R	1-I-1984		1	
The former Yugoslav Republic of Macedonia	27-IX-1991	27-IX-1991	Su	1-XII-1991		1	
Turkey	21-I-1998	31-V-2000	R	1-VII-2000		1	Res26
United Kingdom of Great Britain and Northern Ireland	19-XI-1984	20-V-1986	R	1-VIII-1986	5	1	Res,N26,39
United States of America	23-XII-1981	29-IV-1988	R	1-VII-1988		1	Res24,26
Uruguay		16-XI-1999	A*	1-II-2000		1	
Venezuela	16-X-1996	16-X-1996	R	1-I-1997		1	Res26

1) S = Signature
2) R/A = Ratification or Accession
3) Type
    R   Ratification;
    A   Accession;
        A*   Accession giving rise to an acceptance procedure;
        C   Continuation;
        Su Succession;
        D   Denunciation;
4) EIF = Entry into force
5) Ext = Extensions of application
6) Auth = Designation of Authorities
7) Res/D/N = Reservations, declarations or notifications

6.243

See noter-up to para 6.242

Right to grant where there has been an adoption

6.250

Add to this paragraph:

The status of adoptions defined in s 67 of the Children and Adoption Act 2002 will apply in respect of adoptions made on and after the date on which it is implemented.

6.251

See noter-up para 6.229A for definitions to adoption which the Children and Adoption Act 2002 will apply when it is implemented.

Adoption orders made outside the United Kingdom

6.262

Substitute 'below' for 'overleaf' in the fourth line.

6.264

Commonwealth countries and United Kingdom dependent territories:

Australia	Bahamas	Barbados
Bermuda	Botswana	British Honduras
British Virgin Islands	Canada	Cayman Islands
The Republic of Cyprus	Dominica	Fiji
Ghana	Gibraltar	Guyana
Hong Kong	Jamaica	Kenya
Lesotho	Malawi	Malaysia
Malta	Mauritius	Montserrat
New Zealand	Nigeria	Pitcairn
St. Christopher, Nevis and Anguilla	St. Vincent	Seychelles
Singapore	Southern Rhodesia	Sri Lanka
Swaziland	Tanzania	Tonga
Trinidad and Tobago	Uganda	Zambia

Other countries and territories

Austria
Belgium
Denmark (including Greenland and the Faroes)
Finland
France (including Reunion, Martinique, Guadeloupe and French Guyana)
The Federal Republic of Germany and Land Berlin (West Berlin)

Greece
Iceland
The Republic of Ireland
Israel
Italy
Luxembourg
The Netherlands (including Surinam and the Antilles)
Norway
Portugal (including the Azores and Madeira)
South Africa and South West Africa
Spain (including the Balearics and the Canary Islands)
Sweden
Switzerland
Turkey
The United States of America
Yugoslavia

6.346

Substitute 'determination of probate claim' for 'suit' in the sub-title and paragraph.

6.349

As to expedition of grant, see para **2.39**.

Amount of estate and swearing

6.365

For the practice as to 'amount of estate' and 'swearing', see 'Executor's oath', paras **4.200** ff and **4.223**.

INLAND REVENUE ACCOUNTS

6.387

See noter-up to para 4.249 and Chap 8.

FEES

6.388

The Non-Contentious Probate Fees Order 2004 is reproduced in Appendix III of this supplement.

SOLICITOR'S CHARGES

6.389

See noter-up to para **4.267**.

CHAPTER 7

Minority or life interests and second administrators

Only one child etc of full age

7.29

It should be noted that in respect of births registered on and after 1 December 2003 a father of a minor child who is not married to the mother acquires parental responsibility if he is registered as the father in accordance with relevant provisions of the Births and Deaths Registration Act 1953 and similar provisions in Scotland and Northern Ireland[1]

1   Adoption and Children Act 2002, s 1.

CHAPTER 8

Inland Revenue Accounts

NATIONAL PROBATE AND INHERITANCE TAX HELPLINE

A local rate number is now available for all Probate and Inheritance Tax enquiries, which replaces the Capital Taxes Helpline numbers for Nottingham, Edinburgh and Belfast. The new number is 0845 30 20 900 and lines are open from 9am to 5pm, Monday to Friday. For information on Probate, visit the Court Service website: www.courtservice.gov.uk. For information on Inheritance Tax, visit the Inland Revenue website: www.inlandrevenue.gov.uk/cto.

EXCEPTED ESTATES

8.02-8.03

For deaths on or after 6 April 2004, the overall cash limit for the previous category of excepted estates is brought in line with the Inheritance Tax threshold, currently £263,000. The limits for foreign assets, simple lifetime transfers and settled property remain at the 2002 limits.

For deaths on or after 6 April 2003 and before 6 April 2004, the excepted estate gross value limit to fall within the procedures is £240,000. This increase was authorised by SI 2003 No 1658. The limits for foreign assets, simple lifetime transfers and settled property remain at the 2002 limits.

For deaths on or after 6 April 2002, for a person domiciled in the United Kingdom, the excepted estate gross value limit is £220,000. From that date for the excepted estate procedures to apply, the value of that person's estate must be attributable wholly to property passing under his will or intestacy, or under a nomination of an asset taking effect on his death, or by survivorship in a beneficial joint tenancy or, in Scotland, by survivorship, or additionally under a single settlement in which he was entitled to an interest in possession. Of that property, not more than £100,000 represented value attributable to property which, immediately before that person's death, was settled property, and not more than £75,000 represented value attributable to property which was situate outside the United Kingdom. Also, that person died without having made any chargeable transfers during the period of seven years ending with his death other than specified transfers where the aggregate value transferred did not exceed £100,000.These specified transfers mean cash, quoted shares and securities or an interest in or over land [and furnishings and chattels disposed of at the same time to the same donee and intended to be enjoyed with the land] save to the extent that either sections 102 or 102A[2] of the Finance Act 1986 apply to that transfer or the land [or furnishings or chattels] became settled property on that transfer.

A new category of excepted estate is introduced for deaths on or after 6 April 2004 where the gross value of the estate does not exceed £1m and the net chargeable value, after deduction of liabilities, spouse and/or charity exemption or exemption for a gift for National purposes, does not exceed the Inheritance Tax threshold. No other exemption or relief can be taken into account for this purpose.

Additionally, the following provisions apply for deaths on or after 6 April 2002 for a person who was never domiciled in the United Kingdom or treated as domiciled in the United Kingdom by virtue of section 267[1] of the 1984 Act. If the value of that person's estate situate in the United Kingdom is wholly attributable to cash or quoted shares or securities passing under his will or intestacy, or by survivorship in a beneficial joint tenancy or, in Scotland, by survivorship, and the gross value of which does not exceed £100,000, the excepted estate provisions also apply.

SI 2002 No 1733 refers for deaths on or after 6 April 2002.

The provisions of the third category of excepted estate, where the deceased was never domiciled or treated as domiciled in the United Kingdom, remain at the levels appropriate from 2002.

The provisions of SI 2002/1733 and SI 2003/1688 are revoked in relation to persons who died on or after 6 April 2004.

Every application for a grant/confirmation where the deceased died on or after 6 April 2004 must now be accompanied by basic information about the estate. In England and Wales and Northern Ireland, this means that every application must be accompanied by a revised form IHT205. In Scotland, the Inventory must be accompanied by form C5. The appropriate form must be produced to the Board (in accordance with the regulations) by producing it to:
(a) a probate registry in England and Wales;
(b) the sheriff in Scotland;
(c) the Probate and Matrimonial Office in Northern Ireland.

These changes were authorised by SI 2004/2543.

INHERITANCE TAX AND CAPITAL TRANSFER TAX

Rates of tax

8.13

With effect from 6 April 2004, the taxpaying threshold is increased to £263,000 in line with statutory indexation and rounding rules.[1] The earlier thresholds subsequent to the £242,000 detailed in the main work which was appropriate until 5 April 2002 are as follows:

- 6 April 2002 until 5 April 2003. £250,000[2]
- 6 April 2003 until 5 April 2004. £255,000[3]

In each instance, the rate of tax on the excess over the threshold is 40%.

1   SI 2004 No 771.
2   Finance Act 2002, s 118.
3   SI 2003 No 841.

GRANTS ON CREDIT

8.24

Arrangements are now available for the taxpayer to pay their Inheritance Tax by the Inheritance Tax Direct Payment Scheme. Under this Scheme, participating institutions such as Banks and Building Societies will, on receipt of instructions from the Personal Representatives, transfer money electronically to the Inland Revenue. Further details are provided at para 8.133 of this supplement.

CURRENT FORMS

8.25–8.44

In addition to obtaining forms from the Stationery Section at IR Capital Taxes by post or by telephone, forms may also now be obtained via the website www.inlandrevenue.gov.uk/cto.

PRACTICE

Completion of account

8.45–8.52

Whilst the main work details the full completion of the form IHT 200, in certain circumstances it is now possible for a reduced version of this account to be completed. To qualify for the reduced version:
- the deceased must have been domiciled in the United Kingdom at the date of death;
- some assets must pass under the Will or intestacy to a United Kingdom domiciled spouse [either directly or into a trust under which the surviving spouse has a right to benefit], and/or directly to a charity that is registered in the United Kingdom, and/or directly to a body listed in Schedule 3 of the Inheritance Tax Act 1984, and/or to be held on trusts established in the United Kingdom for charitable purposes only.

If the gross value of any assets passing to beneficiaries other than listed above, plus the value of any other assets chargeable on death, and the chargeable value of any gifts made within seven years of the date of death is less than or equal to the Inheritance Tax threshold, then the reduced form of account may be used. The account is the standard form IHT 200, but only the following details need to be completed:

Page 1 in full;

Page 2. Answer all questions, but it may not be necessary to fill in every supplementary page. If the answer to any of the questions D1 – D6 or D15 is 'Yes', the relevant supplementary page must be completed, though where an asset passes to an exempt beneficiary, an estimated value may be included;

Pages 3–5. Fill in the appropriate boxes for the various assets and liabilities, Again, where an asset is passing to an exempt beneficiary, an estimate may be included;

Pages 6–7. There should not be any tax to pay, but form IHT[WS] should be completed to be sure the taxable value of the estate as a whole does not exceed the threshold. Copy the figures from IHT[WS] to these pages;

Page 8. Complete in full, but do not include items with an estimated value that pass to exempt beneficiaries.

8.61

The reference in this paragraph in the main work should refer to paragraph 8.75 and not 8.875.

Reliefs

Variations: changes in the distribution of the estate on death

INSTRUMENTS OF VARIATION

8.101

With effect from 1 August 2002, whilst there is no longer a need for a formal election to be submitted to the Board of Inland Revenue, the Instrument of Variation must incorporate a statement of intent if the relevant persons want section 142 of the Inheritance Tax Act 1984 to apply to the variation. Additionally, the Instrument of Variation does not have to be referred to the IR Capital Taxes if there is no increase in tax payable as a result of the variation. A new section 218A of the Inheritance Tax Act 1984 places a statutory obligation on the relevant persons to submit the Instrument of Variation to IR Capital Taxes if the variation results in additional tax being payable. An addition to section 245A of the same Act provides for a penalty of up to £100 to be charged if an Instrument of Variation which results in additional tax being payable is not sent to IR Capital Taxes with six months.

8.128

The reference to the 'previous paragraph' in the penultimate line in the main work should refer to para 8.126.

ASSESSMENT, PAYMENT AND DELIVERY

Assessment

8.130

The interest rate of 4% per annum with effect from 6 May 2001 remained appropriate until 5 November 2001. From 6 November 2001 until 5 August 2003, the rate of interest was 3% per annum, effected by a Board's Order dated 19 October 2001. From 6 August 2003 until 5 December 2003, the rate of interest was 2% per annum, effected by a Board's Order dated 21 July 2003. From 6 December 2003 until 5 September 2004, the rate of interest was 3% per annum, effected by a Board's Order dated 17 November 2003. From 6 September 2004, the rate of interest is 4% per annum, effected by a Board's Order dated 10 August 2004. These adjustments were made in accordance with section 178[1] of the Finance Act 1989.

Payment of Tax

8.133

Under a scheme effective from 31 March 2003, a new means is available to the taxpayer to discharge Inheritance Tax from the deceased's Bank or Building Society account directly to the Inland Revenue immediately prior to a Grant of Representation being applied for, providing there are sufficient funds in the account[s]. Taxpayers wishing to use this scheme should contact the IR Capital Taxes to obtain a reference number, either by telephone to the Capital Taxes Helpline on 0845 3020 900, or by completing form D21 which is a new supplementary page to the Inland Revenue Account. Form D21 indicates which office to use and should be submitted to that Capital Taxes office at least two weeks before expected date of submission of the IHT 200. When the form IHT 200 has been completed and the amount of tax that must be paid before the application for a Grant of representation has been calculated, form D20 should be fully completed, including the Capital Taxes reference number, and sent to the Bank or Building Society that will be making the transfer of funds. Form IHT 200, the relevant supplementary pages, form D18 and any other supporting documents should be sent to the appropriate Capital Taxes office at the same time. The Bank or Building Society will transfer the relevant amount directly to the Inland Revenue and, once notification of payment has been received, details will be linked to the IHT 200 and, provided all is in order, the form D18 will be stamped and returned. The whole process may take slightly longer than payment by cheque, and some Banks or Building Societies may charge a fee for the service. It is therefore recommended that early contact be made with the appropriate institution to establish their requirements and to identify the Personal Representatives. Form D20 [Notes] provides further details.

Trust corporations

9.06

Insert: 'now the European Union' after 'European Economic Community'

In the penultimate sentence insert '(now the European Union)'.

Settled land grants

No new material is incorporated in this supplement.

CHAPTER 11

Limited grants

WILL LOST OR NOT AVAILABLE

Proof of will as contained in copy or draft

11.12

Substitute 'a probate claim' for 'an action' at the end of this paragraph.

GRANTS TO ATTORNEYS AND CONSULAR OFFICERS

Execution of power

11.44

Stamp Duty Land Tax which was introduced by the Finance Act 2003 with effect from 1 December 2003 replaces stamp duty. The effect of the new regime removes any need for stamp duty to be paid on a power of attorney for the purpose of obtaining a grant of representation.

Joint grant to attorneys separately appointed

11.89

Current practice when attorneys separately appointed apply for a joint grant is to limit the grant for the use and benefit of the named donor executors until further representation be granted.

11.97

See noter to para 11.89.

11.98

Substitute '11.83' for '11.8283' at the end of the last line.

GRANTS FOR USE OF MINORS

Parents, persons, guardians and local authority entitled in priority

11.149

See noter-up to para 11.156 as to the acquisition of parental responsibility by a father of a minor who was not married to the minor's mother at the death of his birth.

Grant to parents (including adoptive parents)

11.156

Section 4 of the Children Act 1989 was amended by s 111 of the Adoption and Children Act 2002 with effect from 1 December 2003 and is now as follows:

4(1) Where a child's father and mother were not married to each other at the time of his birth, the father shall acquire parental responsibility for the child if-
(a) he becomes registered as the child's father under any of the enactments specified in subsection (1A);
(b) he and the child's mother make an agreement (a 'parental responsibility agreement') providing for him to have parental responsibility for the child; or
(c) the court, on his application, orders that he shall have parental responsibility for the child.

(1A) The enactments referred to in subsection (1)(a) are –
(a) paragraphs (a), (b) and (c) of section 10(1) and of section 10A(1) of the Births and Deaths Registration Act 1953;
(b) paragraphs (a), (b)(i) and (c) of section 18(1), and sections 18(2)(b) and 20(1)(a) of the Registration of Births, Deaths and Marriages (Scotland) Act 1965; and
(c) sub-paragraphs (a), (b) and (c) of Article 14(3)of the Births and Deaths Registration (Northern Ireland) Order 1976.

(1B) The Lord Chancellor may by order amend subsection (1A) so as to add further enactments to the list in that subsection.

(2) [*Unchanged*]

(2A)A person who has acquired parental responsibility under subsection (1) shall cease to have parental responsibility only if the court so orders.

(3)The court may make an order under subsection (2A) on the application-
(a) of any person who has parental responsibility for the child; or
(b) with the leave of the court, of the child himself;

subject, in the case of parental responsibility acquired under subsection (1)(c) to section 12(4).

11.56A

Consequently s 2(2)(b) of the Children Act 1989 is amended so that where a child's father and mother were not married to each other at the time of his birth the father shall have parental responsibility parental responsibility for the child if he has acquired it (and not ceased to have it) in accordance with the provisions of the Act as amended. The effect of these changes is that such father may acquire parental responsibility in one of the three ways mentioned in s 4(1) as amended and on an application for a grant for the use and benefit of the child he must confirm in the oath that he is 'the father of the minor and has acquired parental responsibility for him/her under s2(2)(b) of the Children Act 1989 (as amended) and the parental responsibility is subsisting.' A copy of the document, that is the certified entry of birth or re-registration, court order or registered parental responsibility agreement should be submitted with the application. See noter-up Form 121 in Appendix VI of this supplement.

Persons in whose favour a residence order has been made

11.161

Substitute for this paragraph 'Section 12(2) of the Children Act 1989 provides that where the court make a residence order in respect of a minor in favour of any person who is not a parent or guardian of the minor that person shall parental responsibility for the minor while the order remains in force. CA 1989, s 8 defines 'residence order' as an order settling the arrangements to be made as to the person with whom the child is to live.

Oath and supporting evidence

11.163

See noter-up Form 121 in Appendix VI.

11.183

See noter-up Form Nos 121.

After para 11.323 amend head note to:

ADMINISTRATION PENDING DETERMINATION OF PROBATE CLAIM

and

Grants 'determination of probate claim'

Order required

11.325

Substitute:

'determination of probate claim' for 'suit'.

Issue of grant

11.327

Substitute:

'determination of probate claim' for 'suit' in the first line.

Fees and tax

11.328

The fee for the grant is payable in full, as is also inheritance or capital transfer tax (if any), in respect of all the property of which the deceased was competent to dispose[1].

1   *Re Grimthorpe's Goods, Beal v Grimthorpe* (1905) Times, 8 August (referred to in para **8.17**) where the pending suit grant was limited as to the property to be dealt with.

Subsequent application for full grant

11.329

As the grant of administration pending determination of the probate claim ceases on the determination of the claim, and not upon the extraction of a grant in substitution, the full grant of probate of the will, or letters of administration, as the case may be, following the limited grant, is not regarded as a cessate grant.

11.330

The value of the whole estate is sworn to in the oath, and all the estate is again disclosed in the Inland Revenue account, if required: see Ch 8.

Practice

11.331

Substitute:

'claim' for 'action' in the first line and 'pending determination of probate claim' for 'suit' in the third line.

11.332

The Inland Revenue account for the full grant should be submitted to IR Capital Taxes before lodgment at the registry, with a request for the transfer of the receipt for the tax (if any) paid on the application for the limited grant. A fee of £50 is payable for the grant if the assessed value exceeds £5,000[1].

1   Non-Contentious Probate Fees Order1999, Fee 1.

11.333

Application for the full grant may be made at the Principal Registry or at any district probate registry.

11.337

Substitute 'a claim' for 'an claim' in the first line.

11.348

For form of Inland Revenue account (if required), see noter-up to Ch 8.

CHAPTER 12

Grant where deceased died domiciled out of England and Wales

SECTION II. ENTITLEMENT TO A GRANT WHERE DECEASED DIED DOMICILED OUT OF ENGLAND AND WALES

Grant to, or on behalf of, executor where will is in English or Welsh language

12.83

Unless the estate falls with the concept of an 'excepted estate' as provided for in the Inheritance Tax (Delivery of Accounts)(Excepted Estates) Regulations 2002 as replaced by the Inheritance Tax (Delivery of Accounts) (Excepted Estates) Regulations 2004 and except where the deceased was domiciled in Scotland, an Inland Revenue account must be submitted to IR Capital Taxes before the papers are lodged at the probate registry. The grant will cover the estate in England and Wales only. In other respects the procedure is the same as in the case of a grant to an executor, or the attorney of an executor, of a person dying domiciled in England and Wales (see Chs 4 and 11and noter-up to Ch 8).

12.122

Substitute for this paragraph:

The papers required are the same as if the deceased had died domiciled in England and Wales (see Chs 4, 5 or 6) apart from procedure governing the Inland Revenue account. Where the deceased died domiciled outside the United Kingdom an Inland Revenue account must be submitted to the IR Capital Taxes before probate papers are submitted unless this is dispensed with by the application of the Inheritance Tax (Delivery of Accounts)(Excepted Estates) Regulations 2002 as extended by the Inheritance Tax (Delivery of Accounts)(Excepted Estates) Regulations 2004. Form D18 endorsed by that Office must be lodged with the papers at the registry. Where the deceased died on or after 6 April 2002 and the estate falls within the definition of an 'excepted estate' Form IHT 207 must be submitted with the probate papers. (See noter-up to Ch 8).

Inland Revenue account

12.150

See noter-up to para 12.122 and Ch 8.

12.153

The addresses and telephone numbers of the IR Capital Taxes concerned with the above procedures are as follows:

1.	In England and Wales	IR Capital Taxes	
		Ferrers House	tel 0115 9740000
		POBox 38,	fax 0115 9742432
		Castle Meadow Road,	DX 701201
		Nottingham	Nottingham 4
		NG2 1BB	
2.	In Scotland	16 Picardy Place,	tel 0131 556 8511
		Edinburgh EH1 3NB	
3.	Northern Ireland	Dorchester House,	tel 01232 236633
		52/58 Great Victoria Street,	
		Belfast BT2 7BB	

Chapter 13

Grants 'de bonis non'—Cessate grants—Double probate

PRACTICE IN GRANTS 'DE BONIS NON'

Where granted

13.64

Add to para:

If the widow being entitled to the whole estate has appropriated it the oath should confirm this fact. Where the grant is required for making title only, it may be sworn that the grantee died 'without having completed the administration of the estate'.

13.65

Forms of oath, Nos 169 ff.

Amount of estate

13.66

Add to para:

If the grant is required for the purpose of making title the oath should recite the value as nil (see para 13.64). The administrator will swear to administer the unadministered estate, and the amount of estate sworn to in the oath will be the value of what remains unadministered at the time.

Inland Revenue account

13.74/13.76

For the appropriate form of account, when required, for use on application for a grant de bonis non, see noter up to Ch **8**.

Papers required

13.77

Insert 'IHT 205' after 'D18' in the second line. See also noter-up to Ch 8.

Right of the court to select an administrator – 'Commorientes'

No new material is incorporated in this supplement.

Renunciation and retraction

RENUNCIATION

Form of renunciation

15.05

The effect of Stamp Duty Land Tax introduced by the Finance Act 2003 with effect from 1 December 2003 is that a renunciation under seal is no longer liable for stamp duty.

CHAPTER 16

Amendment and notation of grants

No new material is incorporated in this supplement.

CHAPTER 17

Revocation and impounding of grants

No new material is incorporated in this supplement.

CHAPTER 18

Resealing

COLONIAL GRANTS RESEALED IN ENGLAND AND WALES

Inland Revenue account

18.40

Insert at the end of this paragraph:

Notwithstanding NCPR 39(2) the Inheritance Tax (Delivery of Accounts)(Excepted Estates) Regulations 2002 the concept of 'excepted estates' has been extended in respect of persons who die domiciled outside England and Wales on and after 6 April 2002. Accordingly where these regulations as replaced by the Inheritance Tax (Delivery of Accounts) (Excepted Estates) Regulations 2004 apply Form IHT207 should be submitted with the colonial grant. (See also noter-up to Ch 8).

18.42

As to the practice in relation to Inland Revenue accounts, see noter-up to Ch 8.

Domicile

18.44

Insert after 'Inland Revenue account' in the third line '(Form D18/IHT 207)'.

Documents required

18.70

In sub-para (d) insert after 'Form D18' in the first line 'or Form IHT207' and amend the sentence which follows: Unless the estate is an excepted estate the account itself should be submitted to IR Capital Taxes for control before the papers are lodged at the registry.

Inventory and account

No new material is incorporated in this supplement.

Deposit and registration of wills of living persons

No new material is incorporated in this supplement.

CHAPTER 21

Searches and copies—Exemplifications—Duplicate grants

SEARCHES AND COPIES

Wills proved since 11 January 1858

Searches and copies

21.04

In footnote 3 delete 'see Appendix I to this supplement'.

21.08

Insert after 'address' in the third line 'including postcode'.

Standing search for grant of representation

Fees for searches and copies

21.29

In Fee No 8(a) delete the minus symbol which precedes '£5'

Production of original will for inspection and examination

21.34

Substitute 'claim' for 'action' in the fifth line.

Chapter 22

Affidavits, affirmations and statutory declarations

RULES

22.05

Add to this paragraph:

The Review of Probate Business published in April 2004 accepted the recommendation that signed statements should take the place of sworn oaths so as to bring non-contentious probate procedures into line with other civil jurisdictions. Accordingly when the Non-Contentious Probate Rules are revised signed statements will take the place of sworn oaths and affidavits.

22.09

Add to the end of this paragraph:

Similarly when the deponent is a non-English or Welsh speaker the jurat should confirm that the contents of the oath or affidavit were translated in his/her presence by an interpreter previously sworn and that the deponent appeared perfectly to understand the contents.

JURATS

Forms

22.20A

Non-English/Welsh speaker

Sworn at   [*in the county of*   ] on the   day of   20 , through the interpretation of   , of   he/she first being sworn that he/she had truly and faithfully interpreted the contents of this oath/affidavit and that he would truly and faithfully interpret the oath to be administered to [*the deponent*].

Caveats

ENTRY OF CAVEAT

Commencement of probate claim

23.16

In the fourth line substitute 'determination of probate claim' for 'suit'.

Form of caveat

23.20

Insert after the penultimate sentence:

A caveat signed in the name of the solicitor's or practitioner's firm will not be accepted.

Citations

24.70

Substitute at the end of this paragraph '25.234' for '25.232'.

Applications to district judge, registrar or High Court judge (Non-contentious business)

25.03

Note: The Non-Contentious Probate Rules 1987 have been further amended by the Non-Contentious Probate (Amendment) 2003 (SI 2003 No 185(L.3)) so as to apply Parts 43,44 (except rules 44.9-44.12), 47 and 48 of the Civil Procedure Rules 1998 to non-contentious probate and replace the procedure for taxation of costs. Accordingly a district judge or registrar may make a summary assessment of costs order or conduct detailed a assessment of costs where he or she has made the order. The Rules as amended are reproduced in Appendix II to this supplement.

25.09

Insert 'the' before 'probate department manager' in the third line.

APPLICATIONS WITHOUT NOTICE

25.223

Add to the end of this paragraph:

(see para 25.238 as to the effect of the Human Rights Act 1998 on hearings).

25.237

Summonses to a High Court judge are now heard in private or public at the Royal Courts of Justice. See para 25.238 as to the effect of the Human Rights Act 1998 on court hearings.

25.240

Delete 'in chambers' where it appears in the second and third line.

25.243

Add to the end of this paragraph:

(but see para 25.238 concerning the effect of the Human Rights Act 1998 on hearings in public).

Orders

25.245

At the end of this paragraph replace 'applicant' with 'parties to the summons.

25.248

Substitute 'public' for 'open court' in the fifth and seventh lines.

PART II

Contentious Business

Chapters 26-33

No new material is incorporated in this supplement.

Chapter 34

Defence and counterclaim

34.29

Add: *Tchilingairan v Ouzounian* [2003] WTLR 709.

34.31

For an application of *Parker v Felgate* (1883) 8 PD 171, see —*Clancy v Clancy* [2003] WTLR 1097.

For an example of failure to establish capacity, see *Brown v Deacy* [2002] WTLR 781.

34.50

Add at end:

Although any suspicion aroused by the circumstances of execution or contents of a will would vary from case to case, there is no basis for imposing a burden of dispelling it beyond all reasonable doubt. The question is not whether the court approves of the circumstances in which the will was executed, but whether it is satisfied that it truly represents the testator's testamentary intentions (*Fuller v Strom* [2002] 1 WLR 1097). For a case where suspicious circumstances existed but the burden of proof was discharged, see *Re Good decd, Carapeto v Good* [2002] WTLR 801.

34.70

Re Dickson [1984] LS Gaz R 3012 C.A. is now also reported at [2002] WTLR 1395.

Chapters 35-37

No new material is incorporated in this supplement.

CHAPTER 38

Interim applications

38.08

In the second paragraph for 'if an order proving' substitute 'if an order pronouncing'. In third paragraph, sub-para (a), for 'he insists that he will' substitute 'he insists that the will'.

CHAPTER 39

Trial

39.13

Reference to paragraph 4.128 should be to paragraph 4.178.

CHAPTER 40

Costs

40.16

Add at end of Note 1:

The principles of *Spiers v English* [1907] P 122 were applied in *Carapeto v Good & Ors (Costs)* [2002] WTLR 1305. As the circumstances were suspicious but undue influence was ultimately not proved, the defendant, who had alleged undue influence, was ordered to pay half of the claimant's costs on the standard basis.

CHAPTER 41

Associated actions

41.03

Note 3 – Substitute CPR 57.15(1)

Procedure in the High Court and county court is now governed by CPR Part 57.14 – 57.16.

Add at end:

A condition in a will will only be struck down if it is truly repugnant to or inconsistent with the nature of the gifts made in the will. A provision in a will that a beneficiary will forfeit a legacy or interest if he applies under the Inheritance (Provision for Family and Dependants) Act 1975 is not void as a claim will still be before the court which can take into account the forfeiture of his interest (*Nathan v Leonard* [2003] 1 WLR 827).

41.04

Substitute notes below for existing notes:

1   CPR 57.16(1).
2   CPR 57.16(1).
3   Chancery Guide Ch. 2 para 2.3.
4   CPR 19.2.
5   CPR 19.7.
6   CPR Part 57 PD 17.
7   *Re McBroom* [1992] 2 FLR 49. [1992] Fam. Law 376.

41.05

Delete first sentence and substitute:

The written evidence filed and served by the claimant with the claim form must have exhibited to it an official copy of the grant of probate or letters of administration to the deceased's estate and every testamentary document in respect of which probate or letters of administration were granted (CPR 57.16(3)). Instead of a witness statement or affidavit the claimant may rely on the matters set out in the claim form if verified by a statement of truth. (CPR 8.5(1)).

At the end of first paragraph after 'or affidavit in answer' insert:

Where a defendant who is a personal representative wishes to remain neutral in relation to the claim, and agrees to abide by any decision which the court may make, he should state this in Section A of the acknowledgement of service form (CPR Part 57 PD 15).

In second paragraph, first line, after 'the affidavit' insert 'or witness statement'.

Omit paragraph beginning 'Every defendant who lodges a witness statement ...' and substitute:

A defendant who wishes to rely on written evidence must file it when he files his acknowledgement of services (CPR 8.5(3)) and if he does so he must also at the same time serve a copy of his evidence on the other parties (CPR 8.5(4)). The time within which a defendant must file and serve an acknowledgement of service and any written evidence is not more than 21 days after service of the claim form on him (CPR 57.16(4)).

41.08

Substitute following:

On the hearing of a claim the personal representatives must produce to the court the original grant of representation to the deceased's estate (CPR Part 57 PD 18.1). If the court makes an order under the Act, the original grant (together with a sealed copy of the order) must be sent to the Principal Registry of the Family Division for a memorandum of the order to be endorsed on or permanently annexed to the grant in accordance with section 19(3) of the Act (CPR Part 57 PD 18.2). The memorandum is endorsed in all cases after trial or settlement (Chancery Guide Ch. 9 para 9.14).

Appendices

Statutes

A1.1

CHILDREN ACT 1989

2 Parental responsibility for children

(1)   Where a child's father and mother were married to each other at the time of his birth, they shall each have parental responsibility for the child.

(2)   Where a child's father and mother were not married to each other at the time of his birth—
  (a)   the mother shall have parental responsibility for the child;
  (b)   the father [shall have parental responsibility for the child if he has acquired it (and has not ceased to have it)] in accordance with the provisions of this Act.

(3)   References in this Act to a child whose father and mother were, or (as the case may be) were not, married to each other at the time of his birth must be read with section 1 of the Family Law Reform Act 1987 (which extends their meaning).

(4)   The rule of law that a father is the natural guardian of his legitimate child is abolished.

(5)   More than one person may have parental responsibility for the same child at the same time.

(6)   A person who has parental responsibility for a child at any time shall not cease to have that responsibility solely because some other person subsequently acquires parental responsibility for the child.

(7)   Where more than one person has parental responsibility for a child, each of them may act alone and without the other (or others) in meeting that responsibility; but nothing in this Part shall be taken to affect the operation of any enactment which requires the consent of more than one person in a matter affecting the child.

(8)   The fact that a person has parental responsibility for a child shall not entitle him to act in any way which would be incompatible with any order made with respect to the child under this Act.

(9)   A person who has parental responsibility for a child may not surrender or transfer any part of that responsibility to another but may arrange for some or all of it to be met by one or more persons acting on his behalf.

(10)   The person with whom any such arrangement is made may himself be a person who already has parental responsibility for the child concerned.

(11)   The making of any such arrangement shall not affect any liability of the person making it which may arise from any failure to meet any part of his parental responsibility for the child concerned.

4 Acquisition of parental responsibility by father

(1)   Where a child's father and mother were not married to each other at the time of his birth([, the father shall acquire parental responsibility for the child if—
   (a) he becomes registered as the child's father under any of the enactments specified in subsection (1A);
   (b) he and the child's mother make an agreement (a "parental responsibility agreement") providing for him to have parental responsibility for the child; or4):
   (c) the court, on his application, orders that he shall have parental responsibility for the child.]

[(1A)   The enactments referred to in subsection (1)(a) are—
   (a) paragraphs (a), (b) and (c) of section 10(1) and of section 10A(1) of the Births and Deaths Registration Act 1953;
   (b) paragraphs (a), (b)(i) and (c) of section 18(1), and sections 18(2)(b) and 20(1)(a) of the Registration of Births, Deaths and Marriages (Scotland) Act 1965; and
   (c) sub-paragraphs (a), (b) and (c) of Article 14(3) of the Births and Deaths Registration (Northern Ireland) Order 1976.

(1B)   The [Secretary of State] may by order amend subsection (1A) so as to add further enactments to the list in that subsection.]

(2)   No parental responsibility agreement shall have effect for the purposes of this Act unless—
   (a) it is made in the form prescribed by regulations made by the Lord Chancellor; and
   (b) where regulations are made by the Lord Chancellor prescribing the manner in which such agreements must be recorded, it is recorded in the prescribed manner.

[(2A)   A person who has acquired parental responsibility under subsection (1) shall cease to have that responsibility only if the court so orders.

(3)   The court may make an order under subsection (2A) on the application—
   (a) of any person who has parental responsibility for the child; or
   (b) with the leave of the court, of the child himself,
   subject, in the case of parental responsibility acquired under subsection (1)(c), to section 12(4).]

(4)   The court may only grant leave under subsection (3)(*b*) if it is satisfied that the child has sufficient understanding to make the proposed application.

Rules, Orders and Regulations

A2.1

NON-CONTENTIOUS PROBATE RULES 1987 (AS AMENDED)
(1987 NO 2024)

1 Citation and commencement

These Rules may be cited as the Non-Contentious Probate Rules 1987 and shall come into force on 1st January 1988.

2 Interpretation

(1)   In these Rules, unless the context otherwise requires—

"the Act" means the Supreme Court Act 1981;

"authorised officer" means any officer of a registry who is for the time being authorised by the President to administer any oath or to take any affidavit required for any purpose connected with his duties;

"the Crown" includes the Crown in right of the Duchy of Lancaster and the Duke of Cornwall for the time being;

["district judge" means a district judge of the Principal Registry;]

"grant" means a grant of probate or administration and includes, where the context so admits, the resealing of such a grant under the Colonial Probates Acts 1892 and 1927;

"gross value" in relation to any estate means the value of the estate without deduction for debts, incumbrances, funeral expenses or inheritance tax (or other capital tax payable out of the estate);

["judge" means a judge of the High Court;]

"oath" means the oath required by rule 8 to be sworn by every applicant for a grant;

"personal applicant" means a person other than a trust corporation who seeks to obtain a grant without employing a solicitor [or probate practitioner], and "personal application" has a corresponding meaning;

["probate practitioner" means a person to whom section 23(1) of the Solicitors Act 1974 does not apply by virtue of section 23(2) of that Act]

["registrar" means the district probate registrar of the district probate registry—

(i) to which an application for a grant is made or is proposed to be made,

(ii) in rules 26,40,41 and 61(2), from which the grant issued, and

(iii) in rules 46,47 and 48, from which the citation has issued or is proposed to be issued;]

"registry" means the Principal Registry or a district probate registry;

["the senior district judge" means the Senior District Judge of the Family Division or, in his absence, the senior of the district judges in attendance at the Principal Registry;]

< . . . >

< . . . >

"the Treasury Solicitor" means the solicitor for the affairs of Her Majesty's Treasury and includes the solicitor for the affairs of the Duchy of Lancaster and the solicitor of the Duchy of Cornwall;

"trust corporation" means a corporation within the meaning of section 128 of the Act as extended by section 3 of the Law of Property (Amendment) Act 1926.

(2)　A form referred to by number means the form so numbered in the First Schedule; and such forms shall be used wherever applicable, with such variation as a [district judge or] registrar may in any particular case direct or approve.

[3 Application of other rules]

[(1)　Subject to the provisions of these rules and to any enactment, the Rules of the Supreme Court 1965 as they were in force immediately before 26th April 1999 shall apply, with any necessary modifications to non-contentious probate matters, and any reference in these rules to those rules shall be construed accordingly.

(2)　Nothing in Order 3 of the Rules of the Supreme Court shall prevent time from running in the Long Vacation.]

4 Applications for grants through solicitors [or probate practitioners]

(1)　A person applying for a grant through a solicitor [or probate practitioner] may apply at any registry or sub-registry.

(2)　Every solicitor [or probate practitioner] through whom an application for a grant is made shall give the address of his place of business within England and Wales.

5 Personal applications

(1)　A personal applicant may apply for a grant at any registry or sub-registry.

(2)　Save as provided for by rule 39 a personal applicant may not apply through an agent, whether paid or unpaid, and may not be attended by any person acting or appearing to act as his adviser.

(3)　No personal application shall be proceeded with if—
   (a) it becomes necessary to bring the matter before the court by action or summons[, unless a judge, district judge or registrar so permits];
   (b) an application has already been made by a solicitor [or probate practitioner] on behalf of the applicant and has not been withdrawn; or
   (c) the [district judge or] registrar so directs.

(4)　After a will has been deposited in a registry by a personal applicant, it may not be delivered to the applicant or to any other person unless in special circumstances the [district judge or] registrar so directs.

(5)   A personal applicant shall produce a certificate of the death of the deceased or such other evidence of the death as the [district judge or] registrar may approve.

(6)   A personal applicant shall supply all information necessary to enable the papers leading to the grant to be prepared in the registry.

(7)   Unless the [district judge or] registrar otherwise directs, every oath or affidavit required on a personal application shall be sworn or executed by all the deponents before an authorised officer.

(8)   No legal advice shall be given to a personal applicant by an officer of a registry and every such officer shall be responsible only for embodying in proper form the applicant's instructions for the grant.

6 Duty of [district judge or] registrar on receiving application for grant

(1)   A [district judge or] registrar shall not allow any grant to issue until all inquiries which he may see fit to make have been answered to his satisfaction.

(2)   Except with the leave of a [district judge or] registrar, no grant of probate or of administration with the will annexed shall issue within seven days of the death of the deceased and no grant of administration shall issue within fourteen days thereof.

7 Grants by district probate registrars

(1)   No grant shall be made by a . . . registrar—
   (a)   in any case in which there is contention, until the contention is disposed of; or
   (b)   in any case in which it appears to him that a grant ought not to be made without the directions of a judge or a [district judge].

(2)   In any case in which paragraph (1)(b) applies, the . . . registrar shall send a statement of the matter in question to the Principal Registry for directions.

(3)   A [district judge] may either confirm that the matter be referred to a judge and give directions accordingly or may direct the . . . registrar to proceed with the matter in accordance with such instructions as are deemed necessary, which may include a direction to take no further action in relation to the matter.

8 Oath in support of grant

(1)   Every application for a grant other than one to which rule 39 applies shall be supported by an oath by the applicant in the form applicable to the circumstances of the case, and by such other papers as the [district judge or] registrar may require.

(2)   Unless otherwise directed by a [district judge or] registrar, the oath shall state where the deceased died domiciled.

(3)   Where the deceased died on or after 1st January 1926, the oath shall state whether or not, to the best of the applicant's knowledge, information and belief, there was land vested in the deceased which was settled previously to his death and not by his will and which remained settled land notwithstanding his death.

(4)   On an application for a grant of administration the oath shall state in what manner all persons having a prior right to a grant have been cleared off and whether any minority or life interest arises under the will or intestacy.

9 Grant in additional name

Where it is sought to describe the deceased in a grant by some name in addition to his true name, the applicant shall depose to the true name of the deceased and shall specify some part of the estate which was held in the other name, or give any other reason for the inclusion of the other name in the grant.

10 Marking of wills

(1)   Subject to paragraph (2) below, every will in respect of which an application for a grant is made—
  (a)   shall be marked by the signatures of the applicant and the person before whom the oath is sworn; and
  (b)   shall be exhibited to any affidavit which may be required under these Rules as to the validity, terms, condition or date of execution of the will.

(2)   The [district judge or] registrar may allow a facsimile copy of a will to be marked or exhibited in lieu of the original document.

11 Engrossments for purposes of record

(1)   Where the [district judge or] registrar considers that in any particular case a facsimile copy of the original will would not be satisfactory for purposes of record, he may require an engrossment suitable for facsimile reproduction to be lodged.

(2)   Where a will—
  (a)   contains alterations which are not to be admitted to proof; or
  (b)   has been ordered to be rectified by virtue of section 20(1) of the Administration of Justice Act 1982,

there shall be lodged an engrossment of the will in the form in which it is to be proved.

(3)   Any engrossment lodged under this rule shall reproduce the punctuation, spacing and division into paragraphs of the will and shall follow continuously from page to page on both sides of the paper.

12 Evidence as to due execution of will

(1)   Subject to paragraphs (2) and (3) below, where a will contains no attestation clause or the attestation clause is insufficient, or where it appears to the [district judge or] registrar that there is doubt about the due execution of the will, he shall before admitting it to proof require an affidavit as to due execution from one or more of the attesting witnesses or, if no attesting witness is conveniently available, from any other person who was present when the will was executed; and if the [district judge or] registrar, after considering the evidence, is satisfied the will was not duly executed, he shall refuse probate and mark the will accordingly.

(2)   If no affidavit can be obtained in accordance with paragraph (1) above, the [district judge or] registrar may accept evidence on affidavit from any person he may think fit to show that the signature on the will is in the handwriting of the deceased, or of any other matter which may raise a presumption in favour of due execution of the will, and may if he thinks fit require that notice of the application be given to any person who may be prejudiced by the will.

(3)   A [district judge or] registrar may accept a will for proof without evidence as

aforesaid if he is satisfied that the distribution of the estate is not thereby affected.

13 Execution of will of blind or illiterate testator

Before admitting to proof a will which appears to have been signed by a blind or illiterate testator or by another person by direction of the testator, or which for any other reason raises doubt as to the testator having had knowledge of the contents of the will at the time of its execution, the [district judge or] registrar shall satisfy himself that the testator had such knowledge.

14 Evidence as to terms, condition and date of execution of will

(1)   Subject to paragraph (2) below, where there appears in a will any obliteration, interlineation, or other alteration which is not authenticated in the manner prescribed by section 21 of the Wills Act 1837, or by the re-execution of the will or by the execution of a codicil, the [district judge or] registrar shall require evidence to show whether the alteration was present at the time the will was executed and shall give directions as to the form in which the will is to be proved.

(2)   The provisions of paragraph (1) above shall not apply to any alteration which appears to the [district judge or] registrar to be of no practical importance.

(3)   If a will contains any reference to another document in such terms as to suggest that it ought to be incorporated in the will, the [district judge or] registrar shall require the document to be produced and may call for such evidence in regard to the incorporation of the document as he may think fit.

(4)   Where there is a doubt as to the date on which a will was executed, the [district judge or] registrar may require such evidence as he thinks necessary to establish the date.

15 Attempted revocation of will

Any appearance of attempted revocation of a will by burning, tearing, or otherwise destroying and every other circumstance leading to a presumption of revocation by the testator, shall be accounted for to the [district judge's or] registrar's satisfaction.

16 Affidavit as to due execution, terms etc, of will

A [district judge or] registrar may require an affidavit from any person he may think fit for the purpose of satisfying himself as to any of the matters referred to in rules 13, 14 and 15, and in any such affidavit sworn by an attesting witness or other person present at the time of the execution of a will the deponent shall depose to the manner in which the will was executed.

17 Wills proved otherwise than under section 9 of the Wills Act 1837

(1)   Rules 12 to 15 shall apply only to a will that is to be established by reference to section 9 of the Wills Act 1837 (signing and attestation of wills).<[:

(2)   A will that is to be established otherwise than as described in paragraph (1) of this rule may be so established upon the [district judge or] registrar being satisfied as to its terms and validity, and includes (without prejudice to the generality of the foregoing)—
    (a)   any will to which rule 18 applies; and

    (b) any will which, by virtue of the Wills Act 1963, is to be treated as properly executed if executed according to the internal law of the territory or state referred to in section 1 of that Act.

18 Wills of persons on military service and seamen

Where the deceased died domiciled in England and Wales and it appears to the [district judge or] registrar that there is prima facie evidence that a will is one to which section 11 of the Wills Act 1837 applies, the will may be admitted to proof if the registrar is satisfied that it was signed by the testator or, if unsigned, that it is in the testator's handwriting.

19 Evidence of foreign law

Where evidence as to the law of any country or territory outside England and Wales is required on any application for a grant, the [district judge or] registrar may accept—
    (a) an affidavit from any person whom, having regard to the particulars of his knowledge or experience given in the affidavit, he regards as suitably qualified to give expert evidence of the law in question; or
    (b) a certificate by, or an act before, a notary practising in the country or territory concerned.

20 Order of priority for grant where deceased left a will

Where the deceased died on or after 1 January 1926 the person or persons entitled to a grant in respect of a will shall be determined in accordance with the following order of priority, namely—
    (a) the executor (but subject to rule 36(4)(d) below);
    (b) any residuary legatee or devisee holding in trust for any other person;
    (c) any other residuary legatee or devisee (including one for life) or where the residue is not wholly disposed of by the will, any person entitled to share in the undisposed of residue (including the Treasury Solicitor when claiming bona vacantia on behalf of the Crown), provided that—
        (i) unless a [district judge or] registrar otherwise directs, a residuary legatee or devisee whose legacy or devise is vested in interest shall be preferred to one entitled on the happening of a contingency, and
        (ii) where the residue is not in terms wholly disposed of, the [district judge or] registrar may, if he is satisfied that the testator has nevertheless disposed of the whole or substantially the whole of the known estate, allow a grant to be made to any legatee or devisee entitled to, or to share in, the estate so disposed of, without regard to the persons entitled to share in any residue not disposed of by the will;
    (d) the personal representative of any residuary legatee or devisee (but not one for life, or one holding in trust for any other person), or of any person entitled to share in any residue not disposed of by the will;
    (e) any other legatee or devisee (including one for life or one holding in trust for any other person) or any creditor of the deceased, provided that, unless a [district judge or] registrar otherwise directs, a legatee or devisee whose legacy or devise is vested in interest shall be preferred to one entitled on the happening of a contingency;
    (f) the personal representative of any other legatee or devisee (but not one for life or one holding in trust for any other person) or of any creditor of the deceased.

21 Grants to attesting witnesses, etc

Where a gift to any person fails by reason of section 15 of the Wills Act 1837, such person shall not have any right to a grant as a beneficiary named in the will, without prejudice to his right to a grant in any other capacity.

22 Order of priority for grant in case of intestacy

(1)   Where the deceased died on or after 1 January 1926, wholly intestate, the person or persons having a beneficial interest in the estate shall be entitled to a grant of administration in the following classes in order of priority, namely—
  (a)   the surviving husband or wife;
  (b)   the children of the deceased and the issue of any deceased child who died before the deceased;
  (c)   the father and mother of the deceased;
  (d)   brothers and sisters of the whole blood and the issue of any deceased brother or sister of the whole blood who died before the deceased;
  (e)   brothers and sisters of the half blood and the issue of any deceased brother or sister of the half blood who died before the deceased;
  (f)   grandparents;
  (g)   uncles and aunts of the whole blood and the issue of any deceased uncle or aunt of the whole blood who died before the deceased;
  (h)   uncles and aunts of the half blood and the issue of any deceased uncle or aunt of the half blood who died before the deceased.

(2)   In default of any person having a beneficial interest in the estate, the Treasury Solicitor shall be entitled to a grant if he claims bona vacantia on behalf of the Crown.

(3)   If all persons entitled to a grant under the foregoing provisions of this rule have been cleared off, a grant may be made to a creditor of the deceased or to any person who, notwithstanding that he has no immediate beneficial interest in the estate, may have a beneficial interest in the event of an accretion thereto.

(4)   Subject to paragraph (5) of rule 27, the personal representative of a person in any of the classes mentioned in paragraph (1) of this rule or the personal representative of a creditor of the deceased shall have the same right to a grant as the person whom he represents provided that the persons mentioned in sub-paragraphs (b) to (h) of paragraph (1) above shall be preferred to the personal representative of a spouse who has died without taking a beneficial interest in the whole estate of the deceased as ascertained at the time of the application for the grant.

23 Order of priority for grant in pre-1926 cases

Where the deceased died before 1st January 1926, the person or persons entitled to a grant shall, subject to the provisions of any enactment, be determined in accordance with the principles and rules under which the court would have acted at the date of death.

24 Right of assignee to a grant

(1)   Where all the persons entitled to the estate of the deceased (whether under a will or on intestacy) have assigned their whole interest in the estate to one or more persons, the assignee or assignees shall replace, in the order of priority for a grant of administration, the assignor or, if there are two or more assignors, the assignor with the highest priority.

(2)   Where there are two or more assignees, administration may be granted with the consent of the others to any one or more (not exceeding four) of them.

(3)   In any case where administration is applied for by an assignee the original instrument of assignment shall be produced and a copy of the same lodged in the registry.

25 Joinder of administrator

(1)   A person entitled in priority to a grant of administration may, without leave, apply for a grant with a person entitled in a lower degree, provided that there is no other person entitled in a higher degree to the person to be joined, unless every other such person has renounced.

(2)   Subject to paragraph (3) below, an application for leave to join with a person entitled in priority to a grant of administration a person having no right or no immediate right thereto shall be made to a [district judge or] registrar, and shall be supported by an affidavit by the person entitled in priority, the consent of the person proposed to be joined as administrator and such other evidence as the [district judge or] registrar may direct.

(3)   Unless a [district judge or] registrar otherwise directs, there may without any such application be joined with a person entitled in priority to administration—
   (a)   any person who is nominated under paragraph (3) of rule 32 or paragraph (3) of rule 35;
   (b)   a trust corporation.

26 Additional personal representatives

(1)   An application under section 114(4) of the Act to add a personal representative shall be made to a [district judge or] registrar and shall be supported by an affidavit by the applicant, the consent of the person proposed to be added as personal representative and such other evidence as the [district judge or] registrar may require.

(2)   On any such application the [district judge or] registrar may direct that a note shall be made on the original grant of the addition of a further personal representative, or he may impound or revoke the grant or make such other order as the circumstances of the case may require.

27 Grants where two or more persons entitled in same degree

[(1)   Subject to paragraphs (1A), (2) and (3) below, where, on an application for probate, power to apply for a like grant is to be reserved to such other of the executors as have not renounced probate, notice of the application shall be given to the executor or executors to whom power is to be reserved; and, unless the district judge or registrar otherwise directs, the oath shall state that such notice has been given.

(1A)   Where power is to be reserved to executors who are . . . partners in a firm, . . . notice need not be given to them under paragraph (1) above if probate is applied for by another partner in that firm.]

(2)   Where power is to be reserved to partners of a firm, notice for the purposes of paragraph (1) above may be given to the partners by sending it to the firm at its principal or last known place of business.

(3)   A [district judge or] registrar may dispense with the giving of notice under

paragraph (1) above if he is satisfied that the giving of such a notice is impracticable or would result in unreasonable delay or expense.

(4)   A grant of administration may be made to any person entitled thereto without notice to other persons entitled in the same degree.

(5)   Unless a [district judge or] registrar otherwise directs, administration shall be granted to a person of full age entitled thereto in preference to a guardian of a minor, and to a living person entitled thereto in preference to the personal representative of a deceased person.

(6)   A dispute between persons entitled to a grant in the same degree shall be brought by summons before a [district judge or] registrar.

[(7)   The issue of a summons under this rule in a registry shall be noted forthwith in the index of pending grant applications.]

(8)   If the issue of a summons under this rule is known to the [district judge or] registrar, he shall not allow any grant to be sealed until such summons is finally disposed of.

28 Exceptions to rules as to priority

(1)   Any person to whom a grant may or is required to be made under any enactment shall not be prevented from obtaining such a grant notwithstanding the operation of rules 20, 22, 25 or 27.

(2)   Where the deceased died domiciled outside England and Wales rules 20, 22, 25 or 27 shall not apply except in a case to which paragraph (3) of rule 30 applies.

[29 Grants in respect of settled land]

[(1)   In this rule "settled land" means land vested in the deceased which was settled prior to his death and not by his will, and which remained settled land notwithstanding his death.pr:

(2)   The person or persons entitled to a grant of administration limited to settled land shall be determined in accordance with the following order of priority:
  (i)   the special executors in regard to settled land constituted by section 22 of the Administration of Estates Act 1925;
  (ii)   the trustees of the settlement at the time of the application for the grant; and
  (iii)   the personal representatives of the deceased.

(3)   Where there is settled land and a grant is made in respect of the free estate only, the grant shall expressly exclude the settled land.]

30 Grants where deceased died domiciled outside England and Wales

(1)   Subject to paragraph (3) below, where the deceased died domiciled outside England and Wales, [a district judge or registrar may order that a grant, limited in such way as the district judge or registrar may direct,] do issue to any of the following persons—
  (a)   to the person entrusted with the administration of the estate by the court having jurisdiction at the place where the deceased died domiciled; or
  (b)   where there is no person so entrusted, to the person beneficially entitled to the estate by the law of the place where the deceased died domiciled or, if there is

more than one person so entitled, to such of them as the [district judge or] registrar may direct; or

(c) if in the opinion of the [district judge or] registrar the circumstances so require, to such person as the [district judge or] registrar may direct.

(2)   A grant made under paragraph (1)(a) or (b) above may be issued jointly with such person as the [district judge or] registrar may direct if the grant is required to be made to not less than two administrators.

(3)   Without any order made under paragraph (1) above—

(a) probate of any will which is admissible to proof may be granted—

(i) if the will is in the English or Welsh language, to the executor named therein; or

(ii) if the will describes the duties of a named person in terms sufficient to constitute him executor according to the tenor of the will, to that person; or

(b) where the whole or substantially the whole of the estate in England and Wales consists of immovable property, a grant in respect of the whole estate may be made in accordance with the law which would have been applicable if the deceased had died domiciled in England and Wales.

31 Grants to attorneys

(1)   Subject to paragraphs (2) and (3) below, the lawfully constituted attorney of a person entitled to a grant may apply for administration for the use and benefit of the donor, and such grant shall be limited until further representation be granted, or in such other way as the [district judge or] registrar may direct.

(2)   Where the donor referred to in paragraph (1) above is an executor, notice of the application shall be given to any other executor unless such notice is dispensed with by the [district judge or] registrar.

(3)   Where the donor referred to in paragraph (1) above is mentally incapable and the attorney is acting under an enduring power of attorney, the application shall be made in accordance with rule 35.

32 Grants on behalf of minors

(1)   Where a person to whom a grant would otherwise be made is a minor, administration for his use and benefit, limited until he attains the age of eighteen years, shall, unless otherwise directed, and subject to paragraph (2) of this rule, be granted to

[(a) a parent of the minor who has, or is deemed to have, parental responsibility for him in accordance with—

(i) section 2(1), 2(2) or 4 of the Children Act 1989,

(ii) paragraph 4 or 6 of Schedule 14 to that Act, or

(iii) an adoption order within the meaning of section 12(1) of the Adoption Act 1976, or

[(aa) a person who has, or is deemed to have, parental responsibility for the minor by virtue of section 12(2) of the Children Act 1989(a) where the court has made a residence order under section 8 of that Act in respect of the minor in favour of that person; or]

(b) a guardian of the minor who is appointed, or deemed to have been appointed, in accordance with section 5 of the Children Act 1989 or in accordance with paragraph 12, 13 or 14 of Schedule 14 to that Act]; [or]

[(c) a local authority which has, or is deemed to have, parental responsibility for the minor by virtue of section 33(3) of the Children Act 1989 where the court has made a care order under section 31(1)(a) of that Act in respect of the minor and that local authority is designated in that order;]

provided that where the minor is sole executor and has no interest in the residuary estate of the deceased, administration for the use and benefit of the minor limited as aforesaid, shall, unless a [district judge or] registrar otherwise directs, be granted to the person entitled to the residuary estate.

[(2)   A district judge or registrar may by order appoint a person to obtain administration for the use and benefit of the minor, limited as aforesaid, in default of, or jointly with, or to the exclusion of, any person mentioned in paragraph (1) of this rule; and the person intended shall file an affidavit in support of his application to be appointed.]

(3)   Where there is only one person competent and willing to take a grant under the foregoing provisions of this rule, such person may, unless a [district judge or] registrar otherwise directs, nominate any fit and proper person to act jointly with him in taking the grant.

33 Grants where a minor is a co-executor

(1)   Where a minor is appointed executor jointly with one or more other executors, probate may be granted to the executor or executors not under disability with power reserved to the minor executor, and the minor executor shall be entitled to apply for probate on attaining the age of eighteen years.

(2)   Administration for the use and benefit of a minor executor until he attains the age of eighteen years may be granted under rule 32 if, and only if, the executors who are not under disability renounce or, on being cited to accept or refuse a grant, fail to make an effective application therefor.

34 Renunciation of the right of a minor to a grant

(1)   The right of a minor executor to probate on attaining the age of eighteen years may not be renounced by any person on his behalf.

(2)   The right of a minor to administration may be renounced only by a person [appointed] under paragraph (2) of rule 32, and authorised by the [district judge or] registrar to renounce on behalf of the minor.

35 Grants in case of mental incapacity

(1)   Unless a [district judge or] registrar otherwise directs, no grant shall be made under this rule unless all persons entitled in the same degree as the incapable person referred to in paragraph (2) below have been cleared off.

(2)   Where a [district judge or] registrar is satisfied that a person entitled to a grant is by reason of mental incapacity incapable of managing his affairs, administration for his use and benefit, limited until further representation be granted or in such other way as the [district judge or] registrar may direct, may be granted in the following order of priority—
-    (a)   to the person authorised by the Court of Protection to apply for a grant;
-    (b)   where there is no person so authorised, to the lawful attorney of the incapable person acting under a registered enduring power of attorney;
-    (c)   where there is no such attorney entitled to act, or if the attorney shall renounce administration for the use and benefit of the incapable person, to the person entitled to the residuary estate of the deceased.

(3)   Where a grant is required to be made to not less than two administrators, and there is only one person competent and willing to take a grant under the foregoing provisions of this rule, administration may, unless a [district judge or] registrar otherwise directs, be granted to such person jointly with any other person nominated by him.

(4)   Notwithstanding the foregoing provisions of this rule, administration for the use and benefit of the incapable person may be granted to such [other person] as the [district judge or] registrar may by order direct.

(5)   [Unless the applicant is the person authorised in paragraph (2)(a) above,] Notice of an intended application under this rule shall be given to the Court of Protection.

36 Grants to trust corporations and other corporate bodies

(1)   An application for a grant to a trust corporation shall be made through one of its officers, and such officer shall depose in the oath that the corporation is a trust corporation as defined by these Rules and that it has power to accept a grant.

(2)
   (a)   Where the trust corporation is the holder of an official position, any officer whose name is included on a list filed with the [senior district judge] of persons authorised to make affidavits and sign documents on behalf of the office holder may act as the officer through whom the holder of that official position applies for the grant.
   (b)   In all other cases a certified copy of the resolution of the trust corporation authorising the officer to make the application shall be lodged, or it shall be deposed in the oath that such certified copy has been filed with the [senior district judge], that the officer is therein identified by the position he holds, and that such resolution is still in force.

(3)   A trust corporation may apply for administration otherwise than as a beneficiary or the attorney of some person, and on any such application there shall be lodged the consents of all persons entitled to a grant and of all persons interested in the residuary estate of the deceased save that the [district judge or] registrar may dispense with any such consents as aforesaid on such terms, if any, as he may think fit.

(4)
   (a)   Subject to sub-paragraph (d) below, where a corporate body would, if an individual, be entitled to a grant but is not a trust corporation as defined by these Rules, administration for its use and benefit, limited until further representation be granted, may be made to its nominee or to its lawfully constituted attorney.
   (b)   A copy of the resolution appointing the nominee or the power of attorney (whichever is appropriate) shall be lodged, and such resolution or power of attorney shall be sealed by the corporate body, or be otherwise authenticated to the [district judge's or] registrar's satisfaction.
   (c)   The nominee or attorney shall depose in the oath that the corporate body is not a trust corporation as defined by these Rules.
   (d)   The provisions of paragraph (4)(a) above shall not apply where a corporate body is appointed executor jointly with an individual unless the right of the individual has been cleared off.

37 Renunciation of probate and administration

(1)   Renunciation of probate by an executor shall not operate as renunciation of any

right which he may have to a grant of administration in some other capacity unless he expressly renounces such right.

(2) Unless a [district judge or] registrar otherwise directs, no person who has renounced administration in one capacity may obtain a grant thereof in some other capacity.

[(2A) Renunciation of probate or administration by members of a partnership—
   (a) may be effected, or
   (b) subject to paragraph (3) below, may be retracted by any two of them with the authority of the others and any such renunciation or retraction shall recite such authority.]

(3) A renunciation of probate or administration may be retracted at any time with the leave of a [district judge or] registrar; provided that only in exceptional circumstances may leave be given to an executor to retract a renunciation of probate after a grant has been made to some other person entitled in a lower degree.

(4) A direction or order giving leave under this rule may be made either by the registrar of a district probate registry where the renunciation is filed or by a [district judge].

38 Notice to Crown of intended application for grant

In any case in which it appears that the Crown is or may be beneficially interested in the estate of a deceased person, notice of intended application for a grant shall be given by the applicant to the Treasury Solicitor, and the [district judge or] registrar may direct that no grant shall issue within 28 days after the notice has been given.h:

39 Resealing under Colonial Probates Acts 1892 and 1927

(1) An application under the Colonial Probates Acts 1892 and 1927 for the resealing of probate or administration granted by the court of a country to which those Acts apply may be made by the person to whom the grant was made or by any person authorised in writing to apply on his behalf.

(2) On any such application an Inland Revenue affidavit or account shall be lodged.

(3) Except by leave of a [district judge or] registrar, no grant shall be resealed unless it was made to such a person as is mentioned in sub-paragraph (a) or (b) of paragraph (1) of rule 30 or to a person to whom a grant could be made under sub-paragraph (a) of paragraph (3) of that rule.

(4) No limited or temporary grant shall be resealed except by leave of a [district judge or] registrar.

(5) Every grant lodged for resealing shall include a copy of any will to which the grant relates or shall be accompanied by a copy thereof certified as correct by or under the authority of the court by which the grant was made, and where the copy of the grant required to be deposited under subsection (1) of section 2 of the Colonial Probates Act 1892 does not include a copy of the will, a copy thereof shall be deposited in the registry before the grant is resealed.

(6) The [district judge or] registrar shall send notice of the resealing to the court which made the grant.

(7) Where notice is received in the Principal Registry of the resealing of a grant issued in England and Wales, notice of any amendment or revocation of the grant shall be sent to the court by which it was resealed.

40 Application for leave to sue on guarantee

An application for leave under section 120(3) of the Act or under section 11(5) of the Administration of Estates Act 1971 to sue a surety on a guarantee given for the purposes of either of those sections shall, unless the [district judge or] registrar otherwise directs under rule 61, be made by summons to a [district judge or] registrar and notice of the application shall be served on the administrator, the surety and any co-surety.

41 Amendment and revocation of grant

(1)   Subject to paragraph (2) below, if a [district judge or] registrar is satisfied that a grant should be amended or revoked he may make an order accordingly.

(2)   Except on the application or with the consent of the person to whom the grant was made, the power conferred in paragraph (1) above shall be exercised only in exceptional circumstances.

42 Certificate of delivery of Inland Revenue affidavit

Where the deceased died before 13th March 1975 the certificate of delivery of an Inland Revenue affidavit required by section 30 of the Customs and Inland Revenue Act 1881 to be borne by every grant shall be in Form 1.

43 Standing searches

[(1)   Any person who wishes to be notified of the issue of a grant may enter a standing search for the grant by lodging at, or sending by post to any registry or sub-registry, a notice in Form 2.]

(2)   A person who has entered a standing search will be sent an office copy of any grant which corresponds with the particulars given on the completed Form 2 and which—
    (a) issued not more than twelve months before the entry of the standing search; or
    (b) issues within a period of six months after the entry of the standing search.

(3)
    (a) Where an applicant wishes to extend the said period of six months, he or his solicitor [or probate practitioner] may lodge at, or send by post to, [the registry or sub-registry at which the standing search was entered] written application for extension.r,:
    (b) An application for extension as aforesaid must be lodged, or received by post, within the last month of the said period of six months, and the standing search shall thereupon be effective for an additional period of six months from the date on which it was due to expire.
    (c) A standing search which has been extended as above may be further extended by the filing of a further application for extension subject to the same conditions as set out in sub-paragraph (b) above.

44 Caveats

(1)   Any person who wishes to show cause against the sealing of a grant may enter a caveat in any registry or sub-registry, and the [district judge or] registrar shall not allow any grant to be sealed (other than a grant ad colligenda bona or a grant under section 117 of the Act) if he has knowledge of an effective caveat; provided that no caveat shall prevent the sealing of a grant on the day on which the caveat is entered.

(2)   Any person wishing to enter a caveat (in these Rules called "the caveator"), or a solicitor [or probate practitioner] on his behalf, may effect entry of a caveat—
  (a) by completing Form 3 in the appropriate book at any registry or sub-registry; or
  (b) by sending by post at his own risk a notice in Form 3 to any registry or sub-registry and the proper officer shall provide an acknowledgement of the entry of the caveat.

(3)
  (a) Except as otherwise provided by this rule or by rules 45 or 46, a caveat shall be effective for a period of six months from the date of entry thereof, and where a caveator wishes to extend the said period of six months, he or his solicitor [or probate practitioner] may lodge at, or send by post to, the registry or sub-registry at which the caveat was entered a written application for extension.
  (b) An application for extension as aforesaid must be lodged, or received by post, within the last month of the said period of six months, and the caveat shall thereupon (save as otherwise provided by this rule) be effective for an additional period of six months from the date on which it was due to expire.
  (c) A caveat which has been extended as above may be further extended by the filing of a further application for extension subject to the same conditions as set out in sub-paragraph (b) above.

[(4)   An index of caveats entered in any registry or sub-registry shall be maintained and upon receipt of an application for a grant, the registry or sub-registry at which the application is made shall cause a search of the index to be made and the appropriate district judge or registrar shall be notified of the entry of a caveat against the sealing of a grant for which the application has been made.]

(5)   Any person claiming to have an interest in the estate may cause to be issued from the [nominated registry] a warning in Form 4 against the caveat, and the person warning shall state his interest in the estate of the deceased and shall require the caveator to give particulars of any contrary interest in the estate; and the warning or a copy thereof shall be served on the caveator forthwith.

(6)   A caveator who has no interest contrary to that of the person warning, but who wishes to show cause against the sealing of a grant to that person, may within eight days of service of the warning upon him (inclusive of the day of such service), or at any time thereafter if no affidavit has been filed under paragraph (12) below, issue and serve a summons for directions.

(7)   On the hearing of any summons for directions under paragraph (6) above the [district judge or] registrar may give a direction for the caveat to cease to have effect.

(8)   Any caveat in force when a summons for directions is issued shall remain in force until the summons has been disposed of unless a direction has been given under paragraph (7) above [or until it is withdrawn under paragraph (11) below].

(9)   The issue of a summons under this rule shall be notified forthwith to the [nominated registry].

(10)   A caveator having an interest contrary to that of the person warning may within eight days of service of the warning upon him (inclusive of the day of such service) or at any time thereafter if no affidavit has been filed under paragraph (12) below, enter an appearance in the [nominated registry] by filing Form 5 < . . . > ; and he shall serve forthwith on the person warning a copy of Form 5 sealed with the seal of the court.

(11)   A caveator who has not entered an appearance to a warning may at any time withdraw his caveat by giving notice at the registry or sub-registry at which it was entered, and the caveat shall thereupon cease to have effect; and, where the caveat has been so withdrawn, the caveator shall forthwith give notice of withdrawal to the person warning.

(12)   If no appearance has been entered by the caveator or no summons has been issued by him under paragraph (6) of this rule, the person warning may at any time after eight days of service of the warning upon the caveator (inclusive of the day of such service) file an affidavit in the [nominated registry] as to such service and the caveat shall thereupon cease to have effect provided that there is no pending summons under paragraph (6) of this rule.

(13)   Unless a [district judge or, where application to discontinue a caveat is made by consent, a registrar] by order made on summons otherwise directs, any caveat in respect of which an appearance to a warning has been entered shall remain in force until the commencement of a probate action.

(14)   Except with the leave of a [district judge], no further caveat may be entered by or on behalf of any caveator whose caveat is either in force or has ceased to have effect under paragraphs (7) or (12) of this rule or under rule 45(4) or rule 46(3).

[(15)   In this rule, "nominated registry" means the registry nominated for the purpose of this rule by the senior district judge or in the absence of any such nomination the Leeds District Probate Registry.]

45 Probate actions

(1)   Upon being advised by the court concerned of the commencement of a probate action the [senior district judge] shall give notice of the action to every caveator other than the plaintiff in the action in respect of each caveat that is in force.

(2)   In respect of any caveat entered subsequent to the commencement of a probate action the [senior district judge] shall give notice to that caveator of the existence of the action.

(3)   Unless a [district judge] by order made on summons otherwise directs, the commencement of a probate action shall operate to prevent the sealing of a grant (other than a grant under section 117 of the Act) until application for a grant is made by the person shown to be entitled thereto by the decision of the court in such action.

(4)   Upon such application for a grant, any caveat entered by the plaintiff in the action, and any caveat in respect of which notice of the action has been given, shall cease to have effect.

46 Citations

(1)   Any citation may issue from the Principal Registry or a district probate registry and shall be settled by a [district judge or] registrar before being issued.

(2)   Every averment in a citation, and such other information as the registrar may require, shall be verified by an affidavit sworn by the person issuing the citation (in these Rules called the "citor"), provided that the [district judge or] registrar may in special circumstances accept an affidavit sworn by the citor's solicitor [or probate practitioner].

(3)   The citor shall enter a caveat before issuing a citation and, unless a [district judge] by order made on summons otherwise directs, any caveat in force at the

commencement of the citation proceedings shall, unless withdrawn pursuant to paragraph (11) of rule 44, remain in force until application for a grant is made by the person shown to be entitled thereto by the decision of the court in such proceedings, and upon such application any caveat entered by a party who had notice of the proceedings shall cease to have effect.

(4)   Every citation shall be served personally on the person cited unless the [district judge or] registrar, on cause shown by affidavit, directs some other mode of service, which may include notice by advertisement.

(5)   Every will referred to in a citation shall be lodged in a registry before the citation is issued, except where the will is not in the citor's possession and the [district judge or] registrar is satisfied that it is impracticable to require it to be lodged.

(6)   A person who has been cited to appear may, within eight days of service of the citation upon him (inclusive of the day of such service), or at any time thereafter if no application has been made by the citor under paragraph (5) of rule 47 or paragraph (2) of rule 48, enter an appearance in the registry from which the citation issued by filing Form 5 and shall forthwith thereafter serve on the citor a copy of Form 5 sealed with the seal of the registry.

47 Citation to accept or refuse or to take a grant

(1)   A citation to accept or refuse a grant may be issued at the instance of any person who would himself be entitled to a grant in the event of the person cited renouncing his right thereto.

(2)   Where power to make a grant to an executor has been reserved, a citation calling on him to accept or refuse a grant may be issued at the instance of the executors who have proved the will or the survivor of them or of the executors of the last survivor of deceased executors who have proved.

(3)   A citation calling on an executor who has intermeddled in the estate of the deceased to show cause why he should not be ordered to take a grant may be issued at the instance of any person interested in the estate at any time after the expiration of six months from the death of the deceased, provided that no citation to take a grant shall issue while proceedings as to the validity of the will are pending.

(4)   A person cited who is willing to accept or take a grant may, after entering an appearance, apply ex parte by affidavit to a [district judge or] registrar for an order for a grant to himself.

(5)   If the time limited for appearance has expired and the person cited has not entered an appearance, the citor may—
   (a)   in the case of a citation under paragraph (1) of this rule, apply to a [district judge or] registrar for an order for a grant to himself;
   (b)   in the case of a citation under paragraph (2) of this rule, apply to a [district judge or] registrar for an order that a note be made on the grant that the executor in respect of whom power was reserved has been duly cited and has not appeared and that all his rights in respect of the executorship have wholly ceased; or
   (c)   in the case of a citation under paragraph (3) of this rule, apply to a [district judge or] registrar by summons (which shall be served on the person cited) for an order requiring such person to take a grant within a specified time or for a grant to himself or to some other person specified in the summons.

(6)   An application under the last foregoing paragraph shall be supported by an affidavit showing that the citation was duly served.

(7)   If the person cited has entered an appearance but has not applied for a grant under paragraph (4) of this rule, or has failed to prosecute his application with reasonable diligence, the citor may—

    (a)   in the case of a citation under paragraph (1) of this rule, apply by summons to a [district judge or] registrar for an order for a grant to himself;

    (b)   in the case of a citation under paragraph (2) of this rule, apply by summons to a [district judge or] registrar for an order striking out the appearance and for the endorsement on the grant of such a note as is mentioned in sub-paragraph (b) of paragraph (5) of this rule; or

    (c)   in the case of a citation under paragraph (3) of this rule, apply by summons to a [district judge or] registrar for an order requiring the person cited to take a grant within a specified time or for a grant to himself or to some other person specified in the summons;

and the summons shall be served on the person cited.

48 Citation to propound a will

(1)   A citation to propound a will shall be directed to the executors named in the will and to all persons interested thereunder, and may be issued at the instance of any citor having an interest contrary to that of the executors or such other persons.

(2)   If the time limited for appearance has expired, the citor may—

    (a)   in the case where no person has entered an appearance, apply to a [district judge or] registrar for an order for a grant as if the will were invalid and such application shall be supported by an affidavit showing that the citation was duly served; or

    (b)   in the case where no person who has entered an appearance proceeds with reasonable diligence to propound the will, apply to a [district judge or] registrar by summons, which shall be served on every person cited who has entered an appearance, for such an order as is mentioned in paragraph (a) above.

49 Address for service

All caveats, citations, warnings and appearances shall contain an address for service in England and Wales.

50 Application for order to attend for examination or for subpoena to bring in a will

(1)   An application under section 122 of the Act for an order requiring a person to attend for examination may, unless a probate action has been commenced, be made to a [district judge or] registrar by summons which shall be served on every such person as aforesaid.

(2)   An application under section 123 of the Act for the issue by a [district judge or] registrar of a subpoena to bring in a will shall be supported by an affidavit setting out the grounds of the application, and if any person served with the subpoena denies that the will is in his possession or control he may file an affidavit to that effect in the registry from which the subpoena issued.

51 Grants to part of an estate under section 113 of the Act

An application for an order for a grant under section 113 of the Act to part of an estate may be made to a [district judge or] registrar, and shall be supported by an affidavit setting out the grounds of the application, and

   (a) stating whether the estate of the deceased is known to be insolvent; and

   (b) showing how any person entitled to a grant in respect of the whole estate in priority to the applicant has been cleared off.

52 Grants of administration under discretionary powers of court, and grants ad colligenda bona

An application for an order for—

   (a) a grant of administration under section 116 of the Act; or

   (b) a grant of administration ad colligenda bona,

may be made to a [district judge or] registrar and shall be supported by an affidavit setting out the grounds of the application.

53 Applications for leave to swear to death

An application for leave to swear to the death of a person in whose estate a grant is sought may be made to a [district judge or] registrar, and shall be supported by an affidavit setting out the grounds of the application and containing particulars of any policies of insurance effected on the life of the presumed deceased together with such further evidence as the [district judge or] registrar may require.

54 Grants in respect of nuncupative wills and copies of wills

(1) Subject to paragraph (2) below, an application for an order admitting to proof a nuncupative will, or a will contained in a copy or reconstruction thereof where the original is not available, shall be made to a [district judge or] registrar.

(2) In any case where a will is not available owing to its being retained in the custody of a foreign court or official, a duly authenticated copy of the will may be admitted to proof without the order referred to in paragraph (1) above.

(3) An application under paragraph (1) above shall be supported by an affidavit setting out the grounds of the application, and by such evidence on affidavit as the applicant can adduce as to—

   (a) the will's existence after the death of the testator or, where there is no such evidence, the facts on which the applicant relies to rebut the presumption that the will has been revoked by destruction;

   (b) in respect of a nuncupative will, the contents of that will; and

   (c) in respect of a reconstruction of a will, the accuracy of that reconstruction.

(4) The [district judge or] registrar may require additional evidence in the circumstances of a particular case as to due execution of the will or as to the accuracy of the copy will, and may direct that notice be given to persons who would be prejudiced by the application.

55 Application for rectification of a will

(1) An application for an order that a will be rectified by virtue of section 20(1) of the Administration of Justice Act 1982 may be made to a [district judge or] registrar, unless a probate action has been commenced.

(2)   The application shall be supported by an affidavit, setting out the grounds of the application, together with such evidence as can be adduced as to the testator's intentions and as to whichever of the following matters as are in issue:—
    (a)   in what respects the testator's intentions were not understood; or
    (b)   the nature of any alleged clerical error.

(3)   Unless otherwise directed, notice of the application shall be given to every person having an interest under the will whose interest might be prejudiced[, or such other person who might be prejudiced,] by the rectification applied for and any comments in writing by any such person shall be exhibited to the affidavit in support of the application.

(4)   If the [district judge or] registrar is satisfied that, subject to any direction to the contrary, notice has been given to every person mentioned in paragraph (3) above, and that the application is unopposed, he may order that the will be rectified accordingly.

56 Notice of election by surviving spouse to redeem life interest

(1)   Where a surviving spouse who is the sole or sole surviving personal representative of the deceased is entitled to a life interest in part of the residuary estate and elects under section 47A of the Administration of Estates Act 1925 to have the life interest redeemed, he may give written notice of the election to the [senior district judge] in pursuance of subsection (7) of that section by filing a notice in Form 6 in the Principal Registry or in the district probate registry from which the grant issued.

(2)   Where the grant issued from a district probate registry, the notice shall be filed in duplicate.

(3)   A notice filed under this rule shall be noted on the grant and the record and shall be open to inspection.

[57 Index of grant applications]

[(1)   The senior district judge shall maintain an index of every pending application for a grant made in any registry or sub-registry.

(2)   Every registry or sub-registry in which an application is made shall cause the index to be searched and shall record the result of the search.]

58 Inspection of copies of original wills and other documents

An original will or other document referred to in section 124 of the Act shall not be open to inspection if, in the opinion of a [district judge or] registrar, such inspection would be undesirable or otherwise inappropriate.

59 Issue of copies of original wills and other documents

Where copies are required of original wills or other documents deposited under section 124 of the Act, such copies may be facsimile copies sealed with the seal of the court and issued either as office copies or certified under the hand of a [district judge or] registrar to be true copies.

[60 Costs]

[(1)   Order 62 of the Rules of the Supreme Court 1965 shall not apply to costs in non-contentious probate matters, and Parts 43, 44 (except rules 44.9 to 44.12), 47 and 48 of the Civil Procedure Rules 1998 ("the 1998 Rules") shall apply to costs in those matters, with the modifications contained in paragraphs (3) to (7) of this rule.

(2)   Where detailed assessment of a bill of costs is ordered, it shall be referred—
   (a)   where the order was made by a district judge, to a district judge, a costs judge or an authorised court officer within rule 43.2(1)(d)(iii) or (iv) of the 1998 Rules;
   (b)   where the order was made by a registrar, to that registrar or, where this is not possible, in accordance with sub-paragraph (a) above.

(3)   Every reference in Parts 43, 44, 47 and 48 of the 1998 Rules to a district judge shall be construed as referring only to a district judge of the Principal Registry.

(4)   The definition of "costs officer" in rule 43.2(1)(c) of the 1998 Rules shall have effect as if it included a paragraph reading—
   "(iv)   a district probate registrar."

(5)   The definition of "authorised court officer" in rule 43.2(1)(d) of the 1998 Rules shall have effect as if paragraphs (i) and (ii) were omitted.

(6)   Rule 44.3(2) of the 1998 Rules (costs follow the event) shall not apply.

(7)   Rule 47.4(2) of the 1998 Rules shall apply as if after the words "Supreme Court Costs Office" there were inserted ", the Principal Registry of the Family Division or such district probate registry as the court may specify".

(8)   Except in the case of an appeal against a decision of an authorised court officer (to which rules 47.20 to 47.23 of the 1998 Rules apply), an appeal against a decision in assessment proceedings relating to costs in non-contentious probate matters shall be dealt with in accordance with the following paragraphs of this rule.

(9)   An appeal within paragraph (8) above against a decision made by a district judge, a costs judge (as defined by rule 43.2(1)(b) of the 1998 Rules) or a registrar, shall lie to a judge of the High Court.

(10)   Part 52 of the 1998 Rules applies to every appeal within paragraph (8) above, and any reference in Part 52 to a judge or a district judge shall be taken to include a district judge of the Principal Registry of the Family Division.

(11)   The 1998 Rules shall apply to an appeal to which Part 52 or rules 47.20 to 47.23 of those Rules apply in accordance with paragraph (8) above in the same way as they apply to any other appeal within Part 52 or rules 47.20 to 47.23 of those Rules as the case may be; accordingly the Rules of the Supreme Court 1965 and the County Court Rules 1981 shall not apply to any such appeal.]

61 Power to require applications to be made by summons

(1)   [Subject to rule 7(2),] a [district judge or] registrar may require any application to be made by summons to a [district judge or] registrar in chambers or a judge in chambers or open court.

(2)   An application for an inventory and account shall be made by summons to a [district judge or] registrar.

(3)   A summons for hearing by a [district judge or] registrar shall be issued out of the registry in which it is to be heard.

(4)   A summons to be heard by a judge shall be issued out of the Principal Registry.

62 Transfer of applications

A registrar to whom any application is made under these Rules may order the transfer of the application to another [district judge or] registrar having jurisdiction.

[62A Exercise of a registrar's jurisdiction by another registrar]

[A registrar may hear and dispose of an application under these Rules on behalf of any other registrar by whom the application would otherwise have been heard, if that other registrar so requests or an application in that behalf is made by a party making an application under these Rules; and where the circumstances require it, the registrar shall, without the need for any such request or application, hear and dispose of the application.]

63 Power to make orders for costs

On any application dealt with by him on summons, the . . . registrar shall have full power to determine by whom and to what extent the costs are to be paid.

64 Exercise of powers of judge during Long Vacation

All powers exercisable under these Rules by a judge in chambers may be exercised during the Long Vacation by a [district judge].

65 Appeals from [district judges or] registrars

(1)   An appeal against a decision or requirement of a [district judge or] registrar shall be made by summons to a judge.

(2)   If, in the case of an appeal under the last foregoing paragraph, any person besides the appellant appeared or was represented before the [district judge or] registrar from whose decision or requirement the appeal is brought, the summons shall be issued within seven days thereof for hearing on the first available day and shall be served on every such person as aforesaid.

[(3)   This rule does not apply to an appeal against a decision in proceedings for the assessment of costs.]

66 Service of summons

(1)   A judge or [district judge] or, where the application is to be made to a district probate registrar, that registrar, may direct that a summons for the service of which no other provision is made by these Rules shall be served on such person or persons as the [judge, district judge or registrar] [may direct].

(2)   Where by these Rules or by any direction given under the last foregoing paragraph a summons is required to be served on any person, it shall be served not less than two clear days before the day appointed for the hearing, unless a judge or [district judge or] registrar at or before the hearing dispenses with service on such terms, if any, as he may think fit.

67 Notices, etc

Unless a [district judge or] registrar otherwise directs or these Rules otherwise provide, any notice or other document required to be given to or served on any person may be given or served in the manner prescribed by Order 65 Rule 5 of the Rules of the Supreme Court 1965.

68 Application to pending proceedings

Subject in any particular case to any direction given by a judge or [district judge or] registrar, these Rules shall apply to any proceedings which are pending on the date on which they come into force as well as to any proceedings commenced on or after that date.

69 Revocation of previous rules

(1) Subject to paragraph (2) below, the rules set out in the Second Schedule are hereby revoked.

(2) The rules set out in the Second Schedule shall continue to apply to such extent as may be necessary for giving effect to a direction under rule 68.

SCHEDULE I
Forms

Rule 2(2)

FORM I
CERTIFICATE OF DELIVERY OF INLAND REVENUE AFFIDAVIT

Rule 42

And it is hereby certified that an Inland Revenue affidavit has been delivered wherein it is shown that the gross value of the said estate in the United Kingdom (exclusive of what the said deceased may have been possessed of or entitled to as a trustee and not beneficially) amounts to £ .. .. and that the net value of the estate amounts to £ .. .. ..

And it is further certified that it appears by a receipt signed by an Inland Revenue officer on the said affidavit that £ .. .. on account of estate duty and interest on such day has been paid.

FORM 2
STANDING SEARCH

Rule 43(I)

In the High Court of Justice Family Division

[The Principal (or .. .. District Probate) Registry]

I/We apply for the entry of a standing search so that there shall be sent to me/us an office copy of every grant of representation in England and Wales in the estate of—

Full name of deceased: .. ..

Full address: .. ..

Alternative or alias names: .. ..

Exact date of death: .. ..

which either has issued not more than 12 months before the entry of this application or issues within 6 months thereafter.

Signed .. ..

Name in block letters .. ..

Full address .. ..

Reference No. (if any) .. ..

FORM 3
CAVEAT

Rule 44(2)

In the High Court of Justice Family Division

The Principal (*or* .. .. District Probate) Registry.

Let not grant be sealed in the estate of (*full name and address*) deceased, who died on the .. .. day of 19 .. .. without notice to (*name of party by whom or on whose behalf the caveat is entered*).

Dated this .. .. day of .. .. 19 .. ..
.. .. .

(*Signed*)   .. .. (*to be signed by the caveator's solicitor* [*or probate practitioner*] *or by the caveator if acting in person*)

whose address for service is: .. ..

Solicitor[/probate practitioner] for the said .. .. (*If the caveator is acting in person, substitute "In person".*)

FORM 4
WARNING TO CAVEATOR

Rule 44(5)

In the High Court of Justice Family Division

[(The nominated registry as defined by rule 44(15))]

To .. .. of .. .. a party who has entered a caveat in the estate of .. .. deceased.

You have eight days (starting with the day on which this warning was served on you):
  (i)   to enter an appearance either in person or by your solicitor [or probate practitioner], at the [(name and address of the nominated registry)] setting out what interest you have in the estate of the above-named .. .. of .. .. deceased contrary to that of the party at whose instance this warning is issued; or
  (ii) if you have no contrary interest but wish to show cause against the sealing of a grant to such party, to issue and serve a summons for [directions by a district judge of the Principal Registry or a registrar of] a district probate registry.

If you fail to do either of these, the court may proceed to issue a grant of probate or administration in the said estate notwithstanding your caveat.

Dated the .. .. day of .. .. 19 .. .. ..
.. .

Issued at the instance of .. ..

(Here set out the name and interest (including the date of the will, if any, under which the interest arises) of the party warning, the name of his solicitor [or probate practitioner] and the address for service. If the party warning is acting in person, this must be stated.) .. .. Registrar

FORM 5
APPEARANCE TO WARNING OR CITATION

Rules 44(10), 46(6)

In the High Court of Justice Family Division

The Principal (*or* .. .. District Probate) Registry Caveat No ..
.. .. dated the .. .. day of .. ..
.. .. 19 .. .. (Citation dated the .. .. day of
.. .. 19 .. ..)

Full name and address of deceased: .. ..

Full name and address of person warning (*or* citor): .. ..

(Here set out the interest of the person warning, or citor, as shown in warning or citation.)

Full name and address of caveator (or person cited).

(Here set out the interest of the caveator or person cited, stating the date of the will (if any) under which such interest arises.)

Enter an appearance for the above-named caveator (*or* person cited) in this matter.

Dated the .. .. day of .. .. 19 .. .. ..
.. .

(Signed) .. ..

whose address for service is: .. ..

.. .. Solicitor[/probate practitioner] (*or* In person).

FORM 6
NOTICE OF ELECTION TO REDEEM LIFE INTEREST

Rule 56

In the High Court of Justice Family Division

The Principal (*or* .. .. District Probate) Registry

In the estate of .. .. deceased.

Whereas .. .. of .. .. died on the
.. .. day of .. .. 19 .. .. wholly/
partially intestate leaving his/her/lawful wife/husband and .. ..

.. .. lawful issue of the said deceased;

And whereas Probate/Letters of Administration of the estate of the said .. .. were granted to me, the said .. .. (and to .. .. of .. ..) at the Probate Registry on the .. .. day of .. .. 19 .. .. .. ;

And whereas (the said .. .. has ceased to be a personal representative because .. ..) and I am (now) the sole personal representative;

Now I, the said .. .. hereby given notice in accordance with section 47A of the Administration of Estates Act 1925 that I elect to redeem the life interest to which I am entitled in the estate of the late .. .. by retaining £ .. .. its capital value, and £ .. .. the costs of the transaction.

Dated the .. .. day of .. .. 19 .. ..

(Signed)   .. ..

To the [senior district judge] of the Family Division.

SCHEDULE 2
Revocations

Rule 69

Rules revoked	References
The Non-Contentious Probate Rules 1954	SI 1954/796
The Non-Contentious Probate (Amendment) Rules 1961	SI 1961/72
The Non-Contentious Probate (Amendment) Rules 1962	SI 1962/2653
The Non-Contentious Probate (Amendment) Rules 1967	SI 1967/748
The Non-Contentious Probate (Amendment) Rules 1968	SI 1968/1675
The Non-Contentious Probate (Amendment) Rules 1969	SI 1969/1689
The Non-Contentious Probate (Amendment) Rules 1971	SI 1971/1977
The Non-Contentious Probate (Amendment) Rules 1974	SI 1974/597
The Non-Contentious Probate (Amendment) Rules 1976	SI 1976/1362
The Non-Contentious Probate (Amendment) Rules 1982	SI 1982/446
The Non-Contentious Probate (Amendment) Rules 1983	SI 1983/623
The Non-Contentious Probate (Amendment) Rules 1985	SI 1985/1232

A2.2

THE INHERITANCE TAX (DELIVERY OF ACCOUNTS) (EXCEPTED ESTATES) REGULATIONS 2002 2002 NO 1733

Citation and commencement

1. These Regulations may be cited as the Inheritance Tax (Delivery of Accounts) (Excepted Estates) Regulations 2002, shall come into force on 1st August 2002 and shall have effect in relation to deaths occurring on or after 6th April 2002.

Interpretation

2. In these Regulations -
   'the Board' means the Commissioners of Inland Revenue;
   'the 1984 Act' means the Inheritance Tax Act 1984;
   'an excepted estate' has the meaning given in regulation 3;
   'the prescribed period' in relation to any person is the period beginning with that person's death and ending -
      (a) in England, Wales and Northern Ireland, 35 days after the making of the first grant of representation in respect of that person (not being a grant limited in duration, in respect of property or to any special purpose); or
      (b) in Scotland, 60 days after the date on which confirmation to that person's estate was first granted;
   'value' means value for the purpose of tax.

Excepted estates

3. - (1) An excepted estate means the estate of a person immediately before his death in either of the circumstances prescribed by paragraphs (2) and (3) below.

(2) The circumstances prescribed by this paragraph are that -
   (a) the person died on or after 6th April 2002, domiciled in the United Kingdom;
   (b) the value of that person's estate is attributable wholly to property passing under his will or intestacy or under a nomination of an asset taking effect on death or under a single settlement in which he was entitled to an interest in possession in settled property or by survivorship in a beneficial joint tenancy or, in Scotland, by survivorship;
   (c) of that property -
       (i) not more than £100,000 represented value attributable to property which, immediately before that person's death, was settled property; and
       (ii) not more than £75,000 represented value attributable to property which, immediately before that person's death, was situated outside the United Kingdom;
   (d) that person died without having made any chargeable transfers during the period of seven years ending with his death other than specified transfers where the aggregate value transferred did not exceed £100,000; and
   (e) the aggregate of the gross value of that person's estate and of the value transferred by any specified transfers made by that person did not exceed £220,000.

(3) The circumstances prescribed by this paragraph are that -
- (a) the person died on or after 6th April 2002;
- (b) he was never domiciled in the United Kingdom or treated as domiciled in the United Kingdom by section 267 of the 1984 Act; and
- (c) the value of that person's estate situated in the United Kingdom is wholly attributable to cash or quoted shares or securities passing under his will or intestacy or by survivorship in a beneficial joint tenancy or, in Scotland, by survivorship, the gross value of which does not exceed £100,000.

(4) For the purposes of paragraph (2) 'specified transfers' means chargeable transfers made during the period of seven years ending with that person's death where the value transferred is attributable to -
- (a) cash;
- (b) quoted shares or securities; or
- (c) an interest in or over land (and furnishings and chattels disposed of at the same time to the same donee and intended to be enjoyed with the land), save to the extent that -
  - (i) sections 102 and 102A(2) of the Finance Act 1986 apply to that transfer; or
  - (ii) the land (or furnishings or chattels) became settled property on that transfer.

Accounts

4. Notwithstanding anything in section 216 of the 1984 Act no person shall be required to deliver to the Board an account of the property comprised in an excepted estate, unless the Board so require by a notice in writing issued to that person within the prescribed period.

5. If any person who has not delivered an account in reliance on regulation 4 discovers at any time that the estate is not an excepted estate, the delivery to the Board within six months of that time of an account of the property comprised in that estate shall satisfy any requirement to deliver an account imposed on that person.

Discharge of persons and property from tax

6. Subject to regulation 7 and unless within the prescribed period the Board issue a notice requiring an account of the property comprised in an excepted estate, all persons shall on the expiration of that period be discharged from any claim for tax on the value transferred by the chargeable transfer made on the deceased's death and attributable to the value of that property and any Inland Revenue charge for that tax shall then be extinguished.

7. Regulation 6 shall not discharge any person from tax in the case of fraud or failure to disclose material facts and shall not affect any tax that may be payable if further property is later shown to form part of the estate and, in consequence of that property, the estate is not an excepted estate.

Transfers reported late

8. Where no account of a person's excepted estate is required by the Board, an account of that estate shall, for the purposes of section 264(8) of the 1984 Act (delivery of account to be treated as payment where tax rate nil), be treated as having been delivered on the last day of the prescribed period in relation to that person.

Revocation

9. The Regulations listed in the Schedule are revoked in relation to deaths occurring on or after 6th April 2002.

SCHEDULE
REVOCATIONS

(1) Regulations revoked	(2) References
The Capital Transfer Tax (Delivery of Accounts) Regulations 1981	**S.I.** 1981/880
The Capital Transfer Tax (Delivery of Accounts) (Scotland) Regulations 1981	**S.I.** 1981/881
The Capital Transfer Tax (Delivery of Accounts) (Northern Ireland) Regulations 1981	**S.I.** 1981/1441
The Capital Transfer Tax (Delivery of Accounts) (No. 3) Regulations 1983	**S.I.** 1983/1039
The Capital Transfer Tax (Delivery of Accounts) (Scotland) (No. 2) Regulations 1983	**S.I.** 1983/1040
The Capital Transfer Tax (Delivery of Accounts) (Northern Ireland) (No. 2) Regulations 1983	**S.I.** 1983/1911
The Inheritance Tax (Delivery of Accounts) Regulations 1987	**S.I.** 1987/1127
The Inheritance Tax (Delivery of Accounts) (Scotland) Regulations 1987	**S.I.** 1987/1128
The Inheritance Tax (Delivery of Accounts) (Northern Ireland) Regulations 1987	**S.I.** 1987/1129
The Inheritance Tax (Delivery of Accounts) Regulations 1989	**S.I.** 1989/1078
The Inheritance Tax (Delivery of Accounts) (Scotland) Regulations 1989	**S.I.** 1989/1079
The Inheritance Tax (Delivery of Accounts) (Northern Ireland) Regulations 1989	**S.I.** 1989/1080
The Inheritance Tax (Delivery of Accounts) Regulations 1990	**S.I.** 1990/1110
The Inheritance Tax (Delivery of Accounts) (Scotland) Regulations 1990	**S.I.** 1990/1111
The Inheritance Tax (Delivery of Accounts) (Northern Ireland) Regulations 1990	**S.I.** 1990/1112
The Inheritance Tax (Delivery of Accounts) Regulations 1991	**S.I.** 1991/1248
The Inheritance Tax (Delivery of Accounts) (Scotland) Regulations 1991	**S.I.** 1991/1249

The Inheritance Tax (Delivery of Accounts) (Northern Ireland) Regulations
1991   **S.I.** 1991/1250

The Inheritance Tax (Delivery of Accounts) Regulations 1995   **S.I.** 1995/1461

The Inheritance Tax (Delivery of Accounts) (Scotland) Regulations
1995   **S.I.** 1995/1459

The Inheritance Tax (Delivery of Accounts) (Northern Ireland) Regulations
1995   **S.I.** 1995/1460

The Inheritance Tax (Delivery of Accounts) Regulations 1996   **S.I.** 1996/1470

The Inheritance Tax (Delivery of Accounts) (Scotland) Regulations
1996   **S.I.** 1996/1472

The Inheritance Tax (Delivery of Accounts) (Northern Ireland) Regulations
1996   **S.I.** 1996/1473

The Inheritance Tax (Delivery of Accounts) Regulations 1998   **S.I.** 1998/1431

The Inheritance Tax (Delivery of Accounts) (Scotland) Regulations
1998   **S.I.** 1998/1430

The Inheritance Tax (Delivery of Accounts) (Northern Ireland)
Regulations 1998   **S.I.** 1998/1429

The Inheritance Tax (Delivery of Accounts) Regulations 2000   **S.I.** 2000/967

The Inheritance Tax (Delivery of Accounts) (Scotland) Regulations
2000   **S.I.** 2000/966

The Inheritance Tax (Delivery of Accounts) (Northern Ireland) Regulations
2000

      S.I. 2000/965

A2.3

THE INHERITANCE TAX (DELIVERY OF ACCOUNTS) (EXCEPTED ESTATES) (AMENDMENT) REGULATIONS 2003 2003 NO 1658

Citation, commencement, and effect

1. These Regulations may be cited as the Inheritance Tax (Delivery of Accounts) (Excepted Estates) (Amendment) Regulations 2003, shall come into force on 1st August 2003, and shall have effect in relation to deaths occurring on or after 6th April 2003.

Amendment to the Inheritance Tax (Delivery of Accounts) (Excepted Estates) Regulations 2002

2. In regulation 3(2)(e) of the Inheritance Tax (Delivery of Accounts) (Excepted Estates) Regulations 2002, for '£220,000' substitute '£240,000'.

A2.4

THE INHERITANCE TAX (DELIVERY OF ACCOUNTS) (EXCEPTED ESTATES) REGULATIONS 2004 2004 NO 2543

Citation, commencement and effect

1. These Regulations may be cited as the Inheritance Tax (Delivery of Accounts) (Excepted Estates) Regulations 2004, shall come into force on 1st November 2004 and shall have effect in relation to deaths occurring on or after 6th April 2004.

Interpretation

2. In these Regulations -
    'the Board' means the Commissioners of Inland Revenue;
    'the 1984 Act' means the Inheritance Tax Act 1984;
    'an excepted estate' has the meaning given in regulation 4;
    'IHT threshold' means the lower limit shown in the Table in Schedule 1 of the 1984
        Act applicable to -
        (a) chargeable transfers made in the year before that in which a person's
            death occurred if -
            (i) that person died on or after 6th April and before 6th August, and
            (ii) an application for a grant of representation or, in Scotland, an
                 application for confirmation, is made before 6th August in that year;
                 or
        (b) chargeable transfers made in the year in which a person's death occurred
            in any other case,

and for this purpose 'year' means a period of twelve months ending with 5th April;
    'the prescribed period' in relation to any person is the period beginning with that
        person's death and ending -
        (a) in England, Wales and Northern Ireland, 35 days after the making of the
            first grant of representation in respect of that person (not being a grant
            limited in duration, in respect of property or to any special purpose); or
        (b) in Scotland, 60 days after the date on which confirmation to that person's
            estate was first issued;
    'spouse and charity transfer' has the meaning given in regulation 5;
    'value' means value for the purpose of tax.

Accounts

3. - (1) No person is required to deliver an account under section 216 of the 1984 Act of the property comprised in an excepted estate.

(2) If in reliance on these Regulations a person has not delivered an account paragraphs (3) and (4) apply.

(3) If it is discovered at any time that the estate is not an excepted estate, the delivery to the Board within six months of that time of an account of the property comprised in that estate shall satisfy any requirement to deliver an account.

(4) If the estate is no longer an excepted estate following an alteration of the dispositions taking effect on death within section 142 of the 1984 Act, the delivery to the Board within six months of the date of the instrument of variation of an account of the property comprised in that estate shall satisfy any requirement to deliver an account.

Excepted estates

4. - (1) An excepted estate means the estate of a person immediately before his death in the circumstances prescribed by paragraphs (2), (3) or (4).

(2) The circumstances prescribed by this paragraph are that -
- (a)   the person died on or after 6th April 2004, domiciled in the United Kingdom;
- (b)   the value of that person's estate is attributable wholly to property passing -
    - (i)   under his will or intestacy,
    - (ii)   under a nomination of an asset taking effect on death,
    - (iii)   under a single settlement in which he was entitled to an interest in possession in settled property, or
    - (iv)   by survivorship in a beneficial joint tenancy or, in Scotland, by survivorship in a special destination;
- (c)   of that property -
    - (i)   not more than £100,000 represented value attributable to property which, immediately before that person's death, was settled property; and
    - (ii)   not more than £75,000 represented value attributable to property which, immediately before that person's death, was situated outside the United Kingdom;
- (d)   that person died without having made any chargeable transfers during the period of seven years ending with his death other than specified transfers where, subject to paragraph (7), the aggregate value transferred did not exceed £100,000; and
- (e)   the aggregate of -
    - (i)   the gross value of that person's estate,
    - (ii)   subject to paragraph (7), the value transferred by any specified transfers made by that person, and
    - (iii)   the value transferred by any specified exempt transfers made by that person,

did not exceed the IHT threshold.

(3) The circumstances prescribed by this paragraph are that -
- (a)   the person died on or after 6th April 2004, domiciled in the United Kingdom;
- (b)   the value of that person's estate is attributable wholly to property passing -
    - (i)   under his will or intestacy,
    - (ii)   under a nomination of an asset taking effect on death,
    - (iii)   under a single settlement in which he was entitled to an interest in possession in settled property, or
    - (iv)   by survivorship in a beneficial joint tenancy or, in Scotland, by survivorship in a special destination;
- (c)   of that property -
    - (i)   subject to paragraph (8), not more than £100,000 represented value attributable to property which, immediately before that person's death, was settled property; and
    - (ii)   not more than £75,000 represented value attributable to property which, immediately before that person's death, was situated outside the United Kingdom;

(d) that person died without having made any chargeable transfers during the period of seven years ending with his death other than specified transfers where, subject to paragraph (7), the aggregate value transferred did not exceed £100,000;

(e) the aggregate of -
   (i) the gross value of that person's estate,
   (ii) subject to paragraph (7), the value transferred by any specified transfers made by that person, and
   (iii) the value transferred by any specified exempt transfers made by that person,
did not exceed £1,000,000; and

(f) the aggregate of -

$$A - (B + C)$$

does not exceed the IHT threshold, where -
A is the aggregate of the values in sub-paragraph (e),
B, subject to paragraph (4), is the total value transferred on that person's death by a spouse or charity transfer, and
C is the total liabilities of the estate.

(4) In Scotland, if legitim could be claimed which would reduce the value of the spouse or charity transfer, the value of B is reduced -
(a) to take account of any legitim claimed, and
(b) on the basis that any part of the remaining legitim fund, which has been neither claimed nor renounced at the time of the application for confirmation, will be claimed in full.

(5) The circumstances prescribed by this paragraph are that -
(a) the person died on or after 6th April 2004;
(b) he was never domiciled in the United Kingdom or treated as domiciled in the United Kingdom by section 267 of the 1984 Act; and
(c) the value of that person's estate situated in the United Kingdom is wholly attributable to cash or quoted shares or securities passing under his will or intestacy or by survivorship in a beneficial joint tenancy or, in Scotland, by survivorship in a special destination, the gross value of which does not exceed £100,000.

(6) For the purposes of paragraphs (2) and (3) -
'specified transfers' means chargeable transfers made by a person during the period of seven years ending with that person's death where the value transferred is attributable to -
(a) cash;
(b) personal chattels or corporeal moveable property;
(c) quoted shares or securities; or
(d) an interest in or over land, save to the extent that sections 102 and 102A(2) of the Finance Act 1986 apply to that transfer or the land became settled property on that transfer;
'specified exempt transfers' means transfers of value made by a person during the period of seven years ending with that person's death which are exempt transfers only by reason of -
(a) section 18 (transfers between spouses),
(b) section 23 (gifts to charities),
(c) section 24 (gifts to political parties),
(d) section 24A (gifts to housing associations),

(e) section 27 (maintenance funds for historic buildings, etc), or
(f) section 28 (employee trusts)

of the 1984 Act.

(7) For the purpose of paragraphs (2)(d) and (e) and (3)(d) and (e), sections 104 (business property relief) and 116 (agricultural property relief) of the 1984 Act shall not apply in determining the value transferred by a chargeable transfer.

(8) Paragraph (3)(c)(i) does not apply to property which immediately before the person's death was settled property, to the extent that the property is transferred on that person's death by a spouse or charity transfer.

Spouse and charity transfers

5. - (1) For the purposes of these Regulations, a spouse or charity transfer means any disposition (whether effected by will, under the law relating to intestacy or otherwise) of property comprised in a person's estate -
  (a) subject to paragraph (2), to the person's spouse within section 18(1) of the 1984 Act; and
  (b) subject to paragraph (3), to a charity within section 23(1) of the 1984 Act or for national purposes within section 25(1) of the 1984 Act.

(2) A transfer is not a spouse transfer within paragraph (1)(a) if either spouse was not domiciled in the United Kingdom at any time prior to the transfer.

(3) A transfer is not a charity transfer within paragraph (1)(b) if the property becomes comprised in a settlement as a result of the disposition.

Production of information

6. - (1) Subject to paragraph (3), a person who by virtue of these Regulations is not required to deliver to the Board an account under section 216 of the 1984 Act of the property comprised in an excepted estate, must produce the information specified in paragraph (2) to the Board in such form as the Board may prescribe.

(2) The information specified for the purpose of paragraph (1) is -
  (a) the following details in relation to the deceased -
      (i)   full name;
      (ii)   date of death;
      (iii) marital status;
      (iv)   occupation;
      (v)   any surviving spouse, parent, brother or sister;
      (vi)   the number of surviving children, step-children, adopted children or grandchildren;
      (vii) national insurance number, tax district and tax reference;
      (viii)   if the deceased was not domiciled in the United Kingdom at his date of death, his domicile and address;
  (b) details of all property to which the deceased was beneficially entitled and the value of that property;
  (c) details of any specified transfers, specified exempt transfers and the value of those transfers;
  (d) the liabilities of the estate; and
  (e) any spouse or charity transfers and the value of those transfers.

(3) Paragraph (1) does not apply if the information specified in paragraph (2) has been produced in an account under section 216 of the 1984 Act of the property comprised in the excepted estate that has been delivered to the Board.

7. - (1) The information specified in regulation 6(2) must be produced to the Board by producing it to -
   (a) a probate registry in England and Wales;
   (b) the sheriff in Scotland;
   (c) the Probate and Matrimonial Office in Northern Ireland.

(2) Information produced in accordance with paragraph (1) is to be treated for all purposes of the 1984 Act as produced to the Board.

(3) The person or body specified in paragraph (1) must transmit the information produced to them to the Board within one week of the issue of the grant of probate or confirmation.

Discharge of persons and property from tax

8. - (1) Subject to paragraph (2) and regulation 9, if the information specified in regulation 6 has been produced in accordance with these Regulations, all persons shall on the expiration of the prescribed period be discharged from any claim for tax on the value transferred by the chargeable transfer made on the deceased's death and attributable to the value of the property comprised in an excepted estate and any Inland Revenue charge for that tax shall then be extinguished.

(2) Paragraph (1) shall not apply if within the prescribed period the Board issue a notice to -
   (a) the person or persons who would apart from these Regulations be required to deliver an account under section 216 of the 1984 Act, or
   (b) the solicitor or agent of that person or those persons who produced the specified information pursuant to regulation 6,

requiring additional information or documents to be produced in relation to the specified information produced pursuant to regulation 6.

9. Regulation 9 shall not discharge any person from tax in the case of fraud or failure to disclose material facts and shall not affect any tax that may be payable if further property is later shown to form part of the estate and, in consequence of that property, the estate is not an excepted estate.

Transfers reported late

10. An account of an excepted estate shall, for the purposes of section 264(8) of the 1984 Act (delivery of account to be treated as payment where tax rate nil), be treated as having been delivered on the last day of the prescribed period in relation to that person.

Revocation

11. The Inheritance Tax (Delivery of Accounts) (Excepted Estates) Regulations 2002 and the Inheritance Tax (Delivery of Accounts) (Excepted Estates) (Amendment) Regulations 2003 are revoked in relation to deaths occurring on or after 6th April 2004.

SECTION IV – CLAIMS UNDER THE INHERITANCE (PROVISION FOR FAMILY AND DEPENDANTS) ACT 1975

[57.14 Scope of this Section]

[This Section contains rules about claims under the Inheritance (Provision for Family and Dependants) Act 1975 ("the Act").]

[57.15 Proceedings in the High Court]

[(1)   Proceedings in the High Court under the Act shall be issued in either—
   (a) the Chancery Division; or
   (b) the Family Division.

(2)   The Civil Procedure Rules apply to proceedings under the Act which are brought in the Family Division, except that the provisions of the Family Proceedings Rules 1991 relating to the drawing up and service of orders apply instead of the provisions in Part 40 and its practice direction.]

[57.16 Procedure for claims under section 1 of the Act]

[(1)   A claim under section 1 of the Act must be made by issuing a claim form in accordance with Part 8.

(2)   Rule 8.3 (acknowledgment of service) and rule 8.5 (filing and serving written evidence) apply as modified by paragraphs (3) to (5) of this rule.

(3)   The written evidence filed and served by the claimant with the claim form must have exhibited to it an official copy of—
   (a) the grant of probate or letters of administration in respect of the deceased's estate; and
   (b) every testamentary document in respect of which probate or letters of administration were granted.

(4)   [Subject to paragraph (4A), the time] within which a defendant must file and serve—
   (a) an acknowledgment of service; and
   (b) any written evidence,

is not more than 21 days after service of the claim form on him.

[(4A)   If the claim form is served out of the jurisdiction under rule 6.19, the period for filing an acknowledgment of service and any written evidence is 7 days longer than the relevant period specified in rule 6.22 or the practice direction supplementing Section III of Part 6.]

(5)   A defendant who is a personal representative of the deceased must file and serve written evidence, which must include the information required by the practice direction.]

Acknowledgment of service by personal representative – rule 57.16(4)

15   Where a defendant who is a personal representative wishes to remain neutral in relation to the claim, and agrees to abide by any decision which the court may make, he should state this in Section A of the acknowledgment of service form.

Written evidence of personal representative – rule 57.16(5)

16 The written evidence filed by a defendant who is a personal representative must state to the best of that person's ability –
- (1) full details of the value of the deceased's net estate, as defined in section 25(1) of the Act;
- (2) the person or classes of persons beneficially interested in the estate, and –
  - (a) the names and (unless they are parties to the claim) addresses of all living beneficiaries; and
  - (b) the value of their interests in the estate so far as they are known.
- (3) whether any living beneficiary (and if so, naming him) is a child or patient within the meaning of rule 21.1(2); and
- (4) any facts which might affect the exercise of the court's powers under the Act.

Separate representation of claimants

17 If a claim is made jointly by two or more claimants, and it later appears that any of the claimants have a conflict of interests –
- (1) any claimant may choose to be represented at any hearing by separate solicitors or counsel, or may appear in person; and
- (2) if the court considers that claimants who are represented by the same solicitors or counsel ought to be separately represented, it may adjourn the application until they are.

Production of the grant

18.1 On the hearing of a claim the personal representative must produce to the court the original grant of representation to the deceased's estate.

18.2 If the court makes an order under the Act, the original grant (together with a sealed copy of the order) must be sent to the Principal Registry of the Family Division for a memorandum of the order to be endorsed on or permanently annexed to the grant in accordance with section 19(3) of the Act.

Fees (Non-Contentious business)

A3.1

THE NON-CONTENTIOUS PROBATE FEES ORDER 2004
2004 NO 3120

Citation, commencement and interpretation

1. - (1) This Order may be cited as the Non-Contentious Probate Fees Order 2004 and shall come into force on the 4th January 2005.

(2) In this Order -
    (a) a fee referred to by number means the fee so numbered in Schedule 1 to this Order;
    (b) 'assessed value' means the value of the net real and personal estate (excluding settled land if any) passing under the grant as shown -
        (i) in the Inland Revenue affidavit (for a death occurring before 13th March 1975), or
        (ii) in the Inland Revenue account (for a death occurring on or after 13th March 1975), or
        (iii) in the case in which, in accordance with arrangements made between the President of the Family Division and the Commissioners of the Inland Revenue, or regulations made under section 256(1)(a) of the Inheritance Tax Act 1984 and from time to time in force, no such affidavit or account is required to be delivered, in the oath which is sworn to lead to the grant,

and in the case of an application to reseal means the value, as shown, passing under the grant upon its being resealed;
    (c) 'authorised place of deposit' means any place in which, by virtue of a direction given under section 124 of the Supreme Court Act 1981 original wills and other documents under the control of the High Court (either in the principal registry or in any district registry) are deposited and preserved;
    (d) 'grant' means a grant of probate or letters of administration;
    (e) 'district registry' includes the probate registry of Wales, any district probate registry and any sub-registry attached to it;
    (f) 'the principal registry' means the Principal Registry of the Family Division and any sub-registry attached to it.

Fees to be taken

2. The fees set out in column 2 of Schedule 1 to this Order shall be taken in the principal registry and in each district registry in respect of the items described in column 1 in accordance with and subject to any directions specified in column 1.

Exclusion of certain death gratuities

3. In determining the value of any personal estate for the purposes of this Order there shall be excluded the value of a death gratuity payable under section 17(2) of the Judicial Pensions Act 1981 or section 4(3) of the Judicial Pensions and Retirement Act 1993, or payable to the personal representatives of a deceased civil servant by virtue of a scheme made under section 1 of the Superannuation Act 1972.

Exemptions, reductions, remissions and refunds

4. Where it appears to the Lord Chancellor that the payment of any fee prescribed by this Order would, owing to the exceptional circumstances of the particular case, involve undue financial hardship, he may reduce or remit the fee in that case.

5. - (1) Subject to paragraph (2) where a fee has been paid at a time -
   (a) where the Lord Chancellor, if he had been aware of all the circumstances, would have reduced the fee under article 4, the amount by which the fee would have been reduced shall be refunded; and
   (b) where the Lord Chancellor, if he had been aware of all the circumstances, would have remitted the fee under article 4, the fee shall be refunded.

(2) No refund shall be made under paragraph (1) unless the party who paid the fee applies within 6 months of paying the fee.

(3) The Lord Chancellor may extend the period of 6 months referred to in paragraph (2) if he considers that there is good reason for an application being made after the end of the period of 6 months.

6. - (1) Where by any convention entered into by Her Majesty with any foreign power it is provided that no fee shall be required to be paid in respect of any proceedings, the fees specified in this Order shall not be taken in respect of those proceedings.

(2) Where any application for a grant is withdrawn before the issue of a grant, a registrar may reduce or remit a fee.

(3) Fee 7 shall not be taken where a search is made for research or similar purposes by permission of the President of the Family Division for a document over 100 years old filed in the principal registry or a district registry or another authorised place of deposit.

Special exemption - Armed Forces

7. Where a fee has been paid or fees have been paid for the application of a grant (other than fee 3.2) and at the time of payment of that fee or those fees -
   (a) the application for the grant was in respect of an estate exempt from Inheritance Tax by virtue of section 154 of the Inheritance Tax Act 1984 (exemption for members of the armed forces etc); and
   (b) was in respect of a death occurring before 20th March 2003;

the Lord Chancellor shall upon receiving a written application refund the difference between any fee or fees paid and fee 3.2.

Revocation

8. The Order specified in Schedule 2 in so far as it was made under section 128 of the Finance Act 1990 shall be revoked.

SCHEDULE 1
FEES TO BE TAKEN

Article 2

Column 1 Number and description of fee	Column 2 Amount of fee
1. Application for a grantOn an application for a grant (or for resealing a grant) other than on an application to which fee 3 applies, where the assessed value of the estate exceeds £5,000	£40
2. Personal application feeWhere the application under fee 1 is made by a personal applicant (not being an application to which fee 3 applies) fee 2 is payable in addition to fee 1, where the assessed value of the estate exceeds £5,000	£50
3. Special applications3.1 For a duplicate or second or subsequent grant (including one following a revoked grant) in respect of the same deceased person, other than a grant preceded only by a grant limited to settled land, to trust property, or to part of the estate	£15
3.2 On an application for a grant relating to a death occurring on or after 20th March 2003 and in respect of an estate exempt from inheritance tax by virtue of section 154 of the Inheritance Tax Act 1984 (exemption for members of the armed forces etc)	£8
4. CaveatsFor the entry or the extension of a caveat	£15
5. SearchOn an application for a standing search to be carried out in an estate, for each period of six months including the issue of a copy grant and will, if any (irrespective of the number of pages)	£5
6. Deposit of willsOn depositing a will for safe custody in the principal registry or a district registry	£15
7. InspectionOn inspection of any will or other document retained by the registry (in the presence of an officer of the registry)	£15
8. Copy documentsOn a request for a copy of any document whether or not provided as a certified copy: (a) for the first copy	£5
(b) for every subsequent copy of the same document if supplied at the same time	£1
(c) where copies of any document are made available on a computer disk or in other electronic form, for each such copy	£31):

(d)   where a search of the index is required, in addition to fee 8
(a), (b) or (c) as appropriate, for each period of 4 years searched after the first 4
years   £3

9. OathsExcept on a personal application for a grant, for
administering an oath,

9.1 for each deponent to each affidavit   £5

9.2 for marking each exhibit   £2

10. Determination of costsFor determining costs   The same
fees as are payable from time to time for determining costs
under the Civil Proceedings Fees Order 2004, (the relevant fees
are set out in fee 5 in Schedule 1 to that Order)

11. Settling documentsFor perusing and settling citations,
advertisements, oaths, affidavits, or other documents, for each document settled £10

SCHEDULE 2
ORDER REVOKED

Title	Article 8 Reference
The Non-Contentious Probate Fees (Amendment) Order 2000	S.I. 2000/642

A3.2

THE NON-CONTENTIOUS PROBATE (AMENDMENT) RULES 2004
2004 NO 2985

1. These Rules may be cited as the Non-Contentious Probate (Amendment) Rules 2004
and shall come into force on 7th December 2004.

2. In the definition of 'probate practitioner' in rule 2 of the Non-Contentious Probate
Rules 1987 after 'section 23(2) of that Act' insert 'or section 55 of the Courts and Legal
Services Act 1990;'.

Rates of Inheritance Tax and Capital Transfer Tax

A4.01

Deaths on or after 13 March 1975 and prior to 27 October 1977. First Table of rates of Capital Transfer Tax (Finance Act 1975, s 37; s 49 and Sch 11, para 1).

Range of value		Cumulative tax to bottom of	Rate of tax on value within
Exceeding	Not exceeding	range	range
£	£	£	%
15,000	20,000	Nil	10
20,000	25,000	500	15
25,000	30,000	1,250	20
30,000	40,000	2,250	25
40,000	50,000	4,750	30
50,000	60,000	7,750	35
60,000	80,000	11,250	40
80,000	100,000	19,250	45
100,000	120,000	28,250	50
120,000	150,000	38,250	55
150,000	500,000	54,750	60
500,000	1,000,000	264,750	65
1,000,000	2,000,000	589,750	70
2,000,000		1,289,750	75

A4.02

Deaths on or after 27 October 1977 and prior to 26 March 1980. First Table of rates of Capital Transfer Tax (Finance Act 1978, s 62 and Sch 10).

Range of value		Cumulative tax to bottom of	Rate of tax on value within
Exceeding	Not exceeding	range	range
£	£	£	%
25,000	30,000	Nil	10
30,000	35,000	500	15
35,000	40,000	1,250	20
40,000	50,000	2,250	25
50,000	60,000	4,750	30
60,000	70,000	7,750	35
70,000	90,000	11,250	40
90,000	110,000	19,250	45
110,000	130,000	28,250	50
130,000	160,000	38,250	55
160,000	510,000	54,750	60
510,000	1,010,000	264,750	65
1,010,000	2,010,000	589,750	70
2,010,000		1,289,750	75

A4.03

Deaths on or after 26 March 1980 and prior to 9 March 1982. First Table of rates of Capital Transfer Tax (Finance Act 1980, s 85 and Sch 14).

Range of value		Cumulative tax to bottom of	Rate of tax on value within
Exceeding	Not exceeding	range	range
£	£	£	%
50,000	60,000	Nil	30
60,000	70,000	3,000	35
70,000	90,000	6,500	40
90,000	110,000	14,500	45
110,000	130,000	23,500	50
130,000	160,000	33,500	55
160,000	510,000	50,000	60

Range of value		Cumulative tax to bottom of	Rate of tax on value within
Exceeding	Not exceeding	range	range
510,000	1,010,000	260,000	65
1,010,000	2,010,000	585,000	70
2,010,000		1,285,000	75

A4.04

Deaths on or after 9 March 1982 and prior to 15 March 1983. First Table of rates of Capital Transfer Tax (Finance Act 1982, s 90 and Sch 14).

Range of value		Cumulative tax to bottom of	Rate of tax on value within
Exceeding	Not exceeding	range	range
£	£	£	%
55,000	75,000	Nil	30
75,000	100,000	6,000	35
100,000	130,000	14,750	40
130,000	165,000	26,750	45
165,000	200,000	42,500	50
200,000	250,000	60,000	55
250,000	650,000	87,500	60
650,000	1,250,000	327,500	65
1,250,000	2,500,000	717,500	70
2,500,000		1,592,500	75

A4.05

Deaths on or after 15 March 1983 and prior to 13 March 1984. First Table of rates of Capital Transfer Tax (Finance (No 2) Act 1983, s 8).

Range of value		Cumulative tax to bottom of	Rate of tax on value within
Exceeding	Not exceeding	range	range
£	£	£	%
60,000	80,000	Nil	30
80,000	110,000	6,000	35
110,000	140,000	16,500	40
140,000	175,000	28,500	45
175,000	220,000	44,250	50
220,000	270,000	66,750	55
270,000	700,000	94,250	60
700,000	1,325,000	352,250	65
1,325,000	2,650,000	758,500	70
2,650,000		1,686,000	75

A4.06

Deaths on or after 13 March 1984 and before 6 April 1985. First Table of rates of Capital Transfer Tax (Finance Act 1984, s 101).

Range of value		Cumulative tax to bottom of	Rate of tax on value within
Exceeding	Not exceeding	range	range
£	£	£	%
64,000	85,000	Nil	30
85,000	116,000	6,300	35
116,000	148,000	17,150	40
148,000	185,000	29,950	45
185,000	232,000	46,600	50
232,000	285,000	70,100	55
285,000		99,250	60

A4.07

Deaths on or after 6 April 1985 and prior to 18 March 1986. First Table of rates of Capital Transfer Tax (SI 1985/429).

Range of value		Cumulative tax to bottom of	Rate of tax on value within
Exceeding	Not exceeding	range	range
£	£	£	%
67,000	89,000	Nil	30
89,000	122,000	6,600	35
122,000	155,000	18,150	40
155,000	194,000	31,350	45
194,000	243,000	48,900	50
243,000	299,000	73,400	55
299,000		104,200	60

A4.08

Deaths on or after 18 March 1986 and before 17 March 1987. Table of rates of tax (Finance Act 1986, s 101 and Sch 19, para 36).

Range of value		Cumulative tax to bottom of	Rate of tax on value within
Exceeding	Not exceeding	range	range
£	£	£	%
71,000	95,000	Nil	30
95,000	129,000	7,200	35
129,000	164,000	19,100	40
164,000	206,000	33,100	45
206,000	257,000	52,000	50
257,000	317,000	77,500	55
317,000		110,500	60

A4.09

Deaths on or after 17 March 1987 and before 15 March 1988. Table of rates of tax (Finance Act 1987, s 57).

Range of value		Cumulative tax to bottom of	Rate of tax on value within
Exceeding	Not exceeding	range	range
£	£	£	%
90,000	140,000	Nil	30
140,000	220,000	15,000	40
220,000	330,000	47,000	50
330,000		102,000	60

A4.10

Deaths on or after 15 March 1988 and before 6 April 1989. Table of rates of tax (Finance Act 1988, s 136).

Range of value		Cumulative tax to bottom of	Rate of tax on value within
Exceeding	Not exceeding	range	range
£	£	£	%
110,000		Nil	40

A4.11

Deaths on or after 6 April 1989 and before 6 April 1990 (SI 1989/468).

Range of value		Cumulative tax to bottom of	Rate of tax on value within
Exceeding	Not exceeding	range	range
£	£	£	%
118,000		Nil	40

A4.12

Deaths on or after 6 April 1990 and before 6 April 1991 (SI 1990/680).

Range of value		Cumulative tax to bottom of	Rate of tax on value within
Exceeding	Not exceeding	range	range
£	£	£	%
128,000		Nil	40

A4.13

Deaths on or after 6 April 1991 and before 10 March 1992 (SI 1991/735).

Range of value		Cumulative tax to bottom of	Rate of tax on value within
Exceeding	Not exceeding	range	range
£	£	£	%
140,000		Nil	40

A4.14

Deaths on or after 10 March 1992 and before 6 April 1995 (Finance Act (No 2) 1992, s 72).

Range of value		Cumulative tax to bottom of	Rate of tax on value within
Exceeding	Not exceeding	range	range
£	£	£	%
150,000		Nil	40

A4.15

Deaths on or after 6 April 1995 and before 6 April 1996 (SI 1994/3011).

Range of value		Cumulative tax to bottom of	Rate of tax on value within
Exceeding	Not exceeding	range	range
£	£	£	%
154,000		Nil	40

A4.16

Deaths on or after 6 April 1996 and before 6 April 1997 (Finance Act 1996, s 183).

Range of value		Cumulative tax to bottom of	Rate of tax on value within
Exceeding	Not exceeding	range	range
£	£	£	%
200,000		Nil	40

A4.17

Deaths on or after 6 April 1997 and before 6 April 1998 (Finance Act 1997, s 93).

Range of value		Cumulative tax to bottom of	Rate of tax on value within
Exceeding	Not exceeding	range	range
£	£	£	%
215,000		Nil	40

A4.18

Deaths on or after 6 April 1998 and before 6 April 1999 (SI 1998/756).

Range of value		Cumulative tax to bottom of	Rate of tax on value within
Exceeding	Not exceeding	range	range
£	£	£	%
223,000		Nil	40

A4.19

Deaths on or after 6 April 1999 and before 6 April 2000 (SI 1999/596).

Range of value		Cumulative tax to bottom of	Rate of tax on value within
Exceeding	Not exceeding	range	range
£	£	£	%
231,000		Nil	40

A4.20

Deaths on or after 6 April 2000 and before 6 April 2001 (SI 2000/967).

Range of value		Cumulative tax to bottom of	Rate of tax on value within
Exceeding	Not exceeding	range	range
£	£	£	%
234,000		Nil	40

A4.21

Deaths on or after 6 April 2001 and before 6 April 2002 (SI 2001/639).

Range of value		Cumulative tax to bottom of	Rate of tax on value within
Exceeding	Not exceeding	range	range
£	£	£	%
242,000		Nil	40

A4.22

Deaths on or after 6 April 2002 and before 6 April 2003 (Finance Act 2002, s 118).

Range of value		Cumulative tax to bottom of	Rate of tax on value within
Exceeding	Not exceeding	range	range
£	£	£	%
250,000		Nil	40

A4.23

Deaths on or after 6 April 2003 and before 6 April 2004 (SI 2003/841).

Range of value		Cumulative tax to bottom of	Rate of tax on value within
Exceeding	Not exceeding	range	range
£	£	£	%
255,000		Nil	40

A4.24

Deaths on or after 6 April 2004 (SI 2004/771).

Range of value		Cumulative tax to bottom of	Rate of tax on value within
Exceeding	Not exceeding	range	range
£	£	£	%
263,000		Nil	40

Costs (Non-Contentious Business)

No new material is incorporated in this supplement.

Forms

OATHS

Substitute the following general notes:

General notes.–

1 **Except where otherwise stated, the following forms are applicable in cases where the deceased died on or after 1 January 1926.**

Every oath should state the address including, if known, the postcode of the deceased.

In every oath to lead a grant of administration (with or without will annexed), the deponent must state whether there is a life interest or a minority interest (NCPR 8(4).)

Where there is a life interest or a minority interest, the grant must be made to a trust corporation, with or without an individual, or to not less than two individuals, unless it appears to the court to be expedient in all the circumstances to appoint an individual as sole administrator.

Where the death occurred on or after 1 January 1926, in every oath to lead a grant of probate or administration (with or without will annexed), the deponent must swear to the best of his knowledge, information and belief whether there was land vested in the deceased which was settled previously to his death (and not by his will) and which remained settled land notwithstanding his death (NCPR 8(3)).

The name, address and occupation of the deponent or status (if a female with no occupation) and, in certain cases, his relationship to the deceased, if any, must be shown (see para 4.91).

Every oath must state the age and where the deceased died in the United Kingdom and the death was recorded in the Register of Deaths the name and dates of birth and death as recorded in the Register should be given. If the deceased was known by any different names those names should also be included in the oath. In those cases in which the exact age is not known, the applicant should give the best estimate he can (Practice Directions [1981] 2 All ER 832, [1981] 1 WLR 1185, [1999] 1 All ER 832).

2 Excepted Estates:

(i) Where the deceased died on and after 5 April 2004 and the gross value plus chargeable value of any transfers does not exceed the prevailing IHT threshold the gross value of the estate should be recited as not exceeding the prevailing threshold and the net value should be rounded up to the next whole thousand and expressed as 'not exceeding £....' (President's Direction 23 March 2002);

(ii) where the deceased died on or after 5 April 2004 and the gross value plus chargeable value of transfers does not exceed £1,000,000 and the net chargeable estate after deduction of spouse and/or charity exemptions only is less than the prevailing IHT threshold the exact gross and net values of the estate should be included in the oath and

(iii) where the deceased died before 5 April 2004 the gross value of the estate should continue to be expressed as not exceeding the prevailing limit for the date of death and the net value should be rounded up to the next whole thousand as in (i) above.

66.

Oath for probate (general form)

(Heading as in Form No 1)

I, C D [*or* we C D and E F] of make oath and say that:

1. I [we] believe the paper writing now produced to and marked by me [us] to contain the true and original last will and testament [with two codicils, *or as the case may be*] of A B of formerly of deceased, who was born on the day of   19   and died on the day of 20 aged years, domiciled in England and Wales;

2. To the best of my [our] knowledge, information and belief, there was [no] land vested in the said deceased which was settled previously to his death, and not by his will, and which remained settled land notwithstanding his death*;

3. I am [We are] the son[s] of the said deceased and the sole executor [*or* two of the executors] [*or* the surviving executors] named in the said will;

[4. Notice of this application has been given to the executor(s) to whom power is to be reserved, save **;]

5. I [We] will:

   (i)   collect, get in and administer according to law the real and personal estate of the said deceased;

   (ii)   when required to do so by the Court exhibit in the Court a full inventory of the said estate and render an account thereof to the Court; and

   (iii) when required to do so by the High Court, deliver up to that Court the grant of probate;

6. To the best of my [our] knowledge, information and belief the gross estate passing under the grant [does not exceed/amounts to] £ and that the net estate [does not exceed/amounts to] £ [and that this is not a case in which an Inland Revenue account is required to be delivered].

Sworn by (both) the

above-named deponent(s)

at

this day of 20

Before me,

A Commissioner for Oaths.

[*   If there is settled land, a general executor may take a grant 'save and except settled land' on swearing simply that there was such settled land, but the value of the settled land must not be included in the oath. In such a case the word 'estate' should be followed by the words 'save and except settled land' in each place where it occurs. For form of oath for probate save and except settled land where there has been a previous grant limited to settled land, see No 85.

** Where there are several executors and they do not all prove, power is reserved to the non-proving executors. See paras 4.50 ff., ante as to the requirements for giving notice to the other executor(s) or dispensing with giving such notice and the relevant statement in the oath.

In clause 6 the alternatives so marked should be deleted as appropriate. See the general notes above as to those cases in which an Inland Revenue account is not required to be delivered (see noter-up to Chap. 8, and the Capital Transfer/Inheritance Tax (Delivery of Accounts) Regulations, pp 930 ff. in the main text and Appendix II to this supplement). (see also paras 4.199 and 4.200, ante).]

Insert

69A.

Oath for probate where directors/members of an incorporated practice/limited liability partnership appointed as executors by reference to them being such directors/members

(Heading as in Form No 1)

I, C D, of solicitor, make oath and say that:

1. I believe the paper writing now produced to and marked by me to contain the true and original last will and testament of A B of deceased, who was born on the day of   19   and died on the day of 20 aged years, domiciled in England and Wales;

2. To the best of my knowledge, information and belief there was [no] land vested in the said deceased which was settled previously to his death, and not by his will, and which remained settled land notwithstanding his death;

3. The deceased named as executors, in the said will, the directors and members at the date of his death in the Y Z Limited/ the members at the death of his death of Y Z llp of;

4. At the date of death of the deceased I was one of the directors/members in Y Z Limited/ Y Z llp and as such I am one of the executors named in the will;

5. E F the only other director/member at the date of death of the deceased in the practice is to have power reserved to him [*or* has renounced probate *or* has since died];

6. I will:

   (i)   collect, get in and administer [etc– *continue as in Form No 66*].

A6.96 Substitute:

89.

Oath for administrators– net estate exceeding £125,000 for death on or after 1 December 1993: widow (or husband) and minor child survive: application by spouse and nominated co-administrator [*for the appropriate lesser sums depending on date of death see para 6.85, ante*]

(Heading as in Form No 1)

We, C D, of and E F, of make oath and say that:

1. A B of deceased, was born on the   day of   19   and died on the day of 20 aged years domiciled in England and Wales intestate, leaving the said C D, his lawful widow [*or* her lawful husband] and G H, his [her] lawful* son, together the only persons entitled to share in his [her] estate;

2. The said G H is now a minor of the age of years;

3. There is no guardian, other person or local authority with parental responsibility for the said minor;

4. The said C D is the mother of the said minor [*or* is the father of the said minor with parental responsibility for him under s.2(1) of the Children Act 1989 *or* is the father of the said minor and has acquired parental responsibility for him under s.4 of the Children Act 1989 under an order [*or* under a duly recorded parental responsibility agreement)];

5. A minority and a life interest arise under the intestacy;

6. To the best of our knowledge, information and belief there was no land vested in the said deceased which was settled previously to his [her] death and which remained settled land notwithstanding his [her] death;

7. The said E F is the person nominated by the said C D as co-administrator of the estate of the said deceased;

8. We will:

    (i)   collect, get in and administer [etc– *complete as in Form No 88*].

[**See note* to Form No 88.*]

[When the father is relying on s.4 of the Children Act 1989 a sealed copy of the order or of the recorded parental responsibility agreement, as the case may be, must be produced on the application.]

A6.119

Substitute:

114.

Oath for administration to attorneys of intestate's husband or widow

(Heading as in FORM No *I)*

We, C D of and F G of make oath and say that:

1. A B of deceased, was born on the   day of   19   and died on the day of 20 aged years, domiciled in England and Wales, intestate, leaving E B her lawful husband [*or* his lawful widow];

2. No minority but a life interest arises under the intestacy;

3. [*add statement as to settled land*];

4. We are the lawful attorneys of the said E B *or [if acting under an enduring power of attorney]* we are the lawful attorneys of the said EB acting under an enduring power of attorney which has not been registered and EB remains mentally capable of managing his/her affairs*;

5. We will:

    (i)   collect, get in and administer according to law the real and personal estate of the said deceased for the use and benefit of the said E B until further representation be granted;

    (ii) when required to do so by the Court, exhibit in the Court a full inventory of the said estate and render an account thereof to the Court; and

    (iii) when required to do so by the High Court, deliver up to the Court the grant of letters of administration;

[etc as in FORM No 66*]*.

This clause may be adapted for forms 115,116 and 157 in the main work.

A.126

Substitute:

121.

Oath for administration to father of minor and nominated co-administrator

(Heading as in FORM No *I)*

We E F of and G H of make oath and say that:

1. A B of deceased, was born on the   day of   19   and died on the day of 20 aged years, domiciled in England and Wales intestate, a single woman leaving C

D her *lawful** son and the only person entitled to her estate who is now a minor aged
years;

2. The marriage of the said intestate with the deponent E F was dissolved by final decree
of the High Court of Justice [*or* of the county court] in England and Wales dated the
day of 20 and the said intestate did not thereafter remarry;

3. The said E F is the father of the said minor with parental responsibility for him under
s.2(1) of the Children Act 1989 [*or* has parental responsibility for him under s.2(2)(b) of
the Children Act 1989 [by virtue of being registered as the minor's father] [by virtue of
a parental responsibility agreement] [under an order of the High Court/.........County/
Magistrates Court dated the ....] and has not ceased to have it;

4. There is no guardian, other person or local authority with parental responsibility for
the said minor;

5. The said E F has by a nomination dated the day of 20 nominated the said G H to be
his co-administrator;

6. A minority but no life interest arises under the intestacy;

7. [*Add statement as to settled land.*]

8. We will:

   (i)   collect, get in and administer according to law the real and personal estate of
          the said intestate, for the use and benefit of the said minor until he attains the
          age of eighteen years;

   (ii)   when required to do so by the Court, exhibit in the Court a full inventory of the
          said estate and render an account thereof to the Court; and

   (iii) when required to do so by the High Court, deliver up to that Court the grant of
          letters of administration;

[**See note** to FORM NO 88.]

[This form may be adapted where the father has parental responsibility by virtue of an adoption
   order made within the meaning of s.12 of the Adoption Act 1976. The oath must state that
   he is the adopter or one of the adopters by such order and a copy of the order must be
   produced.]

A6.133

Substitute:

128.

Oath for administrator pending determination of probate claim

(Heading as in FORM NO 1)

I, C D, of make oath and say that:

1. A B of widow, deceased, was born on the day of   19   and died on the day
of 20 aged years, domiciled in England and Wales;

2. There is now pending in the Chancery Division of the High Court a probate claim entitled E against F, concerning the validity of the will of the said deceased [*or* the estate of the said deceased];

3. By order of the said Chancery Division dated the day of 20 it was ordered that letters of administration of the estate of the said deceased be granted to me, pending determination the said claim;

4. [*add statement as to life or minority interest*];

5. [*add statement as to settled land*];

6. I will:

    (i)   collect, get in and administer according to law the real and personal estate of the said deceased, pending determination of the said claim, under the directions and control of this court, save distributing the residue thereof;

    (ii) when required to so by the Court [etc– *complete as in* **FORM NO 88**].

[Note.– **If the order of the court contains any limitation, this form must be varied accordingly. The grant may be made to one individual administrator notwithstanding any life or minority interest, but the oath must state whether or not such interests arise. Application for the grant may only be made to the Principal Registry because the contention in the case has not been disposed of– see NCPR 7(1)(a).**]

A6.145

Insert after Form 140

140A.

Oath for administration under s 113 of the Supreme Court Act 1981

(Heading as in FORM NO 1*)*

I, C D, of make oath and say that:

1. A B of widow, deceased, was born on the day of   19   and died on the day of 20 aged years, domiciled in England and Wales, intestate;

2. No minority or life interest arises under the intestacy;

3. [*Statement as to settled land.*]

4. On the day of 20 it was ordered by Mr District Judge [*or* Registrar] that letters of administration of the estate of the said deceased limited to [*recite the limitation(s) given in order*] be granted to me under and by virtue of section 113 of the Supreme Court Act 1981];

5. I will:

    (i)   collect, get in and administer according to law the real and personal estate of the deceased [*add, if applicable,* limited as aforesaid];

    (ii) when required to do so by the court [etc– *complete as in* **FORM NO 88**].

A6.155

Substitute:

150.

Oath for administration (will) to legatee in accordance with NCPR 20(c)(ii); whole, or substantially whole, of known estate disposed of by enumeration

(Heading as in FORM No 1)

I, C D, of make oath and say that:

1. I believe the paper writing now produced to and marked by me to contain the true and original last will and testament of A B of deceased, who was born on the day of   19   and died on the day of 20 aged years, domiciled in England and Wales;

2. E F, the sole executor and residuary legatee and devisee in trust named in the said will has renounced probate thereof [*or*, No executor, residuary legatee and/or devisee in trust or residuary legatee and/or devisee is named in the said will];

3. [*add statement as to minority and life interests*];

4. [*add statement as to settled land*];

5. I am a legatee [*or* devisee] named in the said will which disposes of the whole [*or* substantially the whole] of the known estate;

6. I will:

    (i)   collect, get in and administer according to law the real and personal estate of the said deceased;

    (ii) when required to do so by the Court, exhibit in the Court a full inventory of the said estate and render an account thereof to the Court; and

    (iii) when required to do so by the High Court, deliver up to that Court the grant of letters of administration;

[etc– complete as in FORM No 66.*]*

[Note.– **Where application is made by a legatee (or devisee) on the ground that substantially the whole estate is disposed of the case must be submitted to the district judge or registrar for his decision whether the facts bring the case within the terms of the rule, having regard to the size of the estate and the amount disposed of. The following statement should then be added at the end of the oath: '£ of the total value of the known estate of £ is disposed of by the said will'.**

Unless it is clear from the papers that there are kin entitled to share in any undisposed-of estate, a statement to this effect should (if such be the case) be included in the oath. If there are no such kin, notice of the application should be given to the Treasury Solicitor under NCPR 38 (Registrar's Direction, 5 August 1954).]

A6.168

Insert after Form 163

163.

Oath for administration (will) under s 116 of the Supreme Court Act 1981

(Heading as in Form No 1)

I, C D, of make oath and say that:

1. A B of deceased, was born on the day of 19 and died on the day of 20 aged years, domiciled in England and Wales, having made and duly executed his last will and testament;

2. On the day of 20 it was ordered by Mr District Judge/Registrar of this Division that letters of administration (with will annexed) of the estate of the said deceased be granted to me under and by virtue of s 113 of the Supreme Court Act 1981 limited to [recite the limitation(s) given in the order];

3. [Add statement as to life and minority interests.]

4. [Add statement as to settled land.]

5. I believe the paper writing now produced to and marked by me to contain the true and original last will and testament of the said deceased;

6. I will:

    (i)   collect, get in and administer according to law the real and personal estate of the said deceased [*add, if applicable*, limited as aforesaid];

    (ii)   when required to do so by the Court [etc– *complete as in* **Form No 143**].

RENUNCIATIONS

A6.188

Substitute:

183.

Renunciation of probate

(Heading as in Form No 1)

A B of deceased, died on the day of 20 having made and duly executed his last will and testament, bearing date the day of 20 [and codicil(s) dated the day of 20]# and thereof appointed the undersigned CD sole executor [and residuary legatee and devisee [in trust]]:

I, the said C D of do hereby declare that I have not intermeddled in the estate of the said deceased, and will not hereafter intermeddle therein with intent to defraud creditors, and I do hereby renounce all my right and title to probate and execution of the said will (with codicil(s) [and to letters of administration (with the said will (and codicil(s) annexed) of the estate of the said deceased]*.

Signed by the said C D as a deed this

day of 20 in the

presence of.

(Witness's name, address and occupation)

[*These words must be included in the form where the executor is also entitled in a lower character under NCPR 20 and has to be cleared off in that character by the applicant for the grant (Registrar's Direction (1952) 27 November).

Where appropriate references to codicil(s) if any should be made in Forms 184A,185 and 186 in the main text].

Instructions, Statutory Will Forms, probate offices

No new material is incorporated in this supplement.